To Refine Like Silver

By Jeanna Ellsworth

Check out Jeanna Ellsworth's blog and other books by Hey Lady
Publications: https://www.heyladypublications.com
Follow Jeanna Ellsworth on Twitter: @ellsworthjeanna
Like her on Facebook:
https://www.facebook.com/Jeanna.Ellsworth
Like the book's Facebook page:
www.facebook.com/ToRefineLikeSilver
Connect by email: Jeanna.ellsworth@yahoo.com

Acknowledgements

There are so many who have influenced this book, but first and foremost, I need to thank Jed Kassing, whose five-minute devotional inspired me to write this story. His words may have been brief, but the spirit of his message was unforgettable. I hope my words share that message with many others.

Too many years of my life were spent in a black, cold abyss, but I never suffered alone. Many friends and family stood by me, and at times, they literally held my hand. I can never thank them enough.

I'd like to thank my editor, Katrina Beckstrand, who polished this work until it shined. She found all its imperfections and refined each one effortlessly. It is because of her devotion and patience with me that you have this book to enjoy. I can think of no greater compliment than to say this work has been through the refiner's fire.

A special thanks to my cover illustrator, Rebecca Watkins, who somehow managed to see into my head to paint exactly what I wanted—and then made it even better.

Thank you to my readers for taking a chance on this book. I know I am breaking tradition by bringing God into a Jane Austen-inspired novel, but I hope you will see the value of my story. If it brings solace to just one reader, I will consider the work a success. Sometimes we need a light to guide us safely through the fog.

Lastly, I would like to acknowledge God. I thank Him for every day that I am depression-free.

Dedication

For those who have no hope.
Sadness is just a feeling; it cannot consume you

CHAPTER 1

Elizabeth quickly snatched up the letter that lay waiting on the silver tray. Another letter from her father so soon! She had only been in Lambton for two weeks; a second letter was most unexpected. She had been so busy helping Mr. and Mrs. Gardiner move into their new estate that she had written home only once to let them know she had arrived safely. She eagerly began opening the second letter without delay.

Longbourn, Hertfordshire
21 June 1811

My dearest Lizzy,

Dare I say how much your presence is missed here in Longbourn? I suppose starting a letter with such a sentiment may be considered foolish, but I cannot pass up any opportunity to express my love and appreciation.

The tenants here are all asking about you and want to know when you will return. I simply tell them the Lord has His own plan for you. I look forward to your return, but I have a feeling that someday soon Longbourn will no longer be your home. The truth of the matter is you are all grown up now. After all, I cannot expect you to stay here in Meryton forever solely for my comfort.

I hope you will be patient with your uncle; taking over an estate is hard work, especially for one who is used to working in a profession. I

1

suppose I do not have to explain how well I know that concept; it has been almost thirteen years since I gave up the cloth.

When Mrs. Gardiner inherited Saphrinbrooke Estate from her great-uncle, I counseled Mr. Gardiner to look to those in the area for advice. Has he met any neighboring landowners? I have no connections to Derbyshire and can only advise him through letters. Creating connections and friends should be one of his first priorities.

Your help is most appreciated, I am sure. I do not need to remind you that he specifically requested you, over any of your sisters, to assist Mrs. Gardiner in taking control over the estate. You have the most skill, experience, initiative, and spirit to help them make the transition from tradespeople to landowners.

I looked in at the orphanage like you asked of me. Little Richard has become quite adept at using the crutch you had made for him, and the twins have gotten over their coughs. Frances is waiting to hear your next big tale about the adventures of the girl with a golden harp. I assume you know to which tale she is referring. The weather has been quite warm, but I did as you asked and ensured they had enough wood to keep the room heated at night. They all miss you terribly.

However, I was caught off guard when they asked for their treats. I believe they expected that I would bring them sweets from the shop in town. Apparently you have been doing so for years. Is that where your pocket allowance has been going? If I had known you were spending it on the children, I would have given you more.

I know that when you left, you were concerned whether you were the right person for the tasks set before you. You so desperately wanted to see your aunt and uncle succeed. I have full faith in the God in Heaven that you will succeed in your purpose for going to Lambton. Saphrinbrooke Estate will be amazing come the end of the summer, and Mr. and Mrs. Gardiner will be well received. They may have been tradespeople until two weeks ago, but they were raised with all the manners to be accepted among the landed gentry.

But in the meantime, remember that if at first you do not succeed, redefine what you call success. Celebrate the little successes instead of waiting for the grand entrance of a miracle.

But enough of that, for I am attempting to refrain from full sermons in this letter. You have heard enough of them from me in the past. And as kind as you are, you still listen. Thank you for appeasing an old man.

I cannot wait to hear of your adventures. Once again, I want to express my full confidence that you are exactly where you need to be and you are doing exactly what the Lord has intended for you. Go easy on the Gardiners; they do not always understand your wit. But after spending two full months with you, I have no doubt that they will master the skill themselves. I have also included a letter to your uncle. Please give it to him.

From your loving papa,
Thomas Bennet

Elizabeth looked up from the letter and wiped the stray tear from her cheek. Her father always knew what to say. They had a close relationship and often spent hours in deep discussions. He was such a source of knowledge, and he was so kind in his teaching that the hours went by quickly. She couldn't think of a single time when she had ended the discussions; it was always her father who would look at his pocket watch, tell her she was allotted two more questions, and then kiss her on the forehead after he answered them.

This was not the first time she had been away from Longbourn, her family, or the Meryton orphanage. But it would be the longest. She had already been here at the small estate just outside of Lambton in Derbyshire for two weeks, and she was planning on staying another two months.

So far, she had accompanied Mr. and Mrs. Gardiner to see most of the tenants—and the list of needs had grown with each visit. She could sense her uncle's anxiety growing as well. Although he had managed employees in his London trade business, he had never felt the weight of their very livelihood on his shoulders.

Two days ago, he had shared his concerns with her. Elizabeth had considered his problem carefully before advising, "Silence the barking frog, and peace will soon follow." She giggled at the look of confusion on his face for a moment before offering a translation—start with the biggest problem first, and many of the smaller problems will be fixed as a result. She didn't know if her advice had done any good, but she hoped it had eased his burden.

Elizabeth carefully folded her precious letter. Then she picked up the one intended for her uncle and went looking for him. After she knocked on his study door and received no answer, she went to the library, but it too was empty. She walked down the long hallway of sitting rooms, the morning room, and the music

4

room, and finally came to the entrance to the garden, which was becoming a favorite place for all of them.

The gardens were fairly small, about as big as Longborn's gardens, but the natural landscape created private sanctuaries for escape. Gravel paths wound around rosebushes and the hollyhocks were just beginning to bloom. She started walking the main path and soon heard voices from behind a manicured hedge. She turned the corner and saw that her uncle was in deep discussion with a dark-haired gentleman. The stranger's back was to her, but she could see he was tall and broad shouldered. His stood erect with one hand bent behind him. She watched his fingers methodically flexing and contracting into a gentle fist.

Her presence must have been heard, because he turned around. He was not just tall and dark; his features were chiseled and striking. His jaw was strong and had a very stern set to it. But after the briefest of moments, there came a slightly raised eyebrow and a look of surprise, and the corner of his eyes and his brows relaxed. Whoever this man was, he was trying desperately not to show his emotions. She gave him a slight smile as her uncle addressed her.

"I see you have found me again in my hiding spot," Mr. Gardiner said with a smile. "But I confess, I have a purpose in being out here this time. Let me introduce you to our neighbor, Mr. Fitzwilliam Darcy of Pemberley. He owns the grand Pemberley estate located on the other side of Lambton. I believe you said it was a mere five miles from Lambton, no?"

"Indeed," Mr. Darcy replied.

Elizabeth could tell she was being evaluated and scrutinized from head to toe, and for a moment she wished she had taken more time with her hair. She recognized that her manners and appearance would reflect on the Gardiners, especially since this was the first landowner they had met in the area. She gave her best curtsy and smiled again. "It is a pleasure to meet you, Mr. Darcy."

Mr. Darcy stood and looked at the lady in front of him. He didn't know how to express his first impression of her, except to say that she sparkled. Was it her hair? Or was it the way she carried herself? Was it that smile? She was simply bright. She was beautiful, but that was not what took his breath away. It was something else entirely. The stirrings were so foreign that he stood staring at her for many moments before he realized he had not addressed her. "I would say the same to you; however, we have not been properly introduced yet. You now know my name, but yours remains a mystery." Mr. Darcy pulled his eyes away from her intriguing gaze long enough to give proper attention to the gentleman speaking next to him.

"My apologies, sir," Mr. Gardiner chuckled. "This is my favorite niece, Miss Elizabeth Bennet. She is my sister's second eldest child. She will be staying with us for the next two months to help us settle in at Saphrinbrooke." Mr. Gardiner noticed the questioning look on Mr. Darcy's face and added, "Elizabeth has been helping her father run an estate in Hertfordshire for many years. I realize it is unusual for a man like myself to seek counsel from a much younger female, but her wisdom and insight is very valuable."

"I do not doubt it. It is a pleasure, Miss Bennet." Mr. Darcy had never wanted to kiss a lady's hand before, but he wanted to now. Without thinking, he reached out and took her hand and bowed over it, giving it a small kiss. When he looked up, he saw that sparkle again and the corner of her mouth turned up in a teasing manner.

"And how, sir, have you come to such a conclusion? Is it really wise to accept Mr. Gardiner's opinion of my character so readily? For you have nothing to judge me on but my appearance and his word. I have said but five words in addressing you, none of which have been wise or insightful." Elizabeth grinned widely as he dropped her hand and returned his arm to the folded position behind his back. She could only assume his fingers were rhythmically moving as she had seen before. She let out a small giggle to let him know she was teasing him.

Mr. Gardiner chuckled, "And so it is with my niece! I warn you now to always be on your toes with this one. She is quick and intelligent, and she makes for good conversation."

Mr. Darcy stood taller and tried to mask his flushed face as he struggled to frame a response. He wasn't used to being teased; he had been shamelessly praised and showered with flattery by every lady of his acquaintance—but not teased. This was new territory for him. He turned back to Mr. Gardiner and said, "I believe your ideas for the gardens are possible, but I would warn you against planting wheat this late in the year."

Elizabeth had watched Mr. Darcy's cheeks and ears turn pink with her teasing but was surprised that he so quickly changed the subject. "And why is that, Mr. Darcy?" she interjected. "Winter wheat will not be damaged by the winter cold, and it will provide much needed sustenance and income to the property and tenants come next summer. It can be planted as late as September in Hertfordshire. We have had great success in planting it after the fall crops are harvested."

Elizabeth watched the expressions in his eyes—he seemed surprised again, yet curious. If she didn't know better, she would guess he had a lot to say but was restraining himself. After a pause, she continued, "Although my uncle claims I am intelligent, I do not possess the power to read someone's mind. Why do you think wheat would not be appropriate in Derbyshire?"

Mr. Darcy had never discussed crops with a lady, and certainly not a lady who seemed to be educated on the matter. "Winter wheat is different than common wheat. I have not planted it myself, but a friend of mine has, and he insists the crop must be strictly rotated."

Elizabeth tried not to smile. She was very familiar with crop rotation. "And would your friend agree that the best place to plant the wheat is in an area where legumes had been planted the year before? I understand legumes, such as beans, provide much-needed nutrients to the soil, making for a more productive crop the next year."

Mr. Darcy could not help himself and let out a laugh. "Indeed, he would have said the very thing." He reluctantly turned away from this oddity in front of him and addressed Mr. Gardiner, "I may be the one asking for guidance from you and your Miss Bennet. I see my five years as being Master of Pemberley is not sufficient time to obtain any expert advice that Miss Bennet does not already know."

"Sir, I would agree that Elizabeth is unique in her vast knowledge, but I am sorely in need of a local resource for my many questions. Could I interest you in joining us for dinner?"

Mr. Darcy truly considered it for a moment. He wanted to get to know this vibrant, glowing lady in front of him. But he had several things that he needed to do, and he had promised his sister, Georgiana, that he would not be gone long. She had promised to go riding with him before dinner. She was still so fragile right now. Just yesterday she had finally sat in front of the pianoforte. He had hoped she would attempt to resume her practicing, but she never played a note. It had been three very long months since she had even visited the music room.

She didn't read, she didn't embroider, and she didn't do anything but stare out the window or walk the halls mindlessly with that blasted, blank stare. Whenever he caught her with that blank stare, he would give her a reassuring smile, which she returned with a triple blink of her eyes and a small parting of the lips. *It was her attempt to smile back*, he told himself. But the mere fact that she had started to show progress, that she had tried to play yesterday, meant that he could not leave her. He had to see her do something, anything; he couldn't break his promise to go riding with her.

Elizabeth saw the hesitation in Mr. Darcy's eyes. She feared she had offended the gentleman or, at least, made a bad impression. "Mr. Darcy, I assure you, I meant no offense with my comments. We all would truly enjoy some company tonight. And since you are the closest neighbor we have, you simply must come to dinner. You can bring your wife and children as well. We meant to extend the invitation to your entire family."

"I am not married."

"I apologize," Elizabeth stammered. "I truly did not mean to assume anything." *How could a handsome gentleman like him not be married? He must be nearing thirty!* Now she truly had offended him. She blushed in embarrassment. She knew she was making a poor impression. She looked away from his careful, emotion-concealing eyes, but not before she saw them soften towards her.

"Miss Bennet, Mr. Gardiner, my only hesitation is that my dear sister, Georgiana, is at Pemberley with expectations of joining me on a good ride in the country. I must return home. But we do not have any specific plans for dinner. If you truly are asking, then we would be happy to have dinner with our closest neighbors." *Well, I would be happy. Georgiana will not. Then again, she could use a little brightness in her day and Miss Elizabeth Bennet is bursting with it!* With this thought, he made up his mind. "In fact, I accept for the both of us. I look forward to it."

*****

"Please, Georgie. As your brother and guardian, I insist that you accompany me tonight. I am not blind to your pain and sorrow. I do understand how betrayed you feel. I trusted him once too. But you simply must try to forget."

How could she forget what he had done? Georgiana bit her lip and tried to look at her brother. As soon as her eyes met his, she saw the pain in them, but there was something else. She saw something she had never seen before. His eyes were pleading with her to accompany him. Why was it so important that she meet their new neighbors? The very thought of attempting to smile and make conversation was so daunting it made her want to retire to bed right then.

She kicked her horse, Hera, and left William behind without saying a word. Why was William asking this of her? Didn't he know that she was not to be trusted anymore? Her shame was leaking out her eyes, and it obscured her view of the path. She moved the reigns to one hand as she quickly wiped away the tears. She heard William coming up behind her, and she kicked the horse harder.

She knew she was taking terrible risks by riding in this emotional state, but it was the one thing that seemed to calm her. People died all the time on horses. She enjoyed the risk. She flicked the reigns and felt the response in the animal immediately. She felt that brief lightness of heart. Maybe today would be the day. Maybe Hera would throw her today. Maybe she would finally be out of the pain she was trapped in.

Every day it was the same. She was coaxed out of bed by her lady's maid and forced to eat something. She greeted her brother with as much confidence as she could muster. And then the rest of the day was nothing. Blackness. Cold, hard, blackness.

She was sure the sun rose and set, but she didn't notice. She knew she breathed in and out, because there were times she felt like she had to remind herself to do so. Every day she relived that moment when the truth had been revealed. She searched her memories for evidence, for an explanation. Something in the weeks preceding the moment should have warned her of his character, but every day, she found none. She was ruined. She was no longer capable of living. She was simply ruined.

If each day would be like this, she did not know how long she could continue. Blurriness. Darkness. Sadness. Every shade of gray. There was no sun, no peace, and certainly no joy. She was not watching very closely where she was going as she let Hera choose the path she wanted at a pace that Georgiana insisted upon.

Hearing William call her name finally pulled her out of her darkness, and she slowed.

Darcy caught up to Georgiana and saw her tear-stained face, and he knew he could not make her go. He pulled his horse up next to her and grabbed her reigns; she was nearly losing her grip on them anyway. He quieted both horses until they came to a stop. "Georgiana, I am sorry. I know you are not ready for this. I will send our regrets to Miss Bennet and the Gardiners."

Georgiana looked up at him and finally realized what she had seen in his eyes before. It had been hope. Now the hope was gone. She knew that hopeless look well. It was the same one in her eyes. For the last three months, she had refused to look in a mirror for that very reason; she even draped a blanket over her bedroom mirror. She could barely handle hurting. She could barely handle the shame. She could barely handle the darkness, and sometimes all she could handle was breathing for one hour at a time. But she could not handle seeing the same look of hopelessness in her brother's eyes.

She stared at him, looking at him as if she had never seen him before. In truth, she hadn't really looked at him in months. She had tried her hardest not to. She didn't want to see his disappointment in her. She needed no more reminders of what had happened. But as she looked at him now, she was sure of one thing: there had been hope in his eyes a moment ago, and now it was gone. Curious was the wrong word, but it made her feel something. She took a deep breath and softly asked, "Who is Miss Bennet?"

"She is the Gardiners' niece visiting from Hertfordshire. She made quite the impression on me. I must admit I would love for you to meet her. There is something about her that is beyond unique. Beyond impressive."

"Is she that beautiful?"

"Oh no! I mean, yes. No, what I mean to say is she *is* beautiful, but that is not why she impressed me. She has something about her that I have never seen before. She made me laugh. She teased me. She was . . ." Darcy's face flushed beet red as he stammered. "Let us just say I would like to know more about her. But there will be other opportunities. I am sorry. You need not go tonight."

Georgiana was speechless. Her brother had just praised a lady. A single, beautiful lady. His disappointment was very evident in his eyes. The same disappointment she had tried so hard not to see these last three months. It moved something deep inside her. She looked away and bit her lip. Could she do it? Or would her presence ruin her brother's chance at happiness? Would she make a fool out of herself, exposing without intent her many follies and indiscretions? She felt him place his hand on her arm. New tears formed from such a gesture. She sniffed them back and turned back to him. "I will go," she announced.

"No, we do not have to go. It was inappropriate and insensitive of me to ask."

She had been getting good at lying. Every day he asked her how she was doing, and every day she said she was fine. She knew she was not fine. She feared she would not even survive each day. The only thing she looked forward to was her daily ride on Hera. Risks. That was the draw in riding Hera.

And going to this dinner would be the biggest risk of all. She would risk everything to see her brother happy. This dinner would remind her that her heart was still pumping, as there were times she was in doubt. "Brother, I said I would go. Do not fight me. I do not have enough fight in me to argue. Just do me one kindness: if I embarrass you, will you please make our excuses and take our leave as soon as possible?" She felt that gentle squeeze on her arm again.

"You could never embarrass me. But we will not stay long. I will make sure of it."

Georgiana felt her chest tighten and bile rose quickly to her mouth. She quickly leaned over the horse away from William and vomited. She could do this. She had to. If it was the last thing she accomplished in her life, she had to survive this night and she had to smile. She took out her handkerchief and wiped her mouth. She refused to look at William, as she did not wish to see his concern, but that did not keep her from hearing it in his voice.

"Are you ill?"

Oh, how she would love to say yes! But she had to do this for him. She had to leave him with some kind of happiness in his life. "No," she answered.

*****

Elizabeth took her time with her hair before dinner; she was determined to remedy this afternoon's negligence. She had a certain amount of anticipation this evening. It was mostly good anticipation, but there was some trepidation as well. She wanted to represent the Gardiners in the best light, but at the same time she knew she would make fewer mistakes if she simply tried to be herself.

She found Mr. Darcy quite interesting. She was curious why he didn't have a wife. He seemed kind and was fairly amiable. She did sense a certain amount of pride, but only because he was so focused on presenting himself well. It was not pride that shined in his eyes; there was something else there. He would be a good neighbor for the Gardiners. When she heard voices downstairs, she took one last look in the mirror and told herself to stop thinking about Mr. Darcy. She tucked the stray curl behind her ear and headed downstairs.

She didn't know what she was expecting, but she certainly wasn't expecting to see a sister at least ten years his junior. She had golden, blonde hair that was pulled up into a simple, elegant bun. She would have been rather tall, but her shoulders were slumped and her head was down. She glanced up at Elizabeth as she came down the stairs, and that is when Elizabeth saw it.

Her eyes. Deep brown didn't describe them adequately. They were nearly black. And Elizabeth was not describing the color. There was a deep sadness to her that was screaming familiarity. Elizabeth bowed her head. She looked away and pretended to smooth her skirts while she said a quick prayer. "Dear Lord, his sister is lost. Help me to find her in her abyss. Now I know why Aunt Gardiner inherited Saphrinbrooke. Now I know why I am here. It was so I could meet Mr. Darcy's sister. She needs help, and now I know what I must do. Give me the courage to do it."

Marianne Gardiner was greeting them at the door when Elizabeth entered smiling sweetly. "This is my niece, Miss Elizabeth Bennet. I could almost call her a daughter, I know her so well."

Mr. Darcy spoke, fully taking in her beauty, "Yes, we were introduced this afternoon by Mr. Gardiner. Miss Bennet, this is my sister, Miss Georgiana Darcy." He watched as Elizabeth leaned into Georgiana and took her by the shoulders and kissed each cheek.

"I am thrilled to get to know my aunt and uncle's neighbors but even more thrilled that I might have a friend in the neighborhood. Please, call me Elizabeth, or Lizzy for short. Some have called me Eliza, but I do not fancy that as much. Do you like to be called Georgiana?"

Georgiana's cheeks were still warm from her kisses. She knew if she had enough blood pumping in her body, she would have been flushed from the forward nature of the welcome. She chanced a deep breath before speaking to Elizabeth. "I am called Georgiana. But William calls me Georgie."

Her voice was barely audible, and it confirmed exactly what Elizabeth thought. "Good, that is settled then! But what would you have me call your brother? He told me his name was Fitzwilliam, and I was going to have some sport with that name, but now you just called him William, which is such a boring and acceptable name. Where shall I find my fun?"

Elizabeth watched closely for Georgiana's reaction. Shock. Confusion. But that darkness lurked. Elizabeth would have to try harder than that. "Do not worry, I have just met your brother and since he has yet to propose, I will have to settle for calling him Mr. Darcy!" She grabbed Georgiana's arm and tucked it nicely inside her own and started walking. She glanced over her shoulder and saw Mr. Darcy staring at the two of them with the strangest of looks on his face. There was both fear and joy in his eyes. *If only he would speak his mind and not conceal so much.*

Elizabeth led Georgiana through the main room of the estate making small talk, very small talk. She tried not to ask too many questions as Georgiana rarely answered. Elizabeth explained, "My aunt, Mrs. Gardiner, grew up in Lambton, and she just recently inherited the estate from her great-uncle, Jonathan Williams. He owned this estate for over five and forty years. No one ever suspected he would outlive all his children. That is how my aunt inherited it. Mr. Williams was nearly five and seventy when his health started declining, and his brother's granddaughter was the only relative he felt close to."

Elizabeth paused, but Georgiana offered no reply, so she continued, "My aunt used to tell me all kinds of stories about Lambton and her time visiting at Saphrinbrooke. The parties, the game nights, the holidays . . . I have no doubt they were her best childhood memories. The way she tells it, this house was always a happy place for her. Perhaps that is why he decided to will the estate to her. Luckily, my uncle was willing to move from London, or they would have had to sell it. They still own their home in London, but I do not know how long they will keep it. Saphrinbrooke will take most of their time and effort these next few years. It has not been very productive as of late, and so there is much to do to return it to a profitable estate."

Elizabeth had been watching Georgiana closely and could see she was finally showing signs of relaxing. She paused again in her speech and then gently guided Georgiana around the corner and into the music room. She studied Georgiana's reaction as she saw the pianoforte.

Georgiana's heart was pumping hard. Why were they in the music room? What did Elizabeth know about her? Would she ask her to play? She stared at the pianoforte until she realized Elizabeth was talking again. She was saying something about Mozart and her difficulty in a certain area of the piece. Suddenly, Georgiana realized Elizabeth had asked her a question. She tore her eyes from the pianoforte and looked at Elizabeth. "I am terribly sorry, my mind was not engaged. What did you ask me?"

"I asked if you played. You were looking at the pianoforte as if it might bite you!"

Georgiana was confused. She tried to focus on what Elizabeth said. Her head was spinning, and she was beginning to doubt her choice in coming tonight. She blinked a few times and parted her lips to speak. Nothing came out. She didn't have the heart to say that she used to play. That she used to enjoy it. That she used to take pleasure in performing for others. She pulled away from Elizabeth's gentle, guiding arm and went to sit on the sofa. It was all so overwhelming.

"If you would like, I can play what I have been working on," Elizabeth offered. "I would love to hear your opinion on my skill. It is a rare opportunity to hear informed suggestions from an unbiased observer. I usually only play in front of family or close friends, and their suggestions are entirely unreliable."

Elizabeth walked over to the pianoforte, and her fingers started the music. After a few minutes she said, "This next section is where I struggle. It changes keys three times, and I would appreciate your guidance." Elizabeth continued playing, but gave only half her usual effort on the section for two reasons. The first was because she needed Georgiana to comment, and the second was because she needed to keep an eye on Georgiana's reaction. Sure enough, Georgiana's fingers started tapping on her leg, bouncing ever so slightly as if she was playing. Elizabeth put a little more feeling into it and let the emotion and power of the next section fill the room. She ended the piece and stood up, noticing that Georgiana had closed her eyes for a moment at the end.

Georgiana was calmer. Music usually did that to her, but the effort to play herself was too much, and so she was simply lost to this comfort. She opened her eyes and said, "Thank you. I cannot describe how nice that was."

"Have you studied that piece before?" Elizabeth asked.

"Yes. I struggled with the same section, but with enough practice, I was rewarded with the satisfaction of conquering it. It is a good feeling to finish such a task."

"Will you not show me that small section? I could dearly use your help."

Georgiana finally took a good look at Elizabeth. Her eyes were bright and cheerful; they were not judging her in any way. They were kind eyes. Georgiana knew she was being a terrible guest, hardly speaking, distracted by her thoughts, and not even attending to the conversation. She saw in Elizabeth's eyes a tenderness that was rare in the other ladies from the *ton*. She decided that she would make better efforts to help William learn more about this lady.

Without saying a word, she stood up and walked to the pianoforte and sat down. Her hands shook, but after a brief, feather-light touch on the ivory keys, Georgiana started to play. She started at the hardest part, the part where Elizabeth said she struggled, but soon the sensation of emotional release seeped through her fingers onto the instrument, and she let it happen. She let the music win her over. She closed her eyes and played the piece that she had known by heart since she was fourteen.

Elizabeth knew Mr. Darcy was in the doorway, watching. There was both sadness and relief in his eyes this time, but his mouth was hard and his lips tightly pressed together. As the piece neared its end, he turned to leave but first caught Elizabeth's watchful gaze. He dipped his chin in acknowledgement, and a slight smile came to his face. He then turned and left just as Georgiana finished.

Georgiana sighed. It felt good. "I have not played that for many months. It is one of my favorite pieces."

Elizabeth stood and reclaimed Georgiana's arm and led her back to the others. "Come, I believe they are holding dinner for us."

"Your aunt and uncle have a very nice pianoforte."

"I will tell them you said so." They walked arm in arm, and Elizabeth noticed Georgiana was not so flaccid. In fact, she could have sworn that she felt a gentle squeeze as they entered the dining room.

Mrs. Gardiner welcomed everyone, and they all took their seats. Mr. Darcy was seated across from Elizabeth and Georgiana. Mrs. Gardiner sat next to him at the foot of the table, and Mr. Gardiner sat at the head. It was the perfect spot for Mr. Darcy. He could watch both of the women across from him and still converse with the Gardiners. Sitting face-to-face with Georgiana and Elizabeth, it was difficult to conceal his relief. Tonight was the first time his sister had played in months; he recognized he had Elizabeth to thank for it. But he kept his emotions in check. He knew, even now, that any reaction from him would upset Georgiana. He assumed a blank face and tried to steer his mind elsewhere, and he quickly found himself occupied in considering Elizabeth's fine features.

The soup was brought in. Just as Mr. Darcy picked up his spoon, he heard Elizabeth clear her throat loudly. He looked up and saw a mischievous grin on her glowing face.

Elizabeth said, "Now, Mr. Darcy, what if we woke up tomorrow morning and had only what we took the time to thank God for?"

"Excuse me? I do not take your meaning."

Elizabeth put her hands together in front of her and bowed her head, then looked up briefly with one eye open to stare at him. She watched him put down his spoon and put his hands together and bow his head. She then closed her eyes and said, "Our Father in heaven, please accept our gratitude for this meal. We thank thee for the fact that we have it, we thank thee for the hands that prepared it, and we thank thee for our dear friends and neighbors whom we can share it with.

"Please bless Mr. and Miss Darcy that they will gain nourishment to their bodies, and that their health will be improved by this sustenance. Bless them with happiness and joy, and bless all of us to always feel thy love. Help us to see how special we are in thine eyes, and may that knowledge make us strong enough to handle the challenges that we must overcome.

"We thank you for our many blessings that we often take for granted, like the sun that warmed us today, and the rain that fed our crops yesterday. Help us to see clearly the things that Thou would have us do in our lives. Help us to see the needs of others and have the courage to offer assistance. Help us to do thy work and give credit to thee. Amen."

Georgiana didn't dare look up. She whispered amen and focused on eating. She pondered Elizabeth's prayer. Was she special in God's eyes? And could that knowledge help her handle her challenges? Could she overcome this thing threatening to destroy her?

Mrs. Gardiner opened the conversation. "Miss Darcy, did you know I knew your mother and father before they passed? I even held you in my arms once when you were quite small. I was visiting my great-uncle, Mr. Williams, when your father came over to show you off." Darcy smiled and looked over at Georgiana, remembering how small she had once been. "I must have been sixteen or so," Mrs. Gardiner continued. "Your father carried you everywhere and was always cooing over you. He had you wrapped so tightly that I worried you could not move. He told me about how just that morning, you had smiled for the first time when he was playing with you."

"He asked if I wanted to see you smile," she went on, "and of course I said yes. So, we sat there for fifteen minutes, watching a grown man giggle and make funny faces at you until he was blue in the face. Then I asked if I could try. Your father was sure I could not do it, and yet he handed you over to me. There were not three words out of my mouth before you gave me a toothless grin that engulfed your entire face. We all had a good laugh at that. Then your father, with his wounded pride, bet me I could not make you smile again."

Georgiana was all ears. Any story about her father and mother was much appreciated. Her brother rarely talked about them. "What did he bet you?"

"This is silly, but he knew I was partial to animals, so he bet me the pick of the litter from his dog, Augusta."

Mr. Darcy smiled and added, "I remember Augusta. She was the best basset hound we ever owned. She was so loyal and a very good mother. I think we had four or five litters from her before she grew too old."

Georgiana just listened. She remembered Augusta as well. She had died when Georgiana was eight. Everyone died.

Mrs. Gardiner continued, "Of course, I had to offer something for the bet as well. So, I offered to sketch Augusta if I could not make you smile. Once the particulars of the wager were settled, I took out a little feather from my pocket and ran it all over your face while making popping noises with my lips. Sure enough, you grinned widely, and I won the bet. Your father accused me of cheating because I used the feather, but he was just teasing me. He enjoyed a good laugh. Of course, when it was time to go, he asked if he could have my feather so he could show your sweet smile to your mother."

Mr. Darcy said, "I remember him trying to get her to smile with a feather. It worked too, especially when he did it around your neck, Georgiana. Mrs. Gardiner, did you ever get your puppy?"

"He offered one to me, but my parents said they did not have room for a puppy in our small house, so my great-uncle raised the puppy here. He let me come see it anytime I wanted. After I married Mr. Gardiner and moved to London, I saw very little of the dog. But I was quite surprised when I looked at the family plot here at Saphrinbrooke and discovered my great-uncle had buried my dog and had given her a headstone. She lived eleven years, and she was my great-uncle's closest companion."

The next course was brought in, and the soup bowls were removed. Elizabeth turned to Georgiana and asked, "Mr. Darcy said you were going riding today. Did you get a chance to go?"

"Yes."

Elizabeth tried again to draw her out. "I do not understand why people delight in riding so much. What is it that makes it is so enjoyable? I, for one, would much rather walk than race on the back of an animal sixteen hands tall. I feel a dangerous lack of control when on top of a horse, or any creature with a will of its own. What is your horse's name?"

"Hera."

"Ah, the sister of the great Zeus. What a fine name! It is a hopeful name as well. Tender-hearted and known for valuing the sacredness of women and marriage. It is very romantic if you ask me. What made you decide on that name?"

Georgiana tried to give her best smile. She felt awkward in doing it, and it seemed to take every conscious effort to make her face cooperate. She needed Elizabeth to see who her brother was. "I often feel like Hera. Not the part where she is married to a sibling, of course. But I could not ask for a better brother." Although she had spoken a mere three sentences, she felt exhausted. She returned her attention to her plate and tried to eat.

Mr. Darcy saw the small smile on Georgiana's face come and go. It was brief but not forgotten. How is it that a stranger could get her to play the pianoforte after three months of avoiding it? And Georgiana had really felt the music. He knew he had Elizabeth to thank for it.

He pondered what she meant when she had asked, what if we woke up tomorrow morning and had only what we took the time to thank God for? He recited prayers at church, even said a few now and again, but ever since his father died, he didn't really pray.

It was an interesting concept, and it stirred his mind into imagining such a scenario. He was quite wealthy, had a house full of loyal servants, had Georgiana and his cousin, Richard, and had the best friend he could have ever asked for in Bingley. He never wanted for anything. If he wanted a new book, a new carriage, or a new painting, he got it. But he had never thanked God in all these years of luxuries. He was born with them and had never once lived without them. So, what if he really did wake up tomorrow and had only the things he thanked God for? He would have nothing.

He felt a chill run up his spine and shook off the goose bumps on his arms. He stole a glance at Georgiana, who was listening intently to something Elizabeth was saying, and he heard Elizabeth giggle. It was a magical sound. It was soft and naturally feminine, not the forced, high-pitched laugh of so many refined ladies. He watched Georgiana's shocked face as she quickly glanced at him. He suddenly realized the laughter was probably about him.

"Miss Bennet," he said, "I prefer to be a participant in conversations rather than the subject. Do you mind informing me what you said to shock my sister so?"

Elizabeth put down her fork and took a sip of her wine. She smiled back at him and then unknowingly gave him a wink. "I think not. But you are right to chastise me for idle gossip. From now on I promise to never disclose my first impressions of you to anyone."

Darcy contemplated this. She was baiting him to ask her what her first impressions were, but perhaps he should take the higher road and pretend not to care. Her wink was simply adorable. He wondered if she even realized she did it. He found himself unable to resist. He winked back at her and replied, "I doubt you will be able to keep that promise. I am the biggest landowner around, and I am talked about a great deal. Perhaps you would like to restate your promise?"

Did Mr. Darcy just wink at me? She felt her face flush pink, and she looked at her plate. "I suppose I should promise that I will only give glowing insights to your character."

"I do hope you will take proper time to form your glowing insights. I am told I often come across somewhat prideful. But those who know me well do not say so."

Elizabeth giggled. "I will certainly offer you what I offer everyone I meet: an opportunity to impress me. I have a theory about people."

"And what is that?" Mr. Darcy asked.

"People are inherently good, even if their actions indicate otherwise. Even our worst enemies have something good at their core. Do you have any enemies, Mr. Darcy?"

Immediately, George Wickham's face came to mind. "Only one. I am afraid I must disagree with your theory. There is no good in that man." He looked briefly at Georgiana, who had her head bowed. She slowly looked up at him, and she had glossy, dark eyes.

Elizabeth sensed that they had wandered into areas that no one really wanted to talk about. She heard Georgiana sniffle slightly and knew "that man" had everything to do with Georgiana's mood. Elizabeth put her hand on Georgiana's and gave it a gentle squeeze. "I have known much evil in my life, but we are all God's children, and we are all capable and deserving of love. If we cannot find love in our hearts for all men, we should ask God for a bigger heart; we cannot expect God to forgive us of our own follies until we are willing to forgive those who have harmed us. It is easy to love those who love us. It takes no effort at all. I imagine you would sacrifice anything for your brother, am I correct, Georgiana?"

"Indeed. I would do anything for him." *And tonight proves it.*

"And you, Mr. Darcy, would give everything you own to see Georgiana safe and healthy?"

"Anything at all. She knows that."

"But can you say you would forgive this man, your enemy as you say, if her life depended upon it?"

Mr. Darcy simply looked at Elizabeth. What did she know? What had she heard about Georgiana? And what was she thinking, discussing it in front of others so callously? He knew his tone was somewhat harsh as he replied, "You know not of what you speak. I would warn you against judging me or Georgiana. I do not know what you have heard, but it is not true."

Elizabeth was shocked. "I was only discussing things in generalities. I knew nothing of you before today and certainly have heard nothing about Georgiana. Forgive me."

Mr. Gardiner cleared his throat, "Do not take offense at Elizabeth's words, Mr. Darcy. I did warn you that she makes for good conversation. She enjoys the pastime of debate, and I am confident that is all she was doing. I often question my long-held beliefs after engaging Elizabeth in conversation. I would wager that if you gave her any position about a topic and asked her to defend it, she would come out the victor."

"Uncle, do not jest. I am only passionate about certain things."

Mr. Darcy realized he had divulged more personal information in a single dinner conversation with Elizabeth than he had ever divulged to anyone else. He couldn't decide if it pleased him or not. One thing he did know was that the lady before him intrigued him, and he did not want strife between them so early. He tried to patch things up between them. "Miss Bennet, if by certain things, you mean everything, then I would have to agree with you. You are clearly passionate about a great deal. Now, will you pass the buttered potatoes?"

And so, the white surrender flag was waved with the passing of the potatoes.

CHAPTER 2

Tuesday was just a day like any other. As always, Elizabeth crawled out of bed, placed the pillow under her knees, and spoke to the one person she could tell anything to. She reviewed all that had happened the day before. She thanked Him for allowing her to be a part of Georgiana's life, even if it would only be for a few months. She asked Him to guide her in her efforts and to show Georgiana how deeply she cared for her. She prayed that she would be strong enough to assist another.

It had only been four years since she had been lost. Not so long ago, she had seen the familiar darkness of Georgiana's eyes in her own reflection. She had felt it so deeply, and for so long. It hadn't been easy, but she had seen the darkness and made it back whole; she knew Georgiana could escape too. She longed to help her. As usual, she thanked Him for the peace she now felt, a peace that she relished every day. A peace that only He could give.

That morning especially, she thanked Him for finding her when she had been lost, for loving her so purely and completely. And she thanked Him for patiently waiting through her turmoil of emotions until she finally saw her worth. Now she hoped she would be strong enough to lift another out of that darkness.

She referred to it as a darkness, but it was really more like a thick fog. The only thing that one could see or feel was the pain; everything else was a blur. One could hear sounds but couldn't really understand what was happening. It was so easy to get lost.

And Elizabeth had been lost. She had struggled with simple, daily tasks; complicated tasks had been impossible. In thick fog, a carriage driver can see only a short distance ahead.

One's vision becomes shortsighted, seeing only twenty, fifteen, or ten feet ahead. Any slight turn of the road, or hidden bump, can spell disaster, so everything progresses at a slow pace. Elizabeth too had progressed at a slow pace. Not only to avoid the danger that lurked everywhere, but also because it simply took so much effort to accomplish anything.

She could see no way out. But every day God gave her enough perspective to get through that minute, that hour, or occasionally, that day. And every day, as she put one foot in front of the other, the fog cleared ahead of her just a little; but it had lingered for years.

The love of her father and her sister, Jane, had been her lights in the fog; they had helped show the way. But it had still required a steady, onward motion to get out. One step in front of the other, pressing forward, every day. *After every night, there is a dawn,* she had told herself. *After every storm, the sun comes out. Eventually, every storm cloud runs out of rain. Darkness does not last forever. In time, the sun, or the Son, will lift this fog.* That was the lesson she had learned ever so slowly, but its truth was now solid in her heart.

Elizabeth knew what it was like to look in the mirror and see dark, sad, desperate eyes. She knew what it was like to feel nothing but pain. But now the fog had been gone for years. Now she could see, and she could very clearly see that she was meant to help Georgiana. She said her amen and lifted her eyes. It was another sunny day in Derbyshire, for her at least.

She quickly dressed and went downstairs. She found her aunt instructing a servant where to hang the family portraits.

Marianne Gardiner was a special soul. One could call her a soul reader. She was blessed with the ability to discern right from wrong, truth from error. So, when she asked her niece how she was doing and received the response, "I am well," she turned her full attention toward her. It wasn't the words that alerted her; it was the carefully hidden tone of sadness in Elizabeth's voice that alerted her that things were not right. She quickly dismissed the servant.

Elizabeth could tell she had not deceived her aunt. She might as well get it out in the open. "I did not sleep well."

"And why was that, my dear?"

"Mr. Darcy and his sister seemed to pervade my dreams. I kept feeling like I said something wrong or that I missed an opportunity to say something right."

"I think it went quite well. Of course, poor Georgiana was dragged to a dinner that she clearly did not want to attend, but I believe you helped her feel more at ease."

Elizabeth pondered that statement. "I do not know. I would like to pay her a call. Do you think we could do that? I feel this kinship to her that I cannot explain. She needs me, and for some reason, I need her too. It is not that I am lonely—I have kept myself quite busy with everything about the estate—but she reminded me of a time when I had that same look in my eyes. Did you notice it, Aunt?"

"Of course, my dear. Yes, she is going through a rough time. At first glance, one would think she was just shy, but there is something more. Are you sure you are strong enough to help another? Will it not rekindle the feelings that you once had?"

Elizabeth shook her head. "I do not believe so. I have come a long way from those years of sadness. I am a stronger person now. If anyone can help her—"

"It will be you."

"No, it *should* be me. I have a duty to help. I was saved, and now I must help those in the same predicament. I know now why I am here. She is excruciatingly pained, perhaps worse than I was, but I pulled through by scratching my nails and screaming my way out of it. I did not have someone who knew how it felt like to fall into a never-ending, cold, dark pit; I did not have someone who understood to help pull me out. It took me years to scrape my way to the top."

"I know, dear, but you were never really alone. You had your father, your sister, Jane, and you had us. I know your mother made it harder on you, but she was in her own kind of pit. She had lost her only son and felt you were to blame for it."

"I know how she felt. She reminded me every day that it should have been me instead of him."

"But she is better now, is she not?"

"I think I simply have accepted that she will always blame me, and I have learned to tolerate her hurtful behavior."

"You do not truly believe that, do you?"

"I do. She hardly said goodbye when I left for Derbyshire. I have heard nothing from her since I came. Papa has written twice so far."

"Yes, but that is because you are his favorite. Now, about visiting the Darcys; I will send our card to them and ask if we could call on them tomorrow morning. I have some friends on the north of Lambton that I need to look in on. Would you mind going with me to visit them first?"

"Not at all. Tomorrow shall be fine. Do you mind if I send a note with yours specifically for Georgiana? I have a few things I would like to say."

"I think that would be a nice gesture. One more thing: how did you like Mr. Darcy?"

"I think he will make a fine friend and offer Uncle good advice."

"I do not mean what kind of neighbor will he be. How did you like him?"

Elizabeth was taken aback for a moment. Her aunt would see through any falsehoods, and yet she didn't want to admit to how much she really had thought about him. "I suppose most would find him handsome. He takes great care to conceal his emotions, but his eyes are quite revealing. He seems to tolerate advice from a lady, which I find refreshing. I suppose he is amiable."

Madeline Gardiner smiled. "I would agree with you on all accounts, but I had not noticed he was handsome."

Elizabeth flushed in embarrassment. "Well, he is. And you are not the only one who can detect lies. I know you think him a handsome man too."

Mrs. Gardiner laughed, "Yes, dear, you caught me. I would say he is quite handsome."

"Indeed."

*****

Mr. Darcy received Mrs. Gardiner's note just after noon. He read through it quickly and felt his heart pound hard a few times. *Miss Bennet is coming to pay a call on Georgiana! Tomorrow!* His mind immediately began scheming about how he could involve himself in their visit to Georgiana. Perhaps he could offer a private tour of the estate?

He took a moment to put his emotions in check. How did a lady he met just yesterday already have such pull on him? He reviewed his interactions with her and studied her face in his mind. Perhaps it was her warm, chocolate, brown eyes spattered with gold flecks. He wasn't sure if he imagined it, but they seemed to be happy eyes, full of merriment. Her whole face was engaging. Her walk had a bounce to it. She had picked up on Georgiana's shy nature quickly and knew exactly what to do. He was in awe. To find such a knowledgeable, educated, witty person was refreshing, let alone to find one that glowed with . . . what? What did she glow with? He could not say, but he felt as if his soul had taken a long drink from a fresh mountain spring.

He studied the sealed letter addressed to Georgiana in an elegant, feminine hand. He searched for Georgiana and found her sitting in the music room, staring with that blank look at the pianoforte.

He cleared his throat and walked with deliberately heavy footsteps, but she remained oblivious to his presence. He leaned down behind her and whispered her name; she didn't even blink. He tentatively reached a hand out and placed it on her shoulder. She quickly jumped and sucked in a gasp of air. "I am terribly sorry, Georgie," he murmured. "I tried to get your attention, but you were deep in thought. I have a letter for you from Miss Bennet."

Georgiana looked at him and saw his eyes creased with worry. She must do something about her mood! There was nothing she wanted more than to see her brother happy, and she knew, at the moment, that she was only a source of worry for him. Silently, she took the letter and put it on her lap and returned to looking at the pianoforte again.

"Are you not going to read it?"

Georgiana heard something in his voice, and she nodded. "I will, William. I promise."

"You do not need to make me any more promises, Georgie. How can I help you? Was last night as bad as you feared?"

"No."

Mr. Darcy walked around to the front of the sofa and gestured his desire to sit next to her. She nodded. He sat and took her hand in his. "Miss Bennet and Mrs. Gardiner have asked to visit us tomorrow. How do you feel about that?"

Georgiana sighed, which took more effort and energy than she had at the moment. She closed her eyes and reminded herself why she went last night in the first place. William deserved to have someone to love him through what was coming, someone who could make him happy. She knew she could not supply that happiness. She could not even muster enough spirit to give him a polite smile, let alone make him happy. With all her heart she loved William, but even that could not save her.

Sucking in another breath, she turned to look at him. He had hope in his eyes again, and it made her heart lighter for a brief moment. She lied and said, "I think I would like a friend right now." But what she thought was, *What could a friend do for me?* The relief in his eyes was all too evident when she said it. Yes, she would have to be friends with Elizabeth Bennet. And a friend she would be, if it was the last thing she did. She knew she was failing miserably as a sister.

"Splendid! I noticed you looking at the pianoforte earlier. Do you not wish to play? I have not heard you in so long, and I know it brought you great joy before."

"I am as good as can be expected, William. One does not bounce back after . . . after . . ."

He took her shoulders and brought her head to his chest. "I know, pumpkin. I know. But he cannot hurt you now."

"How do you know that? He could come at any time!" She hadn't meant to blurt out her thoughts but they continued. "You told me yourself that he has an evil mindset and does not think like we do. How can we predict what he will do?" Her tears ran as quickly as her mouth. She tried to stifle the sobs, but they came unbidden.

Mr. Darcy was relieved she was talking about it. Talking at all was a good sign. He rubbed her shoulder with one hand and kissed her forehead. "I promise you, you will never see that man again. Wickham will see the gallows before he speaks to you again."

"I do not want his life to be on my head. I only wish it had never happened."

"So do I. So do I."

She wiped her eyes and stiffened as she sat up. She was in much better control of her voice now as she said, "I suppose I should read my letter." *It will avoid the pain for a few short minutes.* That was the best she could do. Distract herself. Distraction was not a permanent solution, but it would help for a moment. Lately it seemed that buying a single moment came at great personal cost. Today's price was reading a letter to make her brother happy.

Darcy released her reluctantly. "Would you like me to leave? I should like to stay. You never talk about what happened with Wickham, and I just thought—"

"No. I am not ready. Please do not ask me to talk."

"I only want to know what you wish to tell me. I do not want to push you into anything. He broke your heart, I recognize that. When you are ready to talk about it, I will drop anything to be there for you."

Yes, but what if you knew the truth? Would you judge me? Would it change how you felt about me? And he broke more than my heart. He broke my spirit. He took everything from me. Everything. "I know, William. You have told me many times." She lifted her hand and flicked her fingers in a gesture that meant for him to leave. Even that small gesture was too much, and she dropped her hand clumsily. She just needed to be alone. No one knew her pain. No one could help.

Georgiana watched as William stood and left the room. Her chin dropped to her chest, and she groaned. Why was everything so taxing? Why couldn't she simply take a deep breath and not feel like the world was on her shoulders? Only she knew the truth, and that was how it would stay for a long time.

She opened the sealed letter and read the following words.

Dear Georgiana,

I want you to know that I have felt the same pain you feel. I have been there. And I will come to you in a heartbeat if you wish to talk.

I had the same look in my eyes years ago, and I needed someone to listen when I did not wish to talk. I needed someone to love me when I felt unloved. I needed someone to share my pain when it overflowed, when I knew not how much longer I could exist in that state. I needed to hear how special and valued I was when I felt so very worthless. I wished so much for a friend. I needed to hear that there was joy in store for me, instead of the deep darkness that surrounded me. I needed so much but knew not how or whom to ask for it.

Please know that I wish to be there for you. I cannot explain it, but I am meant to be here, in Derbyshire, to help you. What you feel right now will not last. The sun will shine again. Trust me. I have been to the depths of hell and survived to tell you about it. I have peace now.

I wish to offer whatever part of me you are ready to accept. I can be a friend, a confidant, or even a sister. I want to help you. You can survive this. Forgive me if I speak too plainly, but it is not in my nature to mince words, especially when I see such a jewel before me in so much pain.

I look forward to seeing you tomorrow. Perhaps in time I can help you see the light this world has to offer.

Remember, sadness is just a feeling; it cannot consume you.

Until tomorrow,
Your friend,
Elizabeth Bennet

Georgiana folded the letter. She tucked it into her pocket and stood up to leave. As she passed the pianoforte, she ran her fingers along the keys. The sound made her stop. She paused and turned back around. *I do not really want to play, do I?* She leaned over and let her right hand pick out a few cords in A minor. They seemed to express what she was feeling. *Sadness is only a feeling;*

it cannot consume you. She played a few measures of a song she knew. Without sitting down, she placed her left hand on the keys and started *Prelude and fugue in A minor* by Bach. The mood of the music seeped into her hands as she played.

She played it slower than usual, the passion for the piece stirring something inside her. She felt her heart start to keep rhythm with the music. Soon, she instructed her fingers to play faster and, sure enough, her heartbeat accelerated. It startled her so much that she retracted her hands immediately. The silence in the room echoed loudly as the notes dissipated.

Pulling out the bench, she sat down and rested her hands on the keys waiting for her heart to calm down. When it had resumed a normal pattern, she started to play. As she did so, her heart picked up and pounded hard in her chest. *There it was again—evidence that I am alive.* Evidence that she felt something other than pain. She immediately stood up and left the room, not even noticing she had knocked the bench over in her haste.

Darcy could hear the music through the halls of Pemberley. It was soulful and sad, but he was glad to hear music again. He knew Miss Elizabeth had something to do with it. After the music ended, he went to look in the music room and saw the bench tipped over. He lifted it back onto its legs and placed it in the proper position. She had played. If only for a moment, she had played. He looked down on the ground and there was Georgiana's letter from Elizabeth. The temptation to read it was brief. He simply picked it up and placed the folded letter on the keys of the pianoforte. It seemed only fitting.

*****

Saphrinbrooke, Derbyshire
25 June 1811

Dear Papa,

I have so much to tell you. We dined last night with Mr. Fitzwilliam Darcy, Saphrinbrooke's closest gentleman neighbor. He is an interesting fellow. He is guardian of his only sister, who is at least ten years his junior, but has no other family. He inherited Pemberley five years ago. I will get to see the grand estate tomorrow.

I have never met anyone more committed to concealing his inner thoughts than Mr. Darcy. He makes good conversation when he opens his mouth, but he is so reticent and mysterious. If only I could compel him to speak! But do not fear; I am trying to be a little guarded around him. I know how important it is to make a good impression, for the Gardiners' sake, as I suspect he has quite a bit of influence in this part of the country.

However, the real reason I am writing is his sister, Georgiana. She is like I once was, and I want to help her. I know a lost soul when I see one. I recognized the look in her eyes immediately, although it was the first time I had seen it in another's eyes. I do not know yet what has her so troubled, but I plan to show her all the kindness you and Jane showed me all those years.

I know I have thanked you a thousand times for not giving up on me, but I cannot tell you how alone I felt; each smile, each reassuring word, and each tender touch gave me strength to endure. So, I just wanted to write a quick note to tell you that I now know why I am here. Georgiana needs a friend to show her that her life is worth fighting for. And, if the opportunity presents itself, perhaps I can also convince Mr. Darcy to speak his mind.

*I will write more in a few days, but I wanted
you to know that I have a purpose and a work to do.
I pray I will be strong enough to help them her.
Thank you again for being my rock for me when my
foundation was crumbling.*

*And do not make too much about my
observations about Mr. Darcy. He is simply a man.*

Your loving daughter,
Elizabeth Bennet

Elizabeth reread her lines and laughed. She had made it
sound like she had two missions: to help Georgiana, and to become
better acquainted with Mr. Darcy. Despite her giggles, she
wondered if that was how she really felt. She knew her father
would laugh at her observations and assume even more, but she
didn't mind. Her father was more than just a parent to her—he was
a wise confidant and a faithful friend.

Certainly in the last four years she had given him little to
discipline her for. Before that had been her blur of darkness. She
remembered very little from that time, but she remembered his
constant protective presence. His mini-sermons, as she liked to call
them, were like catching a wave of heat as you stepped out of the
cold into a warm room. It was a momentary relief from a deep
chill, a chill that never really went away.

She wondered if she should have mentioned what was
happening on the estate, but it could surely wait a few days' time
until she wrote again. After sealing it, she put it with the other
letters to be posted, one to Jane and one to her mother. She did not
expect her mother would write back, but that conclusion did not
vex her.

*****

The carriage ride to Pemberley was spectacular. First, they came to a gate at the entrance to the estate. From there, they traveled a good mile before they reached the main house, and the views of the grounds were amazing.

Mrs. Gardiner patted Elizabeth on the knee and said, "It is the largest estate in all of Derbyshire. If he were not so young, he would probably be the local magistrate. If you are impressed now, wait until you see inside. I toured it several times in my youth. It is finely decorated and yet not adorned with expensive, ornate frivolities."

"It is the grounds that have captured my interest. How lovely! Is that a hedge maze? Oh my! And look at that rose garden! And gardenias in full bloom, and look at that bridge over the river! Have you seen anything like it? I could spend hours walking the grounds and not see all of it. I had not thought him so rich."

"I hear he takes in ten thousand a year. Does that make him any more handsome?" She eyed her niece mischievously.

"Aunt, you know I am not of that persuasion. But do not mention to mother that there is a single man of large fortune in the neighborhood, or she will send Jane out in an instant. Then again, perhaps I should tell her myself; Jane would be a perfect match, and I miss her so much."

Mrs. Gardiner had her suspicions of who Mr. Darcy thought would be his perfect match. The frequent object of his gaze during dinner had been a clear indication, but she just smiled back at her niece. They rolled up to the front entrance, and she was surprised to see the man himself waiting to hand them out of the carriage. He must have been waiting for the carriage, which only added to her suspicions.

"Welcome to Pemberley, Miss Bennet and Mrs. Gardiner." He took Elizabeth's hand and felt his heart race as she firmly grasped it. Did he detect a slight squeeze before she dropped it? He looked at her briefly, but she was engrossed in looking at the grounds around her. He handed Mrs. Gardiner out as well.

"Mr. Darcy, I must tell you something," Elizabeth asserted.

His interest was piqued; she had that look in her eyes that said he should prepare himself for something witty. "And what is that, Miss Bennet?"

"I truly do not know of whom you speak!"

"Pardon me?"

"I see your eyes resting on me, trying to conceal all your deepest thoughts, but I must ask if you are acquainted with my sister, Jane?"

"I do not have that pleasure. Why do you ask?"

"The title of Miss Bennet belongs to her as she is the eldest."

"I vaguely remember Mr. Gardiner saying you were the second eldest. Then shall I call you Miss Elizabeth?" The sound of it rolling off his tongue was like melting butter and honey over a slice of hot, fresh bread.

"I believe you shall if you desire to keep my attention. Then again, seeing your estate might very well take all my attention. I may be so distracted that nothing will be able to garner my senses or make me notice your words. It is truly amazing!" She looked around again and took it all in. She had not even gone inside yet.

"Then I shall be the first to claim that I struck Miss Elizabeth Bennet dumb. I would love to show you the estate after tea if you have time."

"You are quick to examine my character, Mr. Darcy. What makes you think I have never been struck dumb before?" She raised an eyebrow at him saucily and saw that he was restraining a smile to the best of his ability.

Mr. Darcy tried to hold it back, but he knew he could not keep a straight face for long. "Something tells me you have a lot to say on just about any subject, madam. I gather your tongue has less restraint than a child with a farthing in his pocket in a sweet shop."

"Are you calling me impertinent?"

"Does it rain in England in November?"

"It does in Hertfordshire, but I am unfamiliar with the weather in Derbyshire. I must assume that you think me loose-tongued and impertinent. Do you have anything else to accuse me of before I can enter? Is this how you treat all your guests?"

He was hooked. As sure as a fish looking at a floating, squirming worm, he was hooked. "I dare not accuse you of anything. I simply said you had a lot to say and that I doubt you have ever been struck dumb. Loose-tongued and impertinent were your own words."

She resisted laughing outright at him. "Well then, perhaps you could show us in?"

"Indeed. Mrs. Gardiner, I believe you have seen the estate before; may I show you in?" He offered her his arm.

Mrs. Gardiner knew when a man was being polite and when he wished to be turned down. This was one of those times. "I am well, thank you. Perhaps Elizabeth could use a hand on those steps?"

"Certainly. Miss Elizabeth, may I show you in before you further accuse me of defaming your character?"

She looked down at his offered arm and hesitated briefly before placing her arm on his. He very properly guided her into the foyer as any gentleman would do. When inside she expected him to drop her arm, but instead he led her toward a man she assumed was the butler.

"Mr. Reynolds, would you please let Georgiana know that our guests have arrived and have tea sent to the yellow sitting room?"

"Yes, sir. May I take your outerwear and reticule, madam?"

Elizabeth nodded and handed him her shawl and reticule. She felt Mr. Darcy's eyes on her. She turned and, just as she expected, he was watching her. She gave him a smile. His eyes lit up in response, yet his mouth remained motionless. "Mr. Darcy, when a lady smiles at you, it is customary to smile in return. You need not hide behind that stone face of yours."

The corners of Mr. Darcy's mouth crawled upward at a painstakingly slow rate, and then she realized why he hid his smile. He turned from handsome, to devastatingly charming, as his dimples made their appearance. She heard herself take in a breath, and she held it in, truly struck dumb. Her heart started racing, and she felt warm inside.

He smiled wider, waiting for her response, but her intake of breath was surprising. He waited for her to reply, but she said nothing. "Am I to assume you have been struck dumb by the sight of my foyer?"

She looked away as she knew her face was burning bright red. "No, sir," she responded. He led her further down the hall to a large sitting room with windows that faced several rose bushes.

He had requested the curtains be opened prior to their guests' arrival, as the view was one of his favorites. He turned to watch Miss Elizabeth's reaction. If he thought she had glowed before, he was surely wrong. She emanated delight, and her face lit up like a candelabra. He carefully dropped her arm and let her walk to the window. She had a pleasing figure. It was light and narrow in all the right places, but she wasn't too thin, not like some of the women he'd danced with. Suddenly, he was struck with the strongest desire to dance with her. He imagined seeing her float through the air, light on her feet, ever so elegant and graceful. He gathered his thoughts momentarily and checked himself. She was speaking, and he wasn't even attending her.

"Mr. Darcy! How do you ever get any work done when you have such beauty before you ready to be explored?"

"I have a very similar view from my study which we passed as we came down the hall. I admit it is one of the grandest views of all of Pemberley, besides the view from Grecian temple on the hill. From there you see the entire property and the hills and the stream. It truly takes my breath away. I would love to show it to you sometime. Do you enjoy walking, Miss Elizabeth?"

Mrs. Gardiner laughed politely. "Oh my, you have not known Elizabeth long if you feel the need to ask such a question! Elizabeth, how many miles do you think you walk on any given day? Four? Six?"

Elizabeth was so moved by the view from the window, that she simply nodded and murmured her agreement. From where she stood, she saw yellow and red roses directly under the window, followed by an open lawn that sloped down towards a large lake. Its left bank was covered by a beautiful canopy of trees, and she could see a pier, at least fifteen yards long, leading to a small, octagonal gazebo situated in the middle of the lake. On the right were some boulders. She could see gentle ripples of water rubbing up against their mossy bases. "Mr. Darcy, how deep is the lake?"

"Only ten feet deep in the middle; the slope is very gradual. But there is a natural spring by those boulders on the right bank. It is quite deep there." Elizabeth giggled. If he was hooked before, that giggle captured him completely. He couldn't help but ask, "What is so funny about my lake?"

She giggled again and turned to look at him. A small smile was on his face, but it was not big enough to reveal his dimples. He was once again hiding behind his "Mr. Darcy mask", as she liked to think of it. "I simply had the biggest urge to jump into a lake! I have not done that for years!"

"When I was younger, my friends and I used to jump off the boulders into the deep area. But I warn you, that area of the lake is quite cold due to the spring. I doubt you would want to do it twice. You surprise me, Miss Elizabeth. I do not think Georgiana has ever done such a thing."

"I highly doubt that. She has spirit."

"Indeed." Mr. Darcy wondered where his sister was hiding, but just then, Georgiana entered. She was hiding behind a small smile; it looked foreign compared to the blank look she had possessed the last three months.

Georgiana's face felt awkward in her attempts to smile, but she had overheard Elizabeth say she had spirit, and she wanted to show her gratitude. She walked up to Elizabeth and said, "Good morning, Elizabeth. Good morning, Mrs. Gardiner. I am sorry I kept you waiting. I hope my brother has been a gentleman and made up for my absence." The exertion she felt in saying all of that at once was so great that it sapped her energy completely; her smile disappeared. She tried once again to replace it. Who knew one would have to think about smiling at the right times?

Elizabeth stood and took Georgiana's hand and leaned into her and whispered something in her ear just loud enough for Mr. Darcy to hear, "He was telling me all about his boyhood indiscretions. He told me he used to swim in the lake as a boy with hardly an inch of clothing on! Can you believe he would admit such a thing to a lady?"

"I said nothing of the sort!"

The shock in his face was great indeed, and she let out a laugh. "Now he forces me to tell the truth: I must admit he did not mention any clothes at all! But to save me from embarrassment I imagined him wearing at least a little clothing!"

Mrs. Gardiner laughed, and Georgiana's face showed a slight grin on it. It was a weak one, but an honest grin. Elizabeth had made her grin.

It was then Mr. Darcy's turn to show his embarrassment, and he stood and tucked his arm behind him and bowed. "I see now why gentlemen do not take tea with ladies. I shall leave you with Georgiana." He turned to leave after first making eye contact with Georgiana. "If they have time, perhaps we could give them a tour of the estate afterwards."

Georgiana looked to Elizabeth and asked, "Would you like that?"

Elizabeth smiled brightly and said, "I would love a tour. We have finished all our calls for today, so we are free to spend more time."

"Then I shall be in my study. Please let me accompany you. There is nothing I enjoy more than sharing my home with others who I know will appreciate the history and memories it holds."

Elizabeth couldn't restrain herself; he was such an easy target. "Will I be hearing more stories of your indiscretions?"

He smiled at her widely. "I shall admit to only a few. But simply because if I do not give you something to quench your thirst for gossip, I fear you will make up your own stories about me. I worry I will soon have a very different reputation entirely." He saw her bright smile answer him in the affirmative, and he left the room.

What kind of woman is this? She seems to take me to task with every conversation! One minute he felt in control of himself, and the next he wanted to dance with her. He hardly knew her! What kind of power did she possess to manipulate him so? He felt a bounce in his step as he entered his study. He sat down and looked out the window at the same scene Elizabeth had just admired. It truly was a beautiful view. And how did she know he used to jump from the boulders wearing little but undershorts in the heat of the summer?

He shook his head. She hadn't known, but his reaction had confirmed it for her. Again he wondered how a lady could draw his attention so drastically. He seemed to think of little else but Elizabeth Bennet for the next half hour. He thought of her giggle, her teasing, her impertinence, and her sparkle. He did not realize how long he had been sitting, doing nothing but thinking of her, until he heard a knock on the door. He glanced at his pocket watch and realized an entire half hour had passed.

He stood and straightened his vest and combed his fingers through his hair. He opened the door and saw the three women ready and waiting for a tour. "Good day, ladies. How was tea? Did Georgiana reveal my deep, dark past to our you?"

Georgiana's face showed her shock as she replied, "Oh no!"

"I am only teasing you, Georgie," Darcy said. "I know you would never tell tales. For I was an angel of a child and remain the image of perfection as an adult. There are simply no stories to tell."

Elizabeth then smiled and said, "Then this shall be a very dull tour. I was hoping to hear some good stories."

"I shall try not to disappoint you. Do you read, Miss Elizabeth?"

"Indeed. I have loved every book I could get my hands on."

"I seriously doubt you love every book."

Mrs. Gardiner laughed and said, "No, not every book. She has read *Fordyce's Sermons*. Her father prohibited her to read it, and yet she did. She disliked them so much she did not finish volume two."

"Ah, so we are to hear of Miss Elizabeth's indiscretions on this tour. How delightful! What else have you done that your father prohibited? Dare I ask?"

"I would advise against it. Continue your enquiry only if you dare."

"Indeed, I do not dare. We shall start with the library then. It is my favorite room of the entire estate."

Georgiana watched as her brother led Elizabeth down the hall to the library and opened the double doors. Georgiana slowly followed, lingering behind with Mrs. Gardiner. She truly tried to make small talk. But it took a great deal of effort, and she sensed that Mrs. Gardiner could tell. That must be why Mrs. Gardiner kept talking about what Georgiana's parents were like: what they would say; how well they treated others; and how generous they were. Georgiana truly was interested, but she was somewhat distracted by a more pressing concern: studying the interactions between her brother and Elizabeth.

They seemed to be in deep conversation about books. Georgiana watched her brother look thoughtful, surprised, impressed, and curious at different times. Elizabeth too looked impressed, but also seemed genuinely interested in the discussion. There was one moment when they looked to be arguing politely. Elizabeth said something with a raised eyebrow to her brother, who then folded his arm behind him and flex his hand repeatedly, a nervous habit of his.

And then suddenly he was smiling at Elizabeth and bowing respectfully to her, and she curtsied back to him with a flirtatious tilt of the head, and they stared silently at each other for a few moments. William then looked stone-faced, and his hand started flexing again behind him, and he pointed behind her to a bookshelf. She let him guide her to the shelf, but she shook her head no to his question. He persisted, trying to convince her of something.

Georgiana wanted so badly to understand and hear what they were saying, but she knew they needed time alone to become better acquainted. Their battle of wills continued, and finally Elizabeth held out her hand to take something. It seemed they had reached a compromise of some sorts, which made William smile widely. He then reached around behind Elizabeth and selected two books from his shelf of personal favorites and handed them to her. She accepted them and held them close to her chest. Georgiana could just make out Elizabeth's bashful thank-you. They were heading back to the hall now, each with smiles on their faces.

Mrs. Gardiner wrapped her story up quickly and said, "So, that is the rumor of how your father resolved the issue. If the rumor is true, then he was a unique landlord."

Mr. Darcy overheard the end of their conversation and added, "Yes, my father was a very unique landlord. Shall we continue the tour? I thought Georgiana could show you her music room."

And so, the rest of the tour continued in this manner. Mrs. Gardiner occupied Georgiana with stories of her parents and her memories of Lambton while Mr. Darcy guided Elizabeth on a personal tour of the estate.

Elizabeth was fully engaged by Darcy's tour narration. In each room he shared his fond memories of growing up in such a grand place. He told her about the parties he had attended in the ballroom and showed her the sculpture he had recently acquired for the morning room. He spoke little about the size, the magnitude, or the impressive grandiosity of what Pemberley represented. He was clearly quite wealthy, and yet he did not flaunt it. He wasn't trying to impress her. Instead, he just shared his good memories and what the home meant to him. This impressed her more than the estate itself.

Elizabeth noticed that her aunt lingered slightly behind, as did Georgiana, and she kept an eye on them both. It seemed they were keeping an eye on her as well. But there were moments that she admitted she was oblivious to their presence. It was so intriguing to watch the emotions dancing in Mr. Darcy's eyes. He continued to restrain himself for the most part, but there were times she caught him staring at her. When that happened, he would quickly start another story about the home.

She gathered that he rarely gave personal tours of his home. He did not offer any of the facts tourists would want to know: when the house was built, how many rooms it had, how many could dine comfortably at that enormous dinner table, or the number of servants employed. Instead, he shared memories of private family gatherings and traditions. She had visited other great estates, but she had never had a tour like this one.

Although she knew time was passing, she was very much engaged in listening to this man who seemed both at ease with her and quite bumble-headed around her. She would catch glimpses of the man behind the "Mr. Darcy mask", and he seemed a tad shy. One could tell he loved his estate, but his tour showed her that it wasn't just an estate to him; it was his home. Realizing how much he loved his home made him quite charming in her eyes.

As they exited the side doors into the gardens, Mrs. Gardiner said, "If you do not mind, I think I will admire the gardens from here. It has been such a treat to see the estate, but I would like to rest a while."

Georgiana picked up on the hint. "Perhaps Mrs. Gardiner and I could stay here while you two continue, and we can enjoy some refreshments together when you finish. I will ask the cook to make lemonade."

Mr. Darcy was surprised at Georgiana's calmness and hospitality. "That sounds like a fine plan. Miss Elizabeth, would you like to rest or would you like to see the gardens?"

"I do not have a choice in the matter."

Mr. Darcy floundered a little; he had been so sure she would want to see the gardens. "If you are concerned it would be improper, we can stay in view of your aunt."

Elizabeth laughed. Teasing him was too much fun. "I only meant that my mind is so set on seeing the gardens that there is no other viable option. If you were to stop the tour, you might have a lone woman, dead set on seeing all of Pemberley, walking aimlessly around your grounds. And no, I do not fear seeing the grounds with you."

"Aunt," Elizabeth continued, "would you mind holding these books Mr. Darcy loaned me? He insisted I take them. Luckily, I was able to negotiate an agreement: I will read these books, if he will read one of mine. I just so happen to have it with me. My intention was to loan it to Georgiana, but now both of them can benefit from it." Her aunt took the books and gave her a wink and a smile which made her flush slightly.

He offered his arm to her, a gesture that he was beginning to quite enjoy. "Then let us proceed." She gave him one of her cheerful, radiant smiles, and they started walking. As soon as they were out of earshot, he took a deep breath and started what he had wanted to say since the dinner at Saphrinbrooke. "I want to thank you for your efforts in befriending Georgiana. She is very dear to me, and you seem to be a good influence on her."

"How so?"

"It is not anything drastic. Perhaps there are a few small things that, when added up, become substantial. She is quite shy and making friends right now in her life is somewhat difficult. She is not out yet and probably will not be for some time. I have been looking for a companion to encourage her in her studies, but she is resistant to the idea at present."

"I imagine she needs several things, but a companion would have to be carefully selected given her current state."

"Her current state? I do not take your meaning."

Elizabeth looked up at Mr. Darcy and could see fear in his eyes. She tried to be truthful, but careful, in her next statement. "She is struggling emotionally. And if I am not mistaken, quite significantly."

"I did not know it was that obvious. I cannot disclose the cause of her sadness; for in truth, she has not even told me all of what happened. She is only a shell of her former self."

Elizabeth pushed further. "How long has she been this way?"

"Three months tomorrow. I only hope she does not realize the date. I worry she will see it as some sort of anniversary of what happened. I fear a great deal for her. But she will pull through it. She is strong, and like you said, she has spirit."

"Even strong spirits can lose their way. I would counsel you to be patient and watch for any warning signs."

"Warning signs? Warning signs of what?" Darcy looked at her, but Elizabeth made no reply.

"Oh no," he continued, "it is nothing like that. She is just feeling melancholy. You do not think she would actually . . . No, you are mistaken. Not Georgiana. She would never . . . She would never do that to me."

"I must counsel you again. What she is going through is significant. It is more than some excessively long, sad moment. She is ill. I know it. And the pain she feels is so very real. If, and I am only saying if, she is considering anything drastic, it will have nothing to do with you. It will be because she can no longer handle the pain. This thing we are talking about, but not really saying out loud, is a real risk for her. I know that look in her eyes. Please promise me you will watch her carefully."

"How do you know that look in her eyes? And what warning signs should I be looking for?"

Elizabeth didn't know how much she wanted to disclose. She opted for less rather than more. She said a quick prayer that it was the right thing to do. "A person I was extremely close to lived with that kind of pain for years before she found her way through it. It is a dark and lonely place to be. I cannot say more. Does she have access to your weapons?"

He stopped and turned quickly to look at her. He wanted to make this quite clear. "Miss Elizabeth, I assure you that she would never, ever do anything to hurt herself. I know my sister much better than you do." This conversation was officially over. He turned and started detailing the history of the gardens.

Elizabeth was somewhat shocked by his stubborn reply. She had tried to warn him, but he would not listen. They continued their tour of the gardens, but he had on his best "Mr. Darcy mask". His eyes never betrayed him. He was stone faced and seemed committed to staying so. The only indication that her words had affected him was an occasional glimpse of his clenching fist behind his back.

CHAPTER 3

The next two weeks were excessively long and burdensome for Elizabeth. She was quite busy helping her aunt and uncle with the tenants and the estate, but in the back of her mind she was always thinking about Georgiana. *Should I call on her again? Should I send our thanks for the tour? How has she liked my prayer notebook? Has she even read any of it? Is she doing any better? Or, God forbid, is she doing any worse?*

One morning in the butler's pantry, Elizabeth reviewed Mr. Darcy's last words, *I know my sister much better than you do.* She prayed again that he was correct. She also prayed that her aunt's perception of Georgiana as simply being shy was correct—perhaps Georgiana appeared worse than she really was.

The tarnish on the silver-rimmed plates was considerable. It appeared they had not been used in several years. She set aside the worst ones for extra polishing as she considered Mr. Darcy's sudden change of demeanor in the Pemberley gardens. He had made it quite clear that any helpful conversation about Georgiana was impossible. She had never come across such stubborn and proud behavior. During the tour of the house, he had been open and engaging and even a little charming, certainly not proud. Now she didn't know what to make of his character. *What kind of devoted brother would disregard counsel regarding the safety of his sister?*

Elizabeth struggled to keep her mind on counting and sorting plates. After all, it did no good to investigate her feelings about the man. At one point, she had imagined he would be a good match for Jane. She had even written to her mother, detailing the grand Pemberley estate and the bachelor who ran it. She was sure her motives were clearly seen by her father, but her mother had fallen right for the trap and had arranged for Jane to come to Derbyshire immediately; after all, a single man of large fortune *must* be in want of a wife. Tomorrow Jane would arrive. Elizabeth was eager to see her and pleased her plan had worked, but the more she thought about Mr. Darcy's reaction in the gardens—his proud denial and stone demeanor—the more she feared that introducing him to Jane was a poor idea.

Elizabeth put away the dishes and began assessing the state of the silverware. Some forks tines had been bent too far and had snapped off. They were probably not worth saving; her uncle would need to purchase new ones. Elizabeth sighed. Would Jane's passive nature, under Darcy's rule, become even more yielding? Would she be bent too far? Jane was kind and sweet tempered. Her compliant nature made her unlikely to argue or disagree about anything. She smiled and agreed with whatever Elizabeth, or her mother, or her father, suggested. Debating an issue for sake of good conversation was viewed as contention, and Jane strictly adhered to their father's warnings against strife of any kind.

Elizabeth returned the passable silverware to the cabinet and bundled up the damaged forks. Perhaps they could still be put to good use. Jane would know how to use them. She always knew the best way to help people and was ready to give everything and anything to someone in need. Of course, Elizabeth was like that too. More than once, each had given her shawl, coat, or pelisse to someone who needed it more. Both assisted at the orphanage. Both listened closely to what their father taught them. And both tried their best to please their mother.

Of course, Jane was more successful at the latter than Elizabeth. Evidence of that fact was that Jane was in route to Saphrinbrooke, arriving tomorrow afternoon, against her will.

But now that Jane was on her way, Elizabeth hesitated in her matchmaking plan. Did she really want to introduce her dearest sister to such a prideful man? Someone who had dismissed her counsel entirely? She reminded herself that she had to continue to look for the good in people. Since most of the tour of Pemberley and her other interactions with Mr. Darcy had been positive, she concluded that Mr. Darcy may have had his reasons for not listening; it was not her place to judge.

Her father always said that people are inherently good. People may make bad choices, but they themselves are inherently good. Even plates marred by decades of tarnish could be polished to reveal the beautiful silver underneath. This was one of the sermons that helped her darkness and fog to subside and eventually disappear. She had committed herself to seeing the hope in life instead of imagining and reliving the evil in the world.

She was struck with a flash of memory so powerful she shuddered. *No. Not now. I will not relive that moment. I have moved past that and have forgiven him.* But she had to admit that it had taken many years to imagine any good in that man. She shuddered again involuntarily and forced her mind back to the silver cabinets.

*****

The next two weeks were difficult for Mr. Darcy as well. He had a great deal to handle on the estate, but it was hard to focus on anything but Georgiana. She fluctuated from slightly better, to much worse, to bizarre. Most of the time she refused to talk at all, and sometimes she asked odd questions.

Once, she asked which horse was the least tame. Then she asked how the roofer had fixed the leak three years ago. This morning she asked for laudanum for a headache. He informed her they didn't keep laudanum in the house unless prescribed by the doctor, and she became hysterical, crying and begging him to send for the doctor. She insisted her headache was unbearable, and she needed laudanum right away.

Darcy was surprised and concerned. He suggested her lady's maid might be better suited to handle a headache than the doctor and offered to fetch her maid at once, but Georgiana protested and looked defeated, saying she would just rest. Twice, he heard her playing the pianoforte, but it was a weak effort at best.

Twice, he offered Elizabeth's prayer notebook to her. The first time, she had been resistant. "Georgiana," he had begun hesitantly, "Miss Elizabeth wanted you to have her prayer notebook of inspirational thoughts. She gave it to me at the end of the tour. I wanted to loan her two books, but she was being quite stubborn. She said she could not possibly impose on me by borrowing them. She finally agreed to take the books, but only if I would read her notebook and have you read it too." Darcy handed the notebook to her. Georgiana glanced briefly at it and looked away, but made no attempt to take it from him.

"Please, Georgie, I gave her my word. Will you not let me read some of it to you?" Georgiana then gave a slight nod of the head and took a deep breath as if he was asking her to swim across the Atlantic Ocean. He read for a few minutes before noticing the tears in her eyes. She was simply letting them fall, not even wiping them. "I am sorry," he said. "I should let you have your time to yourself again."

He was about to get up when Georgiana gently placed her hand on his arm. Her voice was scratchy, coarse, and deeper than usual, as she whispered, "Read that part about frogs again."

"Are you sure?"

She nodded silently.

"It says, 'A frog has been given the skills to live both in water and on land. It enjoys the benefits of both environments, but it is endangered by every predator that walks or swims. Just like a frog, we will face many foes in many different environments, but we have been given the skills to overcome them if we fully rely on God. FROG.' Each letter of the last word is capitalized. I do not know why. She even drew out the word decoratively with swirls and flowers around the letters."

"Let me see." Georgiana took the notebook from her brother and replied flatly, "It is an acronym, F-R-O-G. Look at the daisies after each letter; they are periods."

She silently handed the notebook back. He studied the page closely until he saw them. "Ah, I can see it now. F-R-O-G." Then he saw tiny words hidden within the decoration and read them aloud, "Fully rely on God. Do you think she came up with that herself?" Georgiana made no reply.

"Well," he tried again, "I gather this notebook is a collection of thoughts that she finds valuable, ideas that offer support in some way. Does this idea about frogs interest you?" He was hoping to engage her in discussion, but her next words made it clear that would not happen.

"William, I am tired. Let us not read into it too much. It is just a silly correlation to a slimy, croaking animal. It is interesting, but it simply has no use."

Darcy heard her guarded words, but her eyes betrayed her. He knew she was thinking about what it would mean to fully rely on God. He was thinking about it too, and yet his trials were miniscule compared to hers. He still didn't really know what had happened at Ramsgate with Wickham. When his mind wondered about the details, his worries became painfully imaginative; and so, he tried quite hard not to think about it.

What he did know was enough make him want to see Wickham flogged. But he could tell Georgiana was holding something back. When he let his mind wonder about what else might have happened . . . well, it had been a shock to discover he had murderous feelings towards a man he had once called friend. The doctor had examined her after they returned to Pemberley, but Georgiana had forbidden him from discussing the results with her brother. Darcy knew it was confirmation that there was more to the story.

When he looked back, he was overcome with gratitude for finding her when he did. He also was grateful that, according to her maid, she had her courses since then. It had been quite embarrassing to ask, but he had tried to be discrete about it. He just wished she would return to the innocent little sister he loved.

He leaned in to kiss her forehead and gently wiped away her treacherous tears with his thumbs.

The next time he offered Miss Elizabeth's prayer notebook to Georgiana, she again refused to read it herself, but she allowed him to read a few lines again like before. She listened, but she offered no discussion. That day he shared one part he found particularly appropriate: "You never know how strong you are until being strong is the only option you have left." She just stared ahead as if she were blind. No tears, just that blasted blank look that lacked luster or expression. Her eyes had no glow in them like Elizabeth's eyes.

A few days later as he was trying to work in his study, he remembered the look in Georgiana's eyes, and he naturally let his thoughts drift to Elizabeth's eyes. A knock on the door returned his attention to the present. "Enter," he called out. The housekeeper, Mrs. Reynolds, came in quickly and closed the door behind her. It was an odd action, indicating she had something private to discuss. "What is it, Mrs. Reynolds?" He grew more concerned as he noticed she was wringing her hands.

"It is Miss Darcy. She is trying to ride the new black stallion, but Nathanial, the stable hand, is refusing to saddle him for her, and she is quite distressed. I have never seen her speak to a servant this way before. I was summoned by the lad who has been cleaning the stables, and I cannot speak any sense to her. That stallion is too big and wild for a lady, but she is insisting."

He stood and grabbed his blue jacket and thanked Mrs. Reynolds as he left his study. He took long paces to the stables and was only half way there when he heard her nearly screaming at Nathanial: he was to saddle the horse or be fired. She then threatened to saddle the horse herself, but from the sounds of it, Nathanial refused to give her the saddle. When Darcy arrived, he saw Georgiana attacking Nathanial with her fists.

"You do not understand! It must be that horse! I must ride him now!" Georgiana screamed, her small hands hitting the man, and her voice reaching a frantic tone.

Nathanial was taking the brunt of her fists in the chest, but when she landed one in the gut, he moaned and doubled over in pain. "Miss Darcy," he groaned, "he is not ready to be ridden yet. He is less than a year old and has not been properly broken. He could endanger your life!"

"It is my life and my decision! You forget your place! Now hand me that saddle, or I shall scream!" She pounded on his chest harder. "I will tell my brother that you refused to obey, and then we shall see who runs this stable. You will be in search of work with no references. Give me that saddle!"

Mr. Darcy was shocked. What had gotten into Georgiana to react this way? He walked behind her and grabbed the raised arm that was ready to strike Nathanial again. He quickly restrained the other hand as well. The surprise in Georgiana's face was great indeed. She had a crazed look in her eyes that spoke of desperation.

"Leave us," he instructed Nathanial. He watched as the stable hand turned and left. When he was out of earshot, Darcy spoke to Georgiana, "What do you think you are doing, young lady? That was despicable behavior! Have you no pride? You should never talk to a servant that way, and you certainly should not be hitting them! Have you ever witnessed Father or me hitting a servant? I am so shocked I have not the words to explain how appalled I am!"

"Unhand me, William!" If she had the energy, she would hunt down the servant who brought her brother into this. Her instinct guessed it had been Mrs. Reynolds.

She was trying to squirm free, but he held her tight. "Not unless you can promise to behave."

"I do not need to be spoken to like a child!"

"If you behave like a child, I certainly shall speak to you like a child."

"I am not acting like a child. I simply wanted to ride the new colt."

"No one is to ride him until he is properly broken in. He is still wild. You can ride any other horse, including mine."

"Yours is too tame. I need that one!"

Darcy loosened his grip on her hands, and she shook free of him completely. Her desperation and insistence was not hidden well. He tried to calm her, but she was not showing any sign of relaxation. "My horse is big and strong," he tried again. "If you need a good ride, he will be happy for the exercise."

"No! Your horse will not do what I need it to!"

"He is fast, he jumps, he climbs. What more do you need it to do?"

"You would not understand." Georgiana considered making a dash for the house. She did not want to have this conversation. She did not want to talk at all. She just needed to ride.

He let out a sigh and took her hand in his. He guided her reluctant person over to a hay bale and made her sit down. "I think we need to talk. I want to understand, I truly do. There is nothing you can say to me that would change the fact that I love you and care deeply for you. You have been in such a melancholy mood lately. I think it is time that we discuss it."

"I do *not* want to talk to you!"

"Then I suggest you come up with someone you can talk to. Do you wish to see the doctor again?"

"He cannot help me."

"Mrs. Reynolds has been like a mother to you. Would you like to speak with her?"

"Not her either."

"But you are willing to talk to someone?"

Georgiana felt trapped again. There was no way out of this anymore. She had designed the perfect plan, but everyone had spoiled it. She finally had a way to be free of this pain, but it hadn't worked; she was not free. "There is no one who could understand. No one can help me. I see that you are worried about me. I can see that my pain is contagious; it is like a disease gone rampant on a tiny ship, taking me, you, and the crew along with it. I do not wish to hurt anyone. If you will let me be, you will see that things will work out. I will not be a burden to you much longer. Just give me some time to work things out."

Mr. Darcy was only catching fragments of her pressured speech because his heart was beating so loudly. His mind was reeling. *She thinks she is a burden? And somehow she will not be a burden much longer? What was she hinting at? Was she really thinking of hurting herself? Had Miss Elizabeth been correct?*

"Georgiana . . . I think I know who you need to talk to. When Miss Elizabeth was here, she said she knew someone who was once very melancholy like you are. She has experience with things like this. She would like to be your friend. I think you should talk to her. I think she is a kind and sensitive person. She will listen; I know it.

"But I must say something more. Your behavior and actions make me worried that I am in real danger of losing you. Please, Georgiana, do not do this! You cannot leave me! You are the only family I have left. I would be lost without you. Please, I do not think I could survive if you were to . . . if you were to . . . if you were to do yourself harm."

Georgiana stood up and started pacing. How did he know? If only Nathaniel had saddled that horse! One terrible accident and it would all be over. She would do anything to escape this darkness that engulfed her. Grey. Every shade of grey was all she could see.

Her mind was reeling with thoughts. She knew she could not leave him, not without seeing him settled with Elizabeth. He hadn't even mentioned her these last two weeks except to read her prayer notebook. Did he still admire her? Elizabeth was her only hope for him to be happy once she was gone. She had to find out how she felt about her. If he no longer admired her, then there was no use waiting.

"Please do not do what I think you are planning," Darcy begged. "I can see in your eyes that you are hurting, but people heal. People experience hard times, and then the pain lessens with time. Please do not do anything drastic. I said earlier that I wanted you to speak to someone. Now I am going to insist upon it. If you do not wish want to talk to me about this, please talk to Miss Elizabeth. I can send for her immediately."

Today was going to be the day she ended that pain, but her chest clenched with the realization that she must endure a little longer. For him. How could she do it? Was it even possible? Now that he suspected her and her intentions, he would be watching closer. He would try to prevent something from happening. She was lost in her thoughts when he spoke softly.

"Will you please talk to Miss Elizabeth?"

Georgiana groaned loudly and put her hands to her face. "Will you first tell me a little more about her? Do you admire her?"

Darcy didn't understand her change of topic and eyed her suspiciously. "I do admire her. I think she is intelligent and witty."

"No, I mean, do you *really* admire her? Is she someone you could love?"

He furrowed his brow and stood up to look her in the eye. "I think that is a very inappropriate question."

Georgiana let out an impatient scream and pushed him hard on the chest. His balance faltered, and he stepped back one step, but she was no match for his size. "Just answer the question! Do you think she could make you happy? I do not have time to be hindered by societal rules about which questions are proper and which questions are not. I need to know if you could love her! I need to know if she is special to you!"

"First tell me why you want to know my feelings for Miss Elizabeth."

She could tell she would have to sacrifice something to get him to talk. "I just need to know. You wanted to talk. So, here we are talking like two grown adults."

"Except you just pushed me like a child."

She ignored his comment and continued. "I promise to talk to Elizabeth if you tell me the truth about how you feel about her."

Mr. Darcy was a private man and did not wish to share his thoughts, but the pleading look on her face and the tone in her voice demanded an exception. He paused a moment longer and then made the decision. "Very well. But will you tell her everything? Even the things you have not told me? I am not so unobservant as you seem to think. I know you have not told me all that happened with George Wickham. I think you need to tell someone."

"Can I not merely talk to her about how I feel? Do I really have to tell her what happened? She will not want to be my friend if I tell her."

"I think she is more loyal than that. Do you want to know how I feel about Miss Elizabeth or not?"

"I do. I will."

"You will what?"

She bowed her head and whispered, "Are you really going to make me say it out loud? Very well. I promise to talk to her, and I will tell her what happened at Ramsgate."

"All of it?"

She snapped up her head and stomped her foot. "Stop it, William! I said I would discuss it with her. Do not badger me!"

Mr. Darcy was getting dizzy from her mood swings, but he was pleased she had agreed to talk with Miss Elizabeth. "Then I suppose I must fulfill my part of the bargain. I will first say that she is unique and has piqued my curiosity. She comes from a small country estate with no brothers, but she seems to have a great deal of knowledge about a wide variety of things. Her knowledge is probably due to her extensive reading."

"William, I do not want to know *about* her. I want to know how you *feel* about her. Do you love her?"

"I know what you want to know. I am trying to tell you the best way I know how. Most women read very little. And those who do, usually only read the latest book that is being discussed at all the fashionable soirees. When I talk to them, I gather that they do not enjoy reading at all. They only read so they could join in fashionable conversations about books.

"I do not know if I am making sense. Let me put it another way. When I speak to other ladies about books, their opinions are simple minded and rehearsed, as if they are reciting another person's review, an opinion that they could have read in newsprint. But discussing books with Elizabeth was intriguing and enlightening; it was refreshing.

"In fact, everything about her is refreshing. You know how I am around people I do not know well. I usually lurk in the corner observing, conversing little except when necessary. People have called me brooding. I was once called aloof. I have a desire to be more outgoing, but I do not enjoy engaging in dull conversation, and I admit I avoid it frequently.

"But I am different around her. She ignites me somehow with her glow. Her very walk, her words, her smiles—they pull me in. I have thought of little else over the last two weeks since I have met her. Considering I have had only three interactions with her, I cannot explain the stirrings I have for her. You asked if I love her. I imagine that if given enough time with her, that will be a very real possibility. She is bright and happy, yet so soulful and passionate at the same time. Everything she does is done with passion. When she is in the room, I cannot draw my eyes from her. I find myself scheming ways to see her again."

Georgiana had strained to listen to what she was hoping to hear from him, but this last part confused her. "Then why have you not called on her or invited the Gardiners over for dinner? Why are you holding back? If she moves you in this way, what is stopping you from courting her?"

Darcy paused to mentally evaluate this line of questioning. Why was Georgiana so interested in his feelings and thoughts about Miss Elizabeth? She started tapping her foot anxiously, and he tried to answer her question. "I suppose I have been busy getting ready for Bingley and his sisters to visit. I also was hoping you would show some interest in seeing her as well, but you have behaved so oddly that I did not want to push you into a friendship when your mood was so poor. But I honestly believe that Miss Elizabeth could help you. She seems to care a great deal about you."

Georgiana would not be deflected. "So, you do not love her yet, but you think you could?"

Mr. Darcy ran his fingers through his hair nervously. It was difficult to voice his inner thoughts on any issue, and Elizabeth was an especially complex issue. He was struggling to find the right words.

"I have not considered the issue that deeply," he began. "But I would like to know her better. I do think she is better qualified to run Pemberley than any lady of the *ton* that I have ever met. I imagine I would be very happy in a union with Miss Elizabeth. Now, before you start getting ideas in your head, I know nothing of her family, apart from the Gardiners. All I know is she is a gentleman's daughter. I suppose her family simply likes to be in the country and makes little attempt to participate in the season. Otherwise, I probably would have met her or heard of her before now."

"She seems like she would be quite the match for you."

"I suppose one could look at it that way, but I have not seriously contemplated any real marital possibilities with her. She will only be here a few more weeks before returning to Hertfordshire. There is not much time for a courtship." He unconsciously sighed in disappointment.

Georgiana sat down and contemplated everything she had heard. Her brother was well on his way to loving Elizabeth and had even evaluated her as a potential Mistress of Pemberley. Although he was unwilling to admit it, she could see he would be happy with her as his wife. She had to do something, something different than what she had planned for today.

For the first time in months, she felt a glimmer of hope. There was a flicker of a sensation deep in her heart, a strange, foreign sensation. As soon as she felt it, she was hit with a powerful, tangible force of emotion as she realized that she very nearly killed herself. She had tried to create a terrible tragedy, an irreversible choice. Her foggy mind was riddled with confusion as she considered her actions.

A few minutes ago, while she was trying to take a reckless ride on a very wild colt, it had seemed the right thing to do. She hadn't been riddled with a guilty conscious at the time. There had been no consequences to debate. It had simply made sense at the time to end the pain in any way possible. There was no viable future in her mind then. She never once thought about the pain she would cause everyone around her if she were to be thrown and killed. She had simply wanted the pain to end.

A stronger wave of emotion filled her breast, and she started to shake with the force of it. She had to fight. She knew it now. She had to overcome this beast that had engulfed her. She had to try harder than she had tried in the past. She had to endure the pain long enough to survive. She had to live. She wanted a future. She wanted to see William happily married. But was it possible? Was it possible to live through what she had been through and still find happiness?

Elizabeth said in her letter that she knew how Georgiana felt. She had said she had been through it before. So, did that mean Elizabeth could help her muddle her way though it? Was the bargain she made with William to speak with Elizabeth a blessing in disguise? She tried to focus on what that meant. Did she have the strength to fight her way out? She concluded that there was no other option. She bowed her head and muttered under her breath, "You never know how strong you are until being strong is the only option you have left."

Darcy sat next to her and put his arm around her. "Miss Elizabeth thinks you are strong. I know you can do this. You can get through it."

"By fully relying on God."

"I suppose that is why Miss Elizabeth gave us her prayer notebook. Now come inside, and I will send for Miss Elizabeth. You need some rest before she arrives. But promise me something." She looked up at him and nodded. "Promise me you will do nothing to risk your life."

"Being strong is the only option I have left. But I need help, a great deal of help."

"I did not hear you promise me."

"I promise. And I am suddenly very tired. I think I shall rest for a while before she arrives."

He took her hand and stood up. When she rose, he wrapped his arms around her and whispered, "I love you, pumpkin. I want to help you in any way possible."

"Hearing you speak of how much you admire Elizabeth has helped a great deal. Will you promise me something too?"

"Anything."

"Can I be the first one to know when you propose?"

"*If* I propose."

"No, w*hen* you propose."

He chuckled and kissed her forehead. "If that day comes, God willing, I promise."

"Then beginning now, I will fully rely on God to make that day come."

*****

Mr. Gardiner opened the letter in front of the rider. The driver had informed him that he had been instructed to wait for and deliver a response immediately.

> *Dear Mr. Gardiner,*
>
> *Forgive me for disturbing you and your household, but I have some urgent needs, and I must call upon my new neighbor for his assistance. Georgiana has taken to her bed and is asking for Miss Elizabeth. She is quite unwell, and I will do whatever she asks to comfort her. It is my hope that Miss Elizabeth will come to Pemberley and attend to her. In fact, I have already ordered my carriage to Saphrinbrooke to escort her here.*
>
> *Forgive me for presuming your approval. I am only anxious for my sister and wish to have Miss Elizabeth here as soon as possible. I would be forever in your debt if you would appease me in this matter and allow Miss Elizabeth to attend to Georgiana this afternoon. I assure you that she will be properly escorted back tonight.*
>
> *Thank you again in advance for your assistance. It is truly a blessing to have a friend so close to call upon when such a crisis develops. There is little more valuable in this life than a dependable friend.*
>
> *Sincerely,*

Fitzwilliam Darcy

He folded the letter and asked the rider to wait in the kitchen while he prepared a response. Mr. Gardiner then found his wife and niece looking over the household ledgers. He cleared his throat and sat down. "I must beg your attention, ladies. Mr. Darcy has made a request, and I am inclined to help. It seems Miss Darcy is ill, and she is asking for Elizabeth to come to Pemberley. In fact, Mr. Darcy has already dispatched his carriage to escort you, and it should be here shortly. I am to send a reply with his rider in the next few minutes."

Elizabeth's heart started to pound. "I will do anything to help. You know that. I can be ready immediately. These ledgers can be done later."

"Yes, Edward, if the Darcys need us, we must help," Mrs. Gardiner agreed.

"I expected I would not have to do too much convincing, and I am glad I was correct. I wonder, though. Perhaps Elizabeth should pack a small trunk in case Georgiana is so ill that she needs tending through the night. He did not invite you to stay overnight, but I want you to be prepared in case there is that need. I know Jane is coming tomorrow, but she will not be here until late afternoon. By then we will have a better understanding of Miss Darcy's needs. Would you feel comfortable staying there tonight if she needs you?"

"Without a doubt. If you will excuse me, I will go pack my trunk immediately." Elizabeth stood and hurried out of the room. She bounded up the stairs and entered her room. The maid was cleaning, and she dismissed her. As soon as the door closed, she quickly went to the bed and kneeled down.

After taking a moment to compose herself and prepare emotionally to talk to the Lord, she started her prayer. She asked for guidance. She asked for patience with Mr. Darcy. She asked to maintain her inner peace. She asked for Georgiana's safety. She asked for a charitable heart. She asked for a lot, and if she had more time, she would have asked for even more.

Something deep inside her was stirring, and she needed to be prepared. Before saying amen, she quickly thanked the Lord once again for helping her through her fog so that she could help others like Georgiana get through it as well. No matter how little time she had to devote to a prayer, she could not end it without gratitude.

*****

Mr. Darcy was waiting for the carriage. He had estimated the time it would take to travel the six miles and back and nervously watched as the minutes tick by. When it finally arrived, he rushed outside to welcome Elizabeth and was overwhelmed by the concern and love on her face. It was so endearing that she was willing to come and that she was so emotionally invested in Georgiana's welfare. He handed her out and said, "Thank you for coming so quickly, Miss Elizabeth."

"How is she?"

"She is resting at the moment. If you do not mind, I would like to discuss her condition with you before I show you to her room."

"I am at your disposal, sir. I will hear whatever you think will be helpful."

Darcy felt a bit selfish when he offered her his arm, it being an act that he relished. He showed her into the music room and left the door open for propriety's sake, but he spoke softly so none of the servants could hear. "I am afraid I owe you an apology. When you suggested that I watch for warning signs, I was not prepared to consider the very real possibility that Georgiana would do herself harm. I see the concern in your eyes, and I want to assure you she is safe, but she has been behaving oddly. I was alerted this morning by my housekeeper of her odd behavior and then it became pointedly clear how much danger she was in. I never imagined she was doing that poorly."

"There is no need to apologize. It is easier to see what makes us comfortable than to face our suspicions."

"That is wise counsel. Is it from your prayer notebook?" He smiled briefly at her. It was too hard not to. Even with a look of concern on her face, she emanated something that was nothing short of beautiful.

She smiled briefly back at him and said, "I am afraid not. That one came out spontaneously. Tell me what happened three and a half months ago to make her mood change."

"It is a long story but an important one. It pains me to share such private details, but I know I can trust your discretion." Elizabeth nodded.

"Georgiana has agreed to tell you all of it," he began, "as there are parts even I do not know, but I will tell you what I can. Last November, I hired a companion for her: a young widow named Mrs. Younge. She was only a few years older than Georgiana but seemed to be a good influence. A few months later, Georgiana asked if she could travel to Ramsgate for a few weeks to enjoy the fresh sea air. It was an easy wish to grant since I had learned to trust Mrs. Younge. Unfortunately, I was unaware that Mrs. Younge was acquainted with a man I once called friend.

"George Wickham is the son of my late father's steward. He and I grew up together and were only a few months apart in age but quite different in temperament. Where I valued honesty and integrity, he did not; but he was charming enough to ensure my father's good opinion, so much so that he was awarded the living at Kympton in my father's will.

"As he grew up, his character deteriorated. And then, after his mother's death, he became an entirely different person. His teasing of animals became blatant cruelty. His sneaking into the kitchen for biscuits before dinner became sleight of hand with the valuables. I could never prove his wrongdoings, but his obsession with money and my inheritance became apparent. He was offered a gentleman's education from my father, but his habits of gambling and cheating soon saw him expelled from university. To this day he insists his financial woes are my fault."

Elizabeth was confused. "Why would they be your fault?"

"After my father's death, Wickham came to me requesting monetary compensation for the living, stating he did not wish to take orders. I was quite relieved and complied immediately since he had neither the moral character to serve in the church nor the dependability required of a parson. The papers were drawn up, and the living was settled for three thousand pounds. He seemed pleased, and I wished him luck and hoped that was the last I would see of him.

"He came to me a few years later asking for the living back, saying he had changed his mind as well as his ways. I knew he was hard up for money, a result of gaming tables and saloons. He appealed to our youthful friendship, and although I refused to give him the living back, I did discharge his debts for him, which were extensive. I once more supposed I would never see him.

"At the end of January this year, Georgiana departed on the trip to Ramsgate. I wrote to her weekly, and she did the same to me. As time went on, I noticed a few subtle changes in her letters. She told me Mrs. Younge was instructing her in proper letter writing, and I attributed the change to that. It was nothing terribly alarming.

"Six weeks passed, and I was missing her terribly. Her letters disclosed less and less as the weeks went by. So, I decided to surprise her unannounced. As soon as I could, I set off for Ramsgate, which was the middle of March. The weather was very fine when I arrived. When she was not in the townhouse, I assumed she was walking the beach. I set out after her and was shocked to see my fifteen-year-old sister in the embrace of George Wickham, publically, in front of all to see. Mrs. Younge was nowhere to be seen."

"Why was Wickham there? And where was Mrs. Younge?"

"I soon learned that my surprise visit was serendipitous, for Wickham and Mrs. Younge had convinced Georgiana to elope with him to Gretna Green the following day. Had I been delayed by weather or business, I would have been forced to turn over Georgiana's thirty-thousand-pound dowry to Wickham, which was undoubtedly his goal in pursuing her."

Elizabeth sighed; she saw where this was going. "And Georgiana thought he loved her."

"Indeed. Of course, I discharged Mrs. Younge and informed Wickham that he would never get a farthing of the dowry. He very loudly and angrily told me she was not worth it anyway. Unfortunately, Georgiana overheard him. She fancied herself in love with him, and her heart was truly broken. I did not exaggerate when I said he was charming, nor did I exaggerate his lack of morals or integrity. He had set up numerous debts in town under my name, claiming to be my brother-in-law.

"Georgiana and I stayed in Ramsgate for two weeks while I cleared my name of his debts. At first, she was angry with me— she said I had ruined everything. She insisted that Wickham really did love her and that he did not mean what he had said. She cried and begged me to let her see him again, but I refused. She became so unwell that she refused to leave the house. I stayed with her as much as I could, but one night I met a business associate for dinner. When I returned, she was different. She suddenly stopped fighting me. She no longer cried. She no longer spoke of him.

"I brought her back to Pemberley as quickly as I could. But she no longer played the pianoforte or did anything that she enjoyed before. When I finally convinced her to see the doctor, she swore him to secrecy. He would only say that there was nothing physically wrong with her; she needed only rest and a peaceful environment. But her mood worsened as the weeks went by."

Elizabeth pondered all she had heard. "So, you suspect there is more to the story."

"I pray not. Is it terrible of me to wish that the only damage is her broken heart?"

"Considering all the possibilities, I would be praying for the same thing."

"She has refused to speak with me about it. But today, she agreed to talk to you. I am sure she still does not want me to know about what really happened, but she promised me she would tell you. I offer you my trust. Take care of her. She is all I have left in this world. I do not mean to make you feel obligated to disclose everything she tells you, but is it too much to ask for some reassurance when you are done talking with her?"

"I will do my best. And my best is all I can offer." She looked in his eyes and saw the deepest pain turn deeper.

"I feel like I have failed her in some way," Darcy murmured. "I have been so busy with the estate as of late. I fear I dismissed her behavior too many times. I should have seen the danger well before it got this severe. It has been a difficult spring, and there were numerous problems with tenants. But I do not intend to make excuses, forgive me."

Elizabeth reached out her hand and placed it on his arm. "Even the best men are mere mortals," she reassured him.

He smiled up at her, an automatic response from the sensation of having her hand on his arm. "Is that another quote from your prayer notebook?"

"I am sure it is in there somewhere. There is only one man who was ever perfect. And although perfection is our goal, He does not expect us to achieve it today, and nor should we. Trials are simply distractions along the way. We must not let allow them to divert us from our goal."

"How can a lady as young as you be so wise? You amaze me. I have never met anyone like you. I am sorry. I did not mean to embarrass you, but I see your blush and fear I have done exactly that. I am afraid you bring out a different man in me; I am usually quite successfully guarded."

There was a very awkward silence between them, and Elizabeth removed her hand and smoothed her skirts. She saw a look in his eyes that surprised her. She saw gratitude, kindness, and admiration, the latter completely discomposing her. "May I go to Georgiana now? I am anxious to see her."

"Certainly. I am sorry if I made you uncomfortable."

Trying to lighten the moment, she teased him, "Perhaps you are more readable than you think. You attempt to hide behind your 'Mr. Darcy mask', but you are not as successfully guarded as you might think—at least not to me."

"My interactions with you certainly have been unguarded. The fact that I have trusted you with this story about Georgiana and Wickham only proves you are correct. And what do you mean by my 'Mr. Darcy mask'?"

She let out a laugh. "You may have disclosed more than usual to me, but that does not obligate me to disclose anything to you. I will leave you to wonder about the 'Mr. Darcy mask' until a later date. For now, all you need to know is that I mean no harm by it. Now, let us not delay my visit to Georgiana any longer." She stood and took a guarded breath, preparing herself for the conversation ahead of her.

CHAPTER 4

Georgiana heard the knock on her door and rolled over in her bed. There was no need to get up. After their talk at the stable, William had instructed her lady's maid to stay with Georgiana until he returned—no matter what Miss Darcy said.

She stared at the wall as her maid opened the door. She knew the time had come for a confession and suddenly feared she would lose the contents of her stomach. She took shallow breaths to keep the bile from rising in her throat. Deciding she should probably at least sit up, in case she did need to use the chamber pot, she slowly raised her shoulders. She was pleased to discover that the movement did not increase her nausea.

Mr. Darcy dismissed the maid and motioned for Elizabeth to enter the room. Elizabeth immediately rushed past him to Georgiana's bedside, embracing her with a soft, rocking motion. Elizabeth's tears fell freely from her face, and she caressed Georgiana's hair while whispering soft reassurances to her. Mr. Darcy was struck speechless. The gesture reminded him of seeing his father comfort Georgiana as a little girl. It was such a private moment; watching them together like that nearly brought him to tears. He backed out of the room and left them alone, silently closing the door behind him.

Georgiana could hardly keep her sobs from stealing her breath. The tightness in her chest was so great that her entire body was convulsing, but Elizabeth continued to hold her close. Georgiana's emotions and stresses released in the embrace, and she just let herself cry, really cry. Elizabeth rocked her and rubbed her back, but ultimately just held her.

Georgiana's tears came so fast and were so large that she felt she was a dam breaking at its base—nothing could stop the flow. She knew not how long Elizabeth held her. She was in no hurry to start talking. In a way, just being held and caressed made her feel better—it made her feel as if she had already disclosed everything. She felt a wave of miraculous peace as she realized Elizabeth would not judge her in any way. Elizabeth truly cared for her and was committed to being the friend she had offered to be in her letter.

Ever so slowly, Georgiana's tears dried and her sobs abated. She took a moment longer to relish the love and acceptance of Elizabeth's embrace before pulling away. She knew her face was a mess, and the evidence of her tears was all over Elizabeth's gown. Georgiana used her hand to wipe at the wet spots.

"Do not fret about it," Elizabeth reassured her. "I brought another gown. If you wish to soil my other shoulder, I am perfectly willing to offer it."

Georgiana smiled slightly. "Be careful what you offer. I did not know I had that many tears in me. Who knows how many are still there?"

"I told you I used to feel like you do now. It was years ago, but it still feels like yesterday at times. And I know that crying is better medicine than any doctor's elixir. Be prepared to do a lot more of it. Let yourself do it. You may need to hide it from some—there are those who will not understand—but you need not hide it from me."

There was a pause, and Georgiana took a deep breath. She knew it was time. "Did my brother tell you about Wickham?" she asked. Elizabeth nodded. "So, you know what William knows. Good. I do not want to start from the beginning. I suppose I should feel nervous. I have everything to lose by telling this story, but your kindness seems to have eased my burden. I have shouldered it alone for so long."

Elizabeth put her hand on her arm. "You need not shoulder it alone. There is one set of shoulders that can carry any burden. And those shoulders carried His own cross. All people will fail us at some point or another—they are simply human—but our Savior will never fail us. He can help you carry your burden. And your brother also desperately wants to help you. He is worried about you. He loves you unconditionally, no matter what happened. You do not need to be alone anymore."

Georgiana knew she was delaying discussing what Elizabeth came here to talk about, but she had to ask her a few things before she told her story. "May I ask you a question before we begin?"

"Certainly. I have all the time in the world. My uncle said I could even stay here overnight if you wish. Whatever you need to know, just ask," Elizabeth said.

"William, he is a good brother, do you not think so?"

"Yes, he appears to be very devoted."

"And did you know he had to take over running Pemberley five years ago when he was just two-and-twenty? He and my cousin, Richard, have been my guardians since my father died."

"He seems very capable. It must take a great man to handle all that responsibility."

Georgiana pressed further, "He is a great man. Do you not think so?"

Elizabeth grinned. It seemed Georgiana and her matchmaking mother had more in common than she realized. "From what I have seen, it seems he would be a good match for many fine ladies. I suspect he has to fight them off with a stick."

"He talks very little to me about his lady friends, all except you, of course. He has talked about you."

Elizabeth wasn't going to fall into the trap. "I have given him much to talk about, no doubt. Now, are we done avoiding the real reason I am here in your bedchamber, or would you like to convince me of your brother's merits a little longer?"

"Was it that obvious? I just mention him because he is the reason I am going to fight this thing that seems to have consumed me. I want to see him happy. I believe you could make him happy; he practically said so."

"Is that so? He has been gossiping about me behind my back? Well, I shall have to think up a suitable punishment for him. Would putting jacks in his boots do the trick, or should I verbally confront him when he least expects it, perhaps publically?" Elizabeth giggled to let Georgiana know she was teasing her.

"He does hate mutton. Perhaps we can suggest to the cook to serve it three meals in a row!"

"But I cannot tease a man for not liking mutton; that only shows his good judgment. Perhaps he is a perfect match for me after all!" Elizabeth grinned and then stood up. "Come with me," she said, pulling Georgiana over to the sofa by the window. "My sister, Jane, and I have a small sofa in my bedroom just big enough for the two of us to curl our legs up under ourselves and look out the window while we talk. It is a pastime that I truly love. You will get a chance to meet my sister soon. She arrives in Lambton tomorrow."

Georgiana followed Elizabeth's example and tucked her feet under her. "Like this?" she asked. Elizabeth nodded. "I would have loved to have a sister," Georgiana said.

"Someday when your brother gets married, you will. Maybe the two of you will sit together, just like this," Elizabeth replied. Georgiana turned and looked at her with desperate, pleading eyes. Elizabeth instantly regretted introducing that particular topic and began to feel embarrassed. "Not me," she tried to explain, "just someone, someday. Not that I would not want to call you sister. I just was trying to say that I am not seeking to marry your brother. Not that marrying him would be a terrible thing, but I simply do not look at him like that." She felt her cheeks blush bright red at the lie and saw Georgiana smile.

"Oh bother," Elizabeth stammered. "I am digging myself into a hole. Let us just drop the subject of your brother for now. Is that fair? We have much different things to talk about. And I believe you promised him you would talk about it. Now I suggest we do just that."

"I have been trying to avoid it," Georgiana replied. "But I suppose it is time. Something tells me you will not judge me."

"When you judge people it does not define them; it only defines you. I am not about to judge you. I do not want that sin hanging over my head."

Georgiana took a deep breath and pulled a blanket around her legs. It was time. She desperately wanted to be free from this darkness, and although she was still not sure that talking would help, she was committed to trying harder. She was committed to living—really living, not being trapped in her own thoughts.

She began the story that had chained her over the last few months. She told Elizabeth everything. She shed more tears full of sorrow and shame. She was surprised that as she spoke, the words came easier. The heaviness on her shoulders lifted with each word. She watched Elizabeth nod and murmur her understanding. Never once did Elizabeth give any indication of shock or disgust. All Georgiana saw in her eyes was love and concern and a great deal of compassion.

After, Georgiana glanced out the window and saw that the sun was about an hour from setting, which meant she had talked for over three hours. She took another deep, cleansing breath and felt the air fill her lungs, and for the first time in months, she felt relief with breathing. It was no longer a chore.

Elizabeth sensed that Georgiana was done. Elizabeth had shed many tears of her own while Georgiana talked. She wiped her eyes and realized that she had made it. She had made it through hearing someone else's story like hers; she did not have an overwhelming rise of her old thoughts and feelings. She squeezed the small hand clasped between her own and whispered, "I am so proud of you."

"Proud? That is the last thing I think you should feel after hearing that story."

"No, you are wrong. I am very, *very* proud. You made the decision to fight this long before I ever did. It took me years to talk about it. And none of what happened to you is your fault. Do you know that now?"

"But I should have sent him away that night. What was I thinking? I am so ashamed. It is all my fault—"

"No, it is not your fault. You did not ask for this to happen. You did not give your consent. You are not being punished by God for your sins. Trust me, these are all thoughts I have had myself. And the steps you are taking now will only make you stronger. You do not have to fight this alone."

"I know I have William, and now I have you. And I do feel better after telling someone about it. I felt so alone."

"You forgot one very important person who has always been there for you. Though life is difficult, God does not abandon us, no matter how much it feels like it."

"I remember William reading something like that to me from your prayer notebook. I have never truly prayed much. I suppose I should start."

"Yes, but first there is something else we need to do. Considering what you disclosed, I think Mr. Darcy needs to know."

Georgiana groaned loudly and bowed her head. Fresh tears formed, and she looked up at Elizabeth. "Please, I cannot be the one to tell him," Georgiana begged. "I could not bear to see that look in his eyes. I simply cannot do it. Will you do it? Will you tell him?"

"Georgiana, it is hardly appropriate for me to discuss such things with an unmarried man of no relation."

"Please? I know I could not do it."

Elizabeth felt her stomach grow tight as she imagined trying to have such a conversation with Mr. Darcy. She stared silently at Georgiana for the longest time. She had promised Georgiana that she would help her in any way possible. She had promised to be a friend, a confidant, or even a sister. If she was helping Georgiana as a sister, then that would make Mr. Darcy her brother. Thinking of him as a brother made the task a little easier. "If you truly want me to tell him, I will."

*****

As the hours passed, Mr. Darcy was nearly ready to jump out of his skin. Should he hold dinner? Should he send a tray to Georgiana's room? What was taking so long? It was nearly time for Elizabeth to be heading home, and yet there was still no movement from behind Georgiana's door.

His imagination threatened to overwhelm him as the minutes and hours ticked by. He started pacing his study a few times, but it brought no relief. He poured himself a brandy and downed the entire glass without even tasting it. He started to pour himself another glass, but then he hesitated. Perhaps they had simply lost track of time, enjoying each other's company in the way ladies do. Working himself into a frenzy would not help, nor would becoming foxed.

When Mrs. Reynolds came in, he asked her to hold dinner a while longer. That was all he could articulate at the moment. She didn't leave the room right away, and when he glanced up at her, he saw a motherly look of affection in her eyes. His heart ached to have his mother there to talk to, to have his father's calm words of advice. But he did not have either anymore. He was all alone.

Instinctively, he boxed up his emotions and acted as if nothing were wrong. He assumed a blank face and nodded at Mrs. Reynolds, and she quietly exited. He made an effort to think rationally about the issue. There were people he could consult with, people who cared for Georgiana and would want to help. He had his cousin, Colonel Fitzwilliam; and his aunt and uncle, Mr. and Mrs. Matlock; and Mrs. Reynolds. She truly had been like a second mother; he trusted her completely. And now, he reminded himself, it seemed he had Miss Elizabeth Bennet.

As he considered that pleasant thought, he picked up her notebook. He opened to a page near the beginning and started to read them aloud. Just speaking them was helpful. "Though life is hard and we face difficulties, God does not abandon us, no matter how much it feels like it."

"It is true you know, but you do not need to take my word for it." Elizabeth's voice jolted him out of his concentration, and he looked up to see her in the doorway. "All you have to do is ask God. May I come in?"

Elizabeth had prayed the entire way down the stairs that she could do this for Georgiana. The butler had directed her that she could find Mr. Darcy in his study; here he was. There was no turning back now.

Mr. Darcy could see the wariness in her face, but yet her small smile was so inviting. Her eyes, though slightly puffy from what he guessed had been a few tearful hours, still glowed. "Certainly," he replied. "Would you like some tea or wine?"

"No, thank you. Could we take a stroll in the gardens? I think some exercise would help me clear my mind."

His fear was in his throat like never before. The last three hours had been torture for him, but he had a sinking feeling that the next hour would be worse. After a moment's hesitation, he answered, "Certainly. The logistics of trying to maintain propriety yet hold a private conversation are a little tricky." It was not a hard decision. He wanted to spend more time with her. Even though he wasn't ready to hear what happened to his sweet sister, he couldn't turn her away. He offered his arm and led the way to the gardens.

They walked towards the lake. The setting sun was reflecting on the water, and the weather was peaceful and calm. He needed all the peace he could get. They walked in silence for some time; neither was truly ready for the conversation that was coming.

When it looked like she was waiting on him for something, he began, "I am hopeful you are here to give me some reassurance."

Elizabeth saw the pleading look in his eyes and pitied for him. He did not want to hear this, and she knew it. "I wish that were the case. I can offer you reassurance to some degree. Georgiana will pull through this. She is stronger than I was." She saw the carefully concealed curiosity in his eyes, and she realized she should explain herself, but now was not the time. "I believe she fully disclosed all that happened. You had a right to be worried. I may as well acknowledge your most pressing unspoken question. I can think of no softer way to say it, so pardon my frankness. She is no longer a maiden and most definitely not by choice. I am truly sorry."

He felt weak in the knees and stepped away from her and sat down on the gazebo bench. The words she spoke were replaying themselves in his mind over and over again. He knew he had heard them, but they had not sunk in yet. He looked at Elizabeth and saw the pain in her eyes, and he knew she was reflecting the pain she saw in his own. *Oh dear Lord! Please say I heard her wrong!*

"I am sorry, Mr. Darcy. You did not hear me wrong."

"Did I say that out loud?"

"Indeed. I would recommend saying all your thoughts out loud when addressing the Lord."

"How can you jest at a time like this?"

"I jest not. I wholly recommend praying. It does much good." She took a seat next to him.

He fully comprehended now what she had just told him. His shock was nearly overwhelming, but the emotion that followed was unbearable and no amount of fine breeding could hold back his reaction. "No God in Heaven would have let that happen to my sister!" He felt his anger rising quickly, and yet he could hold it back no further.

He stood up and began pacing. "How could this have happened? I was supposed to protect her! Why would God do this to her? Does he not love his children? Does he not love Georgiana?"

For a moment he was lost in his thoughts and overwhelming feelings of anger, fear, and what he could only describe as a murderous rage. He had never before raised his voice in the presence of a lady, but he felt unable to stop himself. His voice became louder and louder until he was nearly yelling. "That fiend, Wickham! How did he get to her? I would give my right arm to strangle him until he begs for air then take my knee and place his manhood high enough that women in China will hear him scream for mercy!" Mr. Darcy's pace slowed, and he sat down again. He ran his fingers through his hair and groaned.

When he glanced over at the silent Elizabeth, he saw her sparkle had diminished, and she had a very sad look on her face. Had he done that? Had he made her glow leave? He looked away and said, "I am sincerely sorry, Miss Elizabeth. Speaking to a lady in such a way is ungentlemanly and unforgivable."

Elizabeth reached out her hand and rested it on his until he returned his gaze to her. "Nothing anyone does is unforgiveable."

He let out a manic laugh and asked, "Do you not hear yourself? What Wickham did is unforgivable! He took the virtue of a fifteen-year-old and left her a shell of her former self!"

"I know very well what he did, Mr. Darcy. But before you go in search of him and attempt to make women in China hear him scream, your sister is waiting for you in the house, and she is in desperate need of your reassurance. She is very fragile right now. She has suffered these last three and a half months feeling completely alone. Now it is time to show her she does not have to be alone in this fight. She needs your love and acceptance. Your reaction, your words, the very emotion you show will matter a great deal. I suggest we come up with a plan on how you will behave. Getting red in the face, raising your voice, and pulling out your hair will do her no good."

"But how do I change my instinct? I want to kill the man!"

"My father once told me that the only constant in life is change. Change will always be there, requiring us to be flexible and adjust our actions, our thoughts, and our feelings. Time breeds change, and change takes time. Georgiana is ready to change, but it will take time. There is nothing you can do to alter what has happened. You can only change your reaction to it and learn from it. I suspect that too will take time and a great deal of effort."

"What could I possibly learn from the loss of innocence of my only sister?"

"Mr. Darcy, I am not the instructor in life; God is. He chooses which lessons to give. Sometimes others' choices inflict trials upon us, as with Georgiana's trial. But whether my trials come from God or from the choices of another, I have full faith that He will not give me more than I can handle."

Darcy considered her idea. But then he remembered the pain in Georgiana's eyes. "You say God designs our trials as lessons; if that is so, He has dealt too harshly with Georgiana. She is only fifteen, and I nearly lost her. I do not know if I can forgive Him for that."

Elizabeth could feel the pain in his words. She had felt the same way many times. She hesitated only a moment, considering how much to reveal about her own past. "Although I know God designs my lessons, there were times when I questioned my strength," she replied. "There were times when I wondered whether I would survive such harsh lessons. But I did survive, and I know Georgiana will too. After many years, I have learned that God does love me. When I hurt, He hurts also. When I grow, He rejoices. After all, if I lived an easy, carefree life, I would be a very dull person, having learned nothing."

Dull. Something she said triggered a cascade of thoughts in Mr. Darcy. He looked at her with new eyes. She had said someone close to her had felt like Georgiana. She had said she survived and Georgiana could too. What did she mean by that? He looked at her, and he saw in the gold specks of her eyes that the answer was plain as day. She had been the one who had felt like Georgiana. That was how she had recognized the danger lurking.

The silence between them grew thick, and he knew not what to say. His angry reaction had dulled her sparkle, diminished her radiance. But yet she sat here with her reassuring hand on his, calmly guiding him through his visceral emotional response. Suddenly, they weren't just discussing Georgiana's past. He could see that she was reliving the very worst moments of her life, moments when she too had been quite melancholy, perhaps even suicidal. His heart ached to reach out and comfort her.

How could this glowing, captivating lady ever have been like Georgiana had been these last months? He couldn't imagine her essence and love of life gone out of her eyes, but yet when he looked at her now, he caught a glimpse of dullness. He caught a glimpse of that blank stare. He felt his eyes tingle with the pricks of tears forming. He looked out to the lake and blinked them away. He knew now she had been right. His reaction could make or break Georgiana's success in moving forward.

Elizabeth gave his hand a squeeze. She wondered if her family had reacted this way when they found out about her. She felt herself falter slightly in her inner strength and pulled her hand away. She said another quick prayer and looked up at his face, watching the emotions dance in his eyes. He was struggling. She so desperately wanted to help him, but the last few hours had been draining. Elizabeth had relived that wretched moment years ago at least a dozen times as Georgiana told her story. She wasn't a fool and knew she would always have some pain with the memories, but she thought she had been more prepared than this. Looking down at her hands, she felt a chill go up her spine and knew the temperature was only partly to blame. She was startled when Mr. Darcy's husky voice addressed her.

"Miss Elizabeth, obviously my reaction was all wrong. I do not know how to help her. Can you tell me about the person you once knew who went through something similar? What would have been the right thing to say to her?" He looked at Elizabeth's eyes and saw her smile slightly, her glow slowly making its way back into her face.

"This person needed only one thing: unconditional love. No matter what happened to her, or how she behaved, she needed to know she would be loved and accepted. She felt she had lost control of her life. She felt there was no solid foundation, and she was drowning in mundane tasks as simple as breathing. What got her through it was the unconditional love of her sister and father, but most importantly, she learned that God also loved her unconditionally."

"So, you think Georgiana needs my love, not my anger?"

"I do. She did not want to see your reaction, and I am afraid she was correct in her hesitation. When you see her, you need to embrace her with love. She needs to see that you look at her no differently; you need to forget the images in your head right now. She needs to see that what she went through does not define her. Let her know that this thing that Mr. Wickham did does not diminish her worth as a person. Do you think you can do that?"

"Of course Georgiana's worth is not diminished! If anything, I love her more than ever! To imagine she suffered all these months alone is heartbreaking. I want to be there for her in any way I can! I do not want to let her down."

Elizabeth breathed a sigh of relief and stood. "Good. She will need to hear that. She will need it more than you know." She smiled weakly and started walking back to the house. Mr. Darcy followed her, taking long strides to catch up. He put his hand on her arm and gently stopped her.

"Miss Elizabeth, I am sorry for reacting the way I did. I should have been more in control of myself."

"Mr. Darcy, emotions cannot be helped. One cannot stop the rain from falling, but we can be wise enough to seek shelter instead of getting wet. What I am trying to say is, it is what we choose to do with our emotions that is important. Now, Georgiana said she would be waiting in the yellow sitting room. We have been gone some time now, and the sun has set. I suggest we go find her."

Mr. Darcy didn't offer his arm this time. He needed to focus on Georgiana and controlling his reaction when he saw her. As much as he liked feeling Elizabeth's hand wrapped around his arm, now was not the time to play the gentleman suitor. They entered the house, and they both silently walked to the yellow sitting room. He took one more look at Elizabeth's encouraging face.

Elizabeth put her hand on his arm and whispered, "You can do this. She just needs your unconditional love."

Mr. Darcy opened the door, and they both entered. As soon as he saw Georgiana, he quickly wrapped his arms around her, holding her ever so tightly. He needed to hold her not only because his heart ached for her and all she went through, but because he didn't fully trust himself not to show how horribly angry he was at Wickham. He reminded himself of what Miss Elizabeth had said. She needed unconditional love.

"Georgie, I love you," he whispered. "You are the most important thing in my life and nothing can change that, ever. I cannot imagine how hard these last few months have been as you shouldered this burden on your own. You could have told me. We could have done something about it."

Georgiana pulled away, "No, William, I do not want to do something about it. He did what he did, and it is in the past. Let us leave it be."

"I know, Georgie. You have been so strong. It is nearly over now. All that remains is to find him and—"

"No, William, you do not understand. It is over. There is nothing more to be done. I am not totally confident that forgiving him is possible, but I do feel it is necessary. Miss Elizabeth and I talked a great deal about it, and it is the only way."

"But surely this man needs to be punished. He might do this again to someone else." Mr. Darcy looked at Elizabeth and said, "Surely you do not agree with this, Miss Elizabeth?" He felt his anger rising. Elizabeth walked toward him, giving him a warning look.

"I believe each man will have to face the natural consequences of his actions," Elizabeth began. "And one day God himself will judge us. But I do not think we should seek additional judgment in this case. If our legal courts afforded men and women equal privileges, I might counsel differently. I pray someday things will be different and justice will be served to men who force themselves on innocents.

"But we must accept present circumstances as they are," Elizabeth cautioned. "As it stands, if Georgiana accuses Mr. Wickham of his crimes, what will it serve? Tell me, Mr. Darcy, in this world we live in, whose reputation will be more damaged: the young, wealthy lady or the charming gentleman? Whose reputation does society deem the most fragile? Wickham may deny it and perhaps even accuse her of being a willing partner."

Elizabeth could see Darcy was still unconvinced, his lips pressed tight together in disapproval. She ushered him a few steps away from Georgiana and whispered, "Are you truly prepared to let this go public?" She continued, "Is Georgiana prepared to endure censure from society? She is young and still fragile. Do you think she is prepared to let everyone know she was taken by such a man? And what of her future once everyone is aware of what happened? You know as well as I, that there is little forgiveness and plenty of blame for ladies in our world we live in."

Mr. Darcy frowned. He had reacted badly, and he knew it. Elizabeth was right. He could not listen to her carefully worded warnings any longer, and he interrupted her, "You have said enough, madam. I apologize. I see my emotions have moved me to react."

He walked back to Georgiana and embraced her again. "I am sorry, Georgie. I am doing this all wrong. Please forgive me." He took a deep breath and held her tightly. He snuck a peek at Elizabeth's face and saw it soften. He would have to do a better job of controlling his anger in the future. He released Georgiana and gazed into her eyes: there was a new firmness there. She really did not want to seek retribution. He still wanted all the revenge in the world, but he would try to change if it helped Georgiana. Once again he wondered how Elizabeth could be so wise.

Georgiana saw her brother tuck his arm behind him and clench his fist repeatedly in a very rapid motion. He was clearly agitated and nervous. He wanted to help her, and she knew his intentions were good. But her mind was engaged elsewhere, studying the silent looks and private conversations exchanged between her brother and Elizabeth; it seemed as if they were having a full conversation without her. It was somewhat endearing to know that her brother, whom she had always loved, and Elizabeth, who had come to mean so much to her, had been brought together as a result of what Wickham did to her. For the first time, she had a glimpse, albeit a small glimpse, of what Elizabeth described to her as the healing power of gratitude. It made her smile.

"William," she announced, "it has been many months since I said this, but I do believe I am hungry. Let us go to dinner." He nodded and offered his arm to Georgiana. She frowned; that wasn't what she had hoped for. She leaned in to kiss his cheek and said, "Now, William, we have a guest tonight. You can escort me to dinner any day, but tonight you must accompany Elizabeth." He gave her a suspicious, but knowing, look and then resigned himself to appeasing her. She knew he was not disappointed.

"Miss Elizabeth, may I show you to the dining room? It appears I have my marching orders. I must insist you take my arm, or we shall see a distraught young lady. And I believe I have seen enough of that for today. After dinner Georgiana and I can accompany you home in the carriage."

"No, William, please let her stay!" Georgiana pleaded. "She is prepared to stay the night, and I would very much enjoy her company. I am sorry. I should have told you that we had already decided it. Can she not stay?"

Elizabeth felt awkward for a moment. To fill the silence, she leaned on Darcy's arm a little and whispered, "I shall accompany you to dinner if you desire, but I should warn you I plan to tease you without restraint. And you should know that if you let me stay the night, Georgiana and I plan to gossip about you quite mercilessly. Why she has all but planned our wedding breakfast!"

The fear in his eyes was evident as he wondered what Georgiana might have said, and Elizabeth took pity on him. She smiled, and he recognized her comments as teasing and flashed a large, dimpled, knee-weakening smile. Her heart fluttered, and she felt the heat rise in her face.

Mr. Darcy was more than relieved to see her glow back, and he noticed she was a little pink in the cheeks as well. Seeing her rosy-cheeked and embarrassed was delightful, but for the life of him he couldn't understand why she would be embarrassed when she was the one teasing him. He put his hand over hers and whispered, "And what will we serve at our wedding breakfast?"

"Mutton," she replied with a straight face. She heard his roaring, deep laughter but managed not to smile until she heard Georgiana's giggle from behind them, and then all three of them laughed uncontrollably.

The next morning, Elizabeth rolled over and poked Georgiana. "Was our late-night conversation too much? Or did I kick you? Jane says I kick in my sleep."

Georgiana moaned and squinted at the bright sunlight shining on her. Didn't she leave the curtains closed last night? "I am not awake enough to answer that. The sun has just barely risen over the hills. Why did you wake me?"

"Today is the first day of your new life. And you must know that asking me to sleep in your bed has its downfalls; the first being that I kick at night, the second being that I am an early riser. My father always says that you are free to choose your choices, but you cannot choose your consequences. You begged me to sleep with you, and now you must accept the consequence of that choice. Now, get dressed. We are going walking, and you are going to show me your favorite part of Pemberley grounds."

"That would be the stables then."

"Horses? You know I do not enjoy horses. If I were as skilled as you, perhaps I would, but we are far away from that realm of possibility. Can we not explore on our God-given feet, without a huge beast under us? Or are you hoping for some entertainment?"

Georgiana sat up and looked at her new friend. Even in the morning, she was cheerful and happy. Elizabeth even turned her complaints into compliments. Georgiana told herself she would have to try to be more like her. She pushed back the covers and heard Elizabeth squeal with delight and clap her hands in glee. "Elizabeth, I cannot vouch for my mood, and I certainly do not know the grounds like my brother does. Perhaps he would like to go with us."

"That is perfectly acceptable to me. But let us hurry; the birds are singing and begging us to hear their song."

As they helped each other into their day dresses, Elizabeth noticed a significant improvement in Georgiana's mood. She was still quiet and passive, and Elizabeth still often found her staring blankly at nothing, but when Elizabeth spoke to her, Georgiana would awake herself from her stupor and make healthy attempts to converse. Her giggles last night about serving mutton at the wedding breakfast reassured Elizabeth that Georgiana was heading in the right direction.

As Georgiana got dressed, she reviewed last night's conversation. Elizabeth had taught her how to pray. Elizabeth had told her the most important part of prayer is realizing whom you were talking to. God isn't some vague, mighty being, so removed that He can't be bothered to listen to you. He is a real man who was born of a woman, who lived and died on Earth, and who knew every heartache, joy, and pain anyone has ever felt. He is a perfected being who loves His children more than anything in the whole wide world.

Elizabeth had explained that God would give anything to help us; all we had to do was ask. Elizabeth then explained that if talking to God as a real being was the most important part of a prayer, the second most important thing was to thank Him for all He had given us. Expressing gratitude was much more important than petitioning Him. It was gratitude that would help Georgiana find peace again. Elizabeth had said, "Where gratitude is, happiness follows".

They had spent almost an hour detailing the things Georgiana should be grateful for. Of course there were the obvious things: her home and her brother. But Elizabeth helped her to think of more things, such as her love of music, her talent on the pianoforte, her freedom, her sensitive and shy nature, and her ability to be a good friend.

Then there were the more difficult things. Elizabeth helped her to see how grateful she should be that she had not conceived a child, that she was not physically injured, that her reputation was undamaged, and that she still had a bright future ahead of her. It was hard for Georgiana to give thanks for those things. She was not ready yet to thank God for anything related to what Wickham did. But it had felt good to begin to pray last night.

This morning she was truly grateful for one thing: for the first time in many months, she had no nightmares last night. When she saw Elizabeth on her knees, she knew she owed the Lord her thankfulness for that one small blessing. So, Georgiana knelt down next to Elizabeth. As she bowed her head she felt an overwhelming calmness come over her. Elizabeth grabbed her hand and squeezed. It was simply all Georgiana could do not to break down in tears. At the end of her prayer, she gave thanks for one more thing: Elizabeth.

After finishing their morning preparations, Elizabeth followed Georgiana through the house looking for her brother. After searching several rooms without success, Elizabeth said, "Perhaps he does not wish to be found!"

"Who does not wish to be found?"

Darcy's deep baritone voice sent goose bumps up her spine, and she turned to look at him. He was dressed in riding breeches and a waistcoat that fit his shoulders snuggly. He was adjusting his cravat, and the intimate nature of such a gesture made her look at him in awe. He truly was a handsome man. And just as she thought that, he looked deep into her eyes, as if he knew what she was thinking, and grinned. She felt exposed and transparent and had to look away.

Georgiana smiled, pleased to see the two of them exchange nonverbal greetings that made both of them flush, and then addressed her brother. "Would you like to accompany us on a walk before we break our fast?"

"It would be my pleasure. Let me get my jacket from my study. I was just about to write to Mr. Gardiner and let him know when to expect your return. Have you two discussed your plans?"

He ushered them down the hall, and they made their way towards the entryway.

Elizabeth finally felt her cheeks return to their normal shade, which meant she had found her voice as well. "I will stay if Georgiana needs me to, but my sister, Jane, is coming into town this afternoon. I would like to return to Saphrinbrooke in time to meet her, and then both of us can pay a call here tomorrow morning, if you like. I would love to introduce you to my sister, Jane, Mr. Darcy."

The way she said the last sentence confused him. The words themselves were pleasant and polite; however, there was a tone of reservation that made him think she did not mean them. "That sounds like a fine plan. My close friend, Bingley, and his two sisters are coming tomorrow morning. I would like to introduce you to them. There is not a finer, more pleasant man to be acquainted with. He is part boy and part man. He looks like a grown adult, but he is as excitable as a puppy with a stick when he meets new people. And if your sister is even half as amiable as you are, he will be quite happy to make her acquaintance." Mr. Darcy put his jacket on while the ladies put on their bonnets and pelisses.

"Then he will not be disappointed," Elizabeth replied. "I do not put myself in the same class as my sister. She is everything lovely and kind; traits that do not come naturally to me. I work very hard at mimicking her good qualities, but my impertinence sometimes prevents such characteristics from emerging as dominant traits in my character."

Mr. Darcy said, "I must disagree, Miss Elizabeth. Unless your sister is a saint, I cannot imagine her being any more lovely or kind than you are. And while I am already being far too forward, I might add that those traits seem to be quite dominant; I would say they are the very essence of your character." He saw her jaw drop open and then close without saying a word. Her eyes lit up momentarily, but then he saw them clouded with confusion and embarrassment. "Did I render you speechless again? Amazing, for here we stand in the foyer again. It must be the light. Shall we walk?"

CHAPTER 5

"Darcy! You are beginning to look like an old man!" Mr. Bingley called out cheerfully. He limped into Darcy's study unannounced and sat down in the nearest sofa.

Darcy looked up from his desk and then walked over to greet his friend. "So says the man limping his way into my study! What did you do to your foot?"

"Oh, this? I was catching an old tabby cat for the most beautiful lady you have ever laid eyes on."

"I should have known it involved a lady." Darcy patted him on the back, "How are you, my friend?"

"I would be better if the lady had not been engaged to Sir Samuel Pattington! Why are all the good ones already taken?" Bingley cringed as he gently set his foot up on the edge of a chair.

Darcy poured them two glasses of port and joined him on the sofa. "Well, I have some good news on that topic. We are having company this morning: two fine ladies—Miss Jane Bennet and Miss Elizabeth Bennet. I have only had the pleasure of meeting Miss Elizabeth, but she speaks very highly of her eldest sister. If Miss Bennet is anything like Miss Elizabeth, you will be hard pressed to restrain your fickle heart."

"Do I sense an element of regard for this Miss Elizabeth? Who is she?"

Darcy's face flushed red as he replied, "She is a guest staying with Mr. and Mrs. Gardiner at the Saphrinbrooke estate."

"And the very thought of her makes you blush? Goodness, surely the ever-guarded Darcy has not fallen in love! You only left London four months ago!

"I am not in love. But I do admire her. And just because I do not fall in and out of love on a monthly basis like you does not mean I am not capable of love." Darcy paused for a moment and imagined if he would even recognize the feeling. He certainly was closer to it than ever before. "Miss Elizabeth speaks highly of her sister."

Charles Bingley did like to sport with his friend a little now and then. "Yes, I believe you told me that already. Is your usually meticulous mind being distracted at present by daydreams of a blonde?"

"Brunette."

"I should have known. You do not prefer blondes as I do."

"Indeed, but I know how you enjoy meeting ladies, be they blonde or brunette. And I am happy to inform you that an idea has been rolling around in my head for the last few days that I expect will bring you joy."

"And what idea is that?"

"A ball."

Bingley took his leg off the chair and sat up. Laughing wholeheartedly he said, "Now I know you are in love! When was the last time you held a ball at Pemberley? It has been at least three years!"

Darcy took a drink of his sherry and murmured, "Four."

"By gads! Tell me about her. Where is she from? Do I know her? What is she like? And how in the world did she snare your carefully guarded heart?"

"She is the second of five daughters from an estate in Hertfordshire. She is the niece of Mr. and Mrs. Gardiner, who recently inherited an estate six miles from here. Miss Elizabeth is helping get them settled." Darcy stood up again, too excited to remain seated. His speech, usually so carefully considered, began coming out in a rush. "Her uncle is a fine fellow. He was in trade before the inheritance, but you would not know that from his manners. Oh dear—sorry, Bingley. I meant no offence; I know your family made their money in trade."

"None taken," Bingley replied with a grin.

"Anyway," Darcy continued. "I doubt you know her, but you will know why I am drawn to her the moment you see her. She glows."

Bingley's grin hesitated, and he looked at Darcy with confusion. "She glows? I do not understand what you mean. Does she perspire more than usual?"

Darcy gave him a chastising look, "Of course not! She just glows. Her eyes sparkle. Her walk has a bounce. Her lips turn up in a teasing manner, and she pulls people in like some sort of magnet. It makes you beg for the impertinent remark that you know is coming. She is quite intelligent. Our conversations are so varied and enlightening that one would think she had been schooled at university. And she has something else special about her. I would almost call her mature beyond her years. I feel like she has a perspective on life that makes her . . ." Darcy paused, searching for the right word.

Bingley finished Darcy's thought, "Glow. I get it. Interesting. So, when will this ball be? Do you dare host it while my sisters are here?" Bingley saw Darcy grimace slightly at the mention of his sisters. Caroline Bingley seemed destined to remain a spinster, as she was blind to every bachelor she had ever met but one. She had her heart set on being Mistress of Pemberley. She talked through the whole carriage ride from London about how this was surely the visit when Darcy would finally make his feelings known.

Darcy sighed loudly. "You know how I feel about Miss Bingley, and I do appreciate all your attempts to redirect her attentions away from me. But I should not have to alter my plans or mask my interest in Miss Elizabeth simply to spare her feelings. I have never given your sister any encouragement. I will offer to dance with Miss Bingley only *after* I have danced with Miss

Elizabeth. I think two weeks will be sufficient time for my staff to prepare. The season is over, and many of the local families are back in their country homes. It will not be a big affair. After all, I do have a good excuse to host a ball. Miss Elizabeth's aunt and uncle are Pemberley's closest neighbors, and it would only be polite to introduce them properly."

Charles Bingley let out his friendly laugh again. Darcy was too transparent for anyone to miss the real reason he was throwing a ball: he wanted to dance with Elizabeth. "If that is the excuse you want to give, then you can continue to delude yourself; but if you ask me, a bachelor does not throw a ball to introduce his middle-aged neighbors. You will draw quite the crowd of debutants. It will be the talk of the town! Mr. Darcy of Pemberley, the most sought-after bachelor in all of Derbyshire, is looking for a wife!"

Darcy just rolled his eyes at his friend. "I suppose I should be a proper host and welcome your sisters and Mr. Hurst to Pemberley."

"Oh, yes. One in the company is particularly anxious to see you." Bingley let out another teasing laugh that drew another look of disdain from his friend.

"But first I must ask a favor of you. Georgiana has been a little under the weather, so I am sorry to say that she will occupy a considerable amount of my attention this week. Could you assist me in being a good host and attending to everyone's needs?"

"Not a problem. I can talk anyone's ears off, and you can certainly leave guests to their own devices in an estate this size. I hope Miss Georgiana will not be ill long."

"I am unsure at the moment. I suspect she will need a great deal of rest. She says she will try to make a few appearances, but she will probably be absent more often than not. I gather she does not appreciate Miss Bingley's facade of friendship any more than I appreciate her constant flattery."

"Well then, for the sake of our friendship, I shall occupy my sisters as well as I can. But if Miss Jane Bennet turns out to be a blonde, then I cannot guarantee the task will receive my undivided attention."

*****

"Jane, just look at the gardens! Is it not the most amazing sight?" Elizabeth said. The awe on Jane's face spoke volumes.

"Oh dear! Even in this rainy weather, that is a fine house. Very impressive. I do not think I will be able to speak two coherent sentences to a man so wealthy. And you said he will have guests as well?" Jane asked.

"His friend, Charles Bingley; Bingley's two sisters; and a brother-in-law supposedly arrived this morning. One sister is married, and the other is single. Mr. Darcy did not say any more about them, so I do not know what they are like. He did say that Mr. Bingley is very amiable. And Mr. Darcy is quite amiable himself. Maybe we can fulfill Mamma's greatest wish and find you a wealthy man to marry!"

Jane turned her head and looked at her sister in confusion. "Elizabeth, but surely you cannot be serious," she said. "The way you described Mr. Darcy to me last night made it quite clear that you have some feelings for the man. I could never attempt to 'ensnarl him' as Mamma instructed. But he is probably safe anyway," Jane giggled. "I have no idea how to accomplish such a task, although I received many lectures on the best methods and tactics of ensnarling rich men before I left. I will not forget you purposely told Mamma that he was wealthy and single!"

"Well, how else could I convince her to send you here?"

"You are deflecting the question. Do you care for Mr. Darcy?"

"I have mixed feelings. Do I think you are a good match for him? No, your temperaments are too different. Do I have plans to use my arts and allurements to 'ensnarl' him for the sake of ensuring my financial future? No, I am not that kind of lady. I will only marry for love."

Jane carefully considered all that Elizabeth had said—and all that she had *not* said. It was unlike Elizabeth to hold back her opinion of someone. Her sister had avoided saying whether she cared for him, which could only mean that she did. She did not say what she admired about him, which meant she admired him very much. She also did not say why she got along so well with his sister, but Jane was not sure what that meant for Elizabeth's relationship with Mr. Darcy. Miss Darcy was a sensitive topic. Jane could sense that Elizabeth was close to her, yet her sister had said very little about her.

Jane hoped today's introductions would tell her more about Elizabeth's relationship with the Darcys, especially Mr. Darcy. Some, particularly their mother, accused Jane of being timid and shy, but Jane was not really shy—she was just quiet; and in those silent moments, she was observing those around her. Her skill in seeing what others did not see would be of great service today as she studied the interaction between Mr. Darcy and her favorite sister.

The carriage rolled to a stop, and a footman opened the door and assisted them down. Elizabeth couldn't help but feel disappointed that Mr. Darcy was not there to do the task himself. The other times she had been to Pemberley, he had been waiting for her. The butler led them to the morning room where Mr. Darcy and his guests are already taking tea and announced them.

Jane noticed that there were three gentlemen in the room. Two stood immediately; the third had to be elbowed awake and seemed perturbed that his sleep had been interrupted. Of the two standing gentlemen, one smiled widely at them both and the other bowed quite deeply to Elizabeth, seemingly oblivious to Jane's presence. When he lifted his face, Jane saw a great deal of admiration in his eyes for Elizabeth. She had her answer for which gentleman was Mr. Darcy; she could tell that she was going to largely be ignored by him.

Mr. Darcy started making the introductions. The young lady to the left of Mr. Darcy was his sister, Georgiana; there was something familiar about her that Jane could not quite put her finger on. The smiling, red-haired gentleman was his friend, Charles Bingley. There was also Mr. Bingley's sister, Miss Caroline Bingley, and Mr. Bingley's sister and brother-in-law, Mr. and Mrs. Hurst.

Jane immediately saw the resemblance between Mrs. Hurst and Mr. Bingley. She had a strong, masculine jaw and a rather large nose for a lady. Mr. Hurst still hadn't taken it upon himself to stand and greet them, and yet he was able to lean over the coffee table and pour himself some more brandy.

Miss Bingley had her nose in the air and a look on her face as if there was a distasteful odor to the room. Jane understood that look well. The Bennet sisters had been evaluated from head to toe and were found wanting. It was obvious that Miss Bingley dressed in very fine apparel, and Elizabeth's and Jane's muslin day dresses were not the latest style. Jane understood at once that Miss Bingley was an elitist, full of her own self-importance. All in all, the introductions went smoothly, and Jane did her best to acknowledge each person individually.

Bingley and Darcy gave up their seats for the Bennet sisters, and Georgiana poured more tea. Elizabeth was pleased to see Georgiana so composed. She gave her a wink when Georgiana handed her a cup, and Georgiana smiled weakly back at her. It was a small thing, but Elizabeth was very relieved; she could see that Georgiana would cope today, at least mildly well, even with the extra visitors.

Bingley took a seat next to the fair-haired Miss Bennet and opened the room's conversations. "Miss Bennet, Darcy here tells me you and your sister are from Hertfordshire. What part of the county?"

"Our estate, Longborn, is but a mile from Meryton."

Bingley slapped his knee. "By George!" he exclaimed. "Is it is not a small world? Then that means you would be familiar with Netherfield Park?"

Jane looked confused for a moment. "Yes, indeed," she replied. "Are you acquainted with that estate?"

"Considering I just signed a lease for it, I suppose you could say I am!"

Elizabeth smiled and said, "Then you will be our neighbor! Netherfield and Longbourn are but three miles apart. Jane told me just last night that we were getting new neighbors. How delightful! When will you take it?"

Bingley couldn't keep his eyes off Miss Bennet; she had the longest eyelashes he had ever seen. It was as if they were painted on for dramatic effect. Every time she blinked, his heart raced, and when she would glance his way, his heart stopped altogether as her eyes demurely met his. He realized he had not answered Miss Elizabeth. "I will be here at Pemberley for a few weeks, and then I have a few things to do in town. I expect to be settled at Netherfield by the end of August."

Miss Bingley sat up straighter, if that were possible, and said, "It is so lovely to meet some of the local country folk before we actually move in. You can give us the inside gossip on whom to avoid. Lord knows there are those who pass themselves off as gentlemen and ladies whose behavior leaves much to be improved upon!"

For a moment, Elizabeth was too shocked to respond. "I suppose country folk are quite varied," she carefully replied, "but there will be few to avoid in Meryton. Though it is but a small town, the people make it a very fine place to live. Are you planning to go to Netherfield as well, Miss Bingley?"

"Indeed I am, for Charles could not keep an estate running without me. His mind is always engaged in the nearest shiny object. Oh, do not look at me like that, Charles! You know it is true!" She turned back to Elizabeth and added, "His attention to detail has much to be improved upon, and since this is his first opportunity to run an estate, he will need quite a bit of support. My sister and her husband will come for the first few weeks as well."

Miss Bingley turned to Mr. Darcy and continued, "And if I am not mistaken, Mr. Darcy, you were invited to visit as well. Will you be joining us in Hertfordshire?" But as Miss Bingley watched him to gauge his response, she was surprised to find his attention elsewhere engaged. He was gazing not at Caroline, but at Elizabeth. She had been oblivious to it until now, but there was an undeniable familiarity between Elizabeth and Mr. Darcy. Their eyes were locked on each other, and Mr. Darcy had what looked like a smile on his face. Caroline suddenly felt threatened. *He never smiles at me that way!*

Mr. Darcy tore his eyes away from Elizabeth's. He was so thrilled by this turn of events that it was difficult to form a coherent response. He had been painfully aware that Elizabeth's visit to Derbyshire would be ending soon; now he would have a chance to visit her in Hertfordshire.

"Yes, I told Bingley that I would come see him," he replied. "I have not made any definite plans yet, but I am looking forward to a visit to Hertfordshire." He wished he could say how nothing would bring him greater pleasure than to further his acquaintance with Elizabeth, but he recognized that Miss Bingley was sitting right next to him. Perhaps now was not the right moment.

The conversation continued about the little town of Meryton and all the inhabitants for some time. When the tea was cold and the refreshments eaten, Georgiana thought it would be a good time to speak with Elizabeth. She had endured enough of Miss Bingley's haughtiness for one day. Knowing that Miss Bingley would not venture outside when there was the slightest chance of rain, she set her plan into action: "I am in need of a brisk walk. Would anyone like to accompany me to see the gardens?"

Elizabeth made eye contact with Georgiana and immediately seized the opportunity. "I agree that would be a fine idea," she replied. "I cannot pass up an opportunity to walk through Pemberley's gardens."

Georgiana asked, "Miss Bennet? Miss Bingley? Mrs. Hurst? Would you like to go on a walk? I believe the rain will pass us by today. I have been doing much walking lately and find the exercise invigorating." All the ladies politely declined. When Mr. Darcy accepted the invitation, it looked like for a moment that Miss Bingley would change her mind; but, to Georgiana's relief, she ultimately decided not to chance the weather. Jane agreed to stay behind and share more about Netherfield Park and the previous owners. Mr. Hurst had fallen asleep again, so there was no threat there. And Georgiana knew better than to ask Mr. Bingley; it was clear he was quite enthralled with Miss Bennet.

Mr. Darcy, Georgiana, and Miss Elizabeth made their way outside. It was nearing noon, but the cloud cover was thick, making the air sticky and humid.

Elizabeth took Mr. Darcy's offered arm; the simple gentlemanly act was beginning to be quite endearing. She could feel his strength as she walked next to him. It was both a physical strength as well as an emotional strength. He struggled hard to hide that emotional side of him, but she was not blind to his efforts. Perhaps it was because she was always sensitive to the emotional climate around her that she noticed things like that.

She sensed that he had a lot to say, but she felt she must first check in with Georgiana, so she opened the conversation. "I must say, you did a fine job holding yourself together in there with the Bingleys and Hursts," Elizabeth said. "I only saw a flicker of lugubriousness. I am very proud. It must have been hard for you. How are you this morning?"

"I am surprisingly well. Better than the last several months, but that is not saying much. I admit it was taxing trying to smile at all the right moments and trying to participate in the conversation.

It is difficult to do so even on my best days, but I kept telling myself how important it was to not show any weakness in front of Miss Bingley."

It was just as Elizabeth had suspected; Miss Bingley could not be trusted, and even young Georgiana knew this. "I gather you are not fond of the Bingley sisters."

"I do not want to be rude, but I doubt I will ever call them friends. You saw how judgmental she was about country folk. She did not seem to realize that William and I consider ourselves country folk. We spend most of the year at Pemberley. She is only nice to me because she wants to marry William."

Mr. Darcy laughed. "Are you two going to talk as if I am not even here? And how did you hear that Miss Bingley wants to marry me? Surely she did not tell you that herself."

Elizabeth laughed this time. "You are welcome to join the conversation at any time, Mr. Darcy. You should feel quite privileged to catch a glimpse of the secret conversations between ladies. We evaluate and re-evaluate every word, every gesture, and every tone we see and hear. And Georgiana is only stating the obvious; it is quite clear to everyone in the room that Miss Bingley is very fond of you. She must have complimented you and Pemberley four times before tea was over. And she certainly enjoyed wrapping her arm around yours when you agreed to visit Netherfield. She is no chameleon in her attentions."

"I am uncomfortable discussing this with you two."

"Well then, what would you like to discuss?" Elizabeth asked.

"Anything. You choose, just not Miss Bingley."

Elizabeth smiled at Georgiana and replied, "Very well, I will start my 'no comment' questions."

Georgiana snickered. "Oh dear! Now you are in for it, William!"

"Dare I ask what 'no comment' questions are?"

Elizabeth explained, "I ask a deeply personal question, and you can either choose to answer it with complete honesty, or you can choose to answer with 'no comment'. The difficulty is that I will ask three questions, and you may answer 'no comment' only once, so choose carefully."

Mr. Darcy pondered whether to accept Miss Elizabeth's challenge. He wanted to become better acquainted with her, and yet he was a very private person. What if she asked how he felt about her? What if she asked what he had dreamt about last night? Obviously, the appeal of the game was the opportunity to ask slightly inappropriate, or at the least, private questions. It could be very dangerous.

But he knew Miss Elizabeth would not intentionally embarrass him. And they had already discussed a lifetime of inappropriate topics in their conversations about Georgiana. He weighed the matter thoughtfully. How badly did he want to get to know her? Was he prepared to let her get to know him?

"Do you agree to the rules of the game?" Elizabeth asked.

"I do, on one condition: I get to ask you three questions as well." He looked down at her brown eyes and completely lost his train of thought when she smiled. Just then, a curl fell across her forehead, and he almost reached out to move it out if her eyes. She brushed it away, and he chastised himself for not controlling his impulses.

"I accept that proposal. I have no secrets to hide," Elizabeth said cheerfully. "My first question will be fairly easy, I think, and the other questions will increase in difficulty. Are you ready?"

Mr. Darcy took a deep breath and put his hand on hers, giving it a small squeeze. He asked Georgiana, "Have you played this game with her?"

"Indeed. It was quite invigorating. Her questions really make you think. They provide an opportunity to explore and develop conversations that one normally does not have."

"Well then, if Georgiana survived your 'no comment' questions, there is at least some hope for me. Fire away; I am ready."

Elizabeth knew the first question she wanted to ask and did not hesitate. "Whom do you consider your hero?"

Mr. Darcy looked down at her and smiled. "That is easy. My father. Next question."

Georgiana laughed, "No, William, you have to explain yourself! These questions are designed to create good conversation. You have to tell us why he is your hero."

"Well, that was not part of the rules. I answered the question. I think I should get full marks for that."

Elizabeth grinned at him and said, "Then let me further explain the rules. If I feel you answer a question sincerely, then the next question will stay at the same level of intimacy. If I feel you are holding back, then my questions will become much, much more difficult to answer. Are you ready to risk me asking anything and everything?"

Darcy hesitated. "In that case, let me consider the first question again," he replied. He did not like the sound of "much, much more difficult" questions. There were certain questions he was not prepared to answer. Clearly he would have to do better. He was not used to deep, personal conversations, but this question seemed simple enough.

He began, "My father is my hero because he was truly amazing. He was known for his compassion. He was kind to his tenants and servants and devoted to my mother. He believed in the goodness of people, like you do, Miss Elizabeth. That meant he trusted people, even those who had not yet earned his trust; and most people wanted to live up to his trust.

"He was an intelligent man who valued reading and kept himself educated on a great number of topics. He always took the time to share his wisdom with me. Sometimes it was a financial lesson, other times a moral lesson, but he was always teaching. His words were as precious to me as pure gold. I wish I had written down his advice, so I could have it now. I miss him terribly. If I hope to emulate anyone, it is him. He is my hero."

Georgiana sniffled, "That was a fine answer, William. He truly was all of those things."

Darcy was pensive as a silence hung around the group. It made him nervous. This was why he avoided disclosing things about himself. He had an active imagination, and he could think of a great many reasons why Elizabeth was still silent. Had he said too much? Or, had he not said enough? Would her next question be even more personal?

He anxiously looked at her. She was looking up at him with that sparkle in her eyes. Their depth engulfed him like never before, and all his fears seemed to dissolve away as he looked at her. At the moment, she could ask him anything and he would tell her.

He scanned her lightly tanned face and was truly amazed at the beauty he saw. She was not perfect in her symmetry, but she was beautiful. She had a small nose that was feminine and rounded slightly. Her cheekbones were high but not overwhelming. Her eyes were large and not deep set, but it was not her eyes that drew his attention now. It was her mouth that drew his gaze. Her lips looked so pink and soft, and they were slightly parted in a soft smile. That was when he realized he was looking at her lips and pondering what it would be like to kiss them.

Suddenly, he remembered Georgiana was standing right next to him. The awkwardness of the moment weighed heavily on his shoulders. He had been daydreaming about kissing Elizabeth! Right in front of his sister! This was so unlike him. He was usually in control of his thoughts and emotions, and he was always in control of his actions. He looked away quickly, very nearly in a panic. What was she doing to him? How could he want to kiss a lady he had known less than three weeks?

Elizabeth saw a deep longing in his eyes when he talked of his father, but then a rainbow of expressions revealed themselves. Most of them were easily read. She saw uneasiness, some fear, and some level of self-examination, but when he looked down at her, she saw something she didn't recognize. He had looked at her that way before, but the flash of emotion in his eyes was so quick she could not describe it. Was it admiration? Desire?

Surely Mr. Darcy didn't look at her that way. She was Georgiana's friend, but she knew she was not part of their social class. He was from the finest circles; she certainly was not. She didn't have Jane's beauty of flaxen hair and deep blue eyes. She certainly had no connections or fortune to make her attractive; the look in his eyes puzzled her greatly. She kept looking at him trying to catch a glimpse of it again, but he was looking forward without so much as a blink of an eye to reveal his thoughts. What an unusual man! So guarded, so careful, and so mysterious!

Georgiana had seen the two staring at each other, and it filled her with such joy. It was an unfamiliar feeling of late. William was in very real danger of losing his heart. Now Elizabeth needed to get to know him a little better. "Elizabeth, he answered that one well, did he not?"

Elizabeth looked over to Georgiana and saw a glimpse of mischief on her face. "Indeed! He could not have answered it better. I would have liked to meet your father very much."

Before he could stop himself Darcy responded, "He would have liked to meet you." As soon as the words came out of his mouth, he wished he could take them back. He might as well have made an offer of marriage right there. He chanced a glance down at her face, and she had an amused smile on her face.

Elizabeth couldn't help but see the embarrassment in his cheeks. It was sweet that he would want her to meet his father. She sensed that he was closing all emotional doors, and quickly too, so she pushed him a little further. "Mr. Darcy, are you ready for the next question?"

"If you are ready to ask it," Mr. Darcy answered nervously.

"I usually ask three totally different questions, but your answer has made me want to ask another question on the same topic. My next 'no comment' question is this: what is the hardest part about being Master of Pemberley?"

They had made the loop already and were heading back to the house. The rain clouds had passed, and it was growing quite warm. Mr. Darcy slowed the pace a little. "Complete honesty?"

"Or else . . ." Georgiana reminded him.

"Well then, I would say the hardest part of being the Master of Pemberley is living up to the reputation of my father. He was so good at it; he made it look easy. But it is not easy, not for me. I struggle with trying to meet the expectations of everyone, including you, Georgiana. In fact, especially you. Not only am I supposed to run the estate, but I am your guardian. I feel like I have failed you. If I cannot manage the one life that I am in charge of, what makes me think that I will be able to manage the lives of all the servants and tenants and their families?"

Georgiana reached out and stopped her brother. "William! How can you say that? You are the best brother I could ask for!"

Mr. Darcy gently tugged Georgiana along and continued walking. He tried to explain, "But it is not just that. Every day I am presented with problems that require a decision from me. And every day I worry whether or not I made the right decision. I just wish I could have an easy life, with no trials. No problems to fix. Nothing going wrong. No hurdles to jump."

Elizabeth was quite curious about this line of thinking. "This is not the next question, just a clarification question. Would you really would prefer a life with no problems? Nothing to challenge you to be a better person?"

"I do not think I need challenges to make me a better person. I travel, I read extensively, and I study philosophy. So, yes, I believe I can improve myself without challenges. I certainly would like to try it for a change." They had reached the end of the trail at the garden entrance. Mr. Darcy pulled out the chairs from the porch table for Georgiana and Miss Elizabeth and helped them sit down before joining them.

Elizabeth pondered his answer. There was a great deal of pride in it. He certainly felt he was in a class apart from others. "Truly? Well, that surprises me. Everyone has trials, not just the Master of Pemberley. Problems are what make us better people. The whole purpose of trials is to make us reach beyond our comfort and stretch ourselves."

"But I think I could live a happy, fulfilled life without the drama that comes from the misdeeds of others. Take for example the problem I dealt with this morning. A tenant's fourteen-year-old son was caught poaching on my grounds. The law says I must deal harshly with poachers. But the boy is barely old enough to be called a man! Now I must make a decision that could alter his entire future. His parents were hoping to get him an apprenticeship with the carpenter in Lambton, but that will be impossible if I press charges. And if I don't press charges, word will spread, and a small poaching problem could become much worse."

Mr. Darcy sighed and continued, "I did not ask to be the Master of Pemberley. I did not ask to have the power to make or break the lad. So, if you ask me if I would honestly prefer to live without these trials, then the answer is yes."

"But would you have ever considered the problem of the young poacher unless you were forced to make the decision yourself? If you had an easy life, would you have ever stretched yourself to find solutions that meet both justice and mercy?"

"Certainly. I think that if a neighbor sought my advice on such a problem, I would work very hard to find a fair solution. The world is filled with such stories of woe. I do not require any more examples in my own life to learn those lessons."

"Now I see. Trials that happen to others are acceptable, but when they occur to you, it is unsatisfactory."

"I did not say that. I wish no harm on anyone."

Elizabeth paused. "You intrigue me, Mr. Darcy. Your answer leads me to my third 'no comment' question. Do you believe in God?" She watched him look at her in surprise.

"Of course. I attend church every Sunday." Elizabeth raised her eyebrow at him. "Why do you look at me so? Ah, I see. I did not answer appropriately. Let me try to expand on this answer. I was christened at the parish church in—"

"No, I think you misunderstood the question. I asked if you *believe* in God. I was not asking about your Sunday habits."

"I do not understand. Of course I believe in Him."

"I am not sure I believe you. I see from the confused look on your face that it probably would have been best if you had answered 'no comment.'"

"Miss Elizabeth, I assure you I believe there is a God. What makes you question my Christianity? I am a fair, honest man. I treat others with kindness and give liberally to the poor."

Elizabeth didn't know how far she wanted to go with this. She hesitated, and then decided to go all in. This was something she was especially passionate about and she could not resist the urge to make her opinions known, even if it bordered on impertinence. "You say you believe in God, yet you think you could do a better job of running your life without His interference, without the learning experiences He has given you that you dismiss as unnecessary problems. Mr. Darcy, have you ever read Malachi 3:3?"

"I suppose at some time I have, but I do not recall it at the moment. Should I retrieve my Bible and look it up?"

"I always recommend looking in your Bible, but I can recite this particular passage for you. It says God 'will sit as a refiner and purifier of silver'. Do you know how silver is refined, Mr. Darcy?"

"I do not. I suspect you will tell me."

"No, I shall not. This is something you must learn for yourself. I challenge you to research this passage and try to understand what it means. I think it might help you with all three of your 'no comment' answers. When you feel weak, this scripture might lift you up. When you miss your father and struggle to live up to his reputation, you might find this scripture comforting. When you state that you believe in God, this might make your faith unwavering."

"And this simple scripture will do all that?"

"I am sure of it."

They sat there for many moments looking at each other. Mr. Darcy couldn't help but notice that her hair had a reddish tint in the sunlight. It was radiant. Each curl caught the gleam of the noon sun, and they framed her face in a very flattering way. She truly glowed, especially at this moment. Her small smile reached her eyes, and in them he could see an intelligence he had found in no other lady of the *ton*. He wondered how many of them had even read the Bible, let alone could recite it.

She just pulled him in, like some sort of magnetic force. It made him do and say things that he was not ready to say or do. Like ask her to dance. He wished to see her floating form glide across Pemberley's ballroom, and he wanted to hold her hand and feel her feminine grip. He wanted to feel his heart beat in tune with the music, like it was beating now as he watched her shoulders rise and fall with her breathing.

Elizabeth was getting a little uncomfortable as Darcy stared at her. "Mr. Darcy, do you wish to ask me your 'no comment' questions, or should we go inside and join the others?"

A small smile crept across his face. "Indeed, I do have a question. But it is not one of my 'no comment' questions. I plan on saving those for another day. Two weeks from Friday I plan to host a ball in honor of the Gardiners. I would like to request your hand for the first set. Since you just found out about the ball, can I safely assume no one has requested them yet?"

Georgiana sucked in her breath. Was she ready to play hostess at a ball? She could barely handle the Bingleys for tea! She felt the blackness rise in her chest. She desperately searched for a way out. Maybe she would be indisposed that night. Maybe she could get away with only a small entrance since she was not formally out in society yet.

When her anxiety started to subside, a new wave of feelings flooded into her thoughts. *William has not hosted a ball at Pemberley for nearly four years!* It would be a truly momentous occasion. He hadn't discussed any such plans with her. It was completely out of character. But of course she knew why he was suddenly interested in balls. *He must like Elizabeth very much.*

Georgiana looked at Elizabeth and saw a shocked look on her face. She still hadn't answered him yet. Georgiana gently kicked her under the table. The action had its intended effect.

Elizabeth glanced at Georgiana, giving her a brief scowl. She turned back to Mr. Darcy, who had grown quite nervous in her silence. "Mr. Darcy, are you sure you want to open your own ball with me? Surely there are other ladies of consequence who are standing in line for the privilege."

Mr. Darcy wondered at her modesty. "Perhaps there are, but this is a ball in honor of your aunt and uncle. It would not suit to stand up with anyone but their niece."

"But me?"

"Why not you? Are you refusing me?"

"No, no! Certainly not. I accept, but you have left me speechless once again."

Darcy grinned widely. "And to think we are not even in my foyer!"

Elizabeth had to admit that she would have accepted immediately if he had just smiled at her like that, with his dimples in full bloom. *Handsome indeed.*

CHAPTER 6

"How are you, Georgie? You have hardly left your room these last few days."

Georgiana slowly turned to look at her brother. Everything had been so much easier with Elizabeth. Georgiana had made so much improvement that first day; she had almost dared hope her days of darkness were over. But in her friend's absence, they had returned, just as she had feared. "I miss her," Georgiana murmured.

"Miss Elizabeth?" Mr. Darcy asked even though he knew of whom she was speaking. *I miss her too.*

"Yes. She always had some thought-provoking saying that diverted my attention away from . . . him. It has been so trying to entertain the Bingleys. I fear they see right through me. The smallest conversation about the weather, or lace, or fashion, or your ball simply exhausts me. But when I lay down to rest, my mind just replays everything that happened to me, and I feel consumed again."

Darcy stiffened. Elizabeth had warned him that Georgiana might regress, but it was still painful to hear his sister talk this way. He steeled himself to ask the hard questions Elizabeth had instructed him to ask. Elizabeth had told him that if he didn't ask them, Georgiana would not feel his unconditional love. He had failed to help her before, and he had vowed he would not let her down again. "Pumpkin, how bad is it? Are you having thoughts of harming yourself?"

Georgiana looked up at his concerned, loving eyes and answered weakly, "I am."

He tried to be as unreadable as possible. He knew these questions were just as hard for her as they were for him. "Do you have any plans I should know about?"

"No, no plans. Just a consuming fascination with wishing the pain would end. There are moments when I can control myself and talk myself out of the feeling, but then there are times, like right now, when I just want you to hold my head under water and not let go. I know it is wrong, but the thoughts are so invasive. I wake up dreaming about taking a midnight gallop on Hera along the Ellis trail—the one with the cliff. Knowing my luck, I would just kill the horse and injure myself. But I do not think I need to be watched again. It is not as bad as it was that day in the barn. Back then, I could not see reason. At least now I know that at some point it will get better. Someday I will not feel this colorless abyss."

He put his hand on hers and gave it a gentle squeeze. "Miss Elizabeth promises that after every night, there is a dawn. It will get better, Georgiana."

"I know it will. I may not feel it yet, but I know Elizabeth would not lie to me. She says I need to exercise every day, but it has been so rainy. I hate being confined indoors. I wish I could talk to her again."

He wrapped his arm around her shoulders. "Well," he said, "it is not raining today. And I happen to know that the Bingleys and Hursts are gathered in the blue room. If we are careful, we could sneak out and go see her."

"Could we? I would love to see her again."

"Of course," he smiled. "But how would you feel about me discretely leaking our plans to Mr. Bingley? He has not stopped talking about Miss Bennet since they left, and I fear he will never forgive me if we do not invite him. He seems quite impressed with her."

"I have noticed. He keeps calling her his 'angel'. Is he always this way with ladies?"

"I am afraid so. He gets besotted easily."

"I do hope that he does not dally with her feelings. She seems so sweet and kind; I imagine she could be easily hurt."

Darcy had reached that conclusion as well. If he was going to pursue Elizabeth, and he had begun to realize he wanted to, the last thing he needed was his best friend playing on the affections of her favorite sister. "How soon can you be ready?" he asked. "We will have to sneak out quickly if we are to be back in time for supper."

Georgiana's heart lifted slightly with the thought. "I am prepared to go now."

"Then I will meet you at the stables in ten minutes." He kissed her forehead and left to tell Bingley of his plans.

He found Bingley laughing easily with Reynolds in the front entrance. Darcy clapped his hand on Bingley's shoulder and exclaimed, "Bingley, you have the look of a caged animal! I dare say you are anxious to see the local gentry. Perhaps you would like to accompany Georgiana and I on a visit to an *angelic* estate."

Bingley perked up. "Indeed! I wish for nothing else at the moment!"

Darcy smiled and turned to the butler. "Reynolds, could you have the carriage prepared? But do not bring it round to the front. Leave it at the stables. I would like our departure to go unnoticed by certain guests."

"And do hurry, Reynolds!" Bingley added. "I do not trust this Derbyshire weather to stay fine."

Reynolds tried to hide his smile but knew he was unsuccessful. "Right away, sir."

*****

"It is a pleasure to see you again, Miss Bennet. The rain seems to have had little effect on you as you look even better than the last time I saw you," Mr. Bingley said cheerfully.

Jane blushed slightly. "Thank you, sir. Please sit down. It is wonderful to have you visit us on such a beautiful day."

Elizabeth could immediately tell that the last few days had been trying for Georgiana. There were dark circles under her eyes, and she was avoiding eye contact with everyone but Elizabeth. Elizabeth knew sitting down to tea would only make things worse. Before anyone could take their seats, she said, "Jane, since it is such a nice day, perhaps we could stroll through the gardens. Neither Georgiana nor Mr. Bingley have seen Saphrinbrooke's gardens."

Bingley was more than pleased. He knew Darcy and Georgiana would want to walk with Elizabeth, leaving him the undivided attention of Miss Bennet. "What a splendid idea!" he replied. "Darcy was telling me about its many paths and little nooks."

As they walked out to the gardens, Elizabeth took Georgiana's arm and asked, "Georgiana, would you like to accompany me?"

Darcy tried to conceal his disappointment. Obviously, he was not invited to join them. But no matter how badly he wished to be in Elizabeth's presence, he knew Georgiana needed it more. He watched as his sister and Elizabeth quickly put distance between themselves and the rest of the group. Bingley was laughing at something Miss Bennet had said, and Darcy knew he would largely be ignored on this walk. That would suit him well at the moment.

As he watched the two women turn the corner of the hedge, he felt a pang of anxiety. Although he knew he should be concerned about Georgiana, he found he was quite preoccupied with thoughts of Elizabeth. He admitted this was becoming a common occurrence, and he felt somewhat guilty about that.

Although Miss Jane Bennet was quite beautiful, meeting her had only solidified for him how much he admired her sister. Elizabeth was striking. She was beautiful, but it was more than that. She had something else—life's luster, as he liked to call it. It shone in her eyes and made her glow. She loved life, and she reflected all that was good around her. She was extraordinary. She was everything he needed and wanted in a wife.

As Darcy's group turned the corner, he caught a glimpse of Elizabeth again. Her comforting arm was wrapped around Georgiana's shoulders. It looked like Georgiana was doing most of the talking; Elizabeth was patiently listening. Then, just as quickly, they turned again and disappeared out of sight.

He tried to pay attention, at least intermittently, to the conversation next to him. Bingley was being jovial and charming, and Jane was smiling sweetly back at him. Someone said something humorous, and they both laughed. Darcy's thoughts turned back to Elizabeth again.

He was interested in her, but was she interested in him? She certainly had not shown any preference for him. He was used to dealing with ladies who were desperate to garner his attention. Ladies like Miss Bingley flaunted their accomplishments and made their interest known as soon as they were introduced. They paraded their finest clothes and wore their finest adornments of the latest fashions, but Darcy didn't want a peacock as a wife. He didn't want expensive flavors that taxed the taste buds.

He wanted something radiant. He wanted that life's luster every day of his life. There was such a striking difference between Elizabeth's cheeky teasing, bordering on impertinence, and the catty snobbishness he had seen in other women. Elizabeth seemed to be comfortable in her own skin; she wore casual muslin day dresses that were flattering without flaunting her beautiful attractive frame. And she was quite attractive—thin, but curvy, in all the right spots.

"Do you not think so, Mr. Darcy?" Miss Bennet asked.

Darcy blushed at his thoughts and felt a little sheepish at being caught inattentive. Without knowing what she had asked, he replied, "Some might think differently, but I agree with Bingley."

He hoped it was a safe answer. Bingley was different from Darcy in many respects, but he had a good moral foundation, and they shared many of the same political views.

"Ha! Darcy says that in jest. He does not agree with me in the slightest. If it was up to him, he would never dance and certainly not with anyone more than once. He has very strict rules for himself: Never kiss a lady's hand, even when offered. Never invite a single lady to dine without her parents or a male relation. Always say as little as possible so as to not encourage any lady—"

"Bingley, you make it sound as if I am determined to stay a bachelor." *By gads! They were talking about dancing?* He was so embarrassed that he hardly knew what to say.

Jane observed the color in Mr. Darcy's face and understood all too well that his mind had been occupied on something or someone else. He quickly glanced up ahead at where Elizabeth and his sister were walking. It was not brotherly concern she saw in his eyes. She wondered if his preference for Elizabeth was as strong as it appeared to be. "Mr. Darcy," she asked, "how many guests will be at the ball?"

"I sent out just under forty invitations. It is too early to tell how many will attend. Most of the invitations were sent to neighbors, but I also invited my cousin, Colonel Fitzwilliam, who will most likely attend and stay a few days."

"Splendid!" Bingley exclaimed. "Colonel Fitzwilliam is a fine man. You are lucky to have him as a close relation. A good friend is hard to find."

"Indeed I am," Darcy replied. "That reminds me of one of Miss Elizabeth's sayings. How does it go, Miss Bennet? 'A good friend is hard to find unless . . .'"

Jane smiled and finished his thought, "'Unless one is a friend to all. For then one will be surrounded by good friends everywhere.'"

Once again, Darcy found himself thinking of Elizabeth. It seemed he could think of nothing else. He felt like a cad for being so distracted and decided to put in a few good comments about Bingley to make up for it. "Speaking of good friends, Miss Bennet, Bingley is the best friend a man could ask for. He may irritate with his energy of a border collie puppy learning to guide the sheep, but he is just as loyal."

Bingley eyed Darcy curiously. "What has gotten into you, Darcy? First, a ball, then you agree with me that asking for two dances with the same lady is acceptable, and now you offer unsolicited praise! I hardly know the man before me, Miss Bennet!"

Jane thought she could see the very man Bingley was so loyal to. She caught his eyes and saw what Elizabeth had told her of two nights ago. The man desperately wanted to hide behind his mask, but his eyes were far too revealing. Jane pressed further. "How very strange, Mr. Bingley," she said. "Do you have any theories that might explain your friend's behavior? Has he taken up a new hobby that is distracting him? Is it the fine weather that has altered him so? Or perhaps he has problems with drink and has recently found sobriety."

Mr. Darcy blushed at her guesses. He was becoming more uncomfortable with this conversation the further it went on. "Miss Bennet, I assure you, I have never taken to hard liquor. I simply wanted to tell Bingley how much I appreciate him." He glanced up ahead at Elizabeth and Georgiana and saw that they had slowed slightly.

Jane then saw it in his eyes. He was trying to hide his embarrassment, but she saw where he was looking. She had her assurances: Mr. Darcy admired Elizabeth. "Very well, am I safe to assume Mr. Bingley here is as good as you say he is?"

"He is. Now if you will excuse me a moment, I must speak with Georgiana." Mr. Darcy walked quickly ahead and chastised himself all the while. How had Miss Bennet so completely flustered him in just a few minutes? It was as if she had seen his very thoughts. Did she know he had been thinking about Elizabeth?

If the prospect of Miss Bennet discovering his feelings for Elizabeth was so uncomfortable, he knew he was not ready to declare himself. He could not ask Mr. Gardiner for permission to court Elizabeth, not yet. He wanted to be sure of her regard first. So, in those few yards it took to catch up to his sister and Elizabeth, Mr. Darcy decided he would not take the gamble. Not yet. And then he saw her sparkling eyes, and his resolve went out the window.

*****

The Pemberley party called on the ladies of Saphrinbrooke several times over the next week. Miss Bingley and Mrs. Hurst accompanied them once, but their purpose was more to size up the estate than to be social. The Gardiners' shortcomings became a topic of amusement for Caroline, and the night of the ball found her discussing it again with Mrs. Hurst.

"I still cannot believe the Gardiners are trying to pass as landed gentry! They were in trade!" Miss Bingley laughed.

Mrs. Hurst nodded, eager to agree, but confusion was seeping into her thoughts. "But Father made his money in trade as well," she wondered aloud. Caroline shot her a disapproving look and Mrs. Hurst quickly added, "Although in very different circumstances. There is trade, and then there is *trade*."

Miss Bingley stood looking in the mirror and adjusted the lace in her bodice. She needed to show a little more cleavage. "I completely agree," she sniffed. "If I were to meet them in town, I would hardly admit to knowing them! I wish Mr. Darcy could see what harm he is doing to his reputation by opening the ball with a country nobody. Rumors will begin flying! I know how he pities Miss Elizabeth, her being so plain next to her sister's beauty, but I have told him it is not a wise decision. I believe he will regret it."

Caroline smoothed her dress and looked to her sister. Louisa recognized her cue and nodded again reassuringly.

"At least he will dance with me next," Caroline continued, "and I am sure he will ask for a second set. He must feel such relief in knowing that he will not have to stand up with her again. Country balls can be so limiting in that regard."

"Have you noticed his attentions to me?" Caroline went on. "He certainly desires my company," she said with a smile. "Why, every time I start talking with Georgiana, he finds his way over to us and joins in! I knew Georgiana would be the key to securing him. I can see how eager she is for me to become her new sister. And tonight I shall do everything in my power to show him just what kind of sister I can be. There is so much I could teach her. Clearly she does not know how to be a proper hostess; she disappears for hours on end. Why, I passed the whole afternoon on Tuesday with not a soul to converse with but you and Mr. Hurst!"

Caroline snapped her fingers, and Mrs. Hurst jumped up and adjusted the sleeves of Caroline's dress. "Oh yes, Sister," Louisa answered. "She could learn so much from your example. She seems very distracted of late. Perhaps she is still unwell from her illness."

"Oh, Louisa, you will never understand the Darcys! She is not ill! She simply likes her privacy! That is why she takes to her room so often. It is very tiring for her to have you and Charles and Mr. Hurst here and to be always running off to visit the Bennet sisters. She would much rather stay at home. Mr. Darcy is the same way. He is a very private man."

Caroline sighed again and said, "That is why it means so much that Mr. Darcy invited me to Pemberley. And now he is hosting a ball! Could he be any clearer? He would never say anything openly, but obviously he is planning to court me. He is so very sly. If he opened the ball dancing with me, everyone would know his intentions, and he wants to keep things quiet until he is ready to propose. I do pity Miss Eliza, the way he is playing on her emotions to mask his regard for me. But you see it, do you not?" Caroline paused until Louisa nodded in agreement.

"He has been much more attentive to me on this visit than ever before," Miss Bingley continued. She sprayed a generous amount of perfume on her wrists and neck, then, with a last thought, sprayed some down her cleavage.

"Oh yes!" Louisa answered. "He especially likes it when you talk to Georgiana. He always comes over to join you when you talk to her. He almost takes over the conversation, and there were several times Georgiana left you two to converse privately. I think Georgiana is anxious to see you two together as well."

"Louisa, pay attention, dear; I already said that. But I cannot deny that Mr. Darcy enjoys my attentions to Miss Darcy, and I will plan to pay special attention to her tonight! He is so very shy, but I shall do what I can to help him along. Soon you shall call me Mrs. Darcy!" Caroline beamed and sighed. "As soon as the time is right, he will come to me," she said. "Our feelings for each other cannot stay secret for long."

Louisa nodded vigorously. Just then, they heard the grandfather clock chiming in the foyer. "Well, Mrs. Darcy, you must put on your bracelets and descend those stairs soon. I hear the musicians warming up."

"A real lady is never first to arrive, for who would be there to witness her grand entrance? I shall wait until all the guests have arrived, and then everyone will see how attentive Mr. Darcy is towards me. Yes, that will work nicely."

*****

"Richard, I am glad you could come tonight. I have a favor to ask of you," Mr. Darcy said.

Colonel Fitzwilliam stood and straightened his uniform, "You? You are asking me for a favor?"

"Yes, I know it is unusual, but I need your assistance with Georgiana. She has been better the last two days, but she is still very fragile."

"I will do anything for Georgiana. What do you have in mind?"

"She very much wants to attend to the ball to see Miss Elizabeth and Miss Bennet, but she dreads being followed around by Miss Bingley. How would you feel about occupying Miss Bingley tonight as much as possible?"

Colonel Fitzwilliam groaned. "Normally, I would be delighted to save you from beautiful ladies at a ball, but I am not sure how much help I can be. You know she only has eyes for you. Are you asking me to keep her away from Georgiana or to keep her away from you?" he asked with a grin.

"Just keep her away from Georgiana, please," Darcy chuckled. "I can fend for myself. I think she has it in her mind that if she can win over Georgiana, then I am to follow. If you see her cornering Georgiana, will you please intervene? I wish I could stay with Georgiana, but I must circulate the room and greet my guests."

"Very well. But I do this for Georgiana, not you. If I give up the opportunity of dancing with any pretty ladies tonight to listen to Miss Bingley's praises of you, I will expect some form of recompense, perhaps a bottle of your finest port."

"Understood," Darcy laughed. "Now let us go and greet the guests. They should begin arriving at any moment. Although I have not thrown a ball in four years, I do still remember that I should be present when the guests arrive."

"Yes, and about your special guest—"

"Not now."

"Very well. Then I shall be forced to draw my own imaginative conclusions."

Mr. Darcy and Colonel Fitzwilliam walked to the ballroom where they found two couples already awaiting them. "Mr. and

Mrs. Banse, thank you for coming. How was the ride over? I do hope the roads were pleasant enough."

Mr. Banse bowed and said, "Indeed they were. Have you met my wife's sister? Annie, come over here and meet Mr. Darcy. She is very talented on the pianoforte and speaks French beautifully."

Mr. Darcy steeled himself for another introduction as the most eligible bachelor in Derbyshire. He had known this would happen if he hosted a ball. Bingley had predicted, *"You will be auctioned off to every available single lady within ten miles! Every neighbor you invite will bring at least three young ladies! At least I will be in no want of partners!"*

A girl of no more than seventeen came over demurely and curtsied gracefully.

"Mr. Darcy," Mr. Banse began, "this is Miss Anne Brierley of Bere Ferrers, in Devonshire. Miss Annie, this is Mr. Fitzwilliam Darcy."

"Miss Brierley, I am familiar with Bere Ferrers. Is there not a mine near there?" Darcy asked.

She fluttered her eyelashes and said, "Indeed, it is the lifeblood of the town. Men have been mining there for generations."

Darcy knew he had to dance with others besides Elizabeth during the night, so he swallowed hard and replied, "I would love to hear more about it. May I have the privilege of securing the third set?"

She blushed brightly and looked to her sister before answering, "I have not had that dance taken yet."

Mr. Darcy then introduced the Banses to Colonel Fitzwilliam and Mr. Bingley and made his way to the reverend and his wife. "Mr. Walker, so good of you to come. And, Mrs. Walker, you look dashing tonight. Did you not say your niece, Miss Clara Adams, would be coming?"

"It is so good of you to ask about her. She has truly grown up since you saw her last. I am sure you will be quite impressed. She is over there visiting with Miss Darcy. They have not seen each other for years, although they were so close growing up, you know." Mrs. Walker said.

"Yes. We have missed hearing your sermons at church, Mr. Walker. I was thrilled to hear that you are returning to Kympton! I take it your sister's health has recovered?"

"Indeed. She is comfortably settled with my brother in Yorkshire now. And I am glad to be home," Mr. Walker said.

"We are glad to have you home. No one does a better job caring for my tenants than you. I see I have more guests to welcome. Please, enjoy some lemonade." Mr. Darcy wandered over to the ballroom entrance and greeted his neighbor to the east. Darcy was relieved that at least this neighbor had not brought along a single relative to bid on him.

Next, he greeted Mr. and Mrs. Hagenlocker, along with their daughter, Miss Hagenlocker. Then it was Mrs. Kimble and her three young nieces from London. And then Mr. and Mrs. Schumann with their four daughters, two nieces, and Mrs. Schumann's youngest sister. Bingley had been right; there was no lack of unmarried ladies tonight. Mr. Darcy looked around the room as often as he could but still had not located the one lady he was particularly anxious to meet.

An overly high-pitched, feminine voice with a distinct Dutch accent caught his attention. "Mr. Darcy, it 'as been far too long since Pemberley hosted a ball," announced Miss Gisela Krouse. "And vere may I ask are de guests of honor? De Gardiners, I believe you said?"

Mr. Darcy was beginning to wonder where they were as well. "Yes, they should be here shortly. You look well. Where is your brother?"

"Hubrecht 'as already found de refreshment table." She brushed a lock of red hair from her face and smiled at him.

Darcy wanted to groan. Would all this be worth a single dance with Elizabeth? He bowed, promised to introduce the Gardiners when they arrived, and walked away. There were already thirty people in the ballroom, and half the guests hadn't even arrived yet. He was getting a headache from smiling.

So far, he had been cornered by five single ladies, two of which he had secured dances with, and the other three he had pawned off onto Bingley and Colonel Fitzwilliam. Georgiana had not appeared yet, but he knew that she was probably being detained by Mr. Walker's niece. He walked over to the musicians and asked them to begin the ball with a long, slow song. He wanted as much time as possible to dance with Elizabeth. Suddenly, a quiet lull interrupted the constant chatter, and he turned to see who had garnered the attention.

He had been so preoccupied with the musicians that he had missed the Gardiners and the Bennet sisters being announced. But he missed nothing now. The whole room had turned to evaluate the guests of honor, and he was one of them. The Gardiners were dressed very fine, but that was not why his heart stopped.

It might have been the candlelight or the distance, but she emanated grace and goodness. Her hair was swept up in an intricate braid, wrapped around a flower-embellished bun. She had perfectly polished ringlets on each side of her head and wore elegant pearl earrings. Around her neck hung a single silver chain with a medallion. Her gown was made of white, flowing silk, with a pink ribbon wrapped around her high waist, and matching ribbons flowed from the crown of her head. She stood perfectly erect and seemed to be scanning the room for someone when their eyes met. She gave him a smile and a nod of the head that was so casual and relaxed one would think she was a guest of honor at a ball all the time. He smiled back at her and started making his way over to them.

Jane had seen Mr. Darcy's entire reaction. If she had any remaining doubt of his admiration, it was gone now. She whispered to Elizabeth, "He looks very handsome in his dress clothes."

Elizabeth could not help but blush. His clothes were finely tailored; not a single piece could be improved. His cravat was perfectly tied, his vest clung to his chest, and she could see his pocket watch chain sparkle as he made his way across the room. His shoulders seemed broader than usual, and his dress shoes were so shiny she wondered if he could see his reflection as he walked.

But it was not his clothes that made her face heat up. It was that dimpled smile of his. All the chatter in the room died down as he approached, and she felt dozens of eyes on them. He stopped right in front of her and bowed deeply. She curtsied, and suddenly he was reaching for her hand, and he kissed it gently.

How he wished that ladies did not have to wear gloves in a ballroom! He gently squeezed her hand before reluctantly releasing it and acknowledging the others in her party. He had been so caught up in seeing Elizabeth that he had blundered by not addressing the Gardiners first. "Mr. and Mrs. Gardiner, it is my pleasure to have you as my guests of honor. Miss Bennet, welcome to Pemberley's ball. The music and dancing will start shortly, but let me introduce you to a few guests first." He wanted to offer his arm and escort Elizabeth, but that gesture would be too revealing. He did not want to show an obvious preference yet, so he settled for simply walking beside her as they made their way around the room.

Waiting outside the door to be announced, Miss Bingley had witnessed the entrance of the Gardiners and Bennets. She had not missed the deep bow and kiss for Elizabeth. She felt her face heat up. Just as it did, her name was announced, and she sauntered into the room. She gracefully scanned the room for admirers but found that her glory had been outshined by the guests of honor. Mr. Darcy had not even acknowledged her entrance. She searched for Georgiana but did not see her. She quickly made up her mind to join Mr. Darcy in his introductions.

She slithered over to the group and interlocked her arm with Elizabeth's. "Miss Eliza," she said, "so good of you to join the party. I do hope you will not feel threatened by a gathering of this size. I am sure you have not been to a ball of this magnitude before, but I shall help you in any way possible. For any friend of Mr. Darcy and Georgiana is a friend of mine."

It was obvious to Elizabeth that Miss Bingley would waste no opportunity tonight to either insult her or monopolize Mr. Darcy. Ideally, Caroline would try to accomplish both objectives at once. "Yes," Elizabeth replied. "I will be sure to wait until I am properly introduced before I accost anyone with unwanted attention." She then turned away from her and freed herself by adjusting her gloves, which didn't truly need adjusting.

As they continued around the room, Elizabeth noticed something odd about Mr. Darcy's introductions. When they met with older couples, he was delighted to make personal, friendly introductions; but when a bachelor stepped up, he briefly greeted the guest and moved on as quickly as possible. When Mr. Hubrecht Krouse, with his bright red hair, eyed Elizabeth from across the room, Darcy stiffened and stepped slightly closer to her.

Mr. Krouse walked toward them, bowed, and reached for Elizabeth's hand. "It is truly a pleasure to meet you, Miss Elizabeth," he gushed in an exotic accent. "May I 'ave de pleasure of requesting a dance tonight?"

Elizabeth did not offer her hand although it was obvious he wanted to kiss it. She felt a certain level of loyalty to Mr. Darcy, and if Mr. Darcy felt uneasy about Mr. Krouse, then she would be wise to tread cautiously. "Which dance are you requesting?"

"Perhaps de supper set? Then I could 'ave the pleasure of escorting you to dinner, and I cannot imagine any activity more pleasurable," Mr. Krouse replied with a rakish smile.

Mr. Darcy interrupted with a jovial laugh and said, "I have beaten you to the punch, old friend. Miss Elizabeth has agreed to dance the supper set with me." Darcy turned to Elizabeth with a look that begged her to agree.

Elizabeth didn't know whether to be flattered that Mr. Darcy wanted a second dance, or perturbed that he had assumed her consent. But her feelings quickly evolved to relief. She would be glad not to eat dinner with this man who seemed to be looking through her gown and sizing up her curves. "Indeed, I have already agreed to step on Mr. Darcy's toes during that set." She smiled kindly to Mr. Krouse and then turned to leave.

Once they were far enough away, Mr. Darcy whispered, "I apologize for assuming your consent. It was for your own good. He is a wise business man and would be an asset to Mr. Gardiner, however his reputation with ladies is less than stellar. I question his intentions."

"I gathered as much. Thank you."

"You do not miss much, do you?"

"You are easier to read than you think you are."

He didn't know whether or not that was a good thing. There were certain thoughts he would very much like to keep to himself. Just then the music started, and Mr. Darcy knew the time was upon them. He offered his arm to Elizabeth and escorted her to the front of the room. He made sure Mr. and Mrs. Gardiner were following, along with Miss Bennet and Bingley, who had not failed to secure the hand of his "angel" for the first set. He nodded to the musicians and watched as other couples started forming lines.

As the movements began, Elizabeth felt an overwhelming sensation deep in her chest. It quickened her heart and made it flutter like a hummingbird. She watched his graceful form move ever so elegantly, and she suddenly realized that she had been anticipating this very moment for weeks. Up until that moment, she had not realized that she was so attracted to Mr. Darcy.

She had admired his handsome features, even sized up his qualities, but she had not consciously arrived at any conclusion. But now she realized how much she admired him. He was a decent man. He was kind and loving. He tried so hard to create a perfect, refined persona. All of his quirks—the anxious flexing of the fist behind his back; that genuine, dimpled smile; those expressive, yet guarded, eyes—rendered him simply adorable. She wanted to scoop him up and hold him close like a kitten. The realization made her giddy, and she let out a giggle.

"Are you laughing at my dancing?" Mr. Darcy teased. He was enjoying the dance so much that he had forgotten about his anxiety and all the onlookers; he was simply dancing at Pemberley with Elizabeth. It was indeed pleasant to watch her form move. He had never seen such an elegant dress. It clung to her so beautifully that he could not help but steal a glance at her figure now and then. Whenever he did, it became difficult to keep his thoughts on the dance steps, but the pleasure was worth the torture.

She giggled again, and he saw that sparkle dance in her eyes. The musical sound of her laughter pulled him in as a boat being pulled into harbor. He was at home with that laugh. It felt so right, and he wanted more of it.

Elizabeth tried to hide her smirk. "I was daydreaming about you, sir. That was why I laughed."

"Daydreaming? And you are confessing it to me? I can see through your machinations, Miss Elizabeth; clearly you are after me for my money. I have experience with these things, you know."

"With what things?"

"Ladies who try to flirt with me."

"I was not flirting. If I were flirting, you would know it."

"I see you are not only daydreaming about me, but you have deluded yourself into a state of complete denial," he teased.

"If you must know, I was imagining you with a black fur and whiskers."

He arched his eyebrow at her and gave her his most commanding look. "This is the respect I get? You think I am a cat?"

She let out another laugh. She could tease him forever like this. "Perhaps, but I must admit you are rather too large for a cat."

He smiled at her and played her game. "Too large! Now you are suggesting I eat too much? Perhaps I should advise my tailor to seek new employment."

"Certainly not! I am unable to hold any opinion on that topic. It would be completely inappropriate to admit that I have examined your graceful form."

"Ah, you admit that you find me graceful! It pleases me to know you have such positive opinions of me, even if your mind seems to be plagued by odd thoughts about cats," he teased with a smile. "But I believe I have discovered your secret. You find me so attractive that you must distract yourself by imagining me with a black nose and whiskers to keep some semblance of normalcy in your demeanor. I knew it! You are flirting with me! I see your blushing face; for once I have correctly read a lady's mind!"

"Mr. Darcy, I assure you, if I were that emotionally disheveled by dancing with you, I would certainly be unable to flirt. So, your logic is all warped. If I were truly flirting, there would be flashing eyes and blushes, not daydreams of you with pink paws and soft, black fur."

He smiled widely at her and saw that stolen blush she had spoken of. This pleased him more than it should. It pleased him beyond any moment he had had with her up to this point. Yes, one dance with her was worth the hassle of throwing a ball and being auctioned off to every unmarried female in the county. It mattered not who was in the room at the moment. Only she mattered. Only her opinion mattered.

"But perhaps I am still reading you all wrong," he said. "For I am certain I just saw you blush, and surely calling me 'graceful' constitutes as a compliment. So, by your definition, you are flirting with me."

Between their vivacious conversation and her gorgeous gown, his head was spinning as quickly as the dance steps. For a moment, his mind wandered, and he nearly missed a step in the dance. It was the slightest hesitation; he hoped she had not noticed, but her mischievous smile indicated otherwise.

"Ah! Perhaps you are not as graceful as a cat after all," she teased. *Soft black fur, rather larger than a cat, and somewhat clumsy.* "More like a bear, I think."

"A bear? Do explain yourself."

She giggled again and replied, "That discussion, sir, will have to wait until our next dance for this one is over." She curtsied and spun on her heels and left the dance floor.

Darcy bowed belatedly but couldn't wipe the grin off his face. He had another dance with her, and he knew he would get more of the same. She was amazing! He watched her walk away and admired the gentle sway of her hips and the way the light fabric flowed freely.

Colonel Fitzwilliam chuckled. "I would be careful how low you let that jaw drop, even if she is walking away from you."

"Good evening to you too, Richard. Must you question me here on the dance floor?"

"I must and I will. I have never seen you so oblivious to an entire ballroom full of people. You do not seem to see anything but Miss Elizabeth."

Darcy snapped out of his reverie and became worried. "Did something happen? Is Georgiana well?" He quickly scanned for Georgiana and found her sitting quietly with the reverend's niece. She already looked tired.

"She is doing reasonably well. She does not wish to dance tonight, which leaves me without a partner for the next dance. I do believe there was a little magic behind Miss Elizabeth's eyes. Now, if you will excuse me, I intend to secure my next dance and test out the magician."

Darcy watched Colonel Fitzwilliam walk directly over to Elizabeth and witnessed her acceptance. Suddenly, he was startled by the obscene waft of ladies perfume assaulting him from behind.

He did not need to turn to know who it was. Duty called; it was time for his dance with Miss Bingley. He greeted her politely and gave her the slightest pleasantries, but nothing that would constitute a true compliment.

As he led her out to the dance floor, she began her constant babbling. He managed to stay focused enough to attend to her minimally, but her dull conversation caught little of his true attention. Whenever he could, he stole glances at his cousin and Elizabeth. Every time Miss Bingley twirled, a wave of nausea from her perfume assaulted his senses.

He was suddenly very curious as to what Elizabeth smelled like. It was certainly nothing abrasive or vulgar. He occupied his mind during the rest of the dance trying to remember what she smelled like. She did have a fragrance to her, but he could not place it. *Gardenias! That was it!* He smiled with this revelation. His mother used to smell of gardenias, but he knew his mother used a perfume that was much stronger. *Miss Elizabeth must use a milder form, perhaps a toilette water.* It was very pleasing. Remembering her smell made him smile.

The dance ended, and he escorted Miss Bingley to her brother, who had already abandoned his second partner to attend to Miss Bennet's refreshment needs. Darcy gave the smallest bow and went to find his third partner, Miss Anne Brierley, who heralded from Devonshire's mining region.

Within an hour of surviving Elizabeth's "no comment" questions two weeks ago, Darcy had opened his Bible to Malachi 3:3. But Elizabeth had quoted the verse exactly: "He will sit as a refiner and purifier of silver". Reading it offered no further insight to its meaning. He wasn't sure where to go next. Hopefully Miss Brierly could provide some assistance.

But unfortunately, Miss Brierley knew little about refining silver. She did offer him the name of the mine owner. Darcy decided he would write him tomorrow. Surely a mine owner would be able to explain the metaphor in Malachi 3:3. After the third set concluded, he thanked Miss Annie and found Georgiana.

"How are you holding up?" he asked her.

"I would be worse if it were not for Richard. He keeps winking at me and looking at me with the silliest looks. He is being very solicitous. When not dancing, he is right by my side. Mrs. Gardiner kept me company during the last dance. She is very kind. She never asks me dull questions, and she seems to be comfortable with my silence when I do not feel like talking. We are very lucky to have such great neighbors."

"Indeed we are. I must leave you now and collect my next partner. If it becomes too much, please excuse yourself. Just try to let me know when you leave. I would like to talk to you again before you retire. If you need me, I can leave at any time."

"No, William, this is your ball. I am not even supposed to be here since I am not yet out. No one will notice me leave; they would most definitely notice the host's disappearance."

"I suppose you are correct. But please talk to me before you leave."

"I will."

The next three dances were dull; all three ladies fluttered their eyelashes and praised him unmercifully. They lamented about the season being over. They recited dreadfully boring stories of being in town and dropped names and connections as if they were filling the tithing plate on Easter Sunday. They flashed their jewelry and swayed their hips wantonly, which only irritated him. The only thing that got him through the sixth dance was realizing that the supper set was next. He escorted his dance partner to the refreshment table and briskly walked to the end of the row where Elizabeth had been dancing with Bingley. They seemed to be laughing merrily, but they stifled their giggles and diverted their looks when they saw him coming.

A very chipper Elizabeth bit her lip to hide her laughter. "Mr. Darcy, I see you did not forget our dance was next."

Bingley chuckled, "Hurry out to the dance floor, Miss Elizabeth. He is such *bear* when he does not get his way!" This brought laughter from both Elizabeth and Bingley, and surprisingly, Mr. Darcy as well.

"Do you wish for some refreshment before we dance?" Mr. Darcy asked.

"No, my stomach is not growling; is yours? I am sure you can *barely* stand it." She burst out in laughter once again and said, "Dear me, I apologize. Now I simply cannot get the image out of my mind. You are just like a bear. Intimidating in appearance perhaps, but actually quite bumbling and endearing. I imagine you would have brown fur just the same color as the brown curls sitting on top of your head." Without thinking, she reached up and pushed a stray curl off his forehead. She pulled her hand back quickly and clasped them in front of her. "Forgive me, sir. I did not . . . Perhaps I have had too much wine."

Mr. Darcy had never felt such joy. Her embarrassed cheeks made him feel somewhat hopeless, hopelessly in love. He stood up straighter and looked away quickly. *Love? Certainly not! Or maybe? A little? A smidgen? It is overwhelming, but I believe I love Miss Elizabeth!* He was so shocked by his own thoughts that he hadn't heard what she had said. He turned his attention back to her and, if it were possible, she was an ever deeper shade of red. She was avoiding looking at him and muttering to herself.

"Forgive me," he said. "What did you say? I was distracted."

"I am sorry, sir. I realize I put you in an awkward position. If you would rather not dance with me after my behavior, I understand." Elizabeth was mortified. His shocked facial expressions showed he was obviously disgusted with her behavior. He must think she was throwing herself at him. Why couldn't she keep her hands to herself? What was it about Mr. Darcy that made her talk to him as if he was a confidant and close friend?

She had only known him a month, yet she felt like he was family. Perhaps it was her relationship with Georgiana or the time they had spent together discussing his sister's troubles. Perhaps it was because she saw him as an honorable man. Perhaps it was because he was so kind and charming. Perhaps she felt close to him because he had to have some idea that what had happened to Georgiana had happened to her as well, but he was too much of a gentleman to ask. Now, she couldn't help but feel incredibly disappointed in the fact that she was not going to dance with him again.

She had been surprised several times that night. The realization that she desired his good opinion, that she wanted to dance with him, and that she was sorely disappointed that the experience would not be repeated, were only a few of the surprise realizations she had that night. She saw that strange look in his eyes again. She willed herself to look away but she could not. His gentle eyes seemed to soak up her despair like water in a desert. They were kind and speaking a great deal of forgiveness and a bit of . . . desire? Yes! What she saw was definitely desire!

Suddenly, her heart flipped twice and then pounded in her chest. She tried to listen to what his lips were saying. All she knew was he had taken ahold of her arm and had wrapped it around his own. He placed his warm hand on hers, gently squeezing it and caressing it with his thumb. He was leading her back to the dance floor, and she bravely fought back tears of relief.

Mr. Darcy could sense that she was quite embarrassed, but he was not going to give up his second dance with her. He deserved it after enduring debutantes fighting for his attention all night long. Elizabeth was different. She hadn't meant to ignite the burning in his chest that consumed his whole body like dry kindling. She hadn't meant to stimulate love. But she had. He had never felt this way about anyone. He loved Elizabeth, and he knew it now. All those rules that Bingley rattled off to Miss Bennet that day in Saphrinbrooke's gardens, the ones that had kept him a bachelor all these years, they simply no longer applied.

He wanted Elizabeth. He would pursue her. Of this, he was certain.

CHAPTER 7

Elizabeth reviewed the events of the ball with Jane that night, and they both laughed and giggled like little girls. Mr. Bingley had danced twice with Jane, which pleased both sisters immensely. They reviewed all their new acquaintances as thoroughly as a breeder examining a racehorse. They discussed the meal, the music, and the ladies' dresses, but the most thoroughly discussed topic was the handsome host and his charming friend.

On this subject, they spent the early morning hours in rapid and frequent conversation. Jane disclosed that she had witnessed Mr. Darcy admiration for Elizabeth. Elizabeth shared the look of desire she detected in his eyes during the supper set. Jane giggled about Bingley's solicitousness in seeing to her every need.

They discussed Miss Bingley and her terrible perfume and feathered head adornment, and Elizabeth noted how scandalous it was that Colonel Fitzwilliam had danced with her three times! They both knew he did not admire her, but he had been very persistent in his pursuit. Jane suggested it was some sort of ploy to divert Miss Bingley's attention from Mr. Darcy. Elizabeth kept her thoughts to herself but suspected Miss Bingley was really being diverted from someone else: Georgiana. After an exhaustive review of every possible topic, the two Bennet sisters said goodnight in the wee hours of the morning.

Later, Elizabeth lay awake, reeling from all that happened at the ball. Elizabeth had kept a close eye on Georgiana and conversed with her often. She was pleased that Colonel Fitzwilliam had been so attentive to her. There were moments when Elizabeth had seen a faraway look in her eyes, but Georgiana had recovered herself quickly. In all, she had performed so marvelously that no one could have suspected her of struggling so profoundly. She lasted through hours of dancing, long enough to see Darcy and Elizabeth together again in the supper set.

When Georgiana shyly bid her brother goodnight during supper, Elizabeth quietly excused herself to accompany Georgiana to her room. Outside her door, she told Georgiana how wonderfully she had performed. Georgiana smiled and admitted there had been an element of pleasure in watching some of her favorite people enjoy each other's company. This last comment was said with a knowing look, and Elizabeth blushed deeply. Georgiana then kissed Elizabeth on the cheek and told her, "I must go now. God is waiting for me, and I have much to be thankful for tonight."

Elizabeth could not agree more.

*****

Dear Oscar Featherby,

I am the owner of a large estate in Derbyshire and have recently taken an interest in silver mining. I understand you own the mine in Bere Ferrers. I was referred to you by a Miss Anne Brierly, whose father owns several businesses near the mine.

Forgive this letter from a stranger, but I was hoping you could tell me more about your mine and, specifically, about what methods you use to refine silver. I was recently challenged to research the topic, and a gentleman never backs down from a challenge. If you would not mind detailing for me the generalities of the business, I would be happy to make a generous donation to your enterprise reimbursing you for your time. I would also be very grateful.

I hope this letter finds you and your mine doing well, and I look forward to hearing from you soon.

With sincere thanks,

Fitzwilliam Darcy

Mr. Darcy reviewed the contents and sent it to be posted. It would be at least a week until he received a reply; in the meanwhile, he would expand his inquiries. Miss Elizabeth had asked about his research at last night's ball during supper. He admitted he had pondered it a great deal, but had not yet consulted any experts. Miss Elizabeth had smiled and pointed out, "You know, Mr. Darcy, you will never finish unless you start." Her comment had struck home with him, and he had promised himself that he would start the very next day.

He grabbed his jacket and headed to the stables. Today he would make good on that promise. He pondered Elizabeth's challenge while he galloped to Kympton. Mr. Walker was a man of the cloth and should be able to shed light on the matter. The three-mile ride was over quickly, and soon he was dismounting in front of the parsonage.

"Mr. Darcy, what a pleasant surprise," Mr. Walker said as Darcy entered. "What brings you here, and on the morning after your ball no less? I hope everyone is in good health," the reverend said.

"They were all still sleeping when I left, but I assume they are well." A brief discussion about the ball's success was held and generous praise was given. "But I actually did not come here to discuss the ball," Darcy said. "Do you have some time to discuss doctrine?"

The clergyman hid his surprise well; Mr. Darcy had never shown an interest in doctrine before. "I always have time to discuss doctrine," he replied. "Let me get my Bible. Follow me into my study."

Darcy followed the old man into a study which could be generously characterized as well lived-in. There were piles of papers and books on every corner of the desk. The rug was worn thin in the entry, and Darcy made a mental note to find a way to help. He watched as the man sat down and pulled out a large, oversized Bible and then invited Darcy to speak.

Darcy began, "I had an interesting discussion with Miss Elizabeth Bennet a few weeks ago about Malachi 3:3. Are you familiar with that passage?"

"I read the good book daily, but that scripture does not ring familiar. Let me look it up." He thumbed the pages of the book and quickly found the passage. "I see," he said. "Tell me about the discussion, and I will see if I can help."

"It started with me mentioning some of the difficulties in my life. I stated that I wished I did not have such trials. Miss Elizabeth replied that trials are lessons from God and that I should be grateful for the chance to prove myself to Him. She said this scripture explains it all, but I have no idea how."

"What a fabulous discussion! I would have loved to have been a participant! So, you want to know how our trials refine us?"

"Yes, exactly," Darcy agreed.

Mr. Walker stroked his chin and considered the question for a moment. "Well," he said, "let us begin by considering what it means to be 'refined'. What makes a man refined?" he asked. "How does he differ from an unrefined man?"

"But I do not think Miss Elizabeth was comparing the manners of a gentleman and an impoverished peasant."

"Perhaps not," Mr. Walker shrugged, "but a gentleman is a good example. What makes a gentleman refined?"

This was an easy question for Mr. Darcy. "Education, good breeding, and involvement in the arts and culture."

"Yes. What about spiritual refinement? What makes someone a good man, or a refined man, in the eyes of God?"

Mr. Darcy pondered the question. "Honesty. Giving to the poor. Being a good neighbor."

The clergyman smiled and replied, "I think you are partially there. But the amount one donates to the poor means little if one's heart is not in the right place. Any man can donate money; that does not mean he is refined."

Darcy shifted uncomfortably in his seat. "Miss Elizabeth mentioned something similar."

Mr. Walker sensed Darcy's discomfort and tried a different route. "Let us go back to the word 'refine'," he said. "It means to remove impurities or unwanted elements. What would be some impurities that a man might have?"

Darcy immediately thought of Wickham. "Greed. Lust. A lack of integrity."

"That is a good start. There are many others. What about pride or prejudice? Or let us look at it as things that a man might lack. You mentioned a lack of integrity. What about a lack of faith, or a lack of loyalty, or a lack of virtue?"

"Certainly if a man lacks these things, he would be unworthy of respect. One could not call him refined."

"Then how does a man develop these characteristics? Consider faith, for example. If a lack of faith is an impurity, how does one attain faith?"

Darcy paused. He had never considered the question before. "I suppose one attains faith by believing in something."

The clergyman smiled at the simplicity of Mr. Darcy's definition. "Faith is more than just believing, Mr. Darcy. It is more than hoping for something to be real. If that were the case, then Father Christmas would be real and children all over the world would be called faithful." Mr. Walker paused, choosing his words carefully. "Faith is trusting God with undaunted fervor. It is holding tight when the storms come. It is continuing to do what is right, no matter what. We do not express faith through our beliefs; it is expressed by our behavior, especially in our times of trouble."

Darcy tried to understand the reverend's message. "So, good behavior builds faith?" he asked.

"Not quite," Mr. Walker replied. "It is not our behavior that changes our faith, but rather the other way around. When our faith is strong, when it is deep, it changes our actions. Mr. Darcy, have you ever known a man who says one thing but does another?"

"Yes. Were you familiar with my cousin, Peter?" The reverend nodded. "Then you know my father's brother disowned him for womanizing. But then we found out my uncle had fathered a dozen illegitimate children himself. He certainly said one thing but did another."

"I knew Mr. Darcy's brother. Ernest, was it not?"

"Yes."

"Consider Ernest. He was raised at Pemberley as a second son and given the same education and good breeding as your father. Was he refined?"

"He was socially refined; he was raised as a gentleman and given a gentleman's education. Yet he lacked integrity. He was not refined in God's eyes."

"Precisely. His faith was not deep enough to change his behavior. He was not refined. So, we come back to the question: how does one refine themselves morally?"

"Well, I suspect Miss Elizabeth thinks trials remove our impurities. But it is difficult for me to accept that God intentionally gives us trials. Could He not just tell us what to do and let us improve ourselves?"

Mr. Walker picked up the Bible and tapped his finger on the cover. "He has. But how many read His words? How many put His instructions to the test? Your uncle Ernest knew God's commandments, and yet he was not refined. He did not follow God in his heart. Do you?"

"I certainly follow the ten commandments."

"And do you pray?"

Silence hung in the room for several moments. Each looked at the other waiting for a response. Mr. Darcy wanted to say yes, but he knew it would be a lie. He hoped Mr. Walker would move on, but the seconds ticked by in silence. "I have not truly prayed since my father died," he finally murmured.

"Yet you have thought about praying again, I can see it in your eyes. I suspect you have Miss Elizabeth to thank for that."

Darcy looked away in embarrassment. *Am I an open book to everyone now?*

"Let us return to refining one's self," the clergyman continued. "Take charity for instance. The Lord has commanded us to be charitable. How does one attain charity? Does giving three thousand pounds to an orphanage make one charitable?"

"It is the definition of charity."

"Ah, but charity is much more than giving of one's monetary goods. Paul writes that even if we bestow all our goods on the poor, if we have not charity, it means nothing. So, simply giving away money does not make one charitable. How then are we to become charitable?"

Mr. Darcy pondered the idea. It wasn't enough to simply give charity. It wasn't enough to simply obey the laws.

The reverend continued, "Paul teaches that we do more than give to the poor. It is not enough to give to charity once a year at Christmas. We must learn to love our fellowmen. God asks us to do more than follow a set of rules; he asks us to change our hearts. Each choice refines us just a tiny bit more, and we become better today than we were yesterday."

"But at that rate, developing charity would require an entire lifetime."

"Exactly! Refining one's self *is* the work of a lifetime. It is the sum of small choices made each day. After all, one cannot wake up and decide to be a good person and be done by tea time. It takes time. It also takes trials. I told you faith is doing what is right when life is difficult. If life were never difficult, we would have no opportunities to build our faith. You mentioned Miss Elizabeth's belief that our trials are a way to prove ourselves to God. You said it as if you did not believe it yourself."

"I do not see why a loving God would afflict us with difficulties that could harm us."

"The key phrase is 'could harm us'. We can choose how each trial affects us. Let me tell you a story. One day, a farmer's workhorse fell down a deep hole. The farmer loved this horse very much, but he could see no way to pull it out. After several days of throwing food into the hole, he knew there was only one thing left to do. There was no way the horse could survive without water. He must bury it.

"So, reluctantly, the farmer started shoveling in dirt on top of the horse. The farmer shoveled in pound after pound of dirt, crying the whole time. When the farmer estimated that he had shoveled enough dirt to bury the horse up to the shoulders, he looked in to say his last goodbye. He was quite surprised when he looked down the hole and found the horse was not buried. Why do you think the horse was not buried?"

"Not enough dirt?"

"No, there was plenty of dirt. The horse simply shook off the dirt and stepped up."

Darcy smiled and slowly nodded. "A very clever story," he said. "So, you are saying the dirt is our trials, and we can either let them bury us or save us. We can choose to either lament our challenges or learn from them."

"Exactly. So, why does God give us challenges?"

"I think He wants to see us come out of the hole."

"Yes. He wants to see us shake off our challenges. How we choose to react to each challenge will either bury us or refine us. It took one shovel of dirt at a time to get the horse out of the hole. And because the horse persisted in enduring the dirt that came falling on him, he was saved."

Mr. Walker leaned forward and peered at Mr. Darcy before continuing. "Sir, faith comes to us little by little. Each time we are hit with dirt, we can either choose to rely on man, or we can choose to rely on God. Each trial is our opportunity to make another small change and to show what we truly believe."

Darcy considered the reverend's words. "So, are you saying I should start praying and rely more on God than man?"

"Do you believe it will help?"

"I am not entirely sure," Darcy replied. He leaned back against the chair and gazed out the window as he considered the idea. "It feels like a novel concept," he said, turning back to Mr. Walker. "But I cannot imagine deferring all my decisions to God. How can God tell me what to do with two fighting tenants? Or how can He balance my ledgers? I have not seen God's hand in my life so far, and I have not suffered for the lack of it."

"Just because you have not seen God's hand in your life does not mean He was not there."

"But where do I begin? How do I let God in my life when I have not allowed Him in for so many years?"

"You already have begun. And I think you need to thank Miss Elizabeth for that. If you pray, God will tell you what to do next."

Darcy nodded. Trusting God like that, fully relying on Him, would change everything. He would have to think about it. "But I still do not understand what silver has to do with it," he said. "How will God refine us like a purifier of silver?"

"I am afraid I cannot help you with that question. I do not know how one purifies silver. When you find out, I would very much like to hear about it. Could we discuss this matter again sometime?"

Mr. Darcy stood and offered his hand. "Of course, Mr. Walker. Thank you for your time."

*****

Mr. Darcy did not head back to Pemberley. He needed a long ride to work through his thoughts. He pondered what it would mean to really let God into his daily life. What would it mean to pray every day, multiple times a day? Could he do it? Could he turn Pemberley, Georgiana, his whole life, over to God?

As he pondered these things, he also carefully weighed the benefits. Certainly, he had always believed there was a God, but he had never believed God had a hand in his life. What would it mean to believe in a God who knew him personally and wanted to help him? Things were becoming clearer as the horse moved forward.

Soon, he realized he had already made his decision. He would change. He wanted to have the same radiance Elizabeth had. As the miles passed him, he knew that what he was learning was true. God was real. God wanted him to succeed. God wanted him to be happy. And if facing his trials was a part of that, then he would do it.

He nudged his horse toward Lambton and decided to stop by the bookshop for supplies. He had been considering making his own notebook of thoughts. He wanted to record some of the thoughts Elizabeth had shared with him and many of Mr. Walker's thoughts as well. He could sense that he was slowly evolving; he felt he should keep a record of the change.

He entered the store and found the section for journals and blank ledgers. He fingered them and perused each one. A simple brown one with a black ribbon bookmark caught his eye. He took it to the front of the store to make his purchase.

"Good afternoon, Mr. Darcy," the shopkeeper said. "Did you find what you were looking for? The books you requested a few weeks ago have not come in yet, but I suspect they should be here soon."

"Thank you, Mr. Kassing. I did find what I was looking for. I wonder, Mr. Kassing, have you ever kept a journal?"

A bell rang, indicating that someone had entered the bookshop, and Mr. Kassing nodded over Darcy's shoulder before making a reply. "A fine idea, sir," he responded. "I do keep a journal. Some days it is merely a log of whom I talked with, but other days it is much more than that. I find it helps me work through decisions. Are you thinking of starting a journal, sir?"

"Not exactly. Someone let me borrow her notebook of inspirational thoughts, and I am thinking of starting my own. I hope that putting my ideas down on paper will help me make sense of them."

Mr. Darcy heard a familiar, feminine laugh, and he turned around to see Miss Elizabeth. She was wearing a pale yellow dress with bluebells embroidered on the bodice and sleeves. The sunlight coming in through the window seemed to illuminate every part of her—either the afternoon sun was especially bright today, or she had grown even more radiant since last night. Both scenarios seemed equally possible to him at the moment.

He turned back to Mr. Kassing and said, "Thank you for your suggestions, but I think I have found the expert right here." He examined Elizabeth for a moment and then walked towards her, clearing his throat to speak. She laughed again and smiled sweetly at him.

"Hello, Mr. Darcy."

"Good afternoon, Miss Elizabeth. What brings you to the Lambton bookshop today?"

"My aunt has come to Lambton to do some shopping, and I asked her to drop me off here. I could not think of a better way to pass the time than to peruse a bookshop. What brings you here?"

He lifted the journal. "I suppose my purpose is the same as yours."

She reached for the book he had in his hand and asked, "But what have you found that you do not already own?" She flipped through the blank, lined pages and looked with surprised eyes at him. "It is blank. What do you need a blank book for?"

"I have been doing a lot of thinking lately. Some of my thoughts are circulating through my mind, confusing and elusive, while others are well-formed ideas. Either way, I find I am in need of writing them down."

"Well, it is about time."

"I do not take your meaning."

"You seem to fight very hard, although quite poorly I might add, to refrain from expressing your thoughts. I always see so many thoughts and emotions in your eyes, and yet you share so little."

"It is hard for me to share my thoughts."

"No, sir, it is not. You start by saying, 'I feel,' and then you finish the sentence. Try it."

Mr. Darcy looked around for Mr. Kassing and did not see him. There was no one else in the bookshop. His heart started pounding, and his mind was reeling a mile a minute. He had made this decision last night at the ball. Was now the right time? Could he do it? Was she ready to hear it? How does one share such thoughts?

He took a deep breath and stepped a little closer. He took the journal from her hands and put it down on a table. He then took her hand and clasped it in both of his. He saw her surprise at his bold gesture, but instead of making him more nervous, it only strengthened his resolve. Her entire face showed enlightenment and curiosity.

"I *feel* like a different person when I am around you. I *feel* like you have altered me in such a permanent way that there is no going back. I *feel* like I have found someone I can enjoy a lifetime of happiness with. Miss Elizabeth, forgive me, but I *feel* like I cannot hold back this question a moment longer: will you consent to a courtship? I realize that we have only known each other a month, but I cannot imagine my life without you anymore. Please allow me to get to know you better."

Elizabeth's hand was warm from his hands, but it was nothing in comparison to what she felt in her chest. To say she was surprised was an understatement. He was so rich! So handsome! So wonderful! How could she possibly have won his regard?

"Mr. Darcy," she stammered, "I must admit that unless you have been practicing expressing how you feel, you did a wonderful job in your first efforts. I *feel* very flattered that you even have looked in my direction. But you must know that I am a simple country girl from Hertfordshire. Why would the Master of Pemberley want to court me?"

He sensed she was not refusing him, and he took greater courage in declaring himself. "Miss Elizabeth, I have been introduced to many, many ladies, but I have never met anyone like you. You are like a diamond among pearls. Pearls may have a soft sheen, but diamonds reflect every bit of light in a room. You outshine them all. You emanate goodness. I find myself desperately trying to invent ways to spend time with you. I had not meant to declare myself today, in a bookshop of all places, but here I am, doing just that. I have no script rehearsed. I have no prepared words of admiration, but I *feel* like I may love you. Will you please consent to letting me court you properly?"

Tears were building in her eyes. She looked up at him, and his eyes had more love and admiration in them than she could have ever imagined. He was holding nothing back. There was no "Mr. Darcy mask" now. She smiled at him, and he responded with one of his brilliant, dimpled smiles. If he only knew what his smiles did to her! She was so nervous that she almost could not find her voice, but it finally came softly. "I would like that very much, Mr. Darcy."

He squeezed her hand and then brought it to his lips and kissed it gently. "Forgive me for cornering you like this in a shop. I was not planning to express myself today, but you have made me so happy. Thank you for seeing past my faults and accepting me." His joy was so full he was bursting!

"I rather think you did an excellent job for one unprepared. That book of yours will become full quite quickly if your pen can keep up with your mind."

"Then I shall buy two. Whom should I ask for permission to court you? Would your father allow Mr. Gardiner to act in his behalf? Or should I write to your father? Should I make a trip to Meryton?"

Elizabeth laughed at how ridiculous he was being. "I think any of the above would be acceptable. It is not as if you are asking for my hand in marriage! Although I do believe Georgiana has already planned the wedding breakfast," she laughed again.

He was thrilled to hear her teasing remarks. "As long as it is not mutton," he said.

Mr. Darcy encouraged Elizabeth to continue looking at the books. As she perused the shelves, he told her of his discussion with Mr. Walker and his thoughts during the ride to Lambton. An odd assortment of books caught her eye. At first he was confused, but as he watched her closely, he realized that she was choosing books at random and not really reading them at all. Rather, she was intensely focused on his account of his conversation with Mr. Walker. He grinned at the realization that she was so completely distracted. When she picked up *Fordyce's Sermons*, he couldn't resist teasing her. She blushed and sheepishly returned the book to the shelf.

Elizabeth was impressed. He was really trying to understand the scripture. It was clear he had been genuinely touched. She told him she agreed with the clergyman's advice. "I truly believe God wants to be involved in our lives," she said. "If we just let Him, He will personally direct us in every facet of it."

"But how do you let Him direct it? I have directed my own life for so long. I do not know how to let go and take counsel from someone else."

"It just takes a commitment to doing the right thing every time. I think you already do that. Now, you must pray for guidance so that you know what the right thing is."

"Yes, about that. I must admit I have not prayed much. In fact, not at all recently. I am a little nervous. What if I say the wrong thing?"

She giggled quietly and gently patted his arm with her free hand. "Praying is not like going to a formal dinner, Mr. Darcy. You will not be judged on your eloquence."

"Well, that is unfortunate news," he replied. "I feel much more comfortable eating at a formal dinner than kneeling in prayer."

She smiled and assured him, "There is no wrong way to pray. God will hear you no matter what you say. I would only give two bits of advice: speak from your heart, and be grateful. Before you jump into asking for what you want, spend time expressing your gratitude for what you already have. When we truly see how much we have, our problems seem to shrink, and we can better see how to fix them."

He put his hand on hers and relished the closeness they shared at that moment. They were quite secluded, hidden between the aisles of books and out of view from Mr. Kassing. It felt so private to be talking about such spiritual things with no one to interrupt them. He had the strongest desire to lean in and kiss her, but he held back. This was only a courtship. He would not sully her reputation. He turned the conversation back to what he had learned from Mr. Walker. "So, I suppose now I should welcome adversity, as it is sure to refine me into a better man."

Elizabeth had felt the privacy of the moment as well and struggled with her own burning impulses. She focused on what he had said. "Yes," she replied. "Expecting to live a trouble-free life because you are a good person is like expecting the lion not to eat you because you tipped your hat at him. Even good people are meant to have tribulations."

Mr. Darcy chuckled, "Do you have a secret collection somewhere of thought-provoking comments for every possible conversation topic?"

"I admit I do not know any other way to think."

He lowered his voice and stroked her cheek. "I know. I love that about you." He then pulled his hand away and stepped back. "I believe I must be going. Would you please let Mr. Gardiner know that I would like to call on him tomorrow morning? I believe I have something very important to ask him."

"Indeed you do," she giggled. "Until tomorrow." She watched him walk towards the front door and then she called out, "Mr. Darcy, I believe you forgot to buy your book!"

He turned around and smiled. "Yes, I suppose I am somewhat distracted. After all, a diamond draws the attention of even the most-focused gentlemen."

*****

Elizabeth woke up screaming and drenched in sweat. It had been so real. Jane was instantly at her side, and she heard more footsteps in the hall.

Mrs. Gardiner opened the door and asked, "Elizabeth, are you alright?"

Jane stroked Elizabeth's wet hair from her face. "Yes," Elizabeth gasped. "It was just a bad dream."

Jane asked, "Are they the same ones as before? You have not had those dreams for a while."

"No, this one was about David."

"Tell us about it. Unlike your mother, I think talking about your deceased brother is helpful," Mrs. Gardiner said.

"It was that cold January day all over again. He was skating, and I kept telling him to stay away from the center of the pond. But he would not listen. I was frustrated, and I scolded him.

156

I told him I would tell Papa and he would be sent to bed without supper.

"And just as I said that, his skate slipped out from under him. He landed on the ice and fell right through. Everything was in slow motion then. I saw each hand and heard each deafening scream. I ran out to save him, but my feet were sliding on the ice, and no matter how fast I tried to run, I got no closer to him. Each scream for help was echoed; it sounded like dozens of seven-year-old boys. But the faster I ran, the further he slipped. The harder I pressed myself to reach him, the more the ice started to crack under my own feet.

"And then I fell through the ice. I was just ten feet from him. His cries were quieting, and I could not find him. I was paralyzed and blinded by the freezing water rushing around me. My mind started to slow. I could not think clearly; all I could think about was how cold I was. I could smell the dead, stagnant, winter water. I kept calling for David, but I could not get to him. Somehow I swam over to where he had fallen through. I could see ice crystals in his hair. I called for help as loudly as I could, but my voice was scratchy, and my throat was sore. It was so cold.

"When I finally reached him, I pulled David up out of the water and pushed him out onto the ice, but he did not move. He never moved again. It was awful. I pulled him to shore, but I could not stand. My legs and arms had lost all feeling. I was so cold." Elizabeth pulled her blankets up around her tightly.

Jane rubbed Elizabeth's shoulders and embraced her. "Lizzy, it was not your fault. You must remember that. You were only eleven."

Mrs. Gardiner leaned in and sat on the other side of the bed. "Why do you think you are having these nightmares again? That was nine years ago."

"I do not know."

"Now, you know as well as I that you just lied to me. Tell me, what happened to make you think of this incident?" Mrs.

Gardiner's words may have been reprimanding, but her voice expressed a great deal of love and concern.

"I suppose it is because Mr. Darcy declared himself. I am nobody special. I have no connections, nothing to recommend myself. I am not worthy of a man like him."

Jane sighed, "No! Do not let Mamma's hurtful words make you doubt! Elizabeth, she is wrong! She has been wrong all these years. You did not kill our brother; you nearly died trying to save him. It is not your fault, and she is hateful when she says so."

"Sometimes it is hard to shut out her words. 'It should have been you.' 'Now there is no heir, and we will all starve in the hedge groves because you could not properly watch your only brother.'" Elizabeth began sobbing, and her last words were nearly indecipherable: "'You killed him. No man will want you as the mother of his children.'"

Mrs. Gardiner wiped away the tears in her own eyes. "Franny is very wrong to speak to you like that," she said. "You sacrificed your very life for the boy. You were so sick after that. We did not think you would survive, my dear. You were feverish for weeks and barely conscious. You hardly ate anything, just broth and gruel."

Jane sniffled, "I remember it well, Elizabeth. I remember when you finally turned the corner and started speaking again coherently. You wanted to know how David was, but we were so afraid to tell you that he had been buried months ago. You did not believe us until Mamma started in on you. She was very cruel those first weeks after you regained consciousness. She should have been grateful that she buried only one child instead of two. But it did not matter to her that you had survived. All she could talk about was David."

"But now, you have proven your mother wrong, Elizabeth," assured Mrs. Gardiner. "You have a great deal to offer to a man, and Mr. Darcy just proved it today. He sees your worth even if she does not. All those times she said no man could love you, she was hateful and cruel. Do not think for one moment she is right. You are so beautiful inside and out. You have risen to every challenge placed before you, including your mother!"

"But what if Mr. Darcy hears what Mamma has said about me? What if he believes her?" Elizabeth shuddered to think of her mother and Mr. Darcy in the same room.

Jane said, "No, that will not happen. You know how good I am at observing people. I can see he is a very determined man. Once he commits to something, nothing can change his mind; there is no going back. He loves you, Elizabeth. Nothing can change that now."

"I hope you are right. I hope he still feels that way when he meets Mamma and our younger sisters. Nevertheless, I feel I should tell him about David—just in case."

Mrs. Gardiner leaned in and sternly said, "Just in case of what? Just in case he wants to back out of the courtship? Goodness, Elizabeth, I must know him better than you do if you think he will do that!"

"I just feel like he should know about it. As well as other things."

Tears began rolling down Jane's cheeks, and she silently shook her head. Mrs. Gardiner lifted Elizabeth's chin to look her in the eye. "He does not need to know about that," she said quite firmly. "What is in the past is in the past. Nothing that happened back then has altered your worthiness to be a man's wife."

"But what if he feels differently? How can you be sure?"

Jane wiped her own tears and then reached out and embraced her sister. "Elizabeth," she whispered, "you are worthy of the best man in all of England. I do not know a lady who deserves happiness more than you do, and if I have to tell him that, I will."

"Thank you, Jane. I hope you are right."

*****

Elizabeth met Mr. Darcy the next morning at the entrance of Saphrinbrooke. "Mr. Darcy, would you join me for a walk before you go inside?"

Mr. Darcy didn't like the sound of that. Normally he would welcome a private walk, but her eyes looked tired, and her speech was weak. "Is something troubling you?"

"Not particularly. I just think there are some things you should know before we officially begin a courtship."

Jane came up to Elizabeth from behind. "Are you sure about this, Elizabeth?" she whispered.

Elizabeth nodded to her sister and then turned back to Mr. Darcy. "Jane has offered to accompany us as a chaperone. Shall we begin?"

Mr. Darcy offered his arm and said, "Of course." She smiled weakly back at him. "Please know that you can tell me anything," he added.

Jane whispered to Elizabeth, "I told you so."

Elizabeth held on to Mr. Darcy's arm, and Jane followed behind them from a generous distance. They walked in silence for a few minutes. Then she began the story of her brother David's accident. She left out no detail. She spared no emotion. Mr. Darcy listened closely as she spoke. Then Elizabeth detailed her mother's reaction. It hurt to repeat the things her mother had said, but she did it. When she finished her story, Mr. Darcy stopped walking and turned and looked at her.

"I do not know why you felt the need to tell me this story, for it does not alter my intentions. It has, however, stirred up some less-than-Christian feelings towards your mother."

"I just thought you should know. I was very ill afterwards for many months." Her tears were falling freely, and she wiped at them with her free hand. It was difficult to look at him, but when she did, she saw such compassion and love that she very nearly let out a chest-clenching sob.

"I certainly do not place any blame on you, and neither should you." He looked at the great pain seeping out of her eyes, and he knew he had hit the nail on the head. He paused and took both of her hands in his. "Miss Elizabeth," he whispered, "please know that there is no way I think any less of you. If anything, I admire you all the more. I admire you for having such a bright outlook on life in spite of this difficult tragedy. I most certainly do not blame you. I do not want you to harbor feelings of guilt anymore. You did everything in your power to save him, and later, to survive your own accident."

Elizabeth quietly nodded but continued crying. He looked around and saw they were alone. He gently dropped her hands and widened his arms cautiously. "May I?" he asked quietly. "There is only one thing I know to do when I see a lady cry. I have quite a bit of experience with Georgiana."

Elizabeth let all her emotions go and nodded, and soon she felt his strong, masculine arms around her as she burst into sobs. She cried for many minutes like that. He quietly held her close and rubbed her back. How could she deserve the love of a man like Mr. Darcy?

CHAPTER 8

"Charles! You must be joking! Please tell me Mr. Darcy has not truly entered into a courtship with that country chit!" Miss Bingley cried.

"Caroline, control yourself! He may overhear you. And Miss Elizabeth is a fine lady."

Caroline stood up and started pacing. She had to do something; surely there was something she could do to change Mr. Darcy's mind! "Then we must delay our visit to London. You must see the necessity of staying here and helping him see reason. He is confused! You are his closest friend; you must help him!"

Mr. Bingley put a hand on her shoulder, which she shook off brusquely. "He is his own man, Caroline. Let it go. He has never made any pretentions about his feelings for you. It is time for you to understand that. We will leave in three days as planned, and you will be respectful to the Bennets when they come to dinner tonight. Try to be happy for him; he has found love!" With that, Bingley walked out of the room.

Love? Caroline Bingley doubted it. *Miss Eliza is as mercenary as they come. I will prove it if I have to. What could she possibly have that I do not?*

*****

"Colonel, I certainly can take you as far as London. There is no need to leave today and travel by post when I can deliver you there in three days," Mr. Bingley said.

"Thank you, but I have my orders. I have delayed them long enough." Just then, Darcy walked in, joining Bingley and

Colonel Fitzwilliam in the study. The colonel clapped him loudly on the shoulder. "There is the man of the hour! Congratulations, Darcy! She is an amazing lady."

"Thank you, Richard. She certainly is," Darcy grinned.

"Perhaps she has a wealthy, older sister?" Colonel Fitzwilliam asked.

"Absolutely not," said Bingley. He then cleared his throat loudly, "Excuse me. What I meant to say is, as I understand matters, she does not. The Bennet girls only have fifty pounds apiece upon marriage, and the entire estate is entailed away to a clergyman named Mr. Collins, some distant cousin. I believe they have never even met the man."

"Mr. Collins? My aunt, Lady Catherine, just hired a Mr. Collins as the new rector at Rosings. I wonder if they are the same man," Darcy said.

"I have heard that although Longbourn was once a profitable estate, their father now struggles to make a reasonable income," Bingley added.

"How do you know all this, Bingley?" Colonel Fitzwilliam asked.

"Miss Bennet and I have passed many hours together chaperoning those lovebirds on long walks. But do not accuse me of complaining; it is hardly an onerous responsibility. In fact, it has been more pleasurable than I can express. She is such a joy, a real angel! I look forward to spending more time with her in Hertfordshire."

Caroline Bingley listened closely outside the study door. It was exactly as she expected: Elizabeth had no fortune. She would have to plan her strategy carefully. Tonight's dinner was not the right time. *I must gather more information about her in Hertfordshire. Then I will bring to light Miss Eliza's true intentions.*

*****

"Have Mr. Bingley and his sisters left for London?" Elizabeth asked several days later.

Georgiana sighed and leaned back against the chaise. "Indeed, and just in time; for I could not have endured them a moment longer. I am glad to have two weeks rest before we join them in Hertfordshire."

Elizabeth smiled. "You are coming too?" she asked. "How delightful! I cannot wait to introduce you to Charlotte. She is my dearest friend and saw me through my ordeal four years ago. Speaking of which, I still have not told Jane about what happened to you, but I think she suspects something."

"If you think she should know, you may tell her. I do not mind. She is so sweet and kind. And I am doing so much better lately. Two out of the last three nights I was not plagued with the nightmares. The one night I did have them, they were brief and slightly different."

"Different, how so?"

"I dreamt that he came for me through the window again, but this time I pushed him back out, and he fell and broke his neck. He was so horribly disfigured that I woke up crying, but for the first time in my dreams, he did not succeed in his attempts."

"You mean he did not . . ."

"No, he did not."

"Georgiana, this is wonderful! You have made so much progress these last few weeks! I do not know if you have noticed, but you are smiling more lately. I am so thrilled that things are better!"

Georgiana blushed slightly and sipped her tea. "I do not fully feel myself again, but I do feel measurably better. Prayer helps. Having someone to share my deepest thoughts with makes my fears less burdensome. William has been praying lately too. He told me so, and we always pray before the meal now."

"I noticed that at dinner the other night."

"He has been very kind to me during this whole experience. He is quite considerate."

Elizabeth pondered the changes she had been seeing as well. The other day when she and Jane had arrived at Pemberley for a visit, Mr. Darcy had been waiting for them at the door. After helping them out of the carriage, he had returned Elizabeth's prayer notebook to her. He confessed he had copied a few of them into his own journal and hoped she didn't mind. Elizabeth was flattered and told him she didn't mind at all. She was thankful to have her notebook back. That night she had slept with it close to her chest, happy to know it had last been in his possession.

Just then, someone knocked, interrupting Elizabeth's pleasant thoughts. The sitting room door opened, and Mr. Darcy joined them. "Good morning, Mr. Darcy," she said.

"Good morning, Miss Elizabeth," he answered. He walked straight to her, bowed, and kissed her hand. It was a habit they both enjoyed. "Where is Miss Bennet?"

"My aunt needed her today. But since Georgiana is here, I took a great leap of faith and entrusted myself to her legendary chaperoning skills."

Darcy smiled and greeted Georgiana with a kiss on the cheek. "And are you comfortable taking responsibility of such an impertinent charge? She may be quite a handful."

"I believe I can keep her in line." Georgiana said with a smile.

Elizabeth raised an eyebrow, "I dare say I have not been trying hard enough if you are now under the impression that it is possible to keep me in line! Mr. Darcy has now officially called me impertinent. He cannot take it back."

Mr. Darcy smiled a large dimpled smile at her and Georgiana said, "Tsk, tsk, William; that is no way to court a lady. But perhaps a picnic will soften the blow. Are you ready?"

"Yes. I apologize for delaying you, ladies; I had a difficult problem that needed my attention. It seems Mr. Wilson's wife fell ill last week, and it has been challenging for her to care for the children. I hope you do not mind, but I offered to take them with us on the picnic to give her some rest."

Georgiana smiled. Mrs. Wilson was one of their tenants. She had three young boys, each with excessive energy. It would make for a very entertaining day. "What a wonderful idea!"

"Who is Mrs. Wilson?" Elizabeth asked.

Mr. Darcy said, "A neighbor. Come, they are waiting for us in the carriage."

Elizabeth rose and accompanied him out front where she saw three very rambunctious and disheveled boys. When the boys saw them coming, they tried to stifle their excitement by sitting on their hands, but the youngest was squirmy and swung his legs, accidently kicking the eldest boy. The eldest boy reciprocated with a punch to the shoulder. She could tell from their clothes that they were not the children of a gentleman. She immediately felt a longing to be back at the orphanage with the children she missed so much.

Mr. Darcy had worried about inviting the boys without consulting Georgiana or Elizabeth, but when he saw the smile on Elizabeth's face, he knew he had done the right thing. It had just felt right to offer help to the Wilsons. It was a small gesture, but he relished knowing he could help others in nonmonetary ways. He handed Elizabeth and Georgiana into the carriage. He then stepped in and saw that Georgiana had taken the seat next to the two oldest boys, so the only available seat was next to Elizabeth. He discreetly winked at Georgiana as he sat down. He tapped the carriage roof, and the carriage rocked as it began to move.

"You boys are being very quiet. What are your names?" Elizabeth asked.

"We ain't supposed to talk to no strangers, miss," the eldest boy answered, giving her a wary look.

Elizabeth giggled and said, "You are well trained. Mr. Darcy, would you mind introducing me to these fine young gentlemen? It is not proper for me to recommend myself to them, for I can see from their manners that they are men of quality. I do so desire to make their acquaintance."

Mr. Darcy smiled at her attempts to make them laugh. "This gentleman is Master Jonathan Wilson, the gentleman across from you is Lord Jacob Wilson, and the young man next to you is Sir Jeffrey Wilson. Gentlemen, I would like to introduce you to Miss Elizabeth Bennet. She likes frogs."

"Really?" all three boys asked in unison.

Jonathan was slightly better at controlling his surprise than the other two. "But you're a lady! I don't know no girls who like frogs."

"Oh, but I do! Green ones, slimy ones, brown toads with warts—I love them all! I will even try to catch them with you. In fact, I will wager that I can catch a frog quicker than you can."

"Na uh!" Jacob said. "You're in a dress! You'll get all dirty!"

Jeffrey took his thumb out of his mouth and asked, "Do you like to kiss them? Is that why you like to catch them? Are you a princess?"

Elizabeth laughed and leaned into him and said, "If I am a princess, I do not know it. So, I must kiss a frog to find out. Is that not how the fairytale goes?" She was trying to trick them, and her words brought out a round of laugher.

"Miss Elizabeth, you don't know nothin'! That's not why she kisses him! The princess knows she is a princess, but she don't know the frog is a prince! You're not like none of the girls in the village. They know all the stories about princesses. Are you sure you like frogs?" Jacob asked.

Mr. Darcy chuckled and said, "She likes them so much that she owns a necklace with a frog pendant. Have you ever heard of such a thing? A lady wearing an amphibian on her neck? Trust me; she likes frogs."

This time it was Elizabeth who was surprised. "Mr. Darcy, I am shocked. Rummaging through my jewelry collection? That is highly inappropriate."

"You forget, Miss Elizabeth, that you wore that particular necklace the night of the ball. It was a very curious piece of jewelry to wear at a ball, but the pearls in its eyes disguised it nicely."

She paused and smiled. "You are very observant to have noticed."

"Fully Rely On God. F-R-O-G." Mr. Darcy replied.

They arrived at the meadow, and the boys started scrambling to get out and run to the pond. But Darcy stopped them and demonstrated the proper way to hand a lady out of a carriage. The older boys proudly placed one arm behind their backs, just like Darcy, and each offered a hand to assist the ladies.

Georgiana said, "Thank you, Master Jonathan." She curtsied, and he bowed to her like Darcy had showed them.

Jacob was shorter than Jonathan but was not to be outdone. He reached up for Elizabeth's hand and offered his support. "Welcome to the pond, Miss Elizabeth."

"Why thank you, Lord Jacob. That was very well executed. I do not believe a duke could have done it more elegantly." Elizabeth held her hand out it in front of his face. He just stared at it with a disgusted look.

Mr. Darcy interrupted, "Allow me, Lord Jacob. I would not want you to do something that you do not feel comfortable with." He then took Elizabeth's hand and kissed it, leaving his lips lingering a little longer than necessary, and then he looked up at her brown eyes and smiled.

"Disgustin'! I ain't kissin' a girl's hand for nothin'! I don't care how pretty she is!"

Mr. Darcy and Elizabeth both just laughed. Darcy tucked her hand around his arm, and they followed the boys to the pond. Georgiana had already gone on ahead. The servant placed a blanket on the grass next to the pond and was quickly trying to set out the picnic items. Darcy told her, "We can do all that. You are welcome to go back to Pemberley if you like. We can handle things from here."

"Yes, sir. Much obliged, sir. The wine should be placed in the shade so as to not get too warm."

"Thank you, Sarah," Darcy answered. "Please, take some time for yourself and enjoy the fine weather."

"Thank you, sir!" Sarah curtsied, thrilled that she would not have to stand around or run after little boys.

Elizabeth watched the boys run around, and Darcy started rummaging through a basket. He pulled out a ball and two pieces of rope and left to entertain the boys. Elizabeth kneeled down on the blanket and tucked her legs underneath her. The sun was warm on her arms, and she took off her bonnet to feel the sun on her face. Georgiana sat down next to her and opened a book and began reading. Elizabeth smiled. Reading for pleasure had been impossible for her in her dark years, but Georgiana seemed to be doing so well. It was amazing to see her progress.

Elizabeth occupied herself for the next half hour admiring the boys as they played the rope-and-ball game Mr. Darcy was teaching them. Mr. Darcy ran right along with them, and he seemed to be tolerating it quite well. She wondered what he did to stay in good physical condition. She assumed he did some fencing, as most gentlemen do, and she knew already that he was an avid horseman. She caught herself admiring his form and chastised herself for doing so.

She turned away and decided a nap in the sun sounded pleasant. She folded the extra blanket into a pillow and laid her head down. In no time at all, she was drifting off to sleep.

*****

Mr. Darcy spent an hour entertaining the boys, but by the end, it was clear he was not a young man anymore. He was totally fatigued and longing for a bath. The boys wanted to search for frogs and begged him to wake Elizabeth.

"Ah, please, sir! She said she likes to catch frogs, and she bet us she can catch one faster than us. We have to wake her. She'll be terribly angry if she misses it!"

"Well, we would not want that, would we?" Darcy said. The boys all jumped up and down and yelled their excitement. Mr. Darcy walked over to the sleeping Elizabeth and got down on one knee next to her. He called out her name quietly, but she didn't move. He placed his hand on her shoulder and spoke her name a little louder. She still did not move.

Georgiana giggled. "Perhaps the sleeping beauty needs to be kissed awake."

Darcy looked at Georgiana and gave her a devilish look. He certainly did not need to be encouraged in his desires. He turned back to Elizabeth's sleeping form. He caressed her cheek and then brushed back her chocolate curls from her face. She was exquisitely beautiful sleeping so peacefully. He found himself watching her shoulders rise and fall with her steady breathing, and he felt his heart speed up uncontrollably. He took a deep breath to try to control his physical reaction. He spoke in normal tones and gently shook her shoulder.

"Elizabeth—I mean, Miss Elizabeth—the boys are challenging us to a frog-hunting expedition." He saw her stir, and she opened her eyes. She gave him the sweetest, most dazzling smile he had ever seen. Her eyes were glossed over, and he sucked in his breath. Her starry-eyed, sleepy look was very becoming. His voice was low and coarse as he repeated his invitation. "Miss, Elizabeth, the gauntlet has been thrown down, and the boys are quite determined. They have challenged us to a frog-hunting race. I have already chosen to be on your team as I have great faith in your frog hunting skills."

She sat up and stretched. Seeing the boys antsy to get moving she replied, "Well, I believe we shall beat their knickers off them if you are my partner. You grew up on these lands, so our team will have the advantage." She started to stand, and Mr. Darcy offered both his hands to help her up. She arose and murmured her thanks, but he continued to hold her hands. She looked down at her hands and was overcome with the realization that it felt so right to hold his hands like that.

Mr. Darcy reluctantly let her hands go. He bent one hand behind his back and turned to the boys. "Boys, it is time to be whipped! Are you ready?"

Jacob shouted, "Go!" And they all started running in different directions.

"Miss Elizabeth, come this way!" Darcy grabbed her hand and headed down the hill.

"But the marsh is over that way!"

"Trust me!" he grinned.

Her long dress was slowing her down, so she lifted her skirt and ran with him. They weaved through a few trees, and then a muddy area opened up to them. There were high reeds and cattails waving in the wind. "Perfect!" she exclaimed. They stood there together looking at the marsh without moving. He was still holding her hand. "Sir, I may need my hand back to start searching, unless you intend to offer your services to hold my skirt up away from the mud?" She smiled saucily at him. He turned a scarlet red color that went all the way to his ears and quickly dropped her hand. She let out a laugh. "I was only teasing, Mr. Darcy; I have no problem holding your hand. I rather like it."

He looked into her eyes and felt her admiration, and it brought him such joy. "It is a nice feeling. I enjoy it too." He then turned and started pushing the weeds aside and said a quick prayer of thanks while he searched for frogs. The prayer ended abruptly when Elizabeth hiked her skirt up to her knees and stepped into the marsh. He could not help being a little distracted at the sight of her ankles. He was a man after all; it would take a great deal of praying to direct his thoughts elsewhere. He was so distracted that it was difficult to think about frogs at all. He admitted he was probably a liability now instead of an asset to their team and groaned slightly.

"Are you all right, Mr. Darcy?" Elizabeth asked.

He looked up from the reeds by her feet as she spoke. He would have to do a little better at controlling himself. "Of course. Now, let us find some amphibians."

Elizabeth had seen a flash of frustration in his eyes, and she was confused by it. She turned her attention to the weeds in front of her. She waded out into the water a few inches, and with her free hand, she pushed the reeds from side to side.

Although she was trying to look for frogs, her mind was preoccupied with thoughts of Mr. Darcy. Every once in a while, she would steal a glance in his direction, and she would admire his strong legs or broad shoulders. His breeches must be tailor-made, because they fit him so nicely. The gentle wind was blowing his hair around, and he had one little curl right at the nape of his neck. The stray curl was simply adorable. She was nearly close enough to touch it. She turned her attention back to the weeds.

Then they heard it. It was croaking right between them. They both turned to the sound at the same time, and their heads collided quite forcefully. She giggled and started to apologize. Mr. Darcy stepped back to regain his footing, but the mud was too slippery. He flailed his arms, trying to catch his balance, and then all at once, he fell backwards and landed in the muddy water.

She could see from the flash of embarrassment in his eyes that nothing but his pride was hurt. She let out her amusement in the form of hysterical laughter.

Darcy could not believe he had just fallen in the mud. And right in front of Elizabeth. As he listened to her laughter and saw her eyes sparkle as bright and reflective as ever, he started chuckling himself. He sat there in the mud, laughing and feeling his boots fill up with water. "I fear I have become a liability to our team. I have so much water in my boots that I do not think I can run." Then they heard the croak again. Elizabeth pounced on the frog with both hands, dropping her skirt into the mud.

"Got it!" she called out.

Mr. Darcy quickly stood up and followed Elizabeth out of the marsh. She ran back to the blanket, tightly clasping the prize-winning frog.

"Georgiana! We did it! Master Jonathan, Lord Jacob, Sir Jeffrey!" she called out, "I want to give you my deepest condolences for you have lost to a *girl*! I caught the first frog, and you might as well come back now with your heads hung low." She saw them running towards her, and each of them had mud up to their knees.

Jonathan was first to arrive. "I think you're trickin' us; there is no way you found a frog that quickly! You gotta show us."

Jeffrey came close and leaned over Elizabeth's clasped hands, and she lowered it to his eye level. He gasped as she opened up her hands. "You really done it! And you're a girl!"

Jacob laughed and pointed at Elizabeth. "Told ya you would get your dress dirty."

Elizabeth laughed and said, "Well, speaking of dirty, Lord Jacob, I think you may be even dirtier than Mr. Darcy. Then again, we might have to have a fashion show. Georgiana, you must be the judge. Mr. Darcy must show his dirty, wet backside for you to evaluate who has the most mud on their breeches."

"I will do no such thing! I am not flaunting my wares in front of everyone for your amusement. Your plan will not work. I will simply sit here on the grass until the mud dries."

Georgiana giggled and said, "William, you must! I promise to be a fair and impartial judge. But, in the interest of impartiality, I believe Elizabeth must parade her petticoat as well. For I do believe that she may beat you in the category of 'most mud collected'."

Elizabeth looked down at her skirt. She lifted it slightly and saw at least six inches of mud on her petticoat. "I accept. I never back down from a challenge. Mr. Darcy, would you like to go first or should I?"

"You two have no mercy. I will go first so that I may return your giggles and laughter tenfold." The boys and Elizabeth sat down on the grass by Georgiana. Mr. Darcy flipped his tailcoat out dramatically and paraded in front of them, slowly walking from right to left and back again. Then he stood in the center and turned around full circle, pausing for extra effect while his back was to them to look back at them over his shoulder. He then completed the display with a deep, exaggerated bow, and sat down amidst the boys' giggles.

"You did that like a girl!" Jeffrey yelled.

Jonathan bent over laughing and hugged his middle. "My parents will never believe it! I'm gonna tell everyone how you did that! Mr. Darcy, you're gonna win! You're filthy!"

Mr. Darcy turned to Elizabeth and said, "I believe it is your turn, madam."

"Very well, who will hold the frog?" All three boys' hands went up, but she turned and stretched forth her prize to Georgiana with a smile.

Georgiana squealed and said, "No! How disgusting! Get that away from me!"

"If you wish, but consider it a peace offering and remember my kindness as you make your final judgment."

Darcy said, "You are blackmailing the judge? You cannot do that!"

"I do not believe we stipulated any rules besides allowing you to go first," Elizabeth pointed out.

Georgiana giggled again and said, "That is correct, William. You should have considered bribery."

"A Darcy would never stoop so low," he mockingly scolded Georgiana with a fairly convincing look of disappointment.

Elizabeth handed the frog to Jonathan, and then, in her best Miss Bingley impersonation, she sauntered one way and then the other. She lifted one hand up to her hair, and then with the other hand, she lifted the skirt and stretched out her leg to reveal the dirty petticoat. Laughter erupted, and she tried to hold back her own giggles. She then lifted both sides of her skirt and quickly spun around several times, making the muddy petticoat twirl to full effect. Then she stopped and gave her most dramatic curtsy. All the onlookers clapped loudly, and she returned to the blanket. "What is your verdict, Georgiana?"

"If this were London's fashion show, I would have to say that the award for presentation belongs to Elizabeth. But for pure amusement and quantity of mud, I am afraid to tell you that you won, William. Go along, boys, you may go play with the frog now." The boys ran off towards the middle of the field.

"None of you have a lick of sense!" Mr. Darcy joked. "I thought Miss Elizabeth's petticoat was memorable!"

Elizabeth laughed out right and said, "Are you wishing for me to tell you that your backside was memorable? Because I may catch frogs, but I am still a lady!"

Mr. Darcy just shook his head in disbelief. She was always one step ahead of him. He then had an idea. "Well, if I have won, what shall be my prize?"

She turned to Mr. Darcy and said, "We did not stipulate a prize for the winner. What does the muddy gentleman suggest?" Elizabeth sensed the mood had changed, and the look in his eyes confirmed it. The desire was back.

"I believe the loser must accompany the winner on a walk around the pond." He stood up and reached a hand down to her.

"Very well." She took his hand, and he did not hesitate to wrap her arm around his. He silently led them off towards the pond. "I feel I should ask if we require a chaperone," she said. "The gleam in your eye looks a little untrustworthy."

He gasped in shock. "If there is one thing you should know about me, it is that I am trustworthy," he said. "Now you, on the other hand, delight in impertinent speech," he smirked. "I have been told it is a slippery slope to impertinent behavior."

"Really! Well, perhaps we should go back and let Georgiana decide whose heart is in the right place."

Darcy stopped walking, reached up to her cheek, and brushed it with the back of his hand. He lowered his voice and said, "I know exactly where my heart is."

Elizabeth flushed where his hand had caressed her face. Suddenly, she was quite short of breath. She realized she had been holding her breath, and she let it out. The desire in his eyes suddenly changed to a more reserved look of admiration, and he withdrew his hand and stood up straighter. She did not trust her voice to say anything.

They had been courting for two weeks now, and she was finding he was more than just kind and gentle. He was loyal and committed. He was charming and persuasive. He was sweet and patient. He was romantic. He was humorous, and she enjoyed the laughter they shared frequently. Who knew a man who tried so hard to be proper and refined, could tease and laugh so lightheartedly with little encouragement?

"Shall I tell Georgiana her legendary chaperoning skills are being questioned?" Mr. Darcy asked.

She cleared her throat and said, "She appears to delight in seeing us together. I think she may be intentionally slacking in her duties."

"Yes, I think so too. She owes you a great deal, as do I."

"I do not know about that. I simply offered a service that was once offered to me." She hoped her clue was obvious enough that he would finally ask what had happened to her. Jane and her aunt said that Mr. Darcy didn't need to know about it, but

Elizabeth couldn't get it out of her mind. A courtship was intended to lead to engagement, which leads to marriage. A husband should know certain things about his wife.

They walked in silence for nearly ten minutes. Elizabeth tried to give him all the time in the world to form his questions for her, but yet he did not.

As he listened to her breathing next to him, he concentrated on placing one foot in front of the other. It seemed like she wanted to talk about it, but he really did not want to know. It was hard enough imagining what had happened to his sister; he could not allow himself to consider what had happened to Elizabeth. He chastised himself for being so cowardly. She obviously was comfortable discussing it, but he did not know how to explain his fear.

After nearly making it halfway around the pond, Elizabeth gave into the silence and introduced a new topic, "When can I expect you in Hertfordshire?"

Relief—that was all he felt at the moment. Hertfordshire was a topic he would gladly discuss. "I wanted to discuss that with you. I have freed my schedule and am at your leisure. With your father's permission, I would like to escort you and Miss Bennet to Hertfordshire in my carriage. Georgiana will accompany us too, of course."

"Mr. Darcy, you certainly do not have to do that. We have already made our travel arrangements." She looked up at him and saw disappointment in his entire face. His lip literally had a pout to it. She giggled. "That is not to say that those plans cannot change."

He grinned at her and took her hand and kissed it. "Would you permit me to handle the arrangements? Simply tell me which day you desire to be home, and I shall ensure it to the very hour. You will be much more comfortable in my carriage."

"I will have to ask my uncle what he thinks of the plan. But I certainly would prefer to share a carriage with you rather than a stranger."

"And I have never more eagerly anticipated two days of slow, bumpy travel in a crowded carriage. It pleases me greatly that you have agreed. I suspect the miles will fly by with your pleasant conversation."

"Yes, I believe you have yet to ask me my 'no comment' questions."

"I am saving those for another time. Speaking of the 'no comment' questions, I received a letter back from the owner of the mine in Bere Ferres in Devon. I wrote to him asking how silver is mined and refined."

"Oh? And did he enlighten you?"

"Not exactly. He went into great detail about the mining process but shared no insights about the Biblical metaphor, or at least, not that I could tell. He did tell me that silver is very rarely mined as pure silver nuggets. It is more commonly found mixed with lead and copper. He explained that the ore has to be heated to a very high temperature in order to separate the lead and copper from the silver."

Elizabeth asked, "Is that all he had to tell you?"

"That was the most important part of the letter. Will any of it help me in understanding how God refines us like a purifier of silver?"

"You tell me. Did it help?"

"No, not really. I was hoping for more information about the refining process, but he seemed to focus more on the mining process."

"If you ask a miner about his work, he will tell you about mining."

"I suppose so," he said. They walked in silence for a few more minutes.

"This is a beautiful place," Elizabeth said. "There is a pond just like this near Longbourn." And suddenly she remembered David and that wintery day. Darcy noticed in the change in her and squeezed her hand.

"Are you all right?" Darcy asked gently. She nodded. "I have been meaning to ask you something," Darcy continued. "That day you told me about your brother David's accident, you seemed different afterwards. Obviously, it was difficult for you to talk about it, but you seemed almost . . . relieved."

"I was relieved, I suppose. I was relieved at your response. David's death is something I live with every day and I suppose I have learned to accept it. It is a part of me. Just as a river carves out its path in a canyon after a heavy storm, my life shifted directions with its influence. I do not wish the experience on anyone, but I learned so much from it."

"How so?"

"Well, it is a bit complicated. I was planning to tell you that day, but I was a little overwhelmed. And then someone very handsome distracted me." She smiled up at him before continuing, "After David died, I was not well enough to leave my room and venture outside again until spring. The flowers were in full bloom by that time, and the trees had new young leaves on their branches. I started taking walks that spring to work through all the emotions I felt. Most days it was a necessity to escape the criticism of my mother, but the spring air was good for me in other ways.

"I had begun to believe the things my mother said. I thought our entire future at Longbourn had died, all because of me. So, that spring comforted me; it reminded me of new beginnings. My father started accompanying me on my daily walks. I think he saw me slipping into darkness. He had inherited Longbourn only a few years earlier and was sorely missing his days in the parish. He saw what my mother was doing to me, and he did what he could to divert her words, but I think he was going through his own kind of pain. He had lost his only son too. Nevertheless, I remember one day when we had a very memorable discussion.

"He said to me 'Elizabeth, Longbourn may not have a male heir anymore, but that does not mean you have lost the name of Bennet. I have every hope that you will bring honor to my name.

Since I lack any talent in running an estate, my name may very well be the only possession of value I can give you.'

"I remember seeing tears in his eyes when he said this to me. He did not need to say anything else, for in his simple three sentences, I had learned what he wanted to teach. I am a Bennet, a daughter of Thomas Bennet. I felt a wave of pride in knowing that he was proud of me. I wanted to be the best I could be, simply because I carried his name."

Mr. Darcy said, "My father told me something similar a long time ago. 'Once a Darcy, always a Darcy,' he said."

"Yes," she agreed. "It is very moving to hear that from a parent. I told you that story about my brother David not to elicit sympathy, but rather to help you understand what has made me who I am today. Without that tragedy, I do not think I would be half the woman I am now. I look at life as many small, precious moments, all linked together to create a priceless existence. I am not naive enough to believe my life will always be rosy. But I recognize every trial and tribulation as a chance to prove myself worthy of God's good grace. I do not fight life's conflict anymore. When I am in difficulty, I ask myself, what am I supposed to learn from this experience? How am I supposed to grow? How will this make me a better person?"

"That is an interesting concept. It makes me wonder if you would prefer foresight or hindsight better."

"I do not understand what you mean."

"You said that you try to ask yourself what you will learn from each experience. Would you prefer to understand what you will eventually learn right from the beginning? Would you want to have foresight into God's plan for you? Or would you prefer to find understanding of the trial's purpose at the end, through hindsight?"

"Is this one of your 'no comment' questions?"

"Definitely not," he said with a smile. "I told you, I am saving those."

Elizabeth pondered his question. "I think I would prefer hindsight. I do not see how one could build faith if one had all the answers at the beginning. What about you? Would you prefer hindsight or foresight?"

"Foresight. I think I would be much more patient in enduring a trial if I knew upfront how it would improve me. I would have a better attitude if I knew, 'This will make me more humble', or 'I will learn gratitude'. And I would finish the lesson more efficiently; I would work to be humble or to be grateful quickly so the trial would end," Darcy said with a slight laugh.

She giggled. "I suppose one could look at it like that. But the process of enduring takes time. When you learn how silver is refined, you will see what I mean."

"I suspect you are correct. I just tend to be impatient when a difficulty is at its hottest."

They had come around the last part of the pond, and Georgiana was putting all the food out. Elizabeth stopped walking and looked up at Mr. Darcy. "I just want to say that I think you are a fine man. The best man I know. You are everything any lady could ever hope for, and I am so grateful to have the chance to get to know you."

"I hope we will have many years to get to know each other."

"Is that a proposal?" she teased.

He smiled at her and tucked a curl behind her ear. He took her hand and kissed the inside of her palm, then closed it into a gentle fist. "Not yet. I hope I will have the foresight to propose in such a way that you need not ask if I am proposing."

She felt the intimacy of the kiss that was now locked away in her fist. She had an impulse to bring it to her chest so that it would calm that racing organ inside. "I will be sure to tell you in hindsight if you are correct."

CHAPTER 9

Elizabeth, Jane, and the Darcys decided to leave for Hertfordshire in two days. The end was a whirlwind of goodbyes. Elizabeth knew she would miss the house and servants and the village. Most of all, she would miss her aunt and uncle. She spent as much time with them as she could. But she set aside a few hours for a visit to each of her favorite tenants: the Whites, the Lewises, the Harrisons, and the Burns.

She paid a very special call to say goodbye to the three Wilson boys. Their picnic at the pond held special memories, but if she was completely honest, it was not only the boys who had made it memorable.

After their walk around the pond, Mr. Darcy had spent the rest of the picnic by her side. He took off his muddy jacket and joined her on the blanket. He leaned back, propped up on one elbow, and they read together for what seemed like hours while the boys played. She memorized the way his lips spoke the words of Shakespeare. His voice was smooth and creamy and made her insides melt. She had tried not to show how emotional she became as he read. He, on the other hand, had seemed so relaxed and carefree. When he took a lengthy pause, she begged him to continue.

How could a man's voice affect her so completely? She had nearly lost all reason and coherent thought. She smiled thinking about that day and all the kisses he had bestowed on her hand, especially the one on her palm that he wrapped up in her fist.

Jane elbowed Elizabeth. "Why all the smiles?" she asked. "Are you thinking about him again?"

Elizabeth smiled wider. "Yes," she admitted. "I am afraid so. It simply seems too good to be true! He is exactly what I would want in a husband. He is kind, generous, loving, sensitive, honest, loyal, committed—"

"Yes, Elizabeth, we have gone through this before. And you love him."

"I do. I love him. Could this really be happening to me? Could I really deserve a man like Mr. Darcy?"

"As any loyal sister would point out, the question is whether or not he deserves you!"

"But I am nothing compared to him. I only worry he will realize it one day."

Jane saw a flash of fear in Elizabeth's eyes. She put her arms around her shoulders and said, "Mamma cannot chase him away. Do not be afraid."

*****

Their trunks were packed, and every detail was prepared. Any minute now, Georgiana and Mr. Darcy would be arriving with the carriage. Elizabeth was excited but nervous as well. Last night, she had finally told Jane about Georgiana, and they had discussed it a great deal. Jane admitted she had suspected Georgiana was more than just melancholy, but she was shocked nonetheless. Jane and Georgiana had become close friends, being thrown together so often as chaperones for Elizabeth and Mr. Darcy. Jane promised to not treat their new companion any differently.

At the sound of the carriage, both sisters rushed downstairs. Minutes later, a devilishly handsome Mr. Darcy appeared. Elizabeth's cheeks flushed, embarrassed by her pleasure in seeing him again.

"Are you ladies ready? We have several long days ahead of us," Mr. Darcy said, admiring the rosy glow in Elizabeth's cheeks.

Mr. Gardiner stepped into the entry. "Could I speak with you for a moment, Mr. Darcy?" he asked.

"Certainly."

Mr. Gardiner shooed his nieces away. "Ladies, have the footman see to your trunks."

"Yes, Uncle," Jane replied. She took Elizabeth's arm and led her out.

Mr. Darcy followed Mr. Gardiner into the study. It was much better organized than it had been two months ago when he had first met Mr. Gardiner and Elizabeth. The change was impressive. Clearly, Elizabeth had been working her magic here. Darcy found himself remembering his favorite moments with Elizabeth when Mr. Gardiner stiffly offered him a seat. It seemed Mr. Gardiner had something to discuss.

Mr. Gardiner cleared his throat and began, "I received a letter from Mr. Bennet the day before yesterday, and I felt that, in light of your courtship with Elizabeth, you should know what it contains before you leave for Longbourn. I would not want you to be blindsided. It concerns my sister, Elizabeth's mother. I understand Elizabeth has told you a little about her."

"She has."

"There is no excuse for a mother who behaves that way to her own child. We have exhausted every recourse in trying to correct Franny's behavior but to no avail. She continues to insult and belittle Elizabeth at every opportunity. Elizabeth has spent the last nine years of her life hearing how she is not good enough, not pretty enough, not smart enough, and not worthy enough. I have watched her blossom as an oasis in a desert, bringing life to everyone around her. I know I am not her father, but I am the next closest thing."

Mr. Darcy had an idea of where Mr. Gardiner's conversation was headed and began to feel slightly uncomfortable. "I assure you my intentions are honorable," he replied.

"Oh no, I have no doubt about that. That is not why I asked to talk to you. Here is the letter I received from Mr. Bennet. Please read it." He offered the folded letter, and Darcy took it.

Was Mr. Bennet refusing the courtship? Did he disapprove of Darcy escorting his daughters back to Hertfordshire? Darcy carefully unfolded the letter and prayed that it would not confirm the fears creeping through his mind.

Dear Mr. Gardiner,

I am glad to hear that things are falling into place and that Saphrinbrooke is beginning to run smoothly. I am glad Elizabeth was able to guide you in the right direction. She has been invaluable to me and, I daresay, invaluable to you as well. However, there is a pressing matter concerning Elizabeth that you need to be aware of, more precisely, that Mr. Darcy needs to be aware of.

At some point before they depart for Hertfordshire, please disclose to Mr. Darcy that I have told Elizabeth's mother nothing about their courtship. I can imagine your jaw dropped to the floor at that revelation, and therefore, I shall explain myself. In no way do I retract my permission for their courtship. However, considering her behavior towards Elizabeth, I felt it prudent to delay communication of their courtship to Mrs. Bennet as long as possible.

Let me state this plainly. Unless Mrs. Bennet hears of the attachment directly from Mr. Darcy, she will never believe it. I am sure you know that Mrs. Bennet fancies Jane to be a much better match for any single, wealthy gentleman, regardless of temperament or compatibility.

If I tell Mrs. Bennet that Elizabeth is being courted, I fear she will be incredulous and treat Elizabeth cruelly. I can imagine all sorts of colorful language coming from her mouth. Perhaps something along the lines of how Elizabeth must have tried to drown her elder sister to secure her own future. You know Mrs. Bennet well enough to understand my concern. But if Darcy is the one to tell her of the courtship, then there can be no doubt. Perhaps she will be humbled enough to stay tight-lipped.

Elizabeth has shared a great deal in her letters about how strongly she feels for Mr. Darcy, and I gather that the feeling is mutual. But you have a much better understanding of their attachment. If Mr. Darcy seems devoted, please ask him to communicate that devotion to Mrs. Bennet at the very first opportunity. Ask him to be as commanding as necessary to silence her comments. I believe a few words from him will silence her on the matter. However, if the courtship is unlikely to continue much longer, it will be better that Mr. Darcy remains silent and Mrs. Bennet remains ignorant. Please use your discretion and arrange things as you see fit.

I know I ask a great deal of both you and Mr. Darcy. But Elizabeth deserves great happiness, and I am willing to try anything to secure it. Mrs. Bennet is determinedly deaf to any positive remark about Elizabeth that originates from either myself or Jane. But if she were to hear admiration from such a handsome, rich, and respected gentleman, perhaps she would finally listen.

I have written my own letter to Elizabeth, informing her that her mother is unaware of the courtship. However, I did not disclose my hope that Mr. Darcy will be able to silence Mrs. Bennet. I do not want Elizabeth to worry any more than necessary. May God be with you in this matter. Your brother,

Thomas Bennet

Darcy folded the letter and handed it back to Mr. Gardiner. "Is Mrs. Bennet really as bad as that?"

Mr. Gardiner took off his glasses and rubbed his nose. "I am afraid so. As much as I love my sister, Franny has never been one to control her tongue."

"Then how will what I do or say make any difference?"

"May I speak plainly?"

"Certainly. Please do."

"You are rumored to make ten thousand a year; that will be more than enough to make a difference. You may have heard that Longbourn is entailed away to Mr. Collins, a distant cousin. My sister worries constantly about what will happen to her when Mr. Bennet dies. She would do anything to secure her financial future. If she is under the impression that your wealth will bring her stability, she will probably find a new favorite daughter."

"Do you mean Miss Elizabeth?"

"Exactly. I feared showing you the letter for a number of reasons, but not because of Mr. Bennet's concerns. He questioned whether your affections were secure enough to elicit your assistance. Correct me if I am wrong, but—"

"You are not wrong. I care very deeply for Miss Elizabeth. I do not know yet how strongly she feels for me, but every time I see her it is a struggle not to propose. But if you knew that, what were your concerns?"

Mr. Gardiner put his glasses back on and turned away from him to pour a bit of brandy. He offered a glass to Mr. Darcy as well but he declined. "At that first dinner, the day you met Elizabeth, I could see you were attracted to my niece. As any near-father relation would, I asked around about you. I found out very little. Wherever I inquired, it was the same story. Generous. Fair landlord. Private. Somewhat prideful and aloof."

Mr. Gardiner sipped his brandy and continued, "You wanted people to respect you. You valued your station in life, and even though the limelight was not always your favorite place to be, you still saw yourself as a man of means. A man who was entitled to anything he desires."

"I am not sure I like the portrait you are painting of me, sir." Darcy tried not to squirm.

"On the contrary. I was speaking of the past. You slowly opened up, and a different man was revealed. Elizabeth does that to people. She encourages honesty of thought and feeling, both mentally and spiritually. You were no exception. My concern is not your level of affection for Elizabeth. My concern is that I cannot tell how deeply she has changed you. Has your core been altered or just the surface? I fear the shock of the Bennets' behavior will shake your newfound admiration for my beloved niece."

"Certainly not. And it cannot be as bad as you say. Miss Elizabeth and Miss Bennet both have excellent manners. Considering how refined they are, I cannot imagine Mrs. Bennet being as poor mannered as all that."

"If only Mrs. Bennet were the only problem," Mr. Gardiner murmured. "Are you really prepared to meet Elizabeth's family? Are you ready to be introduced to her mother, who married into the genteel life and has completely failed to learn proper etiquette? Or how about her sister, Mary, who seems incapable of holding a conversation without criticizing the morality of everyone in the room? What of her two youngest sisters, who are as flirtatious and obnoxious as any girls in England? Are you prepared to witness all of these behaviors and still stand by Elizabeth?"

"Of course I will stand by Elizabeth," Darcy replied. "Mr. Gardiner, surely, you are being too harsh on your relations."

Mr. Gardiner sipped his brandy again. Darcy could see that the man in front of him was worried. "Well, you will be able to judge that for yourself soon enough," Mr. Gardiner replied after a pause. "Come, I have kept you from your journey too long already."

*****

Mr. Darcy took in the scenery. Hertfordshire was beautiful country. As they drove by fields of lavender, their rich scent permeated the air. He looked back at Elizabeth as she squealed in delight. She truly glowed. As they entered Meryton, she began showing Georgiana all the sights.

"That is the bookshop," Elizabeth pointed out. "It is a second home for me. And behind it, that brown, wooden building is the orphanage. If you look over there, you can see the path that leads to the parish church. We go every Sunday and sit in the third row on the left. The reverend, Mr. Peterson, is amazing! After you meet him, you will understand what I mean. He makes you feel like you are the most important person in the whole congregation."

Darcy felt a twinge of unkind feelings towards this reverend. He had hoped he was the only one who made her feel that way. He listened quietly as she continued.

"Do you see that peak to the west? That is Oakham Mount. When I am not helping at the orphanage, one can usually find me walking the path to the top. It is only four miles round trip, and it is such a beautiful view. We must all climb it while you are here." She looked around, and her eyes landed on Mr. Darcy.

Mr. Darcy smiled at her, "You can count on it."

Georgiana giggled, "I suppose I should offer my illustrious chaperoning skills again. Is it strenuous? I enjoy leisurely strolls, not climbs."

Jane said, "Do not fret, Georgiana. It is no more difficult than hiking to the Grecian temple at Pemberley. It just takes a little longer."

Georgiana said, "Oh, what an enjoyable day that was! I am sure Mr. Bingley remembers it well; I do not think he left your side for more than five minutes, Miss Bennet. But of course, he was planning on leaving the next day. Are you looking forward to seeing him again?"

Jane blushed and looked at her hands. "Any time with Mr. Bingley is enjoyable. He is very amiable."

"Now be careful, Georgiana," Mr. Darcy warned. "You must not say things that are not proper. You might as well have asked Jane her feelings for the man. Can you not see she is embarrassed?"

Georgiana put her hand up to her mouth. "Oh dear!" she said. "I am truly sorry! I did not intend to make you uncomfortable!"

Jane reached over and placed her hand on Georgiana's, "It is quite all right. I said nothing that you had not already perceived on your own."

Thick silence engulfed the carriage. After a few minutes, the carriage turned down a drive. Mr. Darcy could see from the excitement in Elizabeth's face that this was home. The house was much smaller than he had imagined. It probably only had two sitting rooms: one for the family and one to receive guests in. It seemed to be in good repair although the corners were slightly weathered. He supposed they probably only needed a handful of servants to make it run smoothly. To be fair, the gardens were nicely kept.

The carriage pulled to a stop, and the footman approached to open the door. But before the door opened, Mr. Darcy heard an abrasive, screeching voice. He looked over to Elizabeth, who had a mortified look on her face. He assumed he was about to meet Mrs. Bennet. He gave Elizabeth's hand a squeeze and exited the carriage.

"Oh, you must be Mr. Darcy of Pemberley! How handsome you are! Just look at those shoulders; one would think you would not fit into a carriage, but I can see from the elegance of the thing that it's very large and comfortable. It always amazes me that a man can be six feet tall but own a small carriage! Why, who would ever do such a thing! But I can see from the wheels alone that this must have cost you a fortune, and it's so stylish! Jane? Jane? Where are you? Mr. Darcy, won't you hand Jane out to me; I miss her terribly. She is everything lovely, is she not?"

He watched her in amazement, jumping from one topic to the next, and when she finally stopped talking, she sucked in a breath and cocked her head in a squirrelly way, obviously waiting for him to comment on Jane. He gave her a silencing look and turned his frame towards the door of the carriage. He reached in specifically for Elizabeth's hand even though she was farther away.

"Miss Elizabeth, welcome home, I believe your mother is here to welcome you." Elizabeth put her tiny hand in his and stepped out of the carriage. Mr. Darcy bowed deeply over her hand and kissed it, pausing to look up at her afterwards before standing up. He turned his attention back to Mrs. Bennet. "Mrs. Bennet, I presume? I must say I thought your gardens were quite picturesque from the road, but now that I see Miss Elizabeth posed so beautifully, I believe they are even lovelier from this view."

"Of course. But where is Jane? I must see her!"

Elizabeth stepped to the side and bowed her head slightly. Mr. Darcy nodded to the driver, who started handing out Miss Bennet and Georgiana.

Mrs. Bennet swatted the driver's arm. "No!" she said. "You mustn't! Let Mr. Darcy hand Jane out!"

The driver looked to Darcy, surprised that he had just been swatted on the arm by a lady. Darcy just nodded for him to continue. Darcy reached again for Elizabeth's hand and tucked it into his arm. In a firm voice, he said, "Mrs. Bennet, please refrain from hitting my driver. I do not look kindly on such behavior. He is perfectly trained to hand out Miss Bennet and my sister." Mrs. Bennet looked at him in confusion as if she had no idea what he was talking about.

Georgiana stepped out first and tried to mask the shock on her face at what she had overheard. She stepped towards her brother, and he offered his other free arm. She sensed a great deal of hostility coming from him. His breathing was deep and rapid, and he was straining to control it.

The driver finally handed Jane out, and Mrs. Bennet flew to her and embraced her dramatically, rocking from side to side. In a low voice, she whispered something to Jane, and Jane flushed deeply.

Jane was well aware of what was happening. She knew Mr. Darcy was not slighting her; he was only trying to show his preference for Elizabeth. Jane whispered back loud enough for all to hear. "Yes, Mamma, it was a very pleasant ride. I sat next to Elizabeth the whole way."

Mrs. Bennet leaned back into her and whispered, "I told you to sit next to him!"

Mr. Darcy struggled not to let his jaw drop open at her lack of manners. "Mrs. Bennet, may I present my sister, Miss Georgiana Darcy. She was first befriended most kindly by Miss Elizabeth, and then by Miss Bennet, but it is Miss Elizabeth's friendship that brings her here to Hertfordshire. Perhaps you would be so good as to invite us in. Miss Elizabeth, allow me to escort you." He looked at Elizabeth. Her head was still bowed slightly, but it did not hide her pain and embarrassment. He felt for her. Her mother had not even spoken to her, not one word.

Elizabeth approached the house with Mr. Darcy and was met at the door by her father, who must have been watching her arrival from his study. "Papa!" She let go of Mr. Darcy to wrap her arms around her father's neck. She stepped back and grinned at her father. "Allow me to introduce Mr. Fitzwilliam Darcy and his sister, Miss Georgiana Darcy. Miss Darcy, Mr. Darcy, this is my father, Mr. Thomas Bennet." The gentlemen bowed. Then Mr. Darcy reached for her arm and tucked it neatly inside his own again.

Mr. Bennet had most definitely seen and heard all that went on in front of the house, and he felt an immediate regard for the man who had so regally shown his preference for Elizabeth. "Mr. Darcy, Miss Darcy, welcome to Longbourn. Jane and Elizabeth have written a great deal about you and your sister. Come in; I will ring for tea and refreshments. I am sure after such long travels that you are in need of a little sustenance. Or would you prefer a drink instead?"

By now Mrs. Bennet had joined the crowd at the door. She literally pushed herself between Mr. Darcy and Elizabeth, breaking the connection.

Elizabeth caught the warning look in her mother's eye and did not miss the hiss of dissatisfaction as she whispered, "Watch it, young lady! You had better not ruin this for Jane like you always do."

Mr. Darcy had heard it as well. "What does Miss Elizabeth always do? She intrigues me to no end, and I would sorely love to return some of the teasing she has heaped on me. Do tell me, Mrs. Bennet, what does Miss Elizabeth always do?" He moved even closer to Mrs. Bennet and towered over her short but well-rounded body.

"By now you know Elizabeth—"

"I most certainly do."

Mrs. Bennet's eyes narrowed slightly, and she flashed a sharp look to Elizabeth. "Then you know how she is."

Jane murmured quietly, "Mamma, please. Not now."

Mrs. Bennet looked at Jane's embarrassed face and decided quickly that it would do little good to discuss Elizabeth in front of their guests. "Very well," she sighed. "Send Elizabeth for the tea, Jane, dear. She knows how we like it."

Elizabeth blushed in shame, and there was an awkward silence.

"Yes, Lizzy, my love, please ring for tea," Mr. Bennet added. "I am sure Hill is nearly beside herself with excitement to see you again. It would be cruel to keep her waiting any longer." Elizabeth managed a weak smile for her father and nodded, but avoided eye contact with Mr. Darcy and Georgiana.

"Come, Lizzy. Georgiana and I will assist you," Jane offered.

Mr. Darcy carefully watched the three ladies file out of the room together. Jane lovingly took her arm, but Elizabeth's walk had no bounce to it. Her face was dull, and her eyes were dark. He suddenly felt an overwhelming surge of anger at the vulgar woman in front of him who had altered Elizabeth so dramatically in the span of a few minutes.

As soon as they were gone, Mr. Darcy turned hard on his heels and looked down on Mrs. Bennet, giving her his most disdainful look.

She stumbled back a step and invited him to follow her into the parlor. "Please sit down—anywhere you like, Mr. Darcy. A man of your consequence doesn't need to wait for my invitation!" She cocked her head to the side and drummed her fingers against themselves close to her bosom and said, "Do you really make ten thousand a year? For those are the rumors. You certainly carry yourself like a lord. Why aren't you titled?"

It was the most abrupt and abrasive inquiry to his wealth and status he had ever been confronted with. He grasped his hands behind his back and walked to the fireplace. He then stood there for a moment and pretended to brush some dust off the mantel. He flashed a look at Mrs. Bennet who had followed him, obviously hungry for the financial details.

"Mrs. Bennet, if I may be clear about something, let it be this. I am a man who is used to getting his way. A man who makes *more* than ten thousand a year does not like to be told 'no'. A man who runs a household of sixty-two servants is not questioned as to his motives. He is listened to, respected, and honored. Always. Do I make myself clear?"

"More than ten thousand?"

He cleared his throat loudly to silence her. "He is never interrupted, and his words are received and executed with exactness. Do you understand me?" She nodded silently.

"Good. Now understand these next words: I am in love with your daughter, Elizabeth. Not your eldest daughter; Elizabeth. I am in love with Elizabeth. And seeing as I usually get my way, I intend on marrying her. I will not—and I repeat—I will *not* allow you to say or do anything that defames, belittles, disparages, demeans, or criticizes my future wife in any way. Not one word, not one look, not one gesture will be tolerated. You will speak respectfully to her regardless of whether or not I am present. She is the most important thing in my life. Do I make myself clear?"

"Surely you mean Jane—"

He took two quick steps in her direction and stood as closely as he dared without actually touching her. "I believe my words were quite clear, Mrs. Bennet." He then turned and walked towards the silent Mr. Bennet. "Miss Elizabeth mentioned you fancy French brandy. I collect the stuff myself," he said.

Mr. Bennet smiled and gestured with his arm to his study, "I shall retrieve the best I have. Please, come to my study."

*****

That night at Netherfield, Darcy related the experience to Bingley. "It was horrid, Bingley! I have never witnessed such vulgar, poor manners in all my life! I have seen stable hands deliver calves with more finesse!" Mr. Darcy exclaimed.

Bingley took his mark on the pool table and scattered the balls in different directions. "And what did Mr. Bennet do during all this?"

"He just stood there. Afterwards, in his study, he could not stop praising me on what a fine job I did. I do not know what to make of it. I suppose I should be glad to have earned his respect, but the distaste in my mouth after speaking so harshly to a lady, his own wife, was very unpleasant."

"Then why did you do it?"

Darcy walked around to the other side of the table and aimed. "For Elizabeth," he said. He took his shot and hit the ball hard into the pocket.

"Has she given you permission to call her Elizabeth?" Bingley asked with a grin. Darcy jumped and missed his next shot.

"No. I think I slipped up today in front of her mother and father."

Bingley leaned over and balanced his weight evenly and shot, making the intended mark. "I suppose it does not matter; you will be engaged soon anyway. When are you planning on proposing?"

"I must admit I am a little hesitant after today. Her younger sisters arrived home soon after, and they were as uncouth as they come. The youngest, not a day older than Georgiana, hung on me as if I were her personal bodyguard. She flirted mercilessly, and when I shook her off the third time, she had the gall to tell me how boring I was! Must I declare my feelings for Elizabeth to everyone in the household before they will behave appropriately? I do not like using such a heavy hand."

Bingley missed his ball and stood upright and said, "Perhaps it is just the mother and the youngest. What was her name?"

"Miss Lydia. She was dressed so risqué that I was ashamed for her. She had fashioned her afternoon dress like a ball gown and had more bosom showing than hidden! And no, it was not just the youngest. I was accosted by Miss Mary regarding the proper use of riches and the plague of pride that wealth brings. I must have been lectured for over twenty minutes before Miss Bennet suggested Miss Mary play the pianoforte. If I had known how poorly she played and sang, I would have welcomed more lectures!" Darcy realized it was his turn and carelessly shot, nearly missing the target completely. "Your turn," he grumbled.

Bingley looked at the disheveled Darcy and eyed him suspiciously. "You never answered my question. When are you going to propose? Or has the family repulsed you so thoroughly that you cannot feel anything but disgust?" Darcy shot him a warning look. Bingley bent over and took two more shots but missed the third. "I only speak plainly. From the sounds of your ranting, it would seem you are rethinking your intentions to Miss Elizabeth."

"Of course not, but I will say one more thing. Her father and Miss Bennet will be welcome at Pemberley, but I will never allow the rest of them to set one foot on my grounds!" Darcy shot and put the ball into the center pocket.

"Wrong move, Darcy."

"What do you mean? I sunk the ball."

"You cannot shun her family and expect to earn her regard, my friend."

"I suppose you are correct." Just then Darcy and Bingley heard the sound of chiffon skirts rustling outside the door. "Did you hear that?" Darcy asked.

"Probably just one of the maids," Bingley said with a shrug.

CHAPTER 10

"Jane, he may very well be headed back to Pemberley! Our family was at their worst!"

"I am sure he is not going anywhere," Jane reassured her. She tried to mask her concern, but, in all honesty, the evening had not gone well. Not only had Lydia practically thrown herself at Mr. Darcy, but Mary had lectured him severely on the pride of the wealthy. Thankfully, Mrs. Bennet had remained silent. All night, she had looked at Mr. Darcy as if he scared her.

"When Mary started singing, I could see it in his eyes: Elizabeth is not worth all this." Elizabeth tucked her feet under her and looked out at the rain dribbling down the windowpane. She felt as if her heart were leaking tears, one single drop at a time. She placed her hand on the glass and felt the coolness of the weather outside.

Jane took her other hand. "No, Elizabeth, he still loves you. You must not listen to your doubts. When I look in his eyes, I see only his deep love for you. Can you not see it too?"

She nodded. "Yes, but the 'Mr. Darcy mask' was there again. When I asked him if he was well, his face went blank and he simply nodded. I do not think he trusted himself to even look me in the eye."

"What happened when you accompanied him to the carriage?"

"He simply said, 'Miss Elizabeth, I shall see you tomorrow at church. Third row on the left, correct?' Then he kissed my hand, squeezed it briefly, and left."

"What did his eyes show?"

"Compassion, I suppose. And sympathy."

"Then trust in that. He knows how hard the night was for you."

*****

The next morning, Mr. Darcy was early to church for two reasons: to obtain a seat by Elizabeth; and to see who this Mr. Peterson was. In his first purpose, he was successful, securing a seat in the third row. In his second purpose, he was somewhat disappointed. The reverend was a handsome, young man in his late twenties. Darcy had been hoping to find an elderly, bald man in his sixties or seventies; he immediately distrusted him. Mr. Peterson smiled too much too. He was not very tall. And his dark blonde hair was trimmed too short.

But as the clergyman eagerly introduced himself, Darcy's misgivings began to soften. "Welcome, Mr. Darcy! You must be the lucky gentleman who is visiting Mr. Bingley," Mr. Peterson said. "He is the finest fellow I have ever met. And he tells me you are courting Miss Elizabeth Bennet! If I had not taken an oath of celibacy, I might have considered pursuing her myself."

Mr. Darcy felt a wave of relief. "Vow of celibacy?" he asked. "I thought only monks did that."

"It is uncommon for a priest, but I consider it a higher calling. If I focus on the parish, I believe I am more productive and more effective in my work. And I cannot think of anything more important than serving God's children. If God were on the earth today, he would be doing the same: healing the sick, administering to the needy, and sharing his love," Mr. Peterson said.

"Mr. Bennet has told me a little about you," the clergyman continued. "Of course, I cannot disclose all that he said; I must keep parishioners' confidences, you know," he chuckled. "Now that Mr. Bennet is no longer a reverend, he gossips like an old woman. Nevertheless, I respect you a great deal if what he says is correct."

Yes, he definitely liked the reverend. "I would not believe all you hear," Mr. Darcy said. "I suspect Mr. Bennet was informed by his daughter, so his opinion may be somewhat biased."

"And so what if it is? Any man would call himself lucky to be admired by such a fine lady."

"I cannot agree with you more. Is this the pew where the Bennets sit?" Darcy asked with a sincere smile. The man was no threat, even if he did recognize Elizabeth's exceptionally rare value.

"Indeed it is. Now if you will excuse me, I see Mr. and Mrs. Chester. I promised them an answer to their question from the other day." Mr. Peterson bowed, then turned and left.

Darcy took a seat at the end of the row, farthest from the aisle, so he could watch the door for Elizabeth. He sat there for many moments, watching Mr. Peterson move from family to family, always with something kind and deeply personal to say, always encouraging and motivating. He really did make everyone feel like they were the most important person in the congregation. Mr. Darcy vowed to be more like him, to not withhold his good opinion from others. The organist started the prelude music, and he sat back, enjoying the hymns while keeping an eye out for Elizabeth.

*****

Miss Bingley had also come early to church for two reasons. She had heard that the reverend was handsome, and she was never one to miss the opportunity to admire a handsome face even though she had her heart set on Mr. Darcy. Her second reason was the same as Darcy's: she was there to see Elizabeth. She was not disappointed. Instead of arriving by carriage, Miss Bingley was humored to see the whole Bennet family arriving on foot. They must have walked from Longbourn. She smirked and then put on a concerned face and approached Elizabeth.

"Miss Elizabeth, may I have a word? It is very important, and it will only take a moment."

Elizabeth did not trust Miss Bingley for one moment, but she was in a pleasant mood; she was going to sit next to Mr. Darcy during church. While they were in Derbyshire, she and Jane had gone to the Lambton chapel with Mr. and Mrs. Gardiner and Mr. Darcy had always attended the Kympton services. It would be nice to share a pew and hear his smooth voice singing her favorite hymns. She turned to Jane and saw the concerned look on her face. Elizabeth said, "Would you let Mr. Darcy know I will be in soon?"

Jane smiled weakly and said, "Of course." An ominous feeling crept up inside Jane. When she glanced over her shoulder, she saw a self-important and conniving look on Miss Bingley's face.

Elizabeth turned back to Miss Bingley and said, "What is it, Miss Bingley?"

"Oh, call me Caroline, Eliza! We became so close while I was at Pemberley." Miss Bingley took Elizabeth's elbow and guided her over to a maple tree. In a low whisper she said, "And as a close friend, I feel it necessary to warn you so that you may brace yourself for the disappointment."

"I do not know what you mean. What do you have to warn me about?" Elizabeth had only the slightest tingle of fear. She understood the kind of person Miss Bingley was. She knew she liked to gossip and shock people with her rumors.

"I know we have little time, so I will get right to the point. I overheard Mr. Darcy tell my brother some very disturbing tales about your family last night. I am afraid he did not have favorable opinions of them. So much so that he is having second thoughts about . . ."

Elizabeth held her breath and waited for her heart to drop like a glass chandelier falling from the ceiling.

Miss Bingley gave Elizabeth's arm a squeeze in mock sympathy. "You did not really think he would marry you, did you?

I do hope your heart was not touched. Oh dear, I can see that you truly are disappointed! Perhaps it is not so bad. Perhaps he still intends to marry you and will just divide you from your family. I did hear him say at least Jane and your father might be allowed to visit Pemberley." Miss Bingley paused and tried not to smile at the look of despair on Elizabeth's face.

"Oh, Eliza! You poor thing!" she continued in an overly dramatic tone. "If there is *anything* I can do, just say the word. I cannot say that I look forward to meeting your mother and younger sisters, but you can be assured that I will be much less fickle-hearted than Mr. Darcy. Once a friend, always a friend. That is what people always say about me. Please forgive me for distressing you. I just thought you should know so you can prepare for the time when he breaks off the courtship.

"A man like Mr. Darcy could never actually align himself with such a family. I only wish you would have recognized the truth earlier; it would have saved you a great deal of heartache. Oh look, there is Louisa! I promised to sit with her. I will see you after the services. Ta ta!" Miss Bingley sauntered over to her sister and gave her a slight, satisfied nod of the head. They exchanged smirks and entered the chapel together.

Elizabeth finally let out her breath. Was he really considering breaking off the courtship? Did he really say that only Jane and her father would be allowed to visit Pemberley? Her first feelings were shock and fear, but they quickly changed to sadness and resignation. She was a country girl with no connections and had little to offer a man like Mr. Darcy. She had no fortune, no status, nothing that could improve his rank in society. She was a nobody. Just like her mother had always said.

Pain seeped into every pore of her body, and she felt the need to return home immediately. She heard bells chime from the steeple, indicating that she only had a few moments to decide before the service would begin. As she considered the cowardly prospect of running home, she heard Mr. Darcy's deep voice from behind her.

"Miss Elizabeth, are you well? You look a little pale," Mr. Darcy said. She looked more than a little pale; she looked like she would empty the contents of her stomach at any moment.

His voice was so deep and concerned, and his eyes looked so kind. She selfishly decided that if he was going to end the courtship, she would make him wait until after the church service. She wanted to have one last good memory with him. "It is only a little chill. I feel much better now." She clasped her hands in front of her and tried to smile.

Her radiance was lurking beneath a cloudy haze, and he could not fathom why. He offered his arm and tried to tease her, "I have been looking forward to this for some time, you know. Miss Bennet has saved our seats, but if we do not hurry, I worry she might give them away to more-devoted patrons."

She took his arm and firmly told herself to enjoy the next hour, for it would likely be their last. But her resolve was low. "No, Jane, at least is loyal," she murmured.

Mr. Darcy felt confused for a moment. Elizabeth was usually very open, but her words seemed laced with hidden meaning. Loyal? What did she mean? He looked at her for an explanation, but her eyes were determinedly fixed ahead.

He escorted Elizabeth down the aisle and motioned for her to take the seat next to Miss Bennet. She did so silently, with her head bowed slightly, and he sat in the aisle seat next to her. Mr. Peterson was still making his rounds towards the front and getting ready to begin the services. Mr. Darcy took the moment to whisper to Elizabeth, "You look as if you received some distressing news. Is there anything I can help you with?"

She felt the intimacy of his low baritone voice in her ear, and her eyes filled with emotion. It hurt to know that all their stolen looks, escorted walks, and wonderful moments—that it would all end soon. She realized she had not answered him, so she briefly looked at him and shook her head. There was little he could help her with.

She once again tried to shake off her sadness. She wanted to enjoy the moment she had been anticipating. At least for now, he appeared to care for her. The truth of it was she knew he cared. She knew he loved her, but he could not endure her family. She always knew she would be censored for their lack of decorum. But it was still so disappointing; she had believed Mr. Darcy was better than that. She had believed he was one who would not turn away love for the sake of fortune or connections.

She reminded herself that all men are inherently good. Mr. Darcy was a good man, and all his actions up to this point proved it. One moment of brutal honesty from Miss Bingley was not going to change how she felt about him. She would always love him. She slipped her arm into his and leaned into him. In return, he gave her his devilishly handsome, dimpled smile. That was enough to lighten her heart. The organist began playing and the congregation stood to sing.

Be still, my soul; the Lord is on thy side;
Bear patiently the cross of grief or pain.
Leave to thy God to order and provide;
In every change, He faithful will remain.

Yes, she would leave it to God to heal her broken heart. She continued to sing.

Be still, my soul; thy best, heavenly Friend
Through thorny ways leads to a joyful end.

Oh, how she hoped for a joyful end! Even though she was losing Mr. Darcy, she trusted God would guide her back to joy. She truly loved the hope and peace this song brought. She could feel her heart gaining control.

Mr. Darcy listened to Elizabeth's sweet soprano voice and was shocked that he had never heard her sing before. How could she have hidden such a talent from him all these months? He had heard her play the piano many times, but she had never offered to sing. But perhaps that was because Miss Bingley tended to monopolize the evening whenever anyone asked for music. He sung a little softer just so he could hear her pleasant, melodic tones.

She sang the song as if she were sharing her own personal thoughts, and it was more moving than any professional performance he had ever heard at the opera. She had the subtlest vibrato as she hung onto the notes; it was remarkably feminine and tender. It pierced his very soul. He glanced at her and saw her smiling, shining eyes. She was glowing again. Whatever was wrong before was now right. He turned his attention back to the song and tried to master the words and notes, but he was quite distracted by her beautiful performance. He lifted his voice and sang.

> *Be still my soul; thy God doth undertake*
> *To guide the future as He has the past.*

Darcy was pleased by the thought. He very much wanted God to guide his future, a future with Elizabeth.

> *Thy hope, thy confidence, let nothing shake;*
> *All now mysterious shall be bright at last.*
> *Be still, my soul: the waves and winds still know*
> *His voice who ruled them while He dwelt below.*

Elizabeth's arm was interlaced with Mr. Darcy's, and she could feel the vibrations of his chest as his deep baritone voice echoed softly through the crowd. She took courage in this moment. Whatever was to come, she would find peace. God wanted her to be happy, and if being with Mr. Darcy was not in God's plans for her, then she would accept it.

Be still, my soul; the hour is hastening on

She took a deep breath as she sang, knowing that this could very well be the last hour she would have with him.

When we shall be forever with the Lord,
When disappointment, grief, and fear are gone,
Sorrow forgot, love's purest joys restored.

She had always loved this song, but the words meant so much more now. They echoed her thoughts and feelings. She would need to stretch her faith to survive this. And perhaps Miss Bingley was mistaken. Perhaps love's purest joys would be restored. She felt a burning in her bosom at the thought. With all the passion she felt at that moment, she sang the last lines.

Be still, my soul; when change and tears are past,
All safe and blessed we shall meet at last."[1]

A single tear fell from her eye. As she reached for her handkerchief, Mr. Darcy was already offering his. She looked into his eyes and saw deep love and concern and admiration all at once. Never had she been so physically moved by a simple look from a man. *Be still, my soul*, she thought, and she sat down with the congregation.

The service was beautiful. Mr. Peterson spoke of accepting the good with the bad, for life brings both light and darkness. He reminded them to look for things that cheer the heart, even when one is sad, and to remember all that God has given us. He

---

[1] "Be Still, My Soul" by Katharina von Schlegel, translated by Jane Borthwick

explained that time is like a river; you can never touch the same water twice because the flow that has passed will never pass by again. He encouraged them to enjoy each moment in life, for there will never be another moment like it. Elizabeth held tightly to Mr. Darcy's arm and cherished the moment, knowing that the moment may very well be her last.

Mr. Darcy was especially moved by the wise words of the reverend. He imagined how different his life would be if he had not called on Mr. Gardiner that day and been introduced to Elizabeth. The opportunity would have passed him by. He stole glances at the owner of his heart throughout the sermon and gave numerous prayers of gratitude for earning her admiration.

When the sermon ended, Mr. Darcy bowed his head for the prayer and stole a glance at Elizabeth. She had tears in her eyes again. He wondered what was bothering her. Had her mother said something to upset her?

He decided that the only thing to do was to make the engagement official. That would silence her mother once and for all. He felt slightly elated by the thought, and, on impulse, he made the most important decision of his life: he would ask Elizabeth to become his wife.

When the prayer was over, he said, "Miss Elizabeth, may I call on you tomorrow? I have something of great importance to discuss." Now that he had decided to propose, he was incredibly nervous. What would he say? Would she accept him? What if she said no?

Elizabeth turned to him. His eyes held kindness, but there was an element of deep worry as well. Her fears were confirmed. Miss Bingley was right; he wanted to end the courtship. "If that is what you wish." He gave her an apprehensive look and then exited into the aisle. She took the opportunity to depart from his presence as fast as her legs could take her. She was only a few feet away when she saw Miss Bingley smiling at her with false compassion.

Mr. Darcy stood in the aisle and watched Elizabeth walk away. Her words, her body language, and her hasty departure confused him. He didn't know what to make of it. He was considering going after her when Miss Bennet addressed him.

"Mr. Darcy, do you know what is bothering Elizabeth?" she asked.

"No. I have no idea."

"Nor I," Jane replied. She considered telling Darcy about her suspicions about Caroline but hesitated to accuse Bingley's sister. "But try not to worry," Jane reassured him. "She loves you. I will find out what is troubling her and make sure she is at Longbourn tomorrow for your visit."

Mr. Darcy acknowledged her comforting words and turned to watch the lady he loved exit the chapel doors with her head low. He could see her wipe her face as she weaved through the crowd. "Miss Bennet, I will depend on your assistance. My very happiness just left without even a goodbye."

CHAPTER 11

With trepidation, Mr. Darcy tapped the doorknocker at Longbourn. Bingley, nearly giddy, stood at his side. The servant took their names and showed them to the parlor. Darcy's eyes naturally searched for Elizabeth; he found everyone but her.

Mrs. Bennet was not easily deflected and still had plans for Jane and Mr. Darcy. But all that vanished when she saw the handsome gentleman standing beside Mr. Darcy turn to mush in front of Jane. She quickly evaluated his attire and manners and sensed that he must be Mr. Bingley. It was rumored he earned five thousand a year! She immediately went to work.

"Welcome back, Mr. Darcy. And you must be Mr. Bingley! Jane has told me such nice things about you," Mrs. Bennet said.

Jane blushed and whispered, "Mamma, please." She then turned to greet the two gentlemen. Darcy bowed slightly, and Mr. Bingley took the opportunity to kiss her hand. Jane noticed that Mr. Darcy was quite distracted. Obviously, he was looking for Elizabeth.

"Mr. Darcy," she said, "Elizabeth has not yet returned from the orphanage, but she should be here soon." She then walked over to him and whispered, "She received some disappointing news before church. I am sure there is some mistake, but she needs to hear the truth of the matter from you. She is strong, but even she has her limits."

Darcy could sense that something was terribly wrong. He thought of her tears at church and how her glow had wavered.

What could he do to help her? He remembered the advice Elizabeth had given him about Georgiana. *She needs your unconditional love.* That was what Elizabeth needed from him right now. Darcy would not let the opportunity pass him by. "Mrs. Bennet, would you permit me to escort Miss Elizabeth home from the orphanage?" he asked.

"Oh, that chit! Not even here when gentlemen callers come! I swear you could sell her a useless Chinese paper lantern if you told her it had no parents. I am always apologizing for that girl. So distracted! So stubborn! So—"

Darcy took an intimidating step towards Mrs. Bennet. "So humble," he interrupted. "So charitable. So selfless. That was what you were going to say, was it not?" He flashed her a warning look.

Mrs. Bennet sucked in her breath and fumbled her hands. "Of course. That was exactly what I was going to say. Please, go and fetch her. Lord knows she has been there long enough. It is about time she learned not to run off when her suitor is here."

Mr. Darcy gave her one more warning look. He was grieved at the disdain he felt for the woman whom Elizabeth called mother.

As he was leaving, Jane called out that the children were fond of sweets from the shop on Market Street. He nodded and left immediately. The ride was a quick one, and just a mile later he came across the sweetshop and bought several pocketsful. A few streets later, he found the alley Elizabeth had pointed out and saw a brown structure that could only be the orphanage.

The building was old, and there were cracks in a few of the windows. The swing on the porch had a broken chain, leaving it unusable. He investigated further and found that the trouble was simply a link bent out of place. He retrieved a set of pliers from his saddlebag and set about fixing the chain.

He could hear Elizabeth inside, laughing and giggling with the children. As he finished working on the swing, she started telling a story. He could tell she was creating it from her imagination. It was about a girl with a golden harp. He gingerly sat down on the swing to see if it would hold his weight. He sat there listening to her beautiful voice, and he let it seep into his soul.

She was at home with these children, as she probably would be with any child. He let his mind wander, and soon, he was imagining her reading to their children. She would kneel by their beds, tuck stray hairs behind ears, and tell them Bible stories and tales of princesses and heroes. He closed his eyes and gently swung back and forth until he felt the porch swing jostle from someone sitting down next to him.

"Good morning, Mr. Darcy." Elizabeth said. She caught his eyes briefly before she turned away shyly; the look of desire was in his eyes again. There was no denying that he was happy to see her. It helped to know that. It would make it easier to handle her heartache when he broke off the courtship.

"Elizabeth," he whispered. He reached over and put his hand on hers. "Forgive me, I did not mean to use your Christian name. I realize you have not given me permission."

"I suppose I must forgive you, Mr. Darcy, or God will not forgive me of my own sins," she said lightly. She told herself that she had been through a great deal in her short life and was strong enough to handle the disappointment. Never had she loved as deeply, but that did not mean her heart would not heal.

"I cannot imagine you have any sins. But if you do not mind, I would like you to call me Fitzwilliam or William when we are alone."

Elizabeth looked at Mr. Darcy and wondered why he would say such a thing. "Mr. Darcy . . ." She couldn't think coherently enough to finish her question.

Seeing her hesitation, he gently corrected her. "Please, call me William."

She swallowed hard and knew she could not dance around the issue. "William, why would you wish me to address you so informally when you are planning to break off the courtship?"

Shock. Fear. Confusion. They all hit him at the same time. "Why would I do that?"

"Miss Bingley said—"

"Stop right there. Whatever Miss Bingley said has no merit on you and me. I assure you, I am committed to you more than ever."

Relief. Joy. Happiness. They all hit her at the same time. Right there on the porch swing, she flung her arms around his neck and embraced him. Her tears started falling, and he wrapped his arms around her lovingly. He caressed her back and shoulders and kissed her hair a few times. Soon, she heard all the children inside giggling and making kissing noises, and she pulled away.

She turned to the window and said, "Children, I believe you have some reading to do!" Groans and moans erupted, but she giggled and shooed them away from the window. She turned back to Mr. Darcy and smiled at him.

It was heavenly to hold her and give her comfort like that. Her arms fit around his neck like they belonged there. He wanted so badly to kiss her tender lips. *I need a distraction*, he thought. "Could I come inside and meet the children? Then perhaps I can walk you home, and we can further discuss what Miss Bingley does *not* know."

She smiled wider. "That sounds like a fine plan." She led him inside and introduced him to the orphaned children. She could see he was a little uncomfortable at first, but soon he was kneeling beside them and pulling sweets from behind their ears by magic. He had on his dimpled smile for them, and it had an immediate effect on Sarah.

Sarah walked her twelve-year old body over to Mr. Darcy and curtsied to him. Mr. Darcy stood and bowed to her and complimented her on her form. When Sarah did not respond, Mr. Darcy gave Elizabeth a questioning look.

Elizabeth explained, "This is Sarah. She is deaf. But she has excellent instincts about people."

"I see." He then turned back to Sarah. He took her hand and bowed over it and gave it a small kiss. When he stood up, he smiled at her and saw the faintest of blushes on her cheeks. "Sometimes one does not need words, Sarah." She smiled and flitted away like a fairy. He noticed that her dress hem had been let out several times, and he made a mental note to make sure she had a new dress, one that would be less childlike. Elizabeth introduced him to several other children, each eager to get a sweet. He noticed a few other needs and made a mental note of each one.

"That is all of the children, Mr. Darcy. Shall we head back to Longbourn?" The children shouted their displeasure with the plan, and Elizabeth hugged all of them and promised to be back tomorrow.

Mr. Darcy did not think he could see Elizabeth glow any more than she was glowing at that very moment. She was bursting with radiance. It was in her smile, her walk, her gaze, her very speech. He did not know how someone's speech could reflect light, but Elizabeth's did. He was bursting inside from absorbing it. He retrieved his horse, leading him on foot, and wrapped Elizabeth's hand around his arm. Together they started walking to Longbourn. After a brief moment of silence, he asked, "So, what exactly did Miss Bingley say?"

"I am sorry. I should not have listened to her. I should have trusted you, but I was so scared. She said that you were going to end the courtship because of my family. Apparently, she heard you telling Bingley that you would never allow my mother or my younger sisters to visit Pemberley. She said I was foolish to believe you would really marry a lady from a simple country family with no connections."

Darcy felt the color drain from his face. The rustling skirt he had heard while playing billiards with Bingley—it had been Miss Bingley listening at the door. "I must admit that she was not entirely baseless. I was more than a little shocked by your mother's behavior, and I struggled with Miss Mary and Miss Lydia."

"Actually, my mother was on her best behavior. I was stunned by her silence. She not belittle me nor ignore me. Did you have something to do with it?"

"Let us just say I can be very influential when I need to be. But I must apologize. I did say some unkind things about your sisters. In my defense, I was simply expressing my shock and amazement that you and Miss Bennet could behave so admirably when the rest of the family was so strikingly . . ."

"Anyone not used to them would have some strong opinions about them."

"Perhaps, but I should not have voiced them to Bingley. I think you are letting me off the hook a little too easily. I have tried to be a man you would be proud to call husband. I have been reading the Bible and praying. I have tried to live up to my father's reputation. I understand now that life's difficulties can improve us, and I am trying to be grateful for my trials. I really am."

"I know, William. And you should not be so hard on yourself. You were already quite wonderful before you started doing all those things. I am the one who should be trying to live up to the title of Mr. Darcy's wife."

Hearing her say his given name was like chocolate melting in his mouth. He was overcome with emotion. But when she so casually mentioned becoming his wife, he literally felt weak in the knees. Was now the right time?

He looked over at her beautiful face. He so desperately wanted to share his excitement with her, to ask her to share the rest of his life with him. But he had not solved the mystery of Malachi 3:3 yet, and there were still many things they needed to discuss. Deep inside, he knew it was not the right time to propose, but he would burst if he didn't tell her what he was feeling.

He stopped walking, wrapped the leads of the horse around a tree, and then reached for both of her hands. "It warms my heart to know you are considering marrying me," he said. "I love you, Elizabeth. I still have some matters to work out, but I fully intend on offering you all I own when the time is right. Please know my intentions are one hundred percent vested in you. There is nothing I want more than to see you telling your story about the girl with the golden harp to our children."

Elizabeth looked up at him and saw his eyes expressing all he had said. "Then I shall look forward to the day when you have worked things out, and when the time is right, I will be waiting."

"Every moment I spend with you feels like the right time, but I know a man must consider the feelings of the lady as well."

"If you have any doubt about my feelings, you can work that thought out of your head right now. I do not know a better man, and I do not think I could ever give my heart more fully. I love you too, William."

"Say it again."

"Which part?"

"All of it."

"I love you."

"I love you too."

"And, William?"

"Yes?"

"You can call me Elizabeth."

"I love you, Elizabeth."

*****

The next day, Bingley faced the task of dealing with his sister. "Caroline, there will be no argument on the issue. You will apologize to Miss Elizabeth and Mr. Darcy, and you will do it today."

Miss Bingley looked to Mr. Darcy and briefly preened herself before purring in her most feminine voice possible, "Mr. Darcy, I am truly sorry that I overheard your opinions about the Bennets. It was not my intent to eavesdrop. You must know I would never intentionally harm you."

Mr. Darcy tried not to roll his eyes at her ridiculous apology. "Whether or not you intended harm, you certainly inflicted it."

"Well, I am truly sorry for any difficulty I might have caused you," Miss Bingley said, batting her eyelashes. She looked away from Mr. Darcy and addressed her brother, her tone markedly different. "Charles, I owe nothing to Eliza. All I did was tell her the truth of what I heard. And you cannot make me apologize for being honest. I truly felt she was in danger of getting her heart broken."

Bingley stood up and walked over to his sister. "The only one endangering her heart was you, Caroline. You will apologize, or you will not be welcome in my house. If I must, I will send you to visit Aunt Martha."

She laughed. "To the middle of nowhere in the Yorkshire moors? You would not dare. Besides, you could never run this estate without me. We both know that. Be serious, Charles."

"I am being quite serious, Caroline. You will apologize, and you will do it today. We will be leaving for Longbourn at ten o'clock. I expect you to be in the carriage at quarter to ten." Caroline scoffed. "Aunt Martha has written me many times asking whether I can spare you," Bingley continued. "I imagine the solitude is quite dreary for her, and she would so enjoy your company. Besides, you always exclaim how fond you are of the North when we visit Pemberley."

Miss Bingley scowled at her brother and then mockingly said, "Such a gentleman! I suppose if Miss Bennet likes that sort of thing, you need not be worried."

"What is that supposed to mean?" Bingley said.

"Only that sooner or later Miss Bennet will see how heartlessly you treat your single, younger sister. She might be persuaded that you will treat your wife in a similar manner. She may not have the wit that Eliza does, but Jane is still quite intelligent. I suggest you rethink your threat."

Mr. Darcy had enough of her catty snobbishness. "Miss Bingley, I agree wholeheartedly with you," he said.

"See, Charles, Mr. Darcy agrees with—"

"Please allow me to finish," Mr. Darcy interrupted. "I agree that Miss Bennet does not have Miss Elizabeth's wit. However, she is far more observant than most people realize. When she learned of your attempt to ruin the happiness of her favorite sister, as doubtlessly Miss Elizabeth has already confided in her, I suspect it put a quick end to any natural regard she may have felt for you as a potential sister-in-law. I doubt she will feel any pity as you are auctioned off to the first widower in need of a mother for his five spoiled children."

"In fact," Darcy continued over her shrieks, "I know just the man. I believe you met him at Pemberley's ball. Mr. Harwood was his name. You must remember him; you laughed that his jacket was too tight and his breeches were too loose. But that was probably because of his rounded abdomen. He shared a story about the mating rituals of his sheep. You know the man of whom I speak, do you not?"

Miss Bingley stood and walked past the two gentlemen with her nose in the air. "I will be in the carriage at nine forty-five sharp," she announced. "Do not make me wait for you."

*****

Mr. Bennet met the group at the door. "Good morning, gentlemen. Who might this lovely lady be?"

Mr. Bingley introduced his sister. Miss Bingley was cordial, but Mr. Bennet could see that she had no desire to be there. "Welcome to Longbourn, Miss Bingley. My eldest daughters are in the sitting room with some guests and would love to entertain you and Mr. Bingley. However, Mr. Darcy and I are overdue for a chat."

Mr. Darcy did not know which chat they were overdue for, but he was glad for an excuse to extricate himself from Miss Bingley's presence. "I shall be delighted. Bingley, will you inform Miss Elizabeth of where I am?"

Bingley agreed, "Absolutely."

Mr. Darcy followed Mr. Bennet into his study and took a seat in front of the desk. Mr. Bennet sat down behind the desk. "Should I be nervous, Mr. Bennet?"

"Is there a reason to be nervous, Mr. Darcy?" Mr. Bennet grinned mischievously at him.

"Not that I am aware of." Darcy tried not to squirm.

Mr. Bennet laughed and smiled. "Do not worry," he said. "I am simply checking in with you about the courtship. How are things going?"

Mr. Darcy was suddenly reminded of their embrace on the porch swing and him kissing Elizabeth's hair. "There was a small difficulty on Sunday, but we have worked through it. She has a very forgiving nature. I believe she said she learned it from you."

"I cannot claim to be the original source, but I did try to teach her well. Forgive, but never forget. I taught her to learn from her mistakes but not to regret them."

"That is wise counsel. I can see where she gets her supply of thought-provoking comments." Mr. Darcy sat in silence for what seemed like several minutes waiting for Mr. Bennet to begin. Mr. Bennet just looked at him with a half-smile on his face. Mr. Darcy finally broke the silence. "I have a very high regard for Miss Elizabeth. I assure you my intentions are honorable."

Mr. Bennet raised an eyebrow at him. "The road to hell is paved with good intentions."

"Pardon me?"

"Intentions and actions are two different things. If you intend to do something, it means you have not done it yet. One can have all the good intentions in the world but still do nothing of importance."

Mr. Darcy was beginning to see where the conversation was going. "If you are inquiring whether I plan to ask for Miss Elizabeth's hand, I do. I am trying to resolve a few personal questions first."

"And what questions are those? I might be able to help."

Mr. Darcy watched Mr. Bennet change from the role of Elizabeth's father to retired reverend in the blink of an eye. The man was ready to listen without judgment. Mr. Darcy began to tell him about Elizabeth's "no comment" questions and their discussion about Malachi 3:3. Mr. Darcy also explained the research he had done since then, including his discussion with Mr. Walker and the letter to the mine owner. Mr. Bennet nodded his head a few times and leaned back into his chair.

"So, I gather you are not satisfied with the answers you received from these gentlemen." Mr. Bennet said.

"No, neither one could describe the refining process of silver."

"What do you plan to do?"

"I was hoping to find a blacksmith in Meryton. Perhaps he would let me watch the purifying process."

"I think that is a fine idea. I know just the blacksmith. His name is James Rogers. His workshop is on the corner of Market Street and Hampton Avenue. If you feel this will give you your answer, I suggest you visit him."

"Do you think it will give me my answer?"

"As long as you keep asking questions, God will provide the answers."

"Wise counsel, Mr. Bennet. Thank you."

"Now, is there anything else you wish to speak with me about?"

"Actually, there is." Mr. Darcy hesitated. "I know you value honesty," he said, "and I wish to ask you a somewhat impertinent question. Miss Elizabeth told me you were once a man of cloth. The role of a clergyman requires a great deal of selfless service and a certain amount of finesse."

"Mr. Darcy, perhaps you should just ask your question."

Darcy took a deep breath. "I have been rather shocked by Mrs. Bennet's behavior towards Miss Elizabeth. Pardon my frankness, but why do you let Mrs. Bennet act so? Why did you let Miss Elizabeth suffer all these years?"

Mr. Bennet leaned back in his chair. He paused and took a deep breath. "Let me begin by saying that I tried many times to abate the abuse. I devoted hours, months, years even, to disciplining my wife and trying to alter her behavior. I tried withholding pin money. I tried to guide her by example. I tried correcting each misstep in the very moment it happened. Once, I even tried threatening her. Nothing worked.

"I never gave up. The very fact that I was willing to seek your help in correcting her behavior shows how desperate I am to help Elizabeth. You made more progress in two days than I made in nine years! So, I sincerely and humbly thank you.

"I wish I could change my wife's behavior. But one of the greatest lessons I have learned in my life is this: true change comes only from within. No minister, no father, no law can force us. As much as I disapprove of my wife's behavior, I cannot force her to change. I could throw her out, I suppose, but she is a vital part of this family. The girls need her here, even Elizabeth. I believe I have a fairly good idea of why her behavior toward Elizabeth altered so drastically after David's death, and I believe that she will come around.

"So, until that time comes, I will keep doing everything I can for Elizabeth. I have watched her very closely. I have tried to give her all the love and support I can to counteract her mother's behavior."

Darcy pondered this information. He examined the man in front of him and saw true pain in his eyes. He was hurting. Darcy did not want to injure him, but he still had so many questions. "So,

Mrs. Bennet did not treat Miss Elizabeth this way before David died?"

"No. She was actually somewhat partial to her."

"Then why do you think she has changed so dramatically? Her behavior, pardon me, is despicable. It is shocking."

"Mr. Darcy, the human heart is a delicate thing. One never knows how much it can take. Although I cannot reveal my suspicions of why Mrs. Bennet changed so drastically, I do believe that Elizabeth's mother will change her ways in time. Someday, someone will spark change in my wife's heart. God bless you if it is you. Until then, I will love Elizabeth as much as two parents. She is strong; she will endure."

"That is one thing I know without a shadow of a doubt," Darcy replied.

"Yes. I have tried to teach Elizabeth that she is valuable and worthy of the love. But if I am to believe the story of Miss Bingley's interference and your escapade on the swing in front of the children yesterday, perhaps you have taught her even better than I have." Mr. Bennet gave him a sly grin.

Darcy flushed red, remembering the tender embrace he had shared with this man's daughter. He relished the memory but knew it would look very differently from a father's perspective. He cleared his throat and spoke, "I assure you my only intention was only to comfort her."

Mr. Bennet laughed and stood, offering his hand. "I trust that is all it was. I know men have their weaknesses, but since we have already discussed your intentions, I will trust in those as well. Now, is there anything else you would like to discuss?"

"I do not believe so."

"Then the look in your eye tells me you are anxious to see Elizabeth. I will not delay you any further. If anything else comes up, I am always available."

"Thank you, sir." Mr. Darcy stood and shook the hand of what he hoped was his future father-in-law. As he turned to leave, he wondered what had been the purpose of the discussion. It seemed Mr. Bennet already knew about the incident on the swing and his research into silver. Perhaps Mr. Bennet had a hidden agenda. He shrugged off the thought and followed Mr. Bennet out into the parlor.

*****

The early autumn weather held out for the next two weeks, and Bingley and Darcy saw their ladies often. Jane and Elizabeth dined at Netherfield several times, and everyone but Miss Bingley enjoyed their company. One evening, Darcy made sure to ask Elizabeth to sing after dinner, and as she played, he was overwhelmed by a powerful force that begged him to make her his. He very nearly asked for a private audience right there. But he had promised himself that he would solve the mystery of Malachi 3:3 before he proposed. So, he simply sat back and enjoyed the moment. When she finished, he immediately asked for an encore.

If Miss Bingley hadn't interrupted Elizabeth's encore in the last measure, he would have asked for a third song. Instead, as Miss Bingley began playing, he took Elizabeth by the hand, without any words, and started dancing with her. He had seen the waltz at an embassy ball in London, but until then, he did not see what benefits it could provide. They danced until Miss Bingley claimed need of refreshment.

He thought of that moment, holding her in his arms, many times over the next few days. With one hand on her waist, and one clasping her hand, he guided her nervous feet effortlessly, and they seemed to move as one. It was moving to see her eyes burn with desire. He reminded himself that he had better finish that research and get engaged soon. He didn't want to break propriety, but he knew he couldn't go much longer without kissing her.

The following morning, after considerable urging from Mr. Bingley, the Bingley sisters agreed to join Mr. Bingley and Mr.

Darcy in paying a call to Longbourn. When they arrived, Elizabeth met Darcy outside the parlor and pulled him aside while all the others were shown in. She was very nearly in a panic.

"Mr. Darcy, I must speak with you immediately!" she whispered.

The look on her face was grave, and he allowed her to guide him away from the parlor and into the front entrance. "Are you all right? What is the matter?"

"Is Mr. Wickham named George?"

He furrowed his brows. "Yes. Why?"

"I believe he is here, visiting Lydia and Kitty." Elizabeth watched his eyes grow dark; the mask appeared. He stood taller and looked towards the parlor.

Hearing Wickham's unmistakable laugh confirmed it for him. He moved to confront the man when he felt Elizabeth's restraining hand on his arm. He looked back at her and saw the fear in her eyes.

"William, please do not do anything you would regret," she whispered. "You must think of Georgiana. Do not forget that Miss Bingley and Mrs. Hurst are in the parlor as well."

Anger flashed in his eyes. "I make no promises," Darcy replied. Elizabeth's restraining hand let go, and he adjusted his jacket and went into the parlor. His feet propelled him faster than necessary, and he knew his heart was racing. As he entered, he spotted Wickham immediately and froze. It was quite obvious when Wickham saw him. Wickham stood and cautiously bowed.

"Mr. Darcy, what a surprise. What brings you here?" Mr. Wickham asked.

Darcy took a slow breath to calm himself. He made no attempt to bow back. He glared at the man who had nearly destroyed Georgiana. Suddenly, horrific scenes flashed before his eyes. He saw his helpless sister being attacked by the very man standing before him. He heard her screams for help. He tasted the tears she must have shed. He thought of that blank look on her face all those months. Suddenly, he could not take the images anymore, and he stepped forward to Wickham and hit him square in the jaw as hard as he could.

Wickham collapsed on the floor unconscious. Darcy's fist immediately began throbbing. He opened and closed it several times to work out the sensation. Elizabeth hurried past Darcy to check the unconscious man. Darcy did not take his eyes off Wickham as he heard Mr. Bennet speak.

"Is there a reason you assaulted a man in my parlor, Mr. Darcy?"

Darcy made no reply. Elizabeth took out her handkerchief and began dabbing at the blood on Wickham's lip.

Mr. Darcy scoffed. "Do not ruin your linens on that wretch."

Mr. Bennet said sternly, "Mr. Darcy, we shall provide any care necessary to a man in need. Now, do you mind discussing an urgent matter in my study?"

"Certainly, as soon as this man has been thrown out!"

"As you have rendered him unconscious, that option is no longer available. Elizabeth can tend to him for the moment. Come, let us talk rationally."

Mr. Darcy said, "Bingley, the moment that scoundrel wakes up, show him to the door. And tell him that if he ever comes near me, Georgiana, or the Bennets again, he will receive more than a broken jaw." He then turned and followed Mr. Bennet into the study for a second time. He was offered a seat but declined. He was in no mood to sit. He began pacing.

Mr. Bennet offered him a drink, and Mr. Darcy accepted, swallowing half of it in one gulp. Mr. Bennet said calmly, "I believe you have something to explain to me. You will find I am a good listener."

Darcy ran his fingers through his hair and continued to pace. "Forgive me, Mr. Bennet. I should have exercised restraint. But I know that man well. He is no gentleman. He cannot be trusted with your daughters. I cannot divulge more except to say that he has compromised someone dear to me.

"I am ill just thinking about him being in this house. He disgusts me. He deserves no mercy, no kindness, and no leniency. I fear that he may attack again, but unfortunately, there is nothing I can do to stop him. The girl he compromised does not wish to come forward with an accusation. I have been consumed with anger at this man and sorrow for the poor girl. It is overwhelming, and the feelings all came to a head the moment I saw him."

Mr. Bennet put his hands together and pondered what Darcy had just told him. After a moment of silence, he asked, "Do you mind if I tell you a story?"

"No," Mr. Darcy huffed. He took a breath and attempted to calm himself before trying again. "No, I do not mind."

"Very good. Please sit, Mr. Darcy." Mr. Darcy reluctantly took a seat. Mr. Bennet walked around to the front of the desk and leaned back against it, facing Mr. Darcy. "Forgive me if my storytelling is somewhat rusty. This story happened the night Judas betrayed Jesus and led the guards to Jesus. Here was an apostle, a friend, who literally delivered Christ to his captors, knowing that death would be the Master's fate. Peter, in hopes of defending the life of his Lord, drew his sword and smote off the ear of one of the men who had come to take Christ. Christ told Peter to put the sword back in its sheath. Do you know what Christ did next?"

"No, I am not familiar with this story."

"Christ touched the servant's ear and healed it. He healed the man who was taking him to his death." Mr. Bennet observed Mr. Darcy squirm a little in the chair. "Do you know why I tell you this story?"

"I am not inclined to say."

"That is a nice way of saying you have a good guess but do not wish to divulge your thoughts." Mr. Bennet paused. "When someone harms us, what should we do?"

Darcy was determined to say nothing at all. Wickham had harmed him, and he wanted revenge; but Darcy knew that was not the answer Mr. Bennet was seeking. Aggressive thoughts began swirling through his mind as he battled for self-control. He folded his arms in front of him and waited for Mr. Bennet to continue.

"I see you are so enamored with my storytelling abilities that you are waiting with baited breath," Mr. Bennet said with a smile. Without retrieving his Bible, he said, "Matthew 26:52 reads: 'Then said Jesus unto him, Put up again thy sword into his place: for all they that take the sword shall perish with the sword.' Our Lord healed the servant, Peter put away his sword, and Christ gave himself up. Now, I ask you, knowing He was going to his death, why did He go peaceably? Why did He take the time to heal the servant's ear?"

A battle raged in Mr. Darcy's heart, but his defenses were weakening. "I suppose you want me to say that Christ healed the man because He forgave them."

"I do not want you to say anything you do not believe. But let me tell you something an old man has learned. We are taught that we must forgive others in order to be forgiven of our own sins. That is true, but there is a much better reason to forgive. God wants us to forgive one another not only because wrongdoers deserve forgiveness, but because the wronged deserve peace.

"I can tell you are a man who does not easily lose his temper, but that is exactly what just happened in my parlor. You voiced your anger and sadness with your fist. I believe you said a moment ago that your anger is consuming you. So, I pose one more question to you: do you not deserve peace?"

"I do not know," Darcy replied, sounding somewhat defeated. "I know revenge is an ungentlemanly feeling. I suppose it would be a great relief to suppress my ill feelings towards Wickham."

"Not suppress, eradicate. You deserve to be free from the sadness and anger. You deserve peace. I believe forgiveness is not

226

a subject just for sinners. Forgiveness is just as important for those that have been sinned against. Think about it. Christ knows the pain in each human heart. 'He hath borne our griefs, and carried our sorrows'. He knows not just the guilty sorrow of the sinner, but also the victim's anguish. Whatever hurt lies hidden deep inside the souls of men, Christ can heal it, for He has already borne it. Christ knows your heart, Mr. Darcy, and He wants to heal you. He wants to ease your burdens. He can bring you peace."

Mr. Darcy did not trust himself to speak. He was overcome with emotion. Never before had he thought of Christ suffering his pains for him. Mr. Darcy was an honest, hardworking man who never willfully broke any laws. But that is not to say that he did not have sorrow. Like anyone, there were times when he struggled. He had tasted bitter sorrow and paralyzing anxiety.

He never knew Christ's suffering could bring him peace. It was incredible to consider. He could feel his burdens lighten the longer he thought on it. Could Christ really release him of all his fear, his worries, his loneliness, and his anger? Could Christ really bring him peace? When he finally felt in control of his voice, has asked, "What does it take?"

"For what?" Mr. Bennet asked.

Mr. Darcy said, "For the peace to come as you promised."

"Let me make one thing clear: I may have shared a story and a few scriptures, but it is not and never has been my promise. It is Jesus Christ's promise. Matthew 11:28 reads, 'Come unto me, all ye that labor and are heavy laden, and I will give you rest.' It also is the answer to your question. Come unto Him. That is what you must do to find that peace."

"But I have been coming unto Him," Darcy protested. "I have offered my will to Him like never before, and I defer all decisions to Him. What else must I do?"

Mr. Bennet paused before answering. "Consider that question in light of what prompted this discussion," he suggested.

"Wickham. You think I need to forgive him." Darcy looked Mr. Bennet directly in the eyes and watched silence linger in the air between them. The moment grew thick with silence. A battle of wills ensued. Mr. Darcy resisted the notion of forgiving Wickham for compromising Georgiana; the very idea felt like a slap in the face. The longer they looked at each other, the longer Darcy evaluated the remote possibility of offering his forgiveness. Mr. Bennet seemed to be patiently waiting for Darcy to come to his own conclusion as to whether or not Wickham should be forgiven. The battle was lost when Darcy looked down to blink away the emotion brimming in his eyes. "I do not think I can ever forget what he did."

Mr. Bennet smiled. "Let me clarify something," he said. "Do I think you should forgive him? Yes, because you deserve to have peace. But do I want you to forget what he did? No. Forgive, but do not forget. There is no requirement to trust him again. In fact, I think a certain level of distrust would be healthy in this matter. You were right to fear he may repeat his actions. But you were wrong to assume the burden would be on your shoulders. You take too much upon yourself, Mr. Darcy."

They heard a knock on the study door and Darcy stood. "Thank you, sir," Darcy said with a bow. "I do not know if your recommendation is possible, but I am beginning to see the necessity of it."

Darcy was suddenly struck with familiarity of hearing Georgiana say something similar. When he first learned of what wicked deeds Wickham had inflicted on his sister, he had wanted to seek revenge, but Georgiana told him that she just wanted to forgive. She had said she didn't know if it was possible but she saw it was necessary. He felt more compassion than ever for what his sister had gone through and had even more admiration for how far she had come since then.

Mr. Bennet opened the door, and Elizabeth walked in and closed the door behind her. Mr. Bennet asked, "How is the man fairing?"

"Mr. Wickham will be fine. He has only a swollen lip and a bad headache. I came in because I was worried about you, Mr. Darcy. I brought a cool cloth for your hand." She walked over to him and examined his hand and then placed the cloth on it. She looked up at him and couldn't quite make out what his eyes were saying. They were subtly surprised, but there was also a strong amount of curiosity.

"Miss Elizabeth, forgive me for behaving like a common schoolboy. It was terrible of me to lose my temper. I was unprepared for my surge of anger. I am a weak man."

Elizabeth looked at him and said, "Mr. Darcy, may I speak frankly?" Darcy silently nodded. "My devotion was not deterred in the slightest. I am aware of your weaknesses. I know that you are imperfect, and I love you for it. I am only worried about how you will flog yourself for your hasty reaction."

With Darcy's good hand, he brushed the back of his fingers against her glowing cheek. "I do not deserve you," he said.

Mr. Bennet cleared his throat loudly, and Darcy pulled back his hand in embarrassment. "I feel like I have intruded on a private moment," Mr. Bennet said." Perhaps I will check on Mr. Wickham." He turned and exited but pointedly left the door wide open. He may be willing to give them a moment alone, but Mr. Darcy had just showed himself to be a man—a man who occasionally succumbed to his impulses.

CHAPTER 12

Miss Bingley had to act quickly. When Elizabeth left the room, she silently approached Mr. Wickham. "How is your head?" she asked.

Wickham studied the lady in front of him. She was dressed quite fine. She had a long nose and a long face but was still fairly attractive. "It is pounding slightly," he replied. "Nothing I have not handled before."

She lowered her voice and whispered, "I must speak with you privately. Meet me behind the church tomorrow at two o'clock." He eyed her suspiciously before nodding. She returned to her seat just before Mr. Bennet arrived from his study. A moment later, Mr. Darcy and Elizabeth came out as well.

As Mr. Darcy walked over to Wickham, the injured man stiffened. Darcy put up his hands and slowed his approach. "I am not going to hit you again. As much as I would love to, it would be wrong of me. May I speak with you outside?"

Wickham could see that Darcy was angry but not out of control. He nodded and stood up. He handed Elizabeth's soiled handkerchief back to her and passed by Darcy without a word.

Darcy gave Elizabeth's hand a squeeze and followed Wickham out the door. Once outside, he closed the door behind him and swallowed his pride, nearly choking on the effort. "First of all, I apologize for hitting you. Seeing you was more of a shock than I was prepared to handle. I know we used to be friends, but all that is over. I know what you did to my sister." He was hit with a wave of fury but suppressed it. He reminded himself that

Georgiana did not want retribution. She just wanted peace, and so did he. They both deserved peace, and forgiveness was vital to obtaining it.

"I need to express the disgust I feel that you took advantage of her, a child you once played with. I cannot fathom your lack of morals. If it were up to me, you would already be in prison. I have lain awake for hours imagining the pain I would put you through; but the truth of the matter is it would do me no good to see you punished and it would certainly harm Georgiana.

"I also have to say that you may not have considered the effect your actions would have on Georgiana. Allow me to enlighten you. Her self-loathing consumed her for months. She suffered in a dark, lonely abyss that you cannot even imagine. She very nearly killed herself. You almost ruined everything I have left in my life. I was probably justified in hitting you. Nevertheless, it was wrong to react in anger through my fist. That is the closest I can come to apologizing. I wanted to hit you. I wanted to do worse to you. I still do. But I am not the same man you grew up with."

Wickham kept his distance as he considered Darcy's words. Darcy knew what he had done to Georgiana? And yet he was peaceably addressing him? It was incomprehensible! Wickham carefully observed the man in front of him. Darcy stood tall, and his shoulders were broad. His hands were relaxed at his sides, and his eyes said he spoke the truth.

Something was different; Wickham couldn't quite put his finger on it. He studied Darcy a little longer. Then he saw it: Darcy was not clenching his fist behind his back. It had been a habit of Darcy's since he was a young boy. He was not doing it now. Here he was, clearly uncomfortable, but yet in control. Perhaps Darcy had really changed.

Wickham spurred him just a little to test whether the change was permanent. "What was it your father used to say? 'A gentleman never resorts to violence.'" He rubbed his jaw for effect. "But then again, that was a fairly weak punch."

Darcy smiled casually. "Are you offering me another shot?"

Wickham tried not to show his frustration. He had always been able to goad Darcy, to get him to react in accordance with Wickham's plans. That was why Darcy always took the blame when they were children. But yet there he was, calmly smiling back at him. Wickham could sense there was no point in trying to push him. "Certainly not," he responded. "You are simply not as experienced as the men I fight in the brothels. You have kept your gentlemanly hands quite clean until now, I suspect."

"Again, I apologize for hitting you. You are right; it was ungentlemanly. What do you have to say about Georgiana?"

"What would you like me to say, Darcy? Shall we call the magistrate? Are you hoping I will confess my guilty deed so you can tattle on me again?" Wickham replied angrily. In truth, he hardly remembered that day, as he had been completely foxed. "You will not get a confession out of me. Georgiana was the one who—"

"Stop. Spare me your excuses. I do not want to hear your side of the story. I know it happened just as Georgiana said it did because I saw what it did to her. At one point, I thought I would like to hear you admit your wrongdoing, but now I realize I very much do not want to know any details. But I do want to know why you are here in Meryton."

Wickham adjusted his waistcoat and smiled. "I have purchased a lieutenant's commission in our Majesty's militia. We are stationed here for the winter."

"How did you afford a commission?"

"I am not completely void of resources."

Darcy laughed. "Yes, you always were quite resourceful. Listen closely, Wickham; I cannot guarantee that my good behavior will last. I suggest you keep your hands, and any other appendage you may have, close to your person and covered up. Stay completely away from the Bennets, especially Elizabeth."

It was not lost on Wickham that Darcy had just referred to Elizabeth by her Christian name. Wickham walked over to the stone bench and sat down. It was very curious to see a new Darcy. He tried one more time to provoke him. "Very well," he sighed. "I will stay away from the Bennets. But I do not think it fair that I am condemned to the life of a monk simply to avoid your threats of retribution. I am a man after all, and a man has needs."

Mr. Darcy was becoming ill from the colossal amount of self-control he was exerting. He had vile feelings for the man and absolutely no respect for him. He reminded himself he needed to forgive but not necessarily forget.

"I am aware of your 'needs'. That is why I will be watching you, Wickham. I strongly suggest you behave in Hertfordshire. No gentleman within forty miles will admit you into his house if I choose to inform the public about your past. And I plan to have a very frank discussion with your colonel today. You will be watched so closely that you will not be allowed to urinate unsupervised. Now, you have tried my patience long enough. I suggest you return immediately to whatever hole you came out of." Darcy sighed and turned back to the house.

"Wait, Darcy," Wickham called out after him. "Is that all you have to say?"

Darcy turned back to Wickham. "What do you mean?" he asked.

"Why did you really apologize to me? Look me in the eye and tell me the truth."

"I owe you no explanation."

Wickham was genuinely stunned. "What has happened to you?" he asked.

"I have learned a great deal these last few months. I have come to adopt a friend's philosophy."

"What philosophy is that?"

Darcy hesitated. This wasn't a conversation he wanted to have with Wickham. "That people are inherently good," he replied. "Even if their actions indicate otherwise."

"Ah, I see! You believe in me!" Wickham chuckled. "That is why you apologized; you believe I am inherently good!"

"Wickham, you are trying my patience."

"I just need to hear you say it," Wickham said.

Darcy sighed. He knew Wickham wouldn't drop the issue; he might as well say it and be done with it. "Yes, I want to believe that you have some good in you," Darcy said. "Your father was a good man. My father respected and trusted him a great deal. You and I were friends at one point. We have shared good memories. What possessed you to make the choices you have these last eight years instead of trying to further refine yourself is beyond me."

Wickham laughed out right. "Refine myself further? Ha! And become a perfect gentleman like you, I suppose? Since when do you consider me refined?"

"Since I learned the true definition of 'refine'. I have a poor opinion of your current state, but I believe any man can refine himself, given enough time and the appropriate trials. Unfortunately, I think your trials are mostly self-inflicted, and you primarily use them as an excuse to hurt others.

"I can no longer stomach looking at you. I have reached my threshold. Good day." Darcy turned and walked quickly inside the house. He let out a slow breath. He was suddenly very fatigued.

Elizabeth had been watching the scene unfold through the window and felt a surge of compassion for William. His face was tired and strained. His eyes were dark. She met him at the door, silently took his hand, brought it to her mouth and kissed each finger. The knuckles were still red, and the middle one had an abrasion on it, but it was not deep enough to bleed. He looked in her eyes and gave her a weak smile. While they still enjoyed a small amount of privacy, she asked, "What did you say to him?"

"I forgave him. What else could I do? It was overwhelming. No wonder Christ bled from every pore. I felt so much all at once: anger, hatred, sadness, anxiety. Then it slowly turned into pity. When I offered my forgiveness, I do not know who was more surprised: me or him."

"How do you feel now?" Elizabeth asked.

"Actually, I feel better than I have in months. The pain and helplessness are gone. My heart is no longer beating wildly out of my chest every time I think of him."

"You found it."

"I hope so. I hope I found peace."

*****

Darcy immediately made good on his threat. He had no trouble locating Colonel Forster and took little delight in relating Wickham's misdeeds. Darcy kept Georgiana's identity secret, but he detailed the attack and Wickham's lascivious history.

It was depressing to review Wickham's life of poor choices. Here was a man who had felt jilted his whole life because he was not born into wealth or status. It must have been hard to grow up in Darcy's shadow, merely the son of a steward, a charity case. And being kicked out of Cambridge must have been unbearable. What Wickham didn't realize was that he could have succeeded at Cambridge if he had made better choices. It was the cheating, the gambling, and the womanizing that had ruined his chances—not his pedigree.

It seemed to be the story of Wickham's life. He had planned to use the money from the Kympton living to study law, but his gambling debts got in the way. Wickham was always looking for the easy opportunity and shied away from any real work. His greatest problems had always been self-inflicted. There had been so many opportunities, and yet he had thrown them away one by one.

When Darcy finished with Colonel Forster, he felt confident that Wickham would be watched appropriately. He hoped that Wickham understood he was being given one final chance. After that, there was nothing left to do but go home.

Darcy prayed the entire way back to Netherfield. He prayed that it was the right choice to give Wickham another chance. He prayed that Colonel Forster would be trustworthy and keep a tight leash on him. He prayed that he was doing enough to protect the women of Meryton. But he spent most of the ride praying about what to say to Georgiana. The ride was over much too quickly, and he still did not know how to break the news to her.

Darcy handed the reigns over to the stable hand and ran his fingers through his hair. He heard a familiar ring of laughter from the gardens, and he was drawn to Elizabeth like a bee to clover in full bloom. Georgiana was pushing Elizabeth on the rope swing, and the sight was idyllic. Elizabeth had obviously come to comfort Georgiana, but from the looks of things, Georgiana was in still in ignorant bliss.

Darcy approached quietly from behind, and when Georgiana saw him, he put his finger up to his lips to silence her. Darcy waited for Elizabeth to swing back to him, and then he pushed her with both hands, running all the way under, sending her soaring high into the air. He was rewarded with a swell of glorious laughter and squeals of delight. He turned back around and smiled at her widely. She had taken off her bonnet, and the curls around her face waved and fluttered in the wind. She was magnificent. She was perfectly happy, and her entire face was radiant. He tried to control his voice, but it still came out choked from the overwhelming emotion he was feeling. "Good afternoon, Elizabeth," he said.

"Good afternoon, William. I hope you were able to accomplish your tasks as planned."

"I was."

Elizabeth pumped her legs a few times and let the swing take her higher. There was nothing to do now but tell Georgiana. She repeated her prayer for the fifth time that hour: *Bless Georgiana that she will be strong enough to handle the news.* Georgiana had healed a great deal in the last few weeks, but even Elizabeth still got shook up when she saw the man in town who had attacked her, and it had been many years since her attack. She stopped pumping her legs and let the swing slow. She jumped off as it was still moving, and Mr. Darcy instinctively reached out to catch her fall. His arms wrapped around her briefly, and she looked up at him. He stepped away when it was obvious she did not need his help.

Darcy whispered to Elizabeth, "Thank you for coming. Georgiana will need your strength of spirit."

Elizabeth reached for his hand and squeezed it. "She is not the only one suffering. I came here for you as well."

Darcy was too choked up to trust himself to speak. He just nodded and squeezed her hand in return. He brought her hand up to his lips and kissed it gently. He then took his other hand and smoothed the stray curls away from her face. He gave her a smile and hoped it expressed all he felt for her.

Georgiana cleared her throat loudly. "Excuse me. I believe my legendary chaperone skills have been activated. Elizabeth, might I interest you in some lemonade?"

Feeling a little flushed, Elizabeth replied, "Yes, that would be nice. Could we take it in your chambers? We have some news we would like to share with you."

Georgiana looked surprised but smiled mischievously. "William, you promised me you would tell me before you proposed!"

Darcy blushed at Georgiana's teasing. "No, I . . . " he flustered, and then Elizabeth jumped in.

"Mr. Darcy," she said in a convincingly stern voice, "did you propose to someone and forget to tell me? How careless of you!" Georgiana burst into laughter and her brother's face blushed even deeper.

"No, no!" Darcy stammered. "I have not proposed to anyone!"

"Then why did you bring it up, William?" Georgiana reprimanded him. "Do you not see how heartless it is to discuss this in front of Elizabeth?" At this point, Elizabeth could bite her lip no longer and doubled over in giggles. Darcy's cheeks were still hot, but the ladies' laughter was contagious, and he soon joined in.

After they all caught their breath, Georgiana walked over to William and kissed his cheek. "I am sorry, William. Elizabeth is clearly a bad influence on me," she said. Elizabeth gasped dramatically, and Georgiana giggled again. Then she steeled herself for the matter at hand. "What news do you have?" she asked. "Is it pleasant or unpleasant?"

Darcy took a deep breath. "Unpleasant, pumpkin," he said gently. He watched the mirth in her eyes disappear, but she nodded in understanding. If there was ever a time he needed direction from God, it was now. He did not want the blank look to return.

"Very well," Georgiana said. She felt a wave of fear flood over her for a brief moment, but then a calmness started in her chest and moved throughout her body. She was ready for bad news. She took comfort in the fact that her brother and Elizabeth still seemed to be very much in love. Whatever they had to say did not involve them. That meant it involved herself.

She started walking and soon Elizabeth had interlaced her arm with hers and was giving her a gentle squeeze. The calmness returned, and her heart slowed. They entered her chambers, and Georgiana moved to the chaise by the window. She tucked her feet under her and waited.

Elizabeth and Darcy looked at each other as if neither one wanted to start. The silence was thick, and finally, Georgiana giggled. "I feel rather left out of your silent conversation, you know. Do you need me to pick who will be the one to tell me? Perhaps you should both say it aloud at the same time."

Darcy sat down next to her and took her hand in his. "I just fear what our news will do to you. You have come so far in the last two months. I do not wish for another setback. I do not wish to remind you of what happened."

Georgiana's heart pounded in her chest briefly, but then she felt that calmness again. It was like putting on a sun-warmed blanket after swimming in a cold lake. "You can tell me, William. I presume whatever you have to tell me is about Wickham. Has he hurt another lady?"

"No," Elizabeth assured her, "not that we know of."

"And I do not think he will either," Darcy said.

"How do you know that?" Georgiana asked.

"Because I saw the look in his eye today when I threatened to expose him."

Georgiana gave him a most severe look. "William, I asked you not to pursue him. I just want to put it behind me."

Darcy tried not to laugh at his sister's stern face. "I met him quite by chance. If I had been better prepared, I would not have punched him."

"William!" Georgiana shouted.

"I hit him only once. And it felt good. But I did apologize."

"You apologized to him? Why?"

"Well, I was afraid that if I did not make peace with him, I might punch him again and again and again . . ." He paused for effect, and a small grin crept onto Georgiana's face. "No, in all seriousness, I apologized because it was wrong to hit him. I have forgiven him, Georgiana. I hope that does not upset you. My hatred for Wickham has been consuming me for so long. I want to be at peace now. I am so sorry, Georgiana."

"It is all right, William," Georgiana said. "What I do not understand is how did you come to see him? Is he here in Meryton?"

Elizabeth and Darcy both said yes at the same time, and then looked at each other. Darcy gestured for Elizabeth to finish. "He is an officer in the militia and is stationed here in Meryton for the winter. Wickham escorted my sisters home to Longbourn today."

"He was in your house?"

"Yes."

"Are you all right?" Georgiana asked.

"Me? I should be asking if you are all right."

Georgiana glanced at William briefly and then lowered her voice and said, "You know what I mean."

Darcy spoke up, clearly uncomfortable with where the discussion was going. "Perhaps I should go so you two can speak in private."

Elizabeth sensed his trepidation again. One of these days he would need to hear what had happened to her if they were to be married. He couldn't keep avoiding the topic. She walked over to Georgiana and put her hand on her arm. Perhaps a little knowledge said in passing would take the sting out of the revelation when it came time to tell him.

"Georgiana, your brother is too much of a gentleman to ask me what happened to me. But someday when the time is right, he will ask, and I will tell him. As for your question, I am doing fine. I can see why you fancied yourself in love. He is very handsome and has a charming smile. Since my experience was not exactly like yours, I cannot say I experienced any ill feelings towards the man. To me, he was just someone who hurt a dear friend of mine, a man who took things from you that you can never get back. But it is over. He can no longer hurt you. One day you will find a man who will want to know every part of you and will love you anyway. That kind of man is a very special man."

Darcy flinched. He knew she was speaking of him. He knew he should not be so afraid to hear of Elizabeth's experience. But knowing this did not make it any easier. He would love her no matter what happened, so why did he need to know? The details would only give him nightmares. She was perfect in his eyes. He could not bear to hear how someone had scarred her. Couldn't he just love her, the woman she was now? He swallowed hard and looked away when she glanced at him.

Elizabeth saw it in his eyes. He was trying so hard not to show it, but he was afraid. Why? Was he afraid it would change how he felt about her? Or was it something else? She turned back to Georgiana. "How do you feel about him being in town?"

Darcy interjected, "The colonel is watching his every move. There is no way that he can hurt you again. I do not believe he would anyway. I may have threatened him once or twice during the apology."

"I can only imagine such an apology!" Georgiana laughed. "But to answer your question, I do not know how I feel. Part of me wants to head back to Pemberley immediately—"

"And we can do that," Darcy said.

"Let me finish. Part of me wants to head back to Pemberley, but I do not always want to be running. I want to hold my head high, even in the face of tribulation. I want to be worthy of the trust God has placed in me."

"What do you mean?" Darcy asked.

"God gives each of us a unique set of trials, tailored to our specific needs in the hope that we will turn to Him. God never planned for Wickham to hurt me. He would never want that to happen. My particular trial stems from someone else's actions. It is an especially large trial, one that shook me to my very core. It made me question God's love for me. I very nearly failed the test. But I am determined to use this opportunity to prove myself to God, to prove that I will always turn to Him for strength, and that I will never turn from the truth that I now have.

"I have been thinking about what Elizabeth did for me. She did what no one else could because she survived her . . . well, let us just say she survived. God is big and powerful, and we are so small. But even as big as He is, He used Elizabeth's small hands to help me. He needs small people to do His work for Him. I would someday like to do His work and help other ladies the way Elizabeth helped me.

"So, you ask how I am doing? I will tell you: I cannot contain my happiness. I know my life is richly blessed. I will stay right here in Meryton and face Wickham nose to nose, and I will not falter. God has a plan for me, and one man cannot take away that plan." Georgiana took in a deep breath and felt the calmness fill her even more than ever.

Both Mr. Darcy and Elizabeth just sat in awe, dumbstruck by the realization that all their fears were in vain. They each said a silent prayer of thanks.

*****

Assured that Georgiana was really all right, Darcy refocused on his silver research. The next day, he visited the blacksmith shop as Mr. Bennet had suggested. The air was full of the smell of leather, coal, and rich metals. Numerous knickknacks were displayed all over the room along with an impressive assortment of metal and silver—everything from swords and cuff-links, to tools and buckles. An elderly lady greeted him.

"Good afternoon, sir. My name is Mrs. Rogers. Can I help you find something? We have all sorts of items for sale, each uniquely handcrafted. Mr. Rogers is a talented smith of blades, metals, silver, and jewelry. You will never see finer craftsmanship."

The lady motioned to a glass case full of all different kinds of jewelry. As he greeted her politely, he scanned the arrangement of unique bracelets, rings, and hair clips. Each was a one-of-a-kind creation. "Your husband made all of this himself?"

"Oh no, sir, my husband is deceased. It was my son who made these things. Are you looking for a gift for a lady? If you tell me a little about the lady, I can recommend something that will suit her."

"Perhaps. These are quite ingenious. Has your son ever made anything that resembled a frog?"

"He once made a frog necklace for Mr. Bennet, which I believe he gave to his daughter, Miss Elizabeth Bennet. Do you know her?"

"Indeed I do, and I have seen the necklace." Looking at all the beautiful jewelry, Darcy suddenly wished he could give Elizabeth a gift. But the rules of etiquette were quite clear on that point. She would never accept something from a suitor. But, he reasoned, she might accept a small token from Georgiana. And besides, he hoped to be more than just a suitor very soon. On an impulse he added, "In fact, I believe my sister might be interested in buying her a gift."

Mrs. Rogers smiled and replied, "Then you have come to the right place! Miss Elizabeth loves silver. I am sure I can help you and your sister pick out the perfect gift."

"Thank you, madam. I will hold you to that promise. But I am actually here to speak with the blacksmith," Darcy said.

"Of course, sir. Let me see if he is available."

Mrs. Rogers quickly left, and a few moments later, the sound of metal against metal paused. The hammering resumed, and Mrs. Rogers returned.

"He says he is in the middle of something, but you are welcome to follow me back and talk to him while he works."

"That will be fine."

Mrs. Rogers handed him a set of glass goggles. "You may need these."

He fingered the goggles and realized how little he knew about the life of a blacksmith. He followed Mrs. Rogers outside and around the back towards a small workshop. She pushed open the heavy door, and he was assaulted by the smell of sulfur and waves of heat. The blacksmith wore a large leather apron that covered his entire chest and the front of his legs. He had on thick, dirty leather gloves that went past his elbows. In his hand, he held one piece of what appeared to be a bar of iron. The tip of it was red hot, and the blacksmith hammered away at it.

"This is my son, James Rogers. I do not believe I got your name, sir."

"Fitzwilliam Darcy."

"James, this is Mr. Darcy. He wants to speak with you," she shouted.

The hammering stopped, and the man yelled back over the roaring furnace, "I hope you do not mind if I continue. If I stop now, the whole thing will be ruined. You are welcome to stay if you can handle the noise. I am quite accustomed to it. But if it is too loud, we can meet some other time." He hammered away again.

"I do not wish to intrude. I simply had a few questions about the purifying process of silver."

"Silver?"

Darcy raised his voice, thinking he didn't hear him. "I am interested in the purifying process of silver."

"I heard you the first time. I was just curious why you would ask about it." Mr. Rogers continued to hammer away at the metal, turning it over and over after a few well-placed blows.

"I was challenged to research it, and I find myself quite unable to back down. I was hoping to watch the process and see how it is done. I would very much appreciate your help," Darcy yelled. He could already feel beads of sweat building on his brow from the heat.

Mr. Rogers moved the red-hot iron into a barrel of water, and the water sizzled and steamed. He immediately began counting and slowly tapping his foot. When the blacksmith reached thirty, he took out the iron and returned it to the fire.

Taking off his leather arm-length gloves, he turned his full attention to Mr. Darcy. "There, we have a few minutes to talk while it heats up again. I would be happy to show you how silver is refined. In fact, a shipment of ore just arrived today that needs smelting. How about tomorrow? It takes me all day, so I start very early. Can you be here by seven o'clock?"

"Yes, thank you. Would it be all right if I brought two ladies with me? I would like to invite my fifteen-year-old sister and Miss Elizabeth Bennet." Darcy looked around the room. There were all kinds of hammers, molds, and other tools in an organized manner all over the walls.

"Of course. But I would hate to see your sister ruin her fine clothes with dust and soot. And it will be very hot. Tell her to wear a dark-colored, lightweight dress. Does she ride?"

"She is an avid horsewoman."

"Then perhaps she should wear an old riding habit. As for Miss Elizabeth, she will know how to dress. She has watched the process several times."

"Then we will be here at seven o'clock. Thank you."

"You are welcome, sir." Darcy watched Mr. Rogers dip a ladle into a bucket and sip directly from it. "Now, if you will excuse me, I must get back to work." The blacksmith started putting on his gloves.

"Of course," Darcy replied. Darcy wiped his brow and left the hot room. He would be sure to wear something less heavy tomorrow. As he returned to the shop, he handed the goggles to Mrs. Rogers and asked, "Does he ever get a real break during the day?"

Mrs. Rogers smiled sweetly and patted his arm. "Do not worry about my James. He has his father's work ethic. The Rogers have been blacksmiths for seven generations. There are certain things that come with the job; loving the work is one of them."

"I appreciate your help today. I must be going now. But I am returning tomorrow with Miss Elizabeth and my sister to watch Mr. Rogers at work. I will hold you to your promise to help me pick out the perfect gift for Miss Elizabeth. Let me know if anything catches her eye." Darcy gave her a genuine smile.

"Of course, sir. The gift from your sister, right?" Mrs. Rogers asked with a grin.

Darcy blushed but couldn't help smiling as he nodded. Thankfully, there was no one else in the shop to witness his pathetic attempt at a ruse. But he found he didn't really care that Mrs. Rogers had guessed the truth.

All he could think of was Elizabeth. He hoped to be there to see the glow in her eye when she saw something she fancied. How he would love to buy it on the spot and see it in her hair, or around her neck, or even on her finger. He grinned wider. He was close, he could tell. He would solve the metaphor of Malachi 3:3 tomorrow. Once he did that, he knew nothing could stop him from proposing.

Mrs. Rogers gave him a surreptitious smile. "Forgive me for being so forward, sir," she said, "but I have advised many a young man in love over the years. Your secret is safe with me." Then she motioned him over to another glass case. She unlocked it and pulled out a small lockbox. "I believe this item might be of interest to you." She opened the box and unwrapped the velvet cloth covering. She picked up a ring and held it out to examine.

Mr. Darcy took the ring from her and examined it. It had a delicate silver band with a winding, silver ribbon wrapped around it. The silver ribbon met with two leaves before creating an intricate gardenia flower, shaped with numerous petals. "It is beautiful! It must have taken him a great deal of time to shape each petal and then to collect them into such an attractive display. You selected this ring for a reason, did you not?"

"I think this would be very appropriate for Miss Elizabeth."

"You know she smells like gardenias." Mrs. Rogers smiled and nodded. "Has she ever seen this ring before?" Mrs. Rogers smiled wider but shook her head. "And the spot in the middle—is it designed to hold a gem?"

"Yes. He can apply any stone you desire. Is there any specific stone you would like?"

"A diamond. I once told her she sparkled like a diamond."

CHAPTER 13

Elizabeth woke up early, eager for the day to begin. Mr. Darcy would be arriving soon for their trip to the blacksmith. He was finally going to see the process of refining silver, and the mystery would be solved.

Perhaps today she would become engaged. He had never actually told her that he was waiting to understand the metaphor before he proposed, but she sensed that was the case. She only wished she could wear her finest dress for the proposal, but she was too sensible for that. Instead, she pulled out her old dress from two years ago and examined it. It still fit, though the hem was tattered and stained with mud. At least there were no holes in it. She dressed quickly and went downstairs to the kitchen.

"Mrs. Hill, is the picnic basket ready?" Elizabeth asked.

"Yes, Miss Elizabeth, just like you asked. Have a pleasant time today."

Hearing Mr. Darcy's knock at the front door, she quickly kissed Mrs. Hill on the cheek. "Thank you! You are the best! Whatever my father pays you is not enough!" She picked up the basket and snatched a biscuit off the top.

Mrs. Hill just blushed, smiled back at her, and went to answer the door.

As soon as Mrs. Hill exited, Mrs. Bennet walked in and stood in front of the door, blocking Elizabeth's way into the parlor. "Good morning, Mamma," Elizabeth said.

"What crazy plans do you have with a picnic basket?" Mrs. Bennet asked. She fingered Elizabeth's gown sleeve. "And why are you wearing such rags? You look ghastly, completely undesirable. What if Mr. Darcy comes today? Go and change at once. Goodness, child, I do not know what he sees in you! I suppose you have lured him by some artifice. I can see no other reason why any man would want to marry you."

The sting of her mother's words never completely abated no matter how much Elizabeth tried to explain them away. She took a deep breath and replied, "Mamma, Mr. Darcy has already arrived. We are going to the blacksmith's today. I only wore this because I do not want to ruin one of my nice gowns."

"And I do not want to ruin your only chance to get married! Who cares whether your gown gets dirty?" Mrs. Bennet sighed. "Well, there is no time to change now. Just keep on kissing Mr. Darcy and letting him do whatever he wishes until that ring is on your finger and the registry is signed at the chapel. I do not even want to know the things you let him do to you in order to ensnarl him."

Elizabeth would have been shocked if she had not lived with such criticism for years. "He has not so much as kissed me, Mamma. He is the perfect gentleman," she replied.

"Of course! A gentleman! Well, I hate to inform you, but a gentleman of his means will always dally. So, I hope you do not actually believe he will be loyal to you, now nor ever. That is just the way of the things. You should really show some more cleavage to keep his attention, child. But I suppose I do not need to explain these things to you. Mr. Darcy is a man with physical needs; you must already be meeting those carnal needs, or he would never have shown a preference for someone so plain. But after what happened with Mr. Conway six years ago, I cannot say I am surprised. And that ridiculous story you fabricated about him! You actually thought people would believe it! Well, now, everyone can see you are nothing but a—"

At that point, the kitchen door behind Mrs. Bennet sprung open and Mr. Darcy interrupted them. "That is quite enough, Mrs. Bennet!" he said. Mrs. Bennet spun around in surprise. After Mrs. Hill led him in to the parlor, Darcy had overheard most of their conversation as he awkwardly waited for Elizabeth. At first, he had stood there, stunned speechless, he could not imagine what to say. Now, he found he had plenty to say.

"It is bad enough that you accuse me of compromising your daughter, but to treat your own child this way is despicable!" he continued. "I insist that you control your tongue and apologize to Elizabeth. You gave birth to her, madam. You must have loved her at one point. And unless you express some of that love right now, any future request for financial support from me will be summarily denied!"

Mrs. Bennet had flinched at the sound of his baritone voice behind her. But her entire body had winced as he threatened withholding his financial support. Turning back to her daughter and away from Mr. Darcy, she scowled at Elizabeth fiercely. In a labored voice, she said, "Elizabeth, dear, I should not have said such things. I am sure Mr. Conway was in his cups and knew not what he was doing."

Mr. Darcy cleared his throat. "That is not good enough."

She sighed and rolled her eyes. "And I know no daughter of mine would ever disobey her parents and humiliate us as you did."

"Try again."

"Not that you did anything that was humiliating. It was all Mr. Conway's fault."

"Better, but you are far from where you need to be. Keep going," Mr. Darcy said. He looked at Elizabeth's face and saw the deep pain she must be feeling. How many times had she suffered this kind of abuse from her mother? How did she bear hearing such hurtful words?

"I wish to congratulate you on earning Mr. Darcy's regard. A man like that never makes unwise choices." Mrs. Bennet was trying not to grit her teeth.

Mr. Darcy explained, "Although I took offence at your innuendoes, it is not I who should be praised. I will give you one last shot, or I will make good on my threat."

Mrs. Bennet glared at her daughter. She took a deep breath and said, "I think you have turned out to be a fine young lady. Any man would be proud to call you his wife. Forgive me for implying any less. I suppose I lo . . . love you." She turned around and put her hands on her hips and asked, "Mr. Darcy, will that suffice? If not, perhaps you could write down what it is you wish me to say. I have a great many things to do today."

Mr. Darcy studied the small woman standing in front of him. Her face was wrinkled at the lower corners of the mouth as if she had a permanent frown. He wanted so badly to tell her off, but years of good breeding held his tongue. Instead, he looked back to Elizabeth's eyes. She was pleading with him to stop.

Without looking at Mrs. Bennet, he said, "Miss Elizabeth and I will be gone most of the day. If you feel you would like to make another attempt at an apology, we both would dearly love to hear it. But I would suggest one change before your next attempt: mean it. If you are going to say you love someone, mean it. Good day."

He stole a glance at Mrs. Bennet and witnessed a very shocked and fearful expression on her face. Moving past her, he reached for the picnic basket, put his arm around Elizabeth's shoulder, and guided her out the door. He placed the picnic basket in the carriage and then briefly told Georgiana that they would be a few minutes. He led Elizabeth towards the gardens.

It was many minutes before Elizabeth could speak. Every time she resolved to ignore her mother's words, as she had done for the last nine years, she was hit with the realization that William had heard everything. The words had stung, but her embarrassment that he had witnessed it all pierced her heart. She took several deep breaths and willed herself not to cry.

They walked the path in silence. When they were far enough from the house, he stopped walking. He then pulled her into his embrace as she cried gentle tears.

Since David's death, no one had ever forced Mrs. Bennet to say that she loved Elizabeth. Elizabeth had understood for many years that she did not. Today, hearing her mother's cruel pretense hurt even more than her silence.

Elizabeth had always held onto the belief that love does not have to be two-sided. Sometimes love is only given and never received. That was true charity. Christ taught us to love our enemies, and Elizabeth had done that for many years, never expecting anything in return. Her one-way relationship with her mother had been difficult, but not impossible.

Now, being in Mr. Darcy's tender arms filled her with hope that her marriage, at least, would be based on a stronger love. A marriage where love would be both given and received. She suddenly felt the need to tell him how much he meant to her. She pulled away slightly and cupped his face with her palm. "I love you, William. Thank you for standing up for me."

He looked down at her eyes and felt passion surge as a tidal wave. He could no longer help himself. He leaned down to kiss her but stopped as he saw the look in her eyes change. She was scared. A second ago, there had been desire in her eyes. There was no mistaking it. And now, fear was expressed in her entire body language.

She stiffened and looked down and quickly dropped her hand. He pulled away, afraid he had done something she was not ready for.

"My mother's words . . ." she whispered.

He tried to understand what she was trying to say. ". . . are not true."

Elizabeth did not know how to express what she was feeling. "But she will think they are."

"I do not think she can see us."

"But having integrity is doing the right thing even if no one is looking."

Darcy sensed that there was more to her hesitation. He tried to place the foreign look on Elizabeth's face. He had seen that look on her face before: at the gazebo when she told him about Georgiana and Wickham. She had been hurting that day because she knew how Georgiana felt. She had been through something similar.

A wave of understanding hit him hard as he realized he had nearly claimed her lips without even asking her; he had almost compromised her without her permission. He stepped back and released her completely. "Forgive me. I had forgotten that we are still only courting." He had never felt such remorse as he did at that moment.

"William, I need you to understand something. It is not from lack of desire that I pulled away. I have imagined kissing you more times than I care to admit. You did nothing wrong. There are just some things you need to know first. And yes, I would like to be betrothed to you first. Can we talk about this?"

"Elizabeth, please. Do not start a conversation that we cannot finish."

"I understand now is not the right time, not with Georgiana waiting in the carriage. Perhaps we could walk to Oakham Mount this afternoon and talk. I feel like you are avoiding asking about what happened to me, and I can only imagine why. I know you would wish for a wife who is pure and—"

"Elizabeth, I beg of you to understand that whatever happened to you is in the past. It does not affect me. I do not need to know." He was looking at his feet, and he felt all the anxiety the moment could possibly hold. When she said nothing, he looked up at her, and she nodded her head.

She closed the gap between them and took his arm. "Of course. The conversation can wait. Mr. Rogers is expecting us."

*****

"Come in, Miss Elizabeth and Mr. Darcy. You must be Miss Darcy. I am Mrs. Rogers. My son, the blacksmith, will be ready soon. You are free to look around if you would like to." She winked at Mr. Darcy.

He smiled back and gave Mrs. Rogers a knowing look, hoping she remembered her promise to help him select a gift. He knew Elizabeth would never express her interest in front of him, so he turned away from the ladies and examined some swords on the other side of the shop.

It did not take him long to move from feigning admiration to truly seeing their value. He picked up a few. Each was perfectly balanced. The handles were regal and stately but handsome in his hand. One was particularly well-constructed. He held it out and lunged, plunging the sword into an imaginary foe. It was light, and the grip fit his hand perfectly. The door opened, and Mr. Rogers walked over to his side.

"You have good taste. That sword is the finest I have ever made," Mr. Rogers said. The men spoke of its metal components and its length in comparison to the other swords. Mr. Darcy was impressed with his knowledge and expertise. After Mr. Darcy returned the sword back to the shelf, Mr. Rogers asked, "Are you ready to see silver refined?"

By now, Georgiana and Elizabeth had wandered over to the men. "Yes, we are quite ready, Mr. Rogers," Elizabeth answered.

Mr. Darcy agreed, "Indeed. I have been anticipating this moment for quite some time. But first, Mr. Rogers, let me introduce you to my sister, Miss Georgiana Darcy."

"Good morning, Miss Darcy. Follow me, and we will get started." He led them outside to the shop.

Mr. Darcy was pleased that the room was not roasting hot like yesterday. In fact, the furnace was not even lit. Mr. Rogers pulled out a small wooden crate and opened the lid with a pry bar. He took out several small rocks and showed them to his three guests. "Silver is rarely mined as pure silver," he explained. "It is usually mixed in with iron and copper and other metals. But we have some fine specimens today. This small rock is probably ninety percent silver, very rare indeed. If I were to polish it up a bit, it would look almost as good as refined silver."

Mr. Darcy looked at the small piece. It was the size of a few peas and had the shape of a candle flame, thicker at one end and tapering to a point. There were a few rough edges to it, but he could see the raw silver shining through. "Are you going to melt it down?"

"No, I might leave that as it is; I rather like its natural shape. Today I am refining these other pieces of ore." He showed them the pieces and pointed out the rusted iron streaks layered throughout the silver vein. "Now, the first thing one has to do is prepare the ore. These pieces, although smaller than walnuts, are still too big to smelt."

He placed the small pieces of ore onto a large metal anvil that was at least two feet tall and a good ten inches wide. It was the same anvil that Mr. Rogers had been using to hammer the hot metal yesterday. Mr. Rogers explained that the ore must be broken up into smaller pieces in order to melt and release the impurities. "The smaller I make the pieces, the purer the silver will be," he explained.

Elizabeth took Mr. Darcy's hand and held it. "I think I understand the first step," he whispered. "The raw silver must be crushed and humbled before it can be purified, right?" She looked up at him with a smile and nodded.

Mr. Darcy smiled back. He had learned a great deal about humility in the last few months. He had once refused to listen to Elizabeth's warnings about Georgiana, and because of it, he had nearly lost Georgiana. But now, he took counsel easily, even sought it out. Here he was in a blacksmith shop in his less-than-finest clothes, feeling nothing but gratitude for having Elizabeth by his side. To have earned her love was the most humbling knowledge, for he surely did not deserve her.

Mr. Rogers picked up a heavy, metal rolling pin and began rolling it over the ore. The sound of crunching rock against metal filled the room. Mr. Rogers worked in silence for nearly an hour, pressing, gathering the fine powder into the center, and pressing again. Finally, Mr. Rogers paused and put down the rolling pin. "Now you can better see the different types of rock. The powder needs to be about as small as cornmeal before I heat it. Mr. Darcy, would you like to try your hand while I get the furnace going?"

"Certainly." He took the extremely heavy rolling pin from Mr. Rogers and proceeded to roll. Then he brushed the grainy substance into the center of the anvil and rolled again. He repeated the process over and over again. Little by little, he saw the powder become finer. As the room started to heat up, he built up a sweat on his brow from the exertion. The life of a blacksmith was not one he would wish for. His arms began to tremble with the repeated motion of lifting the heavy, metal rolling pin. When Mr. Rogers had the furnace in full flames, he came over to examine the powder.

"Well done. That powder will smelt easily." He took the pin from Mr. Darcy and placed it to the side. "The next step is to get the fire very, very hot. I place this powder into a smelting cup and use tongs to hold it into the hottest part of the fire."

Very carefully, he brushed the powder off the anvil and into the smelting cup. He put on his long, leather gloves and wrapped his apron around himself. He then took a chair and placed it right in front of the open furnace. The heat was incredible, even from across the workshop, yet Mr. Darcy moved closer for a better look. Mr. Rogers sat in the chair and gripped the tongs tightly, locking them in place, and slowly placed the cup into the fire, just above the coal. Mr. Darcy could not take his eyes off the powdered ore.

Mr. Rogers said, "You might as well pull up a chair yourself. There is another apron hanging on the door to protect you from the heat."

"Thank you." Mr. Darcy retrieved the apron and put it on, not giving its dirty, sweaty condition a second thought. He then pulled up a stool next to Mr. Rogers and sat down. The apron helped a little with the heat. He was mesmerized by the process. "How hot do you have to get it before it starts to melt?" Darcy asked.

"It takes quite a bit of patience. Two things will happen. First, it will melt and mold to the cup, and then it will release its impurities."

Mr. Darcy considered that information in light of what Elizabeth had told him. If he were the silver in the metaphor, then he would have to melt and mold into something else before his impurities could be released. He imagined the crushing of the powder, or humbling of himself, was the first step. This next step was molding his will to God's design.

He was much better now at deferring his will to God. In every decision, great or small, he asked God to guide him. He sincerely tried to align his will with God's. Mr. Darcy felt heat rise in his chest, and he knew it was not because of the fire. Elizabeth had shared this metaphor with him because she knew he needed to be refined. He needed to first humble himself and then bend his will, and slowly, the process of refining would begin.

Darcy asked, "How long until it starts to melt?"

"Silver melts at approximately 960 degrees Celsius; iron melts at around 1500; copper at approximately 1080 degrees."

"So, copper and silver melt approximately the same temperature," Mr. Darcy said.

"Yes, that is a key point. Heat it too much, and the copper will melt in with the silver. Heat it too little, and the silver will not melt."

"How do you know when to pull it from the fire?" Mr. Darcy asked.

Mr. Rogers smiled and caught Elizabeth's eye across the room. He then said, "Watch and see."

Mr. Darcy watched for what seemed like another hour as they both sat in front of the furnace. Darcy could not peel his eyes off the smelting cup. There were moments where the heat seemed to die down a little. Then the blacksmith would stir the coal and the heat would return in full force. The process was painstakingly slow. Whenever there was a brief period of relief from the heat, the blacksmith would adjust the coals to increase the temperature. *Much like my life,* Darcy surmised. It was an awe-inspiring metaphor. He was excited to see the conclusion.

He sensed Elizabeth's presence as the ladies joined them, and he looked up at her. She rested her hands on his shoulders. He reached for her hand and held it. Her face was a little shiny from the heat and a small trickle of perspiration was forming on her brow and upper lip. He suddenly was reminded of Bingley's confused look when Darcy said that Elizabeth glowed. *"I do not understand what you mean. Does she perspire more than usual?"* He couldn't help but smile at the memory. He took out his handkerchief and offered it to Elizabeth.

"Thank you, Mr. Darcy, but I brought my own. It looks like you may need it more than I do. Are you getting some answers?"

"I am. The scripture says God will sit as a refiner and purifier of silver. So, in the metaphor, Mr. Rogers is representing God."

"Yes. He is the refiner."

"And I am assuming that the silver is me."

"Yes. Each one of us is the silver that is being refined."

Mr. Rogers said, "Ah, the metaphor of Malachi 3:3. You asked me how I would know it was time to take it out of the fire. Not much longer now, and you will have your answer."

Mr. Darcy took out his pocket watch and noted the time. They had been there three hours already. He looked into the hot furnace and saw the powder was starting to shine. Mr. Rogers swirled the cup gently. The contents had already started to liquefy.

The blacksmith continued to swirl it gently and added more coal to the fire. Darcy could see the flames' reflection in the cup.

Mr. Rogers smiled and said, "Now, Mr. Darcy, ask your question again."

"How do you know when to pull it from the fire? How do you know when it has been refined?"

Mr. Rogers pulled the cup from the furnace and placed it right under Mr. Darcy's nose. "I know because I can see my image in it."

Mr. Darcy looked down at the hot shiny liquid in front of him. He most definitely could see his image. Every hair, his very smile, and the look in his eyes—it was just like a mirror. He heard Georgiana gasp from behind him.

"You look just like father!" Georgiana cried.

Mr. Rogers pulled the silver away from Mr. Darcy and stood up carefully. He walked over to the table and carefully poured the liquid silver into bar molds. Later, he would reheat the solid silver to create masterpieces. "It takes a great deal of patience to purify silver. You must watch it closely. The process is not complete until the refiner's image is reflected in the silver."

Elizabeth asked if he had any questions for the blacksmith, and Mr. Darcy simply shook his head. "Then come, Mr. Darcy, let us eat. It has been a long morning."

The wonder and amazement in Mr. Darcy's heart was overwhelming. He understood now. He must humble himself, bend his will to the Lord's, and endure his trials graciously until his countenance reflected his Creator's. It was all there, so simply. He followed Elizabeth back to the store and then paused. "Elizabeth, would you excuse me for a moment? I thought of a question for Mr. Rogers."

"Of course. We will be outside getting some fresh air."

Mr. Darcy kissed her hand and turned back to the workshop. He cleared his throat to get Mr. Roger's attention.

"Could I see that piece of ore that you said was ninety percent silver?"

"Certainly, it is just beside that crate. Why?"

Darcy picked it up and turned it over in his hands. It was the perfect image of a candle flame. "You said you could polish this up and it would shine like silver. How soon could you have it made into a necklace?"

"It would not take long. But this is simply a silver nugget. Do you not want me to make something out it?"

"Trust me; this is exactly what I want, just without the sharp edges. I will pay whatever you ask if you can have this done by tomorrow morning."

"And you want it in a necklace? It will be a heavy pendant. But I can do that easily enough. Come by tomorrow morning, and I will have it ready for you," Mr. Rogers said.

"Thank you. I was looking for just the right gift, and you showed it to me without even knowing it. I will see you tomorrow." Darcy bowed and left the hot room. The relief he felt as he left the room was not simply because the store was so much cooler; it was because he knew he was ready. He went over to Mrs. Rogers and said, "That ring you showed me? Place the biggest, clearest, most brilliant diamond in its center and have it ready tomorrow morning."

She smiled brightly. "I certainly shall," she said. "And may I be the first to wish you joy?"

"Thank you."

CHAPTER 14

After they finished their picnic lunch, Georgiana and Mr. Darcy returned Elizabeth to Longbourn. Darcy helped her out of the carriage and escorted her to the door. He told her that he wished to return to Netherfield and freshen up, but then he would like to escort her to Oakham Mount. And if she still wanted to talk about her past, he promised he would be ready to listen. Elizabeth's face lit up. She quickly leaned into him and embraced him, wrapping her arms completely around him.

During the short carriage ride back to Netherfield, he relived the moment over and over again. No matter how much he did not want to know what had happened to Elizabeth, he understood now how she desperately needed to tell him. He had seen the relief in her eyes when he agreed to hear her story. Therefore, he made up his mind to listen, no matter how difficult it would be.

He realized he had been selfish. All this time, he had tried to avoid the conversation because of the pain it would cause *him*. But avoiding it was causing *her* pain. She needed his assurance that he loved her, all of her, despite what had happened. *He* knew he loved her, but *she* still wavered in that knowledge. This afternoon, that would not be the case. No matter what she told him, he would make sure she was completely confident in his love. He would show her he loved her unconditionally—just as she had counseled him to do for Georgiana.

The carriage rolled up to Netherfield, and Mr. Darcy said to his sister, "Georgiana, I am going to propose to Elizabeth. I promised you would be the first to know."

"Oh! How wonderful! It took you long enough! When? Will it be today? Will you get down on one knee? Where will you do it?"

Darcy chuckled. "I have a few ideas. But first, I desperately need a bath. Let us talk afterwards." He leaned across and kissed her cheek. "She is amazing, is she not?"

"I do not think you need me to tell you that."

"No, indeed not." He stepped out of the carriage and handed Georgiana out. They walked side by side to the entrance.

The butler stopped them at the door. "Mr. Darcy, there was an urgent letter for you. Since I understood you were at Longbourn, I sent it there. Would you like me to order it back?"

Mr. Darcy was in too good of a mood to worry about a letter at the moment. He had spent the last few hours realizing what it meant to be refined by God. And in doing so, he had cleared the path for his proposal. He was enraptured imagining how and when he would do it. He did not think he could wait another twenty-four hours. Her smile. The brightness in her eyes. Her beautiful spirit. The way her hair caught the sun and shined. Her beautiful, full lips. He had lingered on his examination of that last topic, but he was determined to do it right; he would ask her to be his wife before he kissed her sweet lips.

"Mr. Darcy?" the butler prodded politely.

Georgiana giggled. Snapping out of his delightful reverie, Darcy flushed and stammered, "Forgive me, I was preoccupied. Yes, please send a rider to retrieve the letter. In the meantime, I would like a bath and a shave. Please instruct the kitchen that I would like hot water immediately. And I believe Miss Georgiana would like some hot water as well." Georgiana nodded to the butler and then kissed Darcy's cheek and flitted away to her chambers.

Darcy looked at his pocket watch as he walked to his chambers. It was three o'clock. It had been a long morning, but if things panned out as he hoped, he would soon be an engaged man! He had planned to wait until the ring was ready, but now he couldn't bear to delay even one more day. He would make do without it. He had told Elizabeth he would call on her a little after four. Perhaps a long bath was not possible, but he had time for a quick one with a nice clean shave.

Darcy's valet noted the excitement in his master's countenance. A little later, as Darcy stepped out of the bath, Winston said, "You seem inordinately happy about a simple bath, sir. Am I to wish you joy?"

Darcy smiled and slipped his arms into his dressing gown. "In due time, Winston, in due time. All I am going to say is ask me again tonight. I can think of nothing that will dissuade me from making her an offer."

"Bravo, sir, bravo! Miss Elizabeth is the finest lady who ever walked on Pemberley's grounds."

"That she is. Now give me your finest shave, for I intend to have a special conversation with her this evening. I want to look my best."

"Certainly, sir. I must say, I am becoming quite experienced at shaving your face while you are grinning. I certainly see those dimples more often now, thanks to Miss Elizabeth."

"Yes, they have had a bit of exercise these last few months. It has been nearly three months since I met her, and I have never been more sure of something in my life. It is not like me to be so impulsive. Not in business, not in finances, not in friendships or acquaintances, but she draws it out of me. It reminds me of my youth when I had fewer cares, yet these last few months I have had more on my shoulders than ever before. And I know whom to thank for it."

Winston applied the lathered soap and began the shave. "Miss Elizabeth?" he asked.

"Yes, but it is more than that. She was only the instrument, or in my case, the hot iron, that spurred me along. She showed me the way to God's peace. She is truly remarkable, Winston. She radiates goodness."

"So I have been told, sir, many times. However, if you go on talking about her during your shave, I may scar you with this blade," Winston chuckled. "Now, hold still."

Darcy did as he was told and let his valet continue. They were nearly done when there was a knock on the door. "Would you mind answering that, Winston? I am expecting a letter."

Winston put down the blade and retrieved the letter from the servant. He walked back to Darcy and handed it to him.

Mr. Darcy muttered his thanks and looked down at the letter. His heart stopped in his chest as he recognized the unique handwriting of Mr. Wickham.

Winston saw the surprise and fear in Darcy's eyes. "What is it, sir?"

Darcy tried to hide his alarm. "It is just a letter from an old friend," he said. "Please finish the shave and help me get dressed immediately."

Darcy's stomach lurched. Why had Wickham sent him a letter? Darcy reviewed their last conversation in his mind; there was no good reason for Wickham to contact him. Had he devised some way to turn the situation to his monetary advantage? Was he demanding money to keep quiet about Georgiana? Winston finished the shave and helped Darcy get dressed. Then Darcy dismissed him. He put down the letter and poured himself a drink. He sipped the brandy while looking outside, but he found no solace in the drink or the view. He returned to the letter and opened it.

Darcy,

You may be wondering why in the world I would contact you. If anyone should be keeping their distance from you, it is me. But I have been pondering a certain situation involving Miss Elizabeth Bennet, and I have come to the conclusion to tell you everything.

The day after our chat at Longbourn, Miss Bingley met me secretly in Meryton and made me an offer I almost could not refuse. She wished me to compromise Miss Elizabeth in such a way that her reputation would be tarnished forever. She was quite descriptive in her suggestions. I was to wait for Miss Elizabeth outside of the orphanage and, well, I suppose the particulars are not necessary. Needless to say, there would have been enough witnesses that her reputation would have been muddied quite irrevocably. Miss Bingley offered me two thousand pounds for my service.

You know I am hard up for money, and you are probably asking yourself why I hesitated. I would have gotten a piece of lovely muslin and earned a sizable amount of money for my fun. Well, if it was not for your blasted faith in me, I would have accepted! But you said you believed in me. You said you wanted to believe there was good in me. I know I am not a perfect man, but I like to think I am not a villain. That moment when you apologized for hitting me, well, it cleared a few things up for me. I could either continue doing things that will earn me well-deserved punches, or I could try to be a real gentleman.

So, I hope it is quite obvious which choice I made. I am not going to harm your Elizabeth. I will not deny that I thought long and hard about the offer, but she, and all of Meryton, is safe from me. I did promise you that. For once, you have my word.

If Miss Bingley denies my account, you may be interested to know that Colonel Forster had a man watching me who overheard the whole thing. Perhaps admitting that my superiors knew of Miss Bingley's offer belittles my good deed, but I was unaware of this minor detail when I wrestled with my decision. Had I accepted Miss Bingley's proposal, I doubtlessly would have been caught and court-martialed. Thus, it seems your faith in me saved my neck from the gallows.

I must tell you that you sounded just like your father when we spoke. You are beginning to look like him too. I offer that as a sincere compliment, for I dearly loved him. And although I will not admit to any wrongdoing, please believe that I am sorry my actions have pained Georgiana.

I leave you with my gratitude for believing in me, even when I did not. It takes a good man to forgive someone like me. Perhaps this letter evens the playing field a little. You did me one good deed; now, I have done you one in return.

Do with this information as you chose. But if you would like to speak with me in person, I will be walking the river path at four o'clock.

G.W.

Darcy looked at his watch; it was already ten minutes to four. He quickly went to the writing desk and penned a note to Elizabeth, explaining that he had urgent business to attend to and must postpone their trip to Oakham Mount. He felt a pang of guilt as he realized she was probably already waiting for him.

Hopefully, she would not suspect him of intentionally delaying the topic yet again.

He quickly made his way to the stables. He would have run, but he didn't want to raise Miss Bingley's suspicions. He ordered the stable hand to saddle his horse immediately, and when the man seemed to be taking an enormous amount of time, Darcy anxiously started assisting him. In slightly more time than he had to spare, he mounted his horse in one fluid movement and took off. He knew of only one river in Meryton; he wasn't sure it had a path, but it was the best option he could think of.

He rode hard and fast. All the while, his mind was trying to make sense of the note. He wasn't puzzled by Wickham's accusation—it was all too easy to believe that Miss Bingley would do such a thing. What puzzled him was why Wickham had not accepted her offer. It was out of character for Wickham to turn away easy money. He could not understand it.

He reached the river, and sure enough, there was a path on the bank. Meryton was just one mile north. He looked at his watch and saw that it was already quarter past four. Assuming that Wickham was already on his way back to the barracks, he slowed to a trot and turned the horse south. The path was well worn but meant for walking, not riding. Trees and bushes grazed his legs as he ducked under branches. After a few minutes, he saw two gentlemen up ahead in red coats. He slowed the horse and dismounted just as he came upon them.

Mr. Wickham turned and greeted Darcy. "I see you received my note."

Darcy looked at the other officer suspiciously. "Is there somewhere we can talk?" he asked.

"I would love to dismiss my sidekick, Darcy, but you are the one who convinced the colonel that my every move should be watched. Besides, he may be of some use to our conversation. This is Mr. Churchill. He happens to be the very man who overheard Miss Bingley's proposed plan. We can speak openly in front of him. I thought you might like to question him as to the truthfulness of my tale."

Darcy stood face to face with Wickham, a mere arm's length away from him. "Actually, I do not have any questions," Darcy said slowly. "I do not even know why I came here."

"You do not need Mr. Churchill to verify what happened?"

"No," Darcy replied. "There is some part of me that knows it is not necessary."

"So, you believe me?"

"I do. As much as I question your moral character, I have little doubt that your account is true."

Wickham smiled curiously. "Then why did you come?"

"I do not know."

"Come now, Darcy, why did you come?"

"I was overwhelmed. My mind was reeling, and I had to speak to you."

Wickham put his arms out and walked in a circle. "Speak! What have you got to lose? I only offered to meet with you to prove the truthfulness of what happened. If you do not doubt me, what else is there to say?"

Darcy looked down at his hands. This was very humbling. He looked up and said, "I suppose I need to thank you."

"Thank me? First, you apologize to me, and now, you thank me?"

"Yes. Miss Elizabeth would want me to. If she knew what has happened, she would thank you for having the integrity to say 'no'. Sometimes the easy path is the wrong one. You chose to take the harder path because it was the right thing to do. I thank you for that. I am grateful for Miss Elizabeth's safety. I am grateful you told me of Miss Bingley's plan. I thank you most sincerely, Wickham."

Wickham examined Mr. Darcy. He seemed to be truly sincere. "Then I accept your gracious kindness. I truly did not know what to expect when I saw you galloping towards us. I suppose this is the last we will ever see of each other. Good day, Darcy. I am truly happy for you and Miss Elizabeth." Mr. Wickham extended his hand and shook Darcy's. He then tipped his hat and began walking again.

Wickham wasn't out of ear range before Darcy yelled out to him. "Wait!" He caught up to him and asked, "Is that all? You truly are not going to ask me for money?"

"No. Darcy, I really meant what I said. I may be hard up for money, but you said you believed in me. That is priceless. No one has believed in me for years." Then Wickham grinned and added, "Who knows, perhaps you will make a gentleman out of me yet!"

Darcy watched him walk away for the second time. He was suddenly struck with a memory of something Elizabeth had written in her notebook: each choice has hidden consequences. One is free to make a choice but not to choose the consequences. He could have chosen not to forgive Wickham. He could have chosen to hit him again. He could have exposed Wickham to the whole town. But what would have been the consequence of that choice? What would his vengeance have cost him? It was shocking to consider what had nearly happened.

A gentle peace slowly began to fill Darcy's heart and mind. He realized the consequences of forgiving Wickham were far beyond what he had ever anticipated. He had only hoped for peace, and he had felt a flicker of it after his conversation with Wickham at Longbourn. But that was nothing compared to the peace he felt now. He had chosen to forgive Wickham, and in turn Wickham had chosen to spare Elizabeth.

He continued to watch Wickham walk away. It felt as if this revelation was going to consume him. His knees literally began to shake. He walked back to the horse and put his hands on the saddle, but he could not mount it.

He was overwhelmed. He let go of the horse and knelt down, right there by the river. He almost collapsed onto his knees the pull was so great, and he bowed his head. He thanked God, and he thanked God for a great length of time. He thanked Him until his knees went numb and until his eyes could shed no more grateful tears. He opened his heart to God and poured out everything he had felt and learned this day, both from the blacksmith and from Wickham.

As he knelt there expressing his gratitude, an idea came to him. It came so suddenly, it was as if someone beside him had literally spoken it. The idea was clear as day. He opened his eyes and immediately acted on the thought. He mounted his horse and spurred it towards Longbourn.

*****

Darcy knocked on Mr. Bennet's open study door. "Mr. Bennet," Darcy said, "Could I have a moment of your time?"

"Of course. Please come in. How was the blacksmith's?"

"It was incredible. I have learned a great deal today, and I feel a strong urge to discuss it with someone. Actually, the idea came to me that I should discuss it with you."

Mr. Bennet sat back and put his ledgers away. "Do you wish to talk to the father of Elizabeth or the retired reverend?"

"Both, I think. Let me start from the beginning. Elizabeth, forgive me, Miss Elizabeth, once asked me what I want to be when I grew up. I was quite perplexed by the question. After a moment's thought, I informed her that I was already fully grown and, obviously, my position in life was Master of Pemberley. She looked away with a smile but said nothing. I thought on it many times and considered it a very odd exchange.

"I realize now that I misunderstood the question. She was really asking *whom* I wanted to be when I grew up. If I had understood, I would have said that I wanted to become like my father. He was my hero. He nurtured me, and taught me, and prepared me to inherit a priceless estate. But if you asked me that same question today, I would have a different answer.

"Now, there is only one father I wish to emulate: God the Father. He is refining me and preparing me to receive the greatest inheritance of all. I know now that only by molding my life and submitting my will to His plans can I inherit a place in Heaven. Pemberley is nothing to the mansions there."

Mr. Bennet nodded and listened quietly to his epiphany.

"I learned a valuable lesson today: God really does navigate our lives if we let Him," Darcy continued. "If we are willing to listen to His counsel, He will grant us blessings of infinite number and worth. I never imagined that following God would have such a dramatic impact on my happiness. I had hoped that it would, but I never truly believed it until now."

Mr. Bennet smiled. "Christ tells us in John, chapter 14, verse 11: 'These things I have spoken to you, that my joy may be in you, and that your joy may be full.' Your joy is full, Mr. Darcy. I can see that just by looking at you."

"Yes. For the first time in my life, my choices, however difficult, have led me to the right place at the right time. Suffice it to say, a great number of people were spared a great deal of pain when I chose to forgive Wickham last week. It would have been easy to hate him. It would have been easy to ruin his life, but I did not. In turn, Wickham could have destroyed what I hold most dear, but he did not. It is almost unbelievable. I owe my very happiness to a man I considered my enemy last week."

Mr. Bennet finished his thought for him. "You turned the other cheek, and instead of being struck, you received the peace God promised. It is no small feat to alter one's character so dramatically. I would say you have learned much more than the answer to Malachi 3:3. You have learned that enduring our trials refines us little by little until we have God-like characteristics. You have learned that our trials do not define us, rather they refine us."

Darcy repeated it aloud, stunned with the simplicity of it. "Our trials do not define us, they refine us. Yes, that is exactly what I have learned. I can see that now. God will continue to give me trials and tribulations until I become spiritually refined and reflect His countenance in my every thought, word, and action. My father may have been my hero, and to some extent he still is, but now I wish to emulate Christ. And if it means enduring trials, I will eagerly comply. After all, silver cannot be refined unless it is the hottest part of the fire. And I will not be refined until I reflect the very image of God."

Mr. Bennet sat and listened to the man purge himself of his new found understanding. "You have had a great deal of enlightenment today it seems."

"And I have you and Miss Elizabeth to thank for it. You are a gifted teacher. Miss Elizabeth said people would travel over ten miles to hear you preach. Why did you ever give it up?"

"What makes you think I have?"

Darcy chuckled. "Indeed, you are correct. Without your little sermon on forgiveness, I would have never reached this point."

Mr. Bennet laughed too. "Perhaps I can take off my preacher cloak now and ask you a few questions as the father of Elizabeth."

Darcy smiled and said, "How about I save you from having to ask the question? I am ready now to offer for Miss Elizabeth. For the first time, I feel like someday I may be worthy of deserving her. May I have your permission to love your daughter deeper than imaginable? May I bind myself to her permanently? Will you trust me to ensure her happiness? May I marry Miss Elizabeth?"

"If I know my daughter at all, you are giving yourself too little credit. It is she who feels she is not worthy of you. This will be a very successful marriage when you both start out so humbly. I appreciate you asking me, but it is not me you need to be asking. You have my blessing. And please, save your romantic speeches for Elizabeth." He stood and offered his hand.

Darcy shook his hand and grinned. Things were in place now. All he had to do was be a little patient. "Thank you. May I see Miss Elizabeth now?"

"By all means. Would you like a private audience?"

"Not today. I just want to say hello before I return to Netherfield," Darcy said.

Mr. Bennet opened his study door and motioned for him to exit first. Darcy watched Elizabeth's face light up as he entered the parlor. Mr. Bingley was already sitting next to Jane.

Elizabeth put her embroidery down and stood up. "Good afternoon, Mr. Darcy. How are you?"

He walked over to her and bowed and kissed her hand. "I am sorry I was delayed. I fear it is too late to set off for Oakham Mount as we planned. But perhaps there is still time for a short walk. Would you care to join me?" Elizabeth nodded.

Jane stood and said, "Mr. Bingley, I believe my presence is required in the garden. Can I interest you in a stroll?"

"It will be my pleasure," Bingley replied. He offered his arm, and Jane took it shyly as the group headed out the door.

Rain clouds threatened to spill their contents, but Elizabeth could tell they would have a little bit of time. She slid her arm around William's and simply enjoyed the moment. Every look, every word, and every touch they shared was so special to Elizabeth. She let her mind wander to imagining all sorts of future experiences. She imagined their first Christmas, their first spring at Pemberley, their first baby, and suddenly she was struck with the image of their first kiss. The order seemed a little backwards, and she let out a giggle.

"What prompted that giggle?" Mr. Darcy asked, truly intrigued.

She looked up to him and knew her blush was apparent; she felt the heat of it in her cheeks. "I was just contemplating the great many things the future may bring. Perhaps my active mind is being a little premature. I shall just have to wait and see how accurate my imagination is."

Miss Bennet and Bingley had hurried on ahead of them. When Darcy felt confident in their privacy, he turned to Elizabeth and stopped her from walking. "May I just hold you for a moment?" He felt an overwhelming need to hold what was most dear to him, especially after knowing great harm could have come to her.

Elizabeth looked into his loving eyes and nodded. He reached one hand up to her cheek and gently guided her head to his shoulder. He then slowly, gently, wrapped his arms around her, and rested his cheek against her forehead. He held her like that for several minutes. Then he leaned down until they were cheek to cheek and brushed his cleanly shaven cheek against hers once, then twice. The sensation and intimacy of the embrace made the pre-storm chill a little less noticeable.

She closed her eyes and tilted her head up to him a little more, and she felt his lips brush her cheek as gently as possible. It wasn't quite a kiss, it was simply a tender brush of his lips, but its gentleness sent goose bumps down her spine. She brushed her cheek back against his in response, and he caressed her face and smoothed her hair ever so softly. He leaned into her further and brushed his lips against her ear. The heat she felt rising from such ministrations was overwhelming. Oh, how she wanted to kiss him!

Mr. Darcy heard a feminine, guttural, moan escape from her throat, and he felt the vibrations of it on his lips as they were very near her throat. He reluctantly released her and took both of her hands in his. "Thank you. You lifted me up with that."

She tried to regain some composure and stammered, "I doubt that. I am a great walker but I do not profess to have the strength to lift you. Do you imagine me with arms that rivals Colonel Fitzwilliam's?"

"You were admiring my cousin's arms?"

"And shoulders," she teased.

He chuckled and said, "I shall refrain from telling him so until I have secured your hand. I suppose I will have to lock you in the cellar when he visits." He tried to sound stern. "Remember, a good wife vows to honor and obey."

"Oh dear, perhaps Mamma is right; I shall never make a good wife!"

He squeezed her hands and smiled. She asked him, "Is everything all right? I thought you would not have time to come today after your urgent note. Then I was worried when you spent so long talking to my father." She was trying to control her desire to kiss him, but she was failing miserably at it, probably because he was still caressing her hands.

"I am quite well. Perhaps better than I have ever been before. But I have some disturbing news that concerns you."

He then explained Miss Bingley's thwarted plan, Wickham's change of heart, and his profound gratitude for her safety. "I am confident that Wickham poses no risk to you. Miss Bingley, on the other hand, I cannot vouch for."

She looked ahead to Jane and Bingley and began walking in their direction. "What are you going to do now? Will you tell Mr. Bingley?"

"Yes, I think I must. But I will leave the matter with him. I never imagined that the small bit of faith I put in Wickham would bring so much goodness into my life, so I suppose the only thing to do is to offer the same forgiveness to Miss Bingley." Darcy took her arm and wrapped it around his. He simply wanted to touch her. And if, for propriety's sake, walking arm in arm was the only thing allowed, he would do so and relish every opportunity.

They walked in silence for a moment. "You were very brave today," she said.

"I did not feel very brave," Darcy replied. "I was in a panic when I read that note. I was worried he was after more money. I thought he would make threats against you or Georgiana. But he turned me down, said he did not want any reward. I cannot describe how much it all affected me. I could hardly contain my emotions. I am overwhelmed with gratitude that you were kept safe."

Elizabeth did not know if Mr. Darcy knew he was rubbing her arm or not, but it was very relaxing. A raindrop fell on her cheek, surprising her out of her mesmerized state. "Oh dear," she said, "you had better return to Netherfield, or you will be caught in the rain."

He felt the first few drops as well. He glanced at Bingley and Miss Bennet who had just turned around to head back. They were not even looking in Darcy's direction. He quickly took Elizabeth by the shoulders and leaned in to kiss her on the forehead. "Goodbye, my love. I will see you tomorrow, of that you can be sure. Nothing will keep me from hiking Oakham Mount with you. I promised we would have a very important discussion, and I will do everything in my power to keep my promise." He smiled widely at her.

Elizabeth reached her hand to his newly shaved face and fingered his sweet, little dimple. Without saying another word, she leaned in and kissed the dimple briefly and gave him her best smile.

*****

Darcy decided to wait until after he dressed for dinner to show Bingley the note. Part of him wanted to delay it further. It would be a difficult conversation, and he was not looking forward to it. But it needed to be done.

He thanked his valet and checked his pocket watch. He should have some time before the dinner bell rang.

He had already mentioned to Bingley on the ride from Longbourn that there was a serious matter concerning Caroline that they needed to discuss.

It was as if Bingley hadn't even heard him. It seemed nothing could stop Bingley from beaming for joy; Miss Bennet had agreed to a courtship. Their remaining conversation had centered on the topic of marital bliss with the Bennet sisters. There was no one Darcy would like to call brother more than Bingley.

Darcy slipped Wickham's letter into his pocket and went downstairs. Darcy could hear Bingley playing billiards, and he stood in the doorway.

"Darcy, come in!" Bingley called out. "I can set them up again if you want a fair game."

Darcy took a deep breath. "Perhaps afterwards if you still feel up to it."

"I doubt anything could damper my mood. I will be a married man soon if things go as planned! In fact, I very well may be married before you get around to proposing!"

Darcy laughed and put his hands to his chest as if he had been shot. "You have wounded me!" There was no point in delaying any further. Darcy closed the door behind him and turned to Bingley.

Bingley put the put the end of the stick down and leaned on it a bit. He looked at Darcy for a moment. Darcy was teasing him, but there was an undercurrent of sadness in his eyes. Bingley stood up and put the stick on the table's edge. "Out with it. What has Caroline done now?"

Darcy pulled out Wickham's letter. "I received this letter from George Wickham this afternoon. I think it is self-explanatory." Darcy handed the note over and watched as Bingley read it. He knew immediately when he got to the part that described Miss Bingley's plan. Bingley's face went red, and he gripped the paper more tightly. Darcy patiently waited for him to finish.

Bingley folded up the letter and walked to the side table. He poured himself a bit of port and took his time in drinking it. He was angry at Caroline, angrier than he had ever been in his life, but he had no idea what to say to Darcy. What if Elizabeth had been harmed? How could Caroline have designed such an evil plan? How could she be so blind to Darcy's complete disinterest in her? He had explained to her many times that Darcy did not think of her that way, but it never seemed to sink in. Was she really so desperate that she would stoop this low?

He knew the answers to these questions without even speaking them out loud. He finished his port and turned to his friend. "Darcy, I am so sorry. I do not have the words to express my mortification that Caroline could do such a thing."

Darcy felt sorry for his friend. The news had dampened his jubilant mood. Darcy had never seen him so wretched. "I understand, Bingley, and I do not hold this against you. However you decide to deal with Caroline, I will accept your decision. I am simply grateful that nothing happened. In fact, I am so full of gratitude that I have no room left for feelings of retribution."

"But I should have suspected something!" Bingley exclaimed. "I should have seen how desperate she was. Perhaps I have been too lenient; I do not know. I have no idea how she expected to get her hands on two thousand pounds. I still control her assets and dowry. Perhaps she never intended to actually pay him."

Darcy took the bottle of port and refilled Bingley's glass and poured himself a glass as well. "Let us put a few things in perspective. She felt threatened by Elizabeth. Here was a lady with no connections, no fortune, and yet Miss Bingley felt she was being passed over for her. Perhaps I bear some of the blame. If I had told Miss Bingley myself years ago that I had no interest in her instead of making you handle interference for me, perhaps she would have moved on. She might have allowed herself to be open to the other gentlemen who have shown interest. I should have been more forthright."

"No, Darcy. You cannot take responsibility for everything and everyone. What Caroline did was despicable. But what am I going to do about it?"

Together they discussed several suggestions that might impress upon Caroline the seriousness of her actions. Sending her to her Yorkshire aunt. Withholding pin money and new dresses. Keeping her from the London season next year. Hiring a particularly austere and humorless companion for her.

Bingley sighed. "Well, she cannot stay here, of course. Who knows what she will do when she hears I am courting Miss Bennet? And what if she endangers Miss Elizabeth again? I shall instruct Mr. and Mrs. Hurst to accompany her back to London and keep her there until I marry Jane."

"You mean Miss Bennet, of course," Darcy corrected him with a chuckle.

"Yes, of course," Bingley said with a blush. "I can see the difficulty now! But in all seriousness, Caroline must leave tomorrow at first light."

"Whatever you decide, I will support you, Bingley. Ultimately, the choice is up to you."

"Darcy, I do not know what to say. Not one friend in a hundred would have reacted this way." He stood up straight and shook Darcy's hand. "Thank you for telling me," he said. "I am so sorry. I would have felt miserable if something had happened to Miss Elizabeth."

"You are a good man, Bingley. And from the looks of it, soon we will be calling each other 'brother'." Darcy patted Bingley's shoulder. "Congratulations! Miss Bennet is wonderful."

"Thank you. Now, I must find Caroline. I can hear Georgiana playing in the music room. Perhaps you two can sequester yourself there tonight. Make sure Miss Darcy plays something loud enough to drown out Caroline's protests."

"I will do that." Darcy turned and left Bingley pacing in front of the fireplace.

When he arrived at the music room, he smiled at Georgiana and relaxed into the chair. She was playing with all the passion she had ever played with, perhaps even more. Her talent had grown in the last few weeks. She was practicing daily again for as many hours as she could. He thought of all those months when she didn't even so much as look at the piano, and once again, he was grateful for Elizabeth in his life.

As she played, he considered what his life would be like if he had never meet Elizabeth. She had truly changed the course of his life, just as surely as a flooded river overflows its banks and cuts a new path. He smiled and allowed himself the pleasure of imagining their storybook "happily ever after". He knew their future path would not be easy, but he would welcome the hurdles along the way.

In his heart, he said a quick prayer. *God, thank you for bringing Elizabeth into my life. With her by my side, I will happily endure the heat of the refiner's fire. Selfishly, I ask you to give me a long life with her. Grant me enough time to make myself worthy of her goodness. I know now that my trials do not define me, rather they refine me, but I may need her brilliant radiance to see the stars in the darkness. Please give us many happy years together.*

As Darcy closed his prayer, a warmth spread through his chest, like a fire being stoked into a blaze. The feeling was so peculiar. He had never felt peace in such a concentrated form. Suddenly, he realized God had answered his prayer. He felt sure they would enjoy a long life together. In fact, he had never been more sure of anything in his entire life. The sensation was nearly overwhelming. Elizabeth was his soul mate, and God had granted him the blessing he wanted most—no, *needed* most. A quote from Elizabeth's notebook came to his mind: *"God only gives us what we want if it is also what we need."*

Just as the music reached a beautiful crescendo, Miss Bingley's shrieks echoed from the billiard room, but Darcy and

Georgiana remained blissfully unaware. With a smile, he leaned back, closed his eyes, and enjoyed the music.

CHAPTER 15

Darcy looked outside the next morning, pleased to see that the storm from last night had moved on. The skies were bright and clear. He rang for his valet and anxiously waited for his arrival. When Winston appeared, Darcy noticed he was agitated and fumbled quite a bit with his work.

"Winston, are you well?" Darcy asked.

"Yes, sir. It is just that Miss Bingley is downstairs ordering all the servants around. No one knows what to think of it. She has never risen this early before. She rang for her maid at six o'clock!"

Mr. Darcy had nearly forgotten that Miss Bingley was going to be leaving this morning. He had tried very hard to stay out of her way all night. After he had exhausted Georgiana on the pianoforte with multiple encores, they took their meal privately, and then he read aloud to Georgiana for hours. Finally, they quietly went to bed, successfully avoiding conversation with either of the Bingleys.

But none of that concerned Darcy now. Today was going to be special. He was going to propose to Elizabeth. He wanted it to be just right. While Winston shaved him, he thought about the future moment when he could capture Elizabeth's lips with his own. It was a very pleasant ten minutes.

Mr. Winston had a difficult time shaving his master with all that grinning. But he took his time and even got the dimples. Winston wiped Darcy's face and stepped back. "All done, sir. Perhaps the green waistcoat with the dark blue overcoat?"

"I think I will wear the grey waistcoat today." It wasn't the best choice for hiking, but he wanted to look his best for Elizabeth.

"Very well, sir."

Darcy allowed Winston to finish dressing him and then sent him on his way. As Darcy descended the stairs, he heard Miss Bingley shouting orders at servants like an army sergeant commanding troops in battle. Darcy caught her brother's eyes from across the room and could see from the look on his face that Bingley, although frustrated with his sister, was somewhat amused by her conduct. Darcy quietly poured himself a cup of coffee and tried to escape before Miss Bingley turned around. He was not successful.

"Mr. Darcy!" Miss Bingley cried. Her entire tone instantly changed. She was all smiles and pleasantries again. "Please, sit and break your fast with me."

Shocked was too weak of a word for what Darcy felt. How could she have any notion of continuing a friendship with him after what she had done?

"Caroline, please. Leave him alone," Bingley urged.

"Nonsense, Charles! Mr. Darcy and I are old friends. Mr. Darcy, you may not have heard, but Mr. and Mrs. Hurst have invited me to stay with them in London, and I am leaving very soon. Come join me one last time before I depart." She smiled widely at him, without a trace of remorse or guilt. She seemed determine to carry on as if nothing had changed.

"You are right, Miss Bingley. We are very old friends, and perhaps I should talk to you before you leave," Darcy said. He put down his cup and walked over to her. "I was told once that forgiveness is a virtue. So, I forgive you, Miss Bingley. But hear this well: I will never forget that you plotted to harm the lady I love."

"Why, Mr. Darcy! Do not tell me you actually believe—"

"Hear this as well, Miss Bingley: even if your vicious machinations had succeeded, I still would have offered for

Elizabeth Bennet. I love her, and I do not love you. I will be engaged to her by the end of the day. Furthermore, I could never marry a woman I did not respect. Your wicked scheme has destroyed any vestige of respect I ever had for you. So, as plainly as I can say it, you have no chance of becoming Mistress of Pemberley.

"Truth be told, you were never even in consideration for the position. I should have been honest with you from the start. I apologize for that. But let us forgive one another and wish each other well as old friends."

"But, Mr. Darcy! You cannot—" Miss Bingley started.

"No, Miss Bingley," Darcy continued. "Farewells are all I wish to discuss with you. It is simple. I would very much appreciate it if I could enjoy the rest of my morning without any flattery or flirtations from you. I will say that I wish you a safe journey, and you will say that you wish me well. I doubt we will ever see each other again."

"But Miss Elizabeth is quite unsuitable—" she began.

Darcy's patience was coming to an end. With a firm voice, he interrupted once more, "And, if you ever slander or endanger Miss Elizabeth again, I will not hesitate to share my unflattering opinion of you with the entire *ton*."

Miss Bingley's face paled at Darcy's threat. She looked around the room in a panic. Mr. Darcy's expression made it clear that he was quite serious. Her brother's face was just as severe. Mrs. Hurst was motioning with her hands for Caroline to acquiesce. Miss Bingley took a deep breath. Then she curtsied and lowered her voice in defeat. "Mr. Darcy, I wish you joy."

"And Miss Bingley, I hope the weather stays fine for your journey." He bowed and watched as she left the dining room with Mrs. Hurst.

Bingley patted Darcy on his back and said, "Well done, man. Let me apologize again for—"

"No, that is all in the past now, Bingley. Let us speak of it no more," Darcy interrupted as he filled his plate with ham, eggs, and a muffin. "Actually, I wish to talk about something else entirely. I need your help with Elizabeth today. We are going to hike Oakham Mount, and I was wondering if my two favorite chaperones could find a way to give us some privacy. I would like to have a very important conversation with her."

"Finally! I imagine the poor lady has been waiting weeks for you to propose! Congratulations! And, yes, I can occupy Miss Bennet easily enough. She is an angel!"

"I know, Bingley, you have told me that many times. But I fear we will no longer be friends if we argue about which Bennet sister is the most lovely."

Bingley laughed. "Indeed, for I would win the argument!"

"Hardly. But because I do not want to sow contention between us, I will allow you to claim that Miss Jane Bennet is the fairest. But we both know there is no one more radiant than Elizabeth Bennet."

"I know, I know; she glows."

*****

Darcy stopped by the blacksmith's at a quarter to ten. Mrs. Rogers welcomed him profusely and immediately took out two wooden boxes: a small ring box, and a long, slender box which obviously held the necklace.

"I think you will be very pleased with James's work, sir," Mrs. Rogers said. She opened the boxes and showed him the jewelry.

They were both perfect. "Ah, the necklace is even better than I imagined. She will love it! And the diamond you chose is just right for Elizabeth. It is so brilliant. Thank you, Mrs. Rogers."

"Of course, sir. I had the carpenter make these boxes last night. I just finished putting in the red velvet myself a few minutes ago."

Darcy thanked her and closed the boxes. On the outside of the necklace box, two initials were engraved: E. D. "Elizabeth Darcy. That was very thoughtful of you."

"I only did what I thought Elizabeth would like. She is the finest young woman in all of Meryton. You are very lucky to have earned her affections. I can tell she admires you a great deal. Yes, you are a very lucky gentleman indeed."

Darcy said nothing but knew it was more than luck that had brought Elizabeth into his life; it was God. People often wished each other good luck, and it seemed harmless enough. But in Darcy's mind, saying a person was lucky when good things happened was ignoring God's role in life. There was no such thing as luck, only blessings from God. He made a note to include this realization in his notebook.

He took his bankbook out of his pocket and asked for the amount. He then added a hundred pounds to the amount and handed payment to Mrs. Rogers.

"Sir, this is not the correct amount!"

"I believe it is. Make sure to tell Mr. Rogers thank you." He collected his two boxes. On his way out the door, he turned and said, "Could you hold that sword for me as well? Mr. Rogers will know which one I mean. I cannot take it with me now, but I would like to pick it up another day."

"Certainly, Mr. Darcy."

Mr. Darcy closed the door behind him and tucked the boxes into his horse's saddlebag. He mounted and guided the horse towards Longbourn. It was a short distance. As he approached, he saw Bingley and Georgiana exiting the carriage. They had planned to meet just after ten for their walk to Oakham Mount. They all knocked on the door together and waited to be shown in. But instead of being greeted by Mrs. Hill's familiar face, they were greeted by Mrs. Bennet herself. She seemed to be on her best behavior.

"Welcome! Mr. Darcy, I believe Elizabeth is excited to show you her favorite place to hike. It is a sacred place for her. She goes there often when she is troubled. Miss Darcy, it is so pleasant to have you back at Longbourn. Mr. Bingley, may I say how nice you look? Jane will be speechless. She has talked of nothing else besides the courtship. May I tell both of you gentlemen how proud I am to see my daughters so happy with their suitors? I can hardly contain myself, but I am trying. Come in, come in."

Mr. Darcy tried not to appear suspicious, but Mrs. Bennet seemed to have undergone a drastic change in the last twenty-four hours. She was quite out of character. But his curiosity disappeared as he saw Elizabeth's smiling face shining at him. She was so gloriously beautiful that his breath caught. She was wearing a dress he had never seen before. It was pale green with embroidered, dark green leaves across the bodice. The sleeves were just enough to cover the rounding of her shoulders, but no more. He caught himself admiring the dress' sheer overlay a little too much, and he tried to rein in his diverted thoughts. She was lovely. Bingley would lose this battle. Elizabeth was the angel.

As he walked over to her, he noticed that she had taken great care with her hair today. There were small flowers in her bun, and the ringlets by her face framed her beautiful, brilliant eyes very attractively. She smiled at him, and he saw that life's luster glow even brighter. "Good morning, Mr. Darcy," she said.

Mr. Darcy smiled back one of his dimpled grins that she so adored. "Good morning, Miss Elizabeth." He took her offered hand and kissed it once on the top, and then turned it over and kissed her palm. Then he gently closed her tiny fingers. He winked at her and whispered, "In case you want to save one for later."

She winked back at him and whispered, "I hope I will have others instead."

He looked into her eyes and grinned.

Mrs. Bennet came over and said, "Mr. Darcy, might I have a word with you and Elizabeth?"

He looked to Elizabeth, who gave him a curious look. She seemed equally mystified by Mrs. Bennet's behavior. Darcy was not looking forward to another conversation with Mrs. Bennet, but his good breeding was second nature. "Certainly," he replied politely.

"If you will both follow me," Mrs. Bennet said.

Darcy took Elizabeth's arm and gave it a squeeze. They followed Mrs. Bennet into the library. It was a fairly small room, and there were a great many piles of books, neatly stacked on top of each other because the shelves were too full. Mrs. Bennet motioned for them to take a seat in the chaise by the window.

Mrs. Bennet took a deep breath and started pacing. "As you know, David was my only son. He was so kind and loving and so well behaved. I never had to discipline him for anything. But you know that, Elizabeth. Of all his sisters, you were the one who got down on the floor and played jacks with him. You were the one who showed him how to pump his legs on the swing. You spent more time with him than all the other girls combined.

"And because of that, I had faith in your ability to care for him. I knew he would be safe with you. But you were just eleven. I should have been there watching him instead of you, and I have berated myself ever since. It should have been me who watched David skate. Maybe I would have been able to save him. It should have been me who jumped in after him. It was too much to bear. I didn't know how to cope. I had to bury my only son and see my favorite daughter on her deathbed, all because I wanted to visit Mrs. Long."

Favorite daughter? It was like listening to a foreign language; none of it made any sense. This was not her mother. Everything seemed backwards today. Mrs. Bennet began ringing her hands as she paced. Elizabeth could even see a bit of perspiration forming on her brow.

"You asked me if you could take him skating," Mrs. Bennet said, "and I said yes. I did not know that the lake was thawing. But that does not excuse me. I choose Mrs. Long that day over my responsibility to my children. A mother should know better. I stayed at your bedside for days, but in your confusion, you just kept mumbling and calling out for David. I could not bear it. I could not bear to hear you, or anyone, talk about my dead child.

"Every time I looked at you, I imagined you and David in that freezing water. I remembered the servant rushing into Mrs. Long's parlor and telling me about the accident. All because I wanted to hear the latest gossip from Mrs. Long! So, I left your bedside. When you woke up, I was gone.

"I criticized you and blamed you, hoping to ease my own burden of guilt. Each time I looked at you, all I saw was the reminder of what I had done. My actions almost cost me two of my favorite children. And when things finally started looking better, when it looked like you would survive, it was too late. I knew I could never repair the damage I had done. I could never take back the words I had said to you.

"You were so easy to love; at first, it was difficult to conceal my true feelings. But as the years went by, it became simpler. The more I pushed you away, the less guilt I felt. I know I have been awful, truly awful to you. But I reasoned that your father's love made up for the absence of mine. He spent hours with you every day; I became jealous. Seeing his relationship with you reminded me that I had made the wrong choice.

"Then you came home that day with your dress torn and tattered, only fourteen years old. All the guilt that I had buried deep inside reared its ugly head again. Once again, I had failed to protect my children. I should have been with you that day. But I was not. I was a failure as a mother. I did not know how to help you. It was all my fault. So, I made the decision that day to marry off the other girls as soon as possible. They would be better off with someone else, with anyone but me.

"I have no excuse for the things I have said. But no one ever prepares you for the grief of losing a child. My mother . . . well, you remember Grandmother. She was so critical of everything. Perhaps I learned a bit too much from her."

Elizabeth was shocked. He mother felt guilty for David's death? She did not blame Elizabeth? The revelations were spinning in her head so fast she felt she would collapse. She felt Mr. Darcy's arm around her shoulders. She looked to him and saw the compassion in his eyes.

Mrs. Bennet continued. "So, what I am trying to say is, I love you. I have always loved you, but I made one bad decision after another and pushed you away. I am sorry for what I have done. I know you will never forgive me. I know I am too late to be a mother to you now, but I will try to change."

Elizabeth stood up. She walked over to her mother and took her hands in hers and said, "Mamma, it matters not what you did, but rather what you are currently doing about it."

Mrs. Bennet looked confused. "I do not understand."

"We all have things that we need forgiven for. I can see your sincerity, and I forgive you. I only ask that from now on, you try to treat me respectfully."

"I will, I really will try. And forgive me, Mr. Darcy, for implying anything improper between you two. Out of all of my children, Elizabeth knows best what proper behavior is and why it is so important."

Mr. Darcy smiled politely. "I assure you she has behaved most admirably."

Elizabeth put her arms around her mother's neck and whispered, "I love you too, Mamma. I always have. I love you as much as I miss David."

Mrs. Bennet carefully wrapped her own arms around the daughter she had not held for nine years. The emotion was too much, and she started to shake. "Now go, child, before I get an attack of my poor nerves. I feel them coming on already. Go, I say. Just go." She pushed Elizabeth away and started fanning herself.

"Yes, Mamma. Your smelling salts are in the dining room. Do you want me to fetch them?"

"No!" Tears were welling up in her eyes, and she seemed desperate not to cry in front of them. "I beg of you, please go," she said weakly. She watched her daughter leave with Mr. Darcy, and they closed the door behind them. It was all she could do to take a few steps to the chaise and collapse in fatigue. Who knew that disclosing personal feelings was so fatiguing?

She fingered the locket on her neck that held David's lock of hair and closed her eyes. She pulled the lap blanket over the shoulders and thought of happier times. She was asleep in no time.

*****

Darcy and Elizabeth had quite purposely slowed their pace to the point that Georgiana, Bingley and Jane were out of hearing. Darcy took her hand and asked, "How do you feel?"

"About my mother? I am shocked. All this time, I thought she blamed me for the accident, but she actually blamed herself. I have heard nothing but angry, hurtful words for the last nine years, and today she calls me her 'favorite daughter'. I am still in shock."

"Do you believe her?"

She looked up ahead as the others turned off the road and headed up the trail to Oakham Mount. "I do not know," she said. "It feels unbelievable, but she seemed sincere. I think for the first time, I saw how serious her anxiety really is. I always thought her trembling, fluttering, and shaking were pretend; I thought it was just a show to get attention. But I think she has truly been suffering for a long, long time. I want to believe her. I suppose time will tell if she was in earnest.

"By the way," Elizabeth added, "the children at the orphanage claim a tall, handsome man delivered a box of new clothes and hired a repairman last week. Do you know who it was? I am excessively fond of handsome men and would like to meet such a person."

"As usual, I have no idea what you are referring to."

"That is a relief. They were quite grateful; the headmistress even baked a cake. I was concerned you might have been involved, and then I would have felt obliged to share the cake with you." Darcy chuckled but would not take her bait. Elizabeth was anxious to get to the proposal, so she changed topics. "It was quite an informative trip to the blacksmith yesterday, was it not?"

"I would say so, yes."

"And have you solved the mystery of Malachi 3:3?"

"Yes, I think I finally have. I could not back down from a challenge, especially when it came from such an intriguing lady." He stopped walking and reached for her hands. "Elizabeth, from the first moment I saw you, I have been captivated by your brightness. And now that I understand the mystery of Malachi 3:3, I know why you glow: it is because you have God's image in your countenance," he said. "I want that in my life. I want to see your bright eyes glowing with merriment every moment of my day. I want to hear you spout off deep, thought-provoking comments as we pass through the halls of Pemberley. But it is more than that. I want to reflect God's image as well.

"Knowing you has changed me forever. I am a better man now. I hope to be even better tomorrow than I am today. And if you are by my side, I know I will. Your spirit, your will to survive, your charity towards others—they have all molded you into the perfect woman for me. Will you please do me the great honor of consenting to be my wife?"

Elizabeth was so happy. She wanted to say yes right then and there, but in her heart, she knew there was still another conversation to be had. "Is that a 'no comment' question?" she teased.

Mr. Darcy looked at her and smiled widely. "No, I fully expect an answer."

She turned serious and stopped and looked at him. "Then I suggest you ask your 'no comment' questions first." She watched Darcy bow his head and stand silently for a moment. "Is something wrong?" Elizabeth asked.

He lifted his head, "No, I was just praying."

"What did you pray for?"

"I prayed I would ask the right questions." He caressed her cheek with the back of his fingers. Then he took her hand in his and started walking again.

Elizabeth blushed slightly. This was not going to be a pleasant conversation for either of them.

Darcy took a deep breath and steeled himself for the answer. "My first 'no comment' question is, did something happen to you like what happened to Georgiana?" He knew she would never answer "no comment" to this question; she needed him to know too badly.

Finally, he has asked me about it. Elizabeth walked in silence for a while before she began her story. "I was fourteen," she began. "I had been walking independently all over the countryside for many years. Ever since my father inherited Longbourn, I took to country living like a fish to water. It was natural for me to disappear for hours on end in order to see a new destination. I especially took to it after David died.

"One day six years ago, I hiked through town to get to the hills behind the church. At that time, I was nearly as tall as I am now and just as mature physically. Sometimes, men in the village called out filthy comments as I went by, and I tried to ignore them. So, when the town drunk called out something particularly vile as I passed the church, I just kept on walking. I did not know he was following me.

"His name was Mr. Conway. He still lives in the village with his wife and four sons. A month before all this, my father had hired him to mend some fences on our properties. He only showed up for the work three out of ten days. Therefore, my father only paid him for three days' work. It seems he held a grudge.

"By the time I realized Mr. Conway was following me, I was deep into the hills. I turned and asked him if he needed help. He spat something at me about how my father had not paid him what was promised. I could tell from his foul odor that he was well into his cups. He then started eyeing me rakishly, but not even when he fingered the sleeves of my dress did I have any idea what he might do. Only when he gripped my shoulders firmly and smothered me with his filthy mouth did I truly get nervous. And I was right to be nervous. He pushed me to the ground and ripped my dress in his attempts . . . in his attempts to . . .

"I can still feel the rocks grinding into my hips and shoulders as I fought him off. But he was much stronger than me." She stopped walking and looked at Mr. Darcy. "William, I am not a maiden. I have the scars on my shoulder to prove it." She dropped his hand and turned her back to him and began pushing down the sleeve of her gown to expose her shoulder.

Darcy grabbed her hand to stop her. He slowly brought her hand to his lips and kissed it, and then he leaned towards her shoulder blade and kissed it as well. "Elizabeth, I do not need to see your scars; they do not define you."

Elizabeth turned to face him and saw the love in his eyes. They held more compassion than ever before. He was no longer concealing any of his thoughts as he did when she first met him. "I understand if the things I have just told you alter your intentions," she said, "and I release you from your proposal. Do not worry about me. I will survive the disappointment, and you will find somebody else to marry."

"Elizabeth," he said tenderly, "What happened in your past is behind you. It was not your fault. I wish it had never happened, but I trust God had his reasons. It has refined you into the woman you are, the woman I love. You are perfect, whole, and the only woman I desire as my wife. I do not wish to retract my offer of marriage. Please marry me."

Elizabeth's tears began to fall. "You really still love me?" she whispered.

Darcy had been near tears himself in hearing her tell her story. He felt an overwhelming need to reassure her, and he took her shoulders and pulled her into his arms. "I do! I love you more than life itself! I will gladly face hurdles, obstacles, and trials, if it means I get to hold you like this every day. Now, may I ask my next 'no comment' question?" He heard her murmurs of consent. "Do you love me?"

She looked up at him and said, "More than I thought possible. I thought I was happy before, but this is so much more than I thought I deserved."

Darcy slowly took off her bonnet and placed it on a rock next to them. He cupped her face in his hands and said, "That leads me to my next 'no comment' question. If you really believe all you have told me, all the thoughts in your prayer notebook, all the speeches on forgiveness and the love God has for all His children, and all that talk of trusting God to refine us, how in the world do you not see your own worth?"

Elizabeth simply absorbed the love she felt in his eyes. His tender hands were ever so slowly pulling her face to his. But he stopped before kissing her, holding her face a mere two inches from his lips.

Darcy couldn't stop himself, he brushed his thumb against her lower lip, and it parted. His voice was deep and hoarse. "May I? May I kiss you?"

She smiled at him and raised an eyebrow saucily at him, "You are only allowed three 'no comment' questions. I believe you have used them all up." William gave her a knee-weakening dimpled smile, and she lost the rest of her self-control. She closed the gap and met his lips with hers. She could feel the tenderness in his lips as they moved ever so slowly in perfect unison with hers.

She reached up and put her hands in his hair and pulled him closer. As he wrapped his arms around her and held her close, she felt his chest rise and fall with his rapid breathing. She kissed him again and again and felt the healing love of the man who held her heart.

He pulled away briefly and looked at her. Her eyes were glossed over, and her lips were pink and swollen. He did not mean to kiss her again, but he did. He let his hands run over her back and he thought of how she must have suffered to have scars on her shoulder blades. She was never going to have doubts about his love again.

Daringly, he pressed further and felt her lips accept his desire to deepen the kiss. He tasted of her sweetness, and he felt his heart and body lighten with every movement and kiss. He pulled away again to regain control and laughed softly. "Even your kisses are enlightening! Elizabeth, dearest Elizabeth, you are everything to me." She looked at him with dazzling, bright eyes. They simply gazed at each other. "Have I struck you dumb again?" he asked. "For we are nowhere near my foyer."

"No comment," she answered with a smile on her face.

Darcy laughed and pulled her into his arms again and rested his head on hers. "If I ever do anything to dull your life's luster, now I know what will bring the glow back. All I have to do is kiss you, for I have never seen you glow as brightly as you do now."

Elizabeth held him close and listened to his steady heartbeat. She felt every bit of peace that could possibly come from such a moment. "I love you, William. Nothing could have gone as perfectly as that moment."

But Darcy wasn't done yet. He reached into his satchel and pulled out a small ring box. "Elizabeth, will you allow me to love you deeper than you have ever been loved? Will you allow me to share every thought with you? Will you be patient as I am refined little by little into a man who is worthy of your love? Will you marry me and love me forever?"

"William, you are already everything I have ever wanted. I will marry you, and I promise to love you forever." He grinned at her and pressed the box into her hand. Elizabeth opened it and saw a brilliant diamond in the middle of the flower. "Gardenia! It is my favorite flower! How did you know?"

"Because you smell like gardenias."

"Thank you, William."

"I have one more gift, but I want to explain it first. Since you are the reason I have tried so hard to improve myself, I thought this gift would be appropriate." He took out the necklace box and opened it for her.

"This is the silver nugget Mr. Rogers showed yesterday. It reminded me of you because it is shaped like a candle flame and you are my light. You saw my worth long before I did. I was like this piece of silver—dull and rough around the edges—but you knew my real value. You had faith in me. And with a little patience, you helped me see how I could refine myself. Your glow buffed and polished my rough edges until I shined. And, naturally I would like you to wear a part of me right next to your heart. For it is your heart that I love, not your scars.

Elizabeth's tears ran freely down her face. All these years, she had prayed to know why the attack had happened. Now, she saw that God really did have a purpose in His design. It was her trial that had brought her into Darcy's path. It was because of her pain that she was capable of feeling this much happiness.

Elizabeth said quietly, "I have thought of one more entry for my prayer notebook."

"What is that, my dearest Elizabeth?" Darcy said, stealing another quick kiss.

"I know why I had to go through what I did. I understand now that one must experience darkness to appreciate the light." She then leaned into him and kissed him with all the passion she felt inside. She no longer cared about showing him the view from Oakham Mount.

EPILOGUE

Pemberley, Derbyshire
12 October 1841

Dear Mr. Wickham,

Thank you for your recent letter and for the news of my cousin, Anne de Bourgh. I am glad to hear she is in good health. Thank you for your attentions to her. I know that she values your company, especially since her mother, Lady Catherine, died. You were such a source of strength to them in the end. The parishioners of Rosings are blessed to have you as their rector.

Thank you as well for your interest in the living at Kympton. Yes, it is available once again. Nevertheless, I cannot offer it to you. I know that you have served the church faithfully for more than ten years, and I understand that you would like to return to Derbyshire to make amends to those you once wronged. However, you must know that some here have very, very long memories.

Some still remember the child who threw rocks at their dogs, and the man who flirted with every servant. They do not know the man who has not touched alcohol in thirty years. They have not seen the man who lives solely to serve others. Although it pains me to turn you down, I must tell you that I plan to fill the position from other sources.

I must say that it has been a long thirty years since I decked you soundly! Please know that those feelings are long gone. I still remember how pleased I was when you told me you were taking orders and requested a reference. Although I felt compelled to include an honest account of your history, I also told them they would never find a man so changed for good.

I fully believe you are not the same person. That man, under the influence of the bottle and greed, died many, many years ago. I hardly remember him now. Must I reassure you around every corner?

Do not take my refusal as a personal blow. After all, I believe Anne would be devastated if you left Rosings. She writes me every week, praising your devotion and humility. It is obvious you two care for each other very much. If you are open to a change in your life, I think you will find her open to new proposals as well. I can say no more, but I hope to wish you joy very soon.

Take care and God bless you.

Fitzwilliam Darcy

Darcy looked up from his desk and put his pen in the holder. Once again, he considered those events that autumn thirty years ago. Wickham's life had changed dramatically after their meeting by the river. He gave up alcohol entirely and quickly became the most respected man in the regiment. For more than ten years, he served as Colonel Foster's lieutenant. But eventually, he could no longer suppress the urge to become a servant of God.

Even after thirty years, it was still astonishing that a man could alter his life so drastically because of one small choice Darcy made to forgive and believe in the inherent goodness of man.

Darcy was startled from his thoughts by a familiar hand on his shoulder. It was a sweet hand, a loving and kind hand. He closed his eyes and allowed the hand to caress his face and finger the dimples that were now weathered deep with wrinkles. He felt it pull him around to look at her. He turned around in his chair and gazed at his wife.

The afternoon sun was shining right through the window from behind her, silhouetting her with a halo of light. He saw the roundness of her hips and fullness of her grandmotherly figure and let out a sigh of pleasure. She shined and glowed with a radiance that he understood was the pure light of Christ. He reached for her hand and pulled her onto his lap.

"Mrs. Darcy, my dearest, how did you find me?"

She snuggled her cheek up against his and rubbed it back and forth, "I just needed to hold what is most dear to me, William."

He wrapped his arms around her and continued rubbing his freshly shaved cheek against hers. He whispered, "And how are you doing on this anniversary of your mother's death?"

Elizabeth pondered that a bit. "I imagine I feel as any daughter would feel. I still miss her. I am glad she lived with us here the last four years of her life, but I just keep thinking about those nine years together we lost. I am so glad we mended our bond. I was thinking today of the first time we invited her to Pemberley to come see our little David. Do you remember?"

Darcy smiled at the memory and nodded. It had taken several years of guarded visits before Darcy and Elizabeth could relax around Mrs. Bennet, but her transformation had been nearly as dramatic as Wickham's. "She was so careful with him," he said, "so gentle. No one else could get him to sleep those first few months. She rocked him every night."

"I miss her," Elizabeth sighed. "I really do. She gave me more than I could have asked for. She gave her very heart, and I never expected it after so many years of abuse."

"She was so proud of you, my love. She was always saying that," Darcy said. "I am glad we let her show us that she meant what she said in that library all those years ago. Imagine little Richard never knowing his grandmother, or David never experiencing the tremblings and flutterings of a woman. It is no wonder they are such excellent husbands."

Elizabeth giggled. "William, I agree they are both wonderful husbands, but that is not because of my mother. They learned by watching you."

"Perhaps. But you taught them to full rely on God. And the cufflinks you had made for them will be daily reminders of it. How on earth did you convince the blacksmith to make them into frogs?"

"I can be very persuasive when I need to be. The boys needed a reminder."

Darcy smiled. "Well, I doubt they ate a single bite of food, not even a stolen biscuit, without thanking God first. Speaking of the boys, have you given any more thought to turning Pemberley over to David and Sarah and their family?"

"I have. I know we are getting older, William, but you need not give away your home quite yet."

"I was not suggesting we move out, just move aside. I am nearing sixty, and I am weary. It is a great responsibility to handle an estate as big as Pemberley, and I have been doing it for thirty years now."

"Thirty-five." Elizabeth corrected.

"Yes, dearest, but I have been a great deal more careful and prayerful about it in the last thirty years in particular. But I am serious. We could move to some of the guest suites and let David and Sarah take over the main wing. Their children are at the perfect ages to start their lives and build memories here at Pemberley."

Elizabeth looked up at her husband. "William, I would love to have my grandchildren raised here, and I know David is the heir. But do not rush this. Let us wait until you are ready."

"I believe I am ready. I have lived a good life and done all I could do, but now my body is tired. There is a time and season for all things. Are you ready?"

She looked deep into his eyes and considered the idea. David and Sarah nearby, eating dinner together, children running through the halls again . . . She nodded and broke into a wide grin. "Yes," she said. "Write to David in London and tell him to come home. Home. I am still awed at the idea of Pemberley being home. We have had such wonderful memories here."

Darcy cleared his throat and gently lifted her chin and kissed her wrinkled lips. "Do promise me one thing, sweet wife."

"What is that?"

"No more jumping off the rock into the lake." Elizabeth rolled her eyes at him, but Darcy continued, "Every summer you are determined to be the first to jump in, and every summer I am scared to death that the freezing water from the spring will make you ill."

"But, William, how else could I teach my boys to love life? You were so very protective of me when I was with child; I had to keep you on your toes!"

Darcy shook his head and tried to assume a stern face. "You are fifty now, my dear! If the boys have not yet learned what I learned in the first five minutes of knowing you, then they will never learn! You radiate a love of life. You need not risk your health to prove it."

Elizabeth kissed his stern mouth until his smile returned. "My dear, sweet William," she said. "I do love life and each day that I get to spend with you. I am grateful I can jump, run, walk, sing, play, and cry. Therefore, as long as I can, I will jump every year. Besides, it is a Pemberley tradition. You will never be able to talk me out of it."

"Well," Darcy sighed, "I have been married long enough to know that I cannot talk you out of anything. But the only Pemberley tradition I want to keep is hunting frogs with the grandchildren. Please be careful. I do not want to miss a single day of you waking up by my side. You are the only woman I have ever loved."

"And Georgiana, of course."

"Speaking of Georgiana, did you read her last letter?" With one hand around his wife's shoulders, Darcy reached over to his desk and rifled through some papers until he found what he was looking for. He handed a letter to Elizabeth.

Elizabeth sat up a little straighter. She reached for her glasses, heard his chuckle, and gave him a saucy look. "You just like seeing me in my old woman glasses."

Darcy chuckled again and fixed his own spectacles. "At least now I do not feel so old. Go on, read it."

Elizabeth stuck out her tongue and said, "I will always be younger than you. There is no catching up, old man." She slid her glasses on and read.

London
2 October 1841

Dear William,

I am sorry I have not written for the last few weeks. The ladies' shelter has taken more of my time now that all three children are away at school. Henry sends his love, but I cannot fathom how he has any to spare after all that he showers on me and the children.

I still remember how nervous he was to ask you for my hand twenty-four years ago. I could see the beads of sweat grow on his brow with each passing moment. You really should not have made him worry so much. He was merely a struggling architect back then, but he loved me, and you knew it.

I will never forget the time we were courting, and you sat down in the small, six-inch gap between us, forcing us to move apart! I should have known you would be a little protective after Wickham. Do not fret at the mention of his name; Wickham means little to me anymore. I can nearly look back and remember only the good times I had with him. It does sting a little to remember Ramsgate, but look what that experience has done for me. Now, I can help so many other women at the ladies' shelter.

As you know, most of the women here just need time to regroup and build their self-confidence. Others need a home during their confinement. Others yet are widowed and have no family to turn to. For these women, The Lord's Trust Shelter for Ladies is their only option. I have learned so much from helping them.

Take Miss Genevieve for example. As a servant in Lord Pearson's house, she was cornered and threatened. She had to endure years of unwanted advances and three pregnancies before she escaped to our shelter. Now, she is learning to take in sewing and ironing to support her children.

But that is not why I write today. Do not lecture me on how I should have written earlier, but there is a new arrival at our shelter, one you are quite familiar with: Caroline Ives, nee Bingley. She has been with us for the last few weeks, but she would not let me tell you until now. She has had a difficult life, William. Her first husband, Mr. Stuart, quickly spent her entire dowry and never once gave her any kindness. He did, however, give her four step-children. She quickly dispatched them to other relatives so as to not have them underfoot when her own children arrived.

But apparently, Mr. Stuart refused to share her bed, so there was never any chance of her bearing children of her own. She had always assumed his reluctance was her fault and never told a soul. But when Mr. Stuart died, she learned a horrific fact: Mr. Stuart had kept a mistress and fathered several bastard children by her. In fact, in his will, he gifted the entire estate to the other woman. Caroline's self-esteem plummeted.

She refused Bingley's help out of pride and began working in a factory to support herself. She has remarried twice since then, but both husbands left her a penniless widow. Now, her arthritis is so painful that she can no longer work. She has not heard from her stepchildren for several years. Take pity on her and help her, William.

I must close now, for it is time for dinner, and my dear husband will think I have lost myself again in business. I suppose that is true. I never realized the value of being a Darcy until I had to call in favors from friends and acquaintances to help these poor women. I had no idea that my status and connections could do so much good in the world. "Once a Darcy, always a Darcy," right, brother? Say hello to Elizabeth for me.

With all my love,

Georgiana

Darcy reached his thumb up to Elizabeth's eyes and wiped her tears away. "What are you thinking, Elizabeth?"

She sadly shook her head. "It makes me sad, William," she said. "Jane told me about Caroline. Charles warned her to stay away from Mr. Stuart, but Caroline was so angry with him. She refused to listen. After Bingley finally relented and let them marry, Caroline saw what Mr. Stuart was really like. By then, it was too late."

"But Caroline could have chosen to love her stepchildren; she could have raised them as her own," Darcy said. "With Mr. Stuart as their father, they must have been in desperate need of someone's love. But she showed no interest in them. And now they show no interest in her. Such a wasted opportunity!"

Elizabeth paused and pursed her lips. "I have a confession, William," she said. "Caroline and I have been corresponding for the past few years. She is quite changed. I send her money whenever I can. I know she has made some mistakes, but I would hate to see anything bad happen to her. My father would have urged us to forgive Caroline and help her."

"Yes, he would have. After all, he believed in your mother all those years; he knew she still loved you. I respect him for trying to maintain peace and love when your mother worked so hard to disrupt it. He truly did believe that all people are inherently good. I am glad he started preaching again when Mr. Petersen accidently found himself in love and moved to Scotland with a bride."

"Ah, Mr. Petersen. Now, there was a good man."

Mr. Darcy pinched her bottom and she squealed. "I should have never told you I felt threatened by him," he said.

"And you accused *me* of not trusting your love!"

He kissed her cheek and wrapped his arms around her, and she leaned back against him. They sat together, breathing in and out in unison as the sun set across the lake. "I cannot help but feel a sense of fulfillment as I look out over this view," he said. "I remember the first time you saw it. You said it was amazing I ever got any work done with such a view. After I left you to have tea with Georgiana, your words proved true: I could not get any work done, because all I thought of for a good thirty minutes was you!

"I just pondered you—everything that made you so unique. Your glow, your wit, your impertinent eyebrow. I think I was already in love with you, and it was only our second meeting! I feel so fulfilled now, Elizabeth. This is the same view I had always seen, but I did not truly see it until that day. Now, when I look out, I see a life brimming with joy. I hear you singing 'Be Still My Soul', and it nearly knocks me to my knees. God has blessed me with such depth and quantity of blessings, I cannot number them. I try, every night; I try to thank Him for all I have, but the list goes on and on. But do you know what I thank Him for first and last every night?"

Elizabeth smiled and reached her arms around his neck and let him kiss her fervently. She had heard this monologue many times over the years. First, he would talk about how he fell in love with her, then he would talk about finding gratitude for his trials, then he would come full circle back to her. She never tired of it so she played along. "I have a guess, but I would very much like to hear you say it."

"I thank him for such a wise woman who once asked me 'What if we woke up tomorrow morning and had only what we took the time to thank God for?' Do you know why I thank Him first and last for you?"

"Yes, dear, but tell me again."

"I thank him first for bringing you into my life, and last for keeping you there. I wake up every morning next to the very thing I am most thankful for. I love you, Mrs. Darcy. You are invaluable to me."

Elizabeth fingered her silver candle flame pendent on her neck and brought it to her lips and kissed it. She leaned into him and said, "I love you too, Mr. Darcy. When you gave me this necklace, you said it reminded you that I had seen your worth long before you did. But I must tell you why I still wear it close to my heart after thirty years. The day you proposed, when you listened with unconditional love to my story about Mr. Conway, that was when I realized that *you* saw *my* worth. I could not yet see it myself. You saw silver in me where I only saw streaks of rust."

"So, even you . . ." Mr. Darcy said in awe.

Elizabeth snuggled up against his chest, feeling the security of thirty years of his unwavering devotion. God willing, she would have thirty more. Her joy had never been so full. "Yes, even I have learned what it means to refine like silver."

THE END

Thought Notebook

Some time ago, my life was forever changed by a simple prayer notebook—a collection of inspirational thoughts. That experience has inspired me to create my own notebook. A few of the thoughts are my own; but most of them were related to me by others. Each thought impacted me deeply, and together they have made me the man I am today.

I dedicate this notebook to my sweet wife, Elizabeth. Most of these thoughts—and most of my happiness in life—originated with her.

I pray that someday, my sons, David and Richard, will read this and know that I have learned to believe in God, in my family, in myself, and in the goodness of men.

I pray these thoughts will touch your heart. May they inspire you as you seek to refine yourself.

Sincerely,
Fitzwilliam Darcy

———

- Celebrate the little successes instead of waiting for the grand entrance of a miracle.
- Silence the barking frog, and peace will soon follow.
- What if we woke up tomorrow morning and had only what we took the time to thank God for?
- People are inherently good, even if their actions indicate otherwise.
- If we cannot find love in our hearts for all men, we should ask God for a bigger heart; we cannot expect God to forgive us of our own follies until we are willing to forgive those who have harmed us.
- After every night, there is a dawn.
- Sadness is just a feeling; it cannot consume you.

- A frog has been given the skills to live both in water and on land. It enjoys the benefits of both environments, but it is endangered by every predator that walks or swims. Just like a frog, we will face many foes in many different environments, but we have been given the skills to overcome them if we fully rely on God. F-R-O-G.

- You never know how strong you are until being strong is the only option you have left.

- It is easier to see what makes us comfortable than to face our suspicions.

- Even the best men are mere mortals.

- Although perfection is our goal, God does not expect us to achieve it today, and nor should not we. Trials are simply distractions along the way. We must not allow them to divert us from our goal.

- God is the instructor in life; He chooses which lessons to give.

- Sometimes others' choices inflict trials upon us. But no matter whether trials come from God or from the choices of another, He will never give us more than we can handle.

- God loves you. When you hurt, He hurts also. When you grow, He rejoices.

- If you lived an easy, carefree life, you would be a very dull person, having learned nothing.

- Crying is better medicine than any doctor's prescription.

- There is one set of shoulders that can carry any burden. And those shoulders carried His own cross. All people will fail us at some point or another—they are simply human—but our Savior will never fail us.

- When you judge people it does not define them; it only defines you.

- Though life is difficult, God does not abandon us, no matter how much it feels like it.
- Nothing anyone does is unforgiveable.
- The only constant in life is change. Change will always be there, requiring us to be flexible and adjust our actions, our thoughts, and our feelings. Time breeds change, and change takes time.
- Emotions cannot be helped. One cannot stop the rain from falling, but we can be wise enough to seek shelter instead of getting wet. It is what we choose to do with our emotions that is important.
- Each man will have to face natural consequences of his actions.
- The most important part of prayer is realizing whom you were talking to. God isn't some vague, mighty being, so removed that He can't be bothered to listen to you.
- Where gratitude is, happiness follows.
- Problems make us better people. The purpose of trials is to make us reach beyond our comfort and stretch ourselves.
- A good friend is hard to find unless one is a friend to all. For then one will be surrounded by good friends everywhere.
- You will never finish unless you start.
- Faith is more than just believing. It is more than hoping for something to be real. Faith is trusting God with undaunted fervor. It is holding tight when the storms come. It is continuing to do what is right, no matter what. We do not express faith through our beliefs; it is expressed by our behavior, especially in our times of trouble.
- Charity is much more than giving of one's monetary goods.

- God asks us to do more than follow a set of rules; he asks us to change our hearts. Each choice refines us just a tiny bit more, and we become better today than we were yesterday.
- Refining one's self is the work of a lifetime. It is the sum of small choices made each day.
- One cannot wake up and decide to be a good person and be done by tea time.
- One day, a farmer's workhorse fell down a deep hole. The farmer loved this horse very much, but he could see no way to pull it out. After several days of throwing food into the hole, he knew there was only one thing left to do. There was no way the horse could survive without water. He must bury it.
  So, reluctantly, the farmer started shoveling in dirt on top of the horse. The farmer shoveled in pound after pound of dirt, crying the whole time. When the farmer estimated that he had shoveled enough dirt to bury the horse up to the shoulders, he looked in to say his last goodbye. He was quite surprised when he looked down the hole and found the horse was not buried. The horse simply shook off the dirt and stepped up.
- Just because you have not seen God's hand in your life does not mean He was not there.
- God wants to be involved in our lives. If we just let Him, He will personally direct us in every facet of it.
- Praying is not like going to a formal dinner. You will not be judged on your eloquence.
- There is no wrong way to pray. God will hear you no matter what you say. Just speak from the heart, and be grateful.

- When we truly see how much we have, our problems seem to shrink, and we can better see how to fix them.
- Expecting to live a trouble-free life because you are a good person is like expecting the lion not to eat you because you tipped your hat at him. Even good people are meant to have tribulations.
- Life is made up of many small, precious moments, all linked together to create a priceless existence. Do not be naive enough to believe your life will always be rosy. But recognize every trial and tribulation as a chance to prove yourself worthy of God's good grace.
- Time is like a river; you can never touch the same water twice because the flow that has passed will never pass by again.
- Forgive, but never forget.
- Learn from your mistakes, but do not regret them.
- As long as you keep asking questions, God will provide the answers.
- True change comes only from within.
- God wants us to forgive one another not only because wrongdoers deserve forgiveness, but because the wronged deserve peace.
- Whatever hurt lies hidden deep inside the souls of men, Christ can heal it, for He has already borne it.
- God gives each of us a unique set of trials, tailored to our specific needs in the hope that we will turn to Him.
- God is big and powerful, and we are so small. But even as big as He is, He needs small people to do His work for Him.
- Integrity is doing the right thing even if no one is looking.

- To be refined like silver, we must first be crushed, or humbled, and then we must mold our wills to God's design. It takes a great deal of patience, but if we are diligent, we will at last see the refiner's image reflected in the silver.
- One is free to make a choice but not to choose the consequence.
- Enduring our trials refines us little by little until we have God-like characteristics.
- Our trials do not define us, rather they refine us.
- God only gives us what we want if it is also what we need.
- There is no such thing as luck; everything good that happens is a blessing from God.
- One must experience darkness to appreciate the light.

About the Author

Jeanna is a mother of three daughters, all whom are well versed in *Pride and Prejudice*; they are her best friends and the inspiration for her writing. She also proudly states she is the eighth of thirteen children. When she isn't blogging, gardening, cooking, or raising chickens—or more realistically, writing—she is thoroughly ignoring her house for a few hours at a time in order to read yet another romance novel. Somewhere between being a mom, sister, writer, and cook, she squeezes in three 12-hour shifts each week as a Registered Nurse in a Neurological ICU. She finds great joy in her writing and claims she has never been happier.

Jeanna fell in love again with Jane Austen when she was introduced to the incredible world of Jane Austen-inspired fiction. She can never adequately thank the fellow authors who mentored her and encouraged her to write her first novel. Through writing, Jeanna has gained something that no one can take away from her: hope for her own Mr. Darcy. More than anything, she hopes to prepare her three best friends to look for their own Mr. Darcy and to settle for nothing less.

Jeanna's works include: *Mr. Darcy's Promise, Pride and Persistence, To Refine Like Silver, Hope For Mr. Darcy,* and *Hope For Fitzwilliam.* She recently finished her first attempt at an original Regency romance novel: *Inspired By Grace.* For more information on these books, please visit her website, www.HeyLadyPublications.com

Praise for *Pride and Persistence*

"The perfect book for curling up with after a trying day at work; brilliantly funny and wonderfully romantic, which will leave you feeling perfectly content and with a huge grin on your face." – Sophie Andrews, *Laughing with Lizzie*

"*Pride and Persistence* is such an adorable and admirable variation! Filled with recovery, reflection, romance, rejections, and a plethora of proposals, this novel will be sure to make you laugh, smile, and sigh with delight. I highly recommend!" – Meredith Esparza, *Austenesque Reviews*

"Thank you, Jeanna Ellsworth, for a lovely book. I enjoyed every minute of it and didn't want to put it down." – Janet Taylor, *More Agreeably Engaged*

"*Pride and Persistence* brings us the same characters that we know and love from the original classic, but a brilliant twist adds more to the story than even Jane gave us all those years ago." – Alice, *Reading with Alice*

"I absolutely loved this book! Jeanna Ellsworth knows how to awaken the spirit of *Pride and Prejudice* and Darcy and Elizabeth's growing love—and we get to watch it all through words, and those words certainly came to life." — Elizabeth Cohan